When they hit the dance floor, Judd pulled London snug against his body.

Wrapping one arm around her slender waist, he reached up with his other arm to tuck her head against his shoulder. Her breath warmed his skin through the thin material of his shirt.

He rested his cheek against her bright hair and the golden strands stuck to the stubble of his beard. Reaching between their bodies, he opened her leather jacket and drew her close again, his chest pressing against her soft breasts beneath the silvery material of her dress.

She shifted and her soft lips touched the side of his neck.

He gritted his teeth to suppress the shudder threatening to engulf his body...and for the first time in a very long time and a very long line of women, he felt on the edge of losing control.

Then the door to the bar burst open and London's driver, bloodied and battered, staggered into the room and dropped to the floor.

THE HILL

BY
CAROL ERICSON

MILLS & BOON

Published in Great Britain 2014
by Mills & Boon, an imprint of Harlequin (UK) Limited,
Eton House, 18-24 Paradise Road, Richmond, Surrey, TW9 1SR

© 2014 Carol Ericson

ISBN: 978-0-263-91373-6

46-1014

Harlequin (UK) Limited's policy is to use papers that are natural, renewable and recyclable products and made from wood grown in sustainable forests. The logging and manufacturing processes conform to the legal environmental regulations of the country of origin.

Printed and bound in Spain
by Blackprint CPI, Barcelona

Carol Ericson lives with her husband and two sons in Southern California, home of state-of-the-art cosmetic surgery, wild freeway chases, palm trees bending in the Santa Ana winds and a million amazing stories. These stories, along with hordes of virile men and feisty women, clamor for release from Carol's head. It makes for some interesting headaches until she sets them free to fulfill their destinies and her readers' fantasies. To find out more about Carol, her books and her strange headaches, please visit her website, www.carolericson.com, "Where romance flirts with danger."

To all the ladies at GIAMx2

Chapter One

"Your father was murdered. You could be next."

London Breck jerked her head up from the slip of paper and caught the waiter's arm as he turned away. "I'm sorry. Who gave this to you?"

The young man's eyes widened and London released her death grip on his white jacket.

"Like I told you, Ms. Breck. I found the folded piece of paper on my tray with your name written on the outside. I—I don't know who put it there…and I didn't read it."

She crumpled the note in her fist and dropped it into her evening clutch, trading it for a ten-dollar bill. "That's okay. Thanks for delivering it to me."

The waiter pocketed the money and scurried away without looking back.

Someone had decided to play a joke with that note, or it signaled the opening gambit of some sort of scam. London tucked a stray strand of hair behind her ear. If this con man believed he could pull a fast one on her or Breck Global Enterprises, he hadn't met their legal team.

She straightened her spine and turned to face the room, smiling so hard her cheeks hurt. It was an occupational hazard—if one could call glad-handing and raising money an occupation. But it was the only one she'd ever had, the only one she'd ever trained for.

She swept a champagne flute from a passing tray with practiced ease and turned her attention to the crowd jamming the Fairmont Hotel's ballroom. Which well-heeled donor or wannabe had left that note? Scanning the room, her gaze tripped over the hottie in the corner.

Even though his crisp tux conformed to the dress code for the evening, he had *outsider* scribbled all over his amazing body. The tux couldn't mask the sheer power of the man, and it had very little to do with the way the material puckered and stretched across his massive shoulders, crying out for a good tailor.

His stance, his demeanor—okay, the dark sunglasses—marked him as a member of the bevy of body- and security guards that littered the room, jealously watching their clients or their clients' jewels or both. Probably not the author of the note, but definitely worth a closer inspection.

The note almost forgotten, London squinted at the pretty people bedecked in diamonds and designer duds and wondered which one had invited that powerful panther into the midst of the pampered trust-fund babies and oily politicians.

"Don't you know squinting like that will bring on the wrinkles, my dear?"

London rolled a sip of champagne on her tongue as she eyed her cousin. *Speaking of trust-fund babies...*

"Have you seen Roger tonight?"

"Your square-jawed, preppy suitor?" Niles shook his head. "For someone practically running the company, he sure misses a lot of soirees, doesn't he?"

She drew her fingertip around the rim of her glass. She didn't want to talk about the company. "Did you bid on something fabulous, Niles?"

"Of course I did. It's all rather too late, though, isn't it?" He plucked a cracker brimming with caviar from the tray on the table and studied it before popping it into his mouth.

"Too late?" She steadied herself for one of her cousin's acidic barbs.

He brushed his fingers together. "Here we are raising all this money for heart disease, but your father, Spencer Breck, already bit the dust, leaving you gazillions of dollars and handing you the reins of Breck Global. Should've had this fund-raiser *before* he kicked the bucket."

"I can always count on you to say the right thing at the right moment, bringing light and comfort."

Niles clicked his tongue, a decidedly feminine gesture she was sure Mr. Dark Sunglasses over in the corner had never made in his life.

Then Niles leaned in, his booze-soaked breath tickling her ear. "This is your cousin Niles. You don't have to pretend with me, my dear. I know you despised the man as much as I did."

He threw his silk scarf over his shoulder and waltzed away, throwing a kiss at a dowager across the room.

Maybe Niles had written that note to stir up trouble. She wouldn't put it past him. His own father had left Niles gazillions of dollars, but it was never enough for Niles.

Besides, Niles and his father, her late uncle Jay, might have despised Spencer, but her relationship with him had contained many more nuances than simple dislike.

She placed her champagne glass down next to the plate of caviar. The abrupt action caused the sparkling liquid to slosh over the rim. A waiter appeared as if by magic, whisking away the glass, replacing it with a fresh one and blotting the drops of champagne from the white tablecloth with a thick napkin. He even swapped out the plate of caviar, although none of the liquid had touched it.

The dull throbbing in her head from earlier in the evening made a repeat performance. She had to get away from the chatter.

She turned and collided with a brick wall—a brick wall

in a fine wool suit. The man with the sunglasses caught her arm with a surprisingly gentle grip.

"I'm sorry." His voice was a deep baritone that sent shocks of awareness up her spine.

He wasn't wearing sunglasses anymore and she stared into the bluest eyes she'd ever seen. "M-my fault."

He released her arm and strode past her.

She watched his broad back as he cut a swath through the partygoers. He landed in front of Bunny Harris and ducked as the older woman whispered something in his ear.

Watching the exchange, London sucked in her lower lip. Was he one of Bunny's escorts? If so, the old dame's taste in men had gone up several notches.

London slipped out of the room and headed for the ladies' restroom. On the way, Captain Williams from the San Francisco police department stopped her.

"This is a wonderful benefit, London. I'm sure your father would've been proud."

"Thank you, Captain."

He shook a finger in her face. "How many times do I have to tell you to call me Les? I've known you since you were a little girl, but you're a grown woman now. Les will do."

"I'll try to remember that…Les. If you'll excuse me." She'd been inching away from him during their conversation and was able to turn and make a break for it. If Captain Les Williams thought she had any pull to get him the chief's job, he'd better start kissing someone else's backside. Her father, with his connections to the SFPD, hadn't been able to do it, so she sure as hell couldn't.

She pushed through the ladies' room door. A couple of women were primping at the vanity and stopped their gossip long enough to smile at London in the mirror.

She nodded and swept past them to the restroom. Leaning against the tile counter, she dug into her clutch for an ibuprofen. She cupped some water in her hand from the faucet and swallowed the gelcap.

The voices of the women in the outer room rose and then a man burst through the bathroom door, holding his hand in front of him. "Don't be alarmed, Ms. Breck. I'd just like to ask you a few questions. Ray Lopez from KFGG. You might've seen my show."

She'd need to pop another ibuprofen at this rate. Instead she wedged a hand on her hip. "Really? You're following me into the ladies' room to get an interview?"

"Just a comment."

"You can't call my office?"

He spread his hands as he smiled. "You know and I know it's not that easy to reach you at your…office. Just a quick question about your father's death."

One of the women from the other room had followed the reporter into the bathroom and skewered him with an icy gaze. "Security is on the way."

He shrugged and stepped closer to London.

"I've already done that interview, Mr. Lopez—just not with you." She turned toward the mirror and ran the pad of her thumb over one eyebrow.

"You didn't answer this question. Did you find your father's death suspicious?"

"Not at all." She backed away from the mirror and tucked her bag under her arm, brushing past Lopez. Had he written the threatening note to manufacture some story? Why would he ask that question? She wouldn't give him the satisfaction of asking him about his motives.

As she took one step out of the lounge, a security guard barreled past her. "Sir, you're not allowed in the ladies' room. I'm going to have to escort you out of the hotel."

Lopez craned his head over his shoulder to give her one last look as the security guard hustled him toward the escalator.

She blew out a long breath. She couldn't even escape notice in the ladies' bathroom. She'd had enough, enough of the pretense and the fake smiles and the eager reporters... and the vaguely threatening notes. Her father had passed away just last month—of natural causes. Surely she could be excused for having a headache and leaving the shindig early.

She plucked her phone from her purse and called her driver. "Theodore, I'm ready to go. Meet me in the side alley. I don't want to go through the front entrance."

"Paparazzi stalking you again, Ms. Breck?"

"You have no idea."

"On my way."

When she entered the ballroom, she located her cousin, who was telling some risqué story and taking liberties with the truth. She crooked her finger at him and he broke away from his adoring audience.

"I'm getting out of here. People already think I was terribly brave making an appearance so soon after Dad's death."

"Especially since he did go off rather abruptly."

Was everyone drinking the same water? Lifting her shoulders, she said, "He *did* have heart disease."

"Although all his money allowed him to manage it quite well."

"Did you send me a note tonight, Niles?"

"A note?" His tweezed eyebrows shot to his hairline. "What are you talking about?"

"Nothing. Never mind." Had she really expected him to confess? Of course, maybe she'd just put him on notice.

She flicked her fingers at the room, still buzzing with activity. "Could you please do the honors for me? Announce the winners of the silent auction, thank everyone for coming and so on and son on."

He patted her arm with his long, thin hand. "I'd be happy

to, my dear. You go home and get a good night's sleep and dream of your billions."

She sighed. "You're not exactly in the poorhouse, cousin."

"Ah, but your father was the lucky one—and the greedy one."

"I already have a headache. Let's not get into family politics." She kissed the air somewhere near his cheek and pivoted on her heel.

She nearly bumped into Bunny Harris at the coat check, hanging on to a much younger man's arm, but not the man with the sunglasses. "So sorry, Bunny. Are you off already?"

"Don't worry, London. I made a sizable donation to the cause. Your father was one of my oldest friends. I'll miss him."

"Thank you." London's gaze strayed over Bunny's shoulder to her model-handsome companion lounging against the coat-check window.

Bunny slid her ticket across the counter with one manicured fingertip. "Oh, this is…"

"Lance." The man reached around Bunny, extending his hand. "Ms. Breck."

"Nice to meet you." She shook his hand and then dropped it. "Enjoy the rest of your evening."

Lance draped Bunny's fur around her shoulders and they descended the escalator to the lobby of the hotel.

Shaking her head, London dipped her hand into her purse for the claim ticket and felt the note. She pulled it out with the ticket and examined the block letters written with a black felt-tip pen.

She'd hold on to it for a day or two in case there was a follow-up and then turn it over to Breck Global's security team. It could very well be that reporter trying some angle.

The coat-check clerk plopped her leather bomber jacket on the counter. "Cool jacket."

London smiled, handed her a tip and headed for the escalator, hugging the jacket to her chest. When she hit the first step, she gathered the skirt of her long dress in one hand and lifted it.

She glided into the lobby and a bellhop sprang to life. "Do you need a taxi, Ms. Breck?"

"No, thanks. My driver's waiting." Technically, Theodore was her father's driver, but she didn't have the heart to let him go, even though she felt silly with a driver.

She stuffed her arms into her jacket and pulled out her phone to check the time. If Theodore had taken the car back to her father's Pacific Heights mansion, it shouldn't take him more than ten or fifteen minutes to get here.

She parked herself in front of a rack of flyers and studied the trips to Alcatraz and the wine country for a few minutes. Then she glanced over her shoulder at a few people crisscrossing the lobby. No photographers, no Ray Lopez, although they could be waiting for her out front. She pushed through the side door of the hotel. Lifting her skirts, she traipsed down the steps and shoved open the heavy metal door to the outside.

It slammed behind her.

The dark alley glistened with moisture. Theodore hadn't made it yet. She squinted toward the street, partially blocked by a Dumpster.

He must've taken the car somewhere else on his break. She turned toward the side door and grabbed the handle, pressing it down. The door didn't budge.

A footstep crunched behind her, but before she had time to turn around, an arm hooked around her throat.

She should've braved the paparazzi.

Chapter Two

Locked in a stall in the men's room, Judd slipped the velvet pouch crammed with jewels into the inside pocket of his dinner jacket. He patted his .45 tucked into the shoulder holster on the other side.

He had no idea where Bunny Harris would wind up with that gigolo she'd picked up tonight, but at least her jewelry wouldn't be with her.

He shoved out of the stall and nodded at the man washing his hands at the vanity, who'd caught his eye in the mirror. The dude had been talking to London Breck earlier— probably a relative. As far as he knew, the richest woman in the city didn't have a husband or even a boyfriend. The tabloids linked her with a new man every other month… not that he followed the tabloids except for business.

The man at the sink and London had the same look— blond, Nordic, cold. Although London was a beautiful girl, she wasn't his type, even with all those dollar signs after her name.

Judd washed his hands, accepted a warm towel from the attendant and slipped a five in his basket. He turned toward the door.

"Care for a spritz?"

Judd stumbled to a stop and glanced over his shoulder at the mirror.

The Breck relative held up a bottle of cologne, aiming it at him. "It's a good scent…manly."

"That's okay." Judd held up his hands. "I'm good."

He heard the hiss of the spray bottle behind him as he dodged through the bathroom door. *Rich people.*

Checking his watch, he jogged down the escalator. Bunny had told him she'd send her car back for him at the side entrance to the hotel. He waved to the hotel clerk and gave a fist bump to one of the bellhops.

"Later, man."

He took the steps down to the side door two at a time and pushed through to the alley. Darkness enveloped him as his shoes crunched broken glass. He tilted back his head to look at the lights on the outside of the hotel, which had been smashed.

His head jerked up at the sound of scuffling down the alley, and he noticed a car parked at the end, blocking the entrance to the street, contributing to the darkness.

He plucked a small but powerful flashlight from his pocket and aimed it in the direction of the noise.

A man wearing a ski mask looked up from the woman he was dragging behind him by the throat.

"Hey!" Judd sprinted toward the scene.

The man dropped his victim and rushed to the waiting car at the end of the alley. Tires squealed and the car peeled out before Judd could reach it. He flicked his light at the retreating vehicle, but someone had removed the back license plate.

A woman coughed behind him and he spun around and strode back to her. The sparkly material of her gown was twisted around her legs and she couldn't stand. He scooped her up and set her on her impossibly high heels. No wonder she couldn't run away from her assailant.

She brushed strands of blond hair from her face. That silvery hair seemed to be the only source of light in the alley—that and the sparkles on her black dress and at her throat.

She coughed again, swore like a sailor and spit onto the concrete. "My God, if he wanted the necklace, why didn't he just ask?"

Judd found himself looking into the perfect face of London Breck, a little disheveled and mad as hell, but those qualities only seemed to enhance her beauty.

Her eyes widened and sparkled, matching the diamonds around her neck in brilliance. "You!"

"What the hell are you doing out here in the alley?" He bent over and swept her handbag from the ground. Odd the thief hadn't snatched that.

She grabbed it from him and folded her arms over her body. "Waiting for my driver. You?"

"Waiting for Bunny Harris's driver."

She swayed toward him and he caught her before she toppled over. She smelled…expensive, except for the odor of leather coming from her jacket. Who wore a jacket like that with a haute couture evening dress?

"Whoa." He pointed to her feet. "If you hope to stand upright on your own, you'd better straighten out that dress."

"I hate long dresses." She leaned forward and placed her hands on either side of a hole in her dress below her knees and pulled it apart.

The bottom part of her dress, which seemed to be made of different material from the top, ripped off, and she dropped the silky material, which probably cost more than his motorcycle, into a puddle in the alley.

"There." She thrust out her hand. "London Breck. Thanks for saving me from whatever that was."

"Judd Brody." He clasped her long, slim fingers in his hand, but if he expected a limp, girly handshake from her, he was wrong. She gave his hand a firm squeeze and dropped it.

"That was a robbery, wasn't it?" His gaze shifted to the bright bauble stuck on her right ring finger and the diamond bracelet now peeking from the cuff of the jacket.

She trailed her fingers across her throat. "At first I thought he wanted my necklace, but he was using it to choke me and drag me. He was pulling me to that waiting car."

"A kidnapping?" He lifted one eyebrow. "I suppose you're worth a few bucks."

She snorted. "Yeah, good luck with that. My cousin wouldn't pay one dime for my release, and I'm sure my board of directors would be happy to get rid of me."

A black limo pulled into the alley, bathing it in bright light. Judd cupped a hand over his eyes and squinted.

The car door swung open and a massive figure rolled from the car. "Miss Breck? Are you all right? I'm sorry I'm late. I had a little mishap on the way over."

She waved. "I'm fine, Theodore. Mr. Brody here rescued me from a would-be robber."

"What?" Theodore waddled toward them. "I told you not to be waiting in this alley."

"I expected you to be right here to whisk me away." She patted the big man's arm. "Not that I blame you, Theodore. Sh—stuff happens."

Theodore grabbed Judd's hand and shook his arm as if he wanted to yank it off. "Thank you, sir."

Another limo pulled into the alley and honked.

"Now, who is that?" Theodore tugged his cap over his eyes to shield out his headlights.

"I believe that's Ms. Harris's driver for me." Judd straightened his jacket and patted the hidden jewels.

Theodore tilted his head at him. "You one of Bunny's young men?"

London coughed and clapped a hand over her mouth. As long as Theodore had been working for the upper crust of the city, he'd never learned to filter his speech. She liked that.

"God, no. I'm working for her tonight…as a bodyguard."

"Can I buy you a drink?" London sniffed and ran her hand beneath her nose. "It's the least I can do. Theodore can take us."

"That I can," her driver added.

A drink with the rich and beautiful London Breck? Why not? Another way to make his older brothers jealous.

"Sure."

"I'll go tell Bunny's driver. I know him." Theodore turned and made his way down the alley, momentarily blocking out the headlights and casting him into darkness again with London.

She suddenly looked vulnerable with her silvery-blond hair half-down on one side and her ripped couture dress.

Judd tapped his neck. "Are you okay?"

"Throat's a little rough, but I'll live."

"Do you want to report it to the cops?"

"Did you get a license plate or a good look at the driver or my attacker?"

"The car didn't have a license plate and the driver was wearing a ski mask just like your assailant's, except for the white zigzag down the front."

"Then, no. I don't need the publicity."

Theodore shifted his formidable presence to the side and the headlights lit up the alley again. The beams picked up London's sparkles—her hair, her jewels, her dress—and she blazed to life. How had he ever imagined this woman had one vulnerable bone in her body?

"You get a lot of that, don't you? Publicity, I mean."

Spreading her hands, she shrugged. "Comes with the territory."

Theodore called from behind her, "I sent Mrs. Harris's driver away. Are you ready, Miss Breck?"

"After the night I just had? You bet."

She spun around on her high heels and picked her way through the puddles in the alley to the waiting town car.

Judd's gaze locked onto her swaying hips in the glittering material below the bomber jacket and the endless legs below the jagged hem of the skirt. London had a tall, slim build, but he wouldn't call her skinny.

Wouldn't kick her out of bed, either.

He motioned for the driver to get in the car first and held open the door as Theodore squeezed behind the wheel. Judd slammed the door after Theodore and ducked into the backseat.

It smelled like brand-new leather, which felt as smooth as butter beneath his fingertips as he adjusted himself on the seat next to London.

The glass between the front and backseats slid open. "Where to, Miss Breck?"

"How about Sneaky Pete's in the Lower Haight?"

"I don't think it's very safe down there, Miss Breck."

"I'm going to be with Bunny Harris's bodyguard, and he's—" she patted his chest "—packing heat."

"It's that obvious?"

"To the practiced eye." With her hand still on his chest, she ran those practiced eyes down to his thighs and a slow heat simmered his blood.

"And here I thought we were headed someplace upscale and trendy."

"I just want a quiet drink. Disappointed?" She snatched her hand back and dropped it into her lap where her ripped dress had ridden up, exposing her creamy thighs.

"Doesn't make any difference to me, but if we're headed that way, I need to make a stop first. Is that a problem?"

"Not for me." She leaned forward in her seat. "Theodore?"

"Not a problem, sir. Where to?"

Judd pulled the bag of jewels from his pocket and tossed

it on the seat between him and London. "I need to make a deposit at Bunny's house."

"I know exactly where the Harris house is. It's not too far from Mr. Breck's residence. We'll be there in less than fifteen minutes." The privacy glass magically slid into place while Theodore backed the car out of the alley and rolled onto the street.

"I'm sure this was your idea." London caressed the velvet pouch. "Bunny is notoriously careless, especially when she's met a new young stud."

"I noticed."

"Do you guard her body or her possessions?"

"This is a one-night gig for me. I was helping out a buddy, and the directive was to watch the jewels. When it was clear she'd made plans after the gala with someone she'd just met, I insisted she leave her jewels with me."

"You're one of *those* Brodys, aren't you?"

Why wouldn't she know his family? Hers had been in this city longer than his. He hunched forward and inspected the mobile liquor cabinet in front of him. "Yep."

"Congratulations."

"For what?" He lifted the lid from a cut-glass decanter half-full of dark amber liquid and sniffed the rich aroma.

"After all these years, it looks as though your brother and that true-crime writer uncovered the truth that your father wasn't the Phone Book Killer."

"I guess so." He investigated another decanter.

"You seem rather nonchalant about it all."

"Happened a long time ago." And he'd sealed off that part of his life in a cold little box in one corner of his heart. He'd let his older brothers gnash their teeth over the stain on the family name. He'd schooled himself not to think about it…or his father.

Her hand covered his, grasping the decanter. "Do you want a drink?"

That smooth skin against his did things to his insides. Was she that smooth all over? That perfect? He'd have fun getting her a little dirty.

His gaze wandered to the tinted glass. Would Theodore mind? This backseat afforded plenty of room to twist this leggy blonde into a pretzel. But she deserved more than a quickie.

He stared into her murky green eyes. "I can wait."

As her hand left his, she trailed her short, polished fingernails across his skin and he suppressed a shiver.

This one might be made of ice, but she liked to play with fire. He'd seen the tabloids—London Breck jumping naked into a fountain, London Breck running away from home at seventeen to join a rock band on tour, London Breck getting arrested in Qatar for having one of the world's largest diamonds in her possession, which she'd claimed a married sheikh had given her.

Slumming it with a lowly P.I. could be her next crazy prank.

Hell, he was game.

What made him think she wasn't his type? Any gorgeous woman who was up for a good time was his type.

The car slid to a smooth stop at the gates of a mansion in Pacific Heights. The city lights created a twinkling river before them.

The intercom clicked on and Theodore's voice rumbled across the speaker. "I don't know if we can get past the security gates, sir."

"Mrs. Harris and I made arrangements. Pull up to the call box, Theodore."

The car turned into the driveway and stopped at the intercom at the gate. Judd punched the button and held it in.

"Hello?"

"This is Judd Brody."

"Of course, Mr. Brody. Mrs. Harris left instructions."

The gate eased open and Theodore drove the car around the short, circular drive in front of the Victorian mansion. Did London live in a place like this up here?

"I'll be right back." Judd swung open the door before Theodore could get out and open it for him. He strode up the front porch and rang the doorbell, which chimed somewhere deep in the house.

The door opened a crack and an eyeball assessed him. Then the crack widened and the pinched face of Bunny's butler appeared.

Judd held out the pouch. "Mrs. Harris wants these to go right back in the safe."

"Yes, of course." The butler snatched the pouch with long, bony fingers and pressed it to his heart. "Thank you, Mr. Brody, for looking after Bunny's treasures."

"I think someone else is looking after her treasures now."

He left the butler standing at the door with his mouth gaping open, launched off the porch and grabbed the handle of the car door.

He fell onto the seat and ran a hand through his hair. "On to Sneaky Pete's."

The car lurched forward and London fell against his shoulder. She took her time getting back into her own space. So she felt it, too?

He'd better maintain control. The drive to the Haight wasn't that long—not nearly long enough for what he planned for London.

He cleared his throat. "Do you live in Pacific Heights?"

"No." She shook her head and her hair shimmered. "I live on Nob Hill, but my father has a place here. I'm not moving."

He shot a quick glance at her luscious lips, now pressed

into a determined line. His simple question had changed the mood in the car.

London kept her hands in her lap and stared out the window. She seemed to have lost interest in their flirtation, so maybe he wouldn't be getting lucky with an heiress tonight.

Theodore pulled the car to the curb, but this time Judd didn't beat him to the door. Theodore opened London's door with a wrinkled brow beneath his cap. "I don't like this, Miss Breck."

"It's all good, Theodore. Do you want to join us for a drink?"

He crossed his arms, resting them on his big belly. "I don't drink and drive. Never have, never will."

Judd clambered from the car and eyed the seedy bar with the psychedelic mural on the outside wall and a flickering red neon sign. "I'll take care of her, Theodore."

"Thank you, sir."

London heaved an exaggerated sigh, but she didn't protest. "You can take the car home, Theodore. We can get a taxi later."

"I have my own code. I take you somewhere, and I bring you back. Call when you're ready."

"If you insist." She winked at Judd.

"Hold on." Judd shed his dinner jacket, shrugged out of his cummerbund and pulled off his bow tie. He tossed them into the backseat of the car. "I don't want to be overdressed."

London tugged her motorcycle jacket closed over the sparkly material of her dress. "You have a point."

Judd opened the door of the bar and ushered her through. The neon motif from outside carried forward to the interior. Standard-issue neon beer signs flashed on the walls, and a jukebox in the corner cranked out a hard-rock tune. If smoking in bars were allowed in this city, this would be a smoke-filled room.

Instead patrons cracked peanut shells and dropped them on the floor as they gathered around tables or hunched over the bar. A few couples danced on the wood floor of a small room off the main bar. Nobody looked at them twice.

Rolling up the sleeves of his white shirt, Judd led London to a table near the jukebox and slid onto the wood bench across from her. "Come here often?"

"Every once in a while." Her gaze scanned the tattoos spilling down one of his arms, and she pointed to the long bar of scarred wood. "We can order at the bar. The waitresses here are few and far between."

"I'm in no hurry, are you?" He caught the eye of a waitress in a pair of short shorts and a tie-dyed T-shirt tied under her breasts.

She scurried over, balancing a tray of drinks with one hand. "What can I get you?"

"I'll have a beer, whatever you have on tap."

"I'll take the same." London turned wide eyes on him. "How did you get her to come over here so fast?"

He shrugged. "I just made eye contact. It works better than yelling."

Her gaze dropped from his face and meandered across his chest, where he'd undone the first few buttons of his shirt. His flesh warmed in the wake of her inventory.

"Yeah, whatever." She folded her arms on the table. "So what do you normally do for a living when you're not helping out friends guarding jewels for rich, frisky matrons?"

"Guard jewels for rich, frisky matrons."

"Really?"

He stretched his legs out to the side of the table. "I'm a private investigator and bodyguard. Usually my assignments are more long-term than this one. I just got back from a job in Saudi Arabia."

"I know a few people in that part of the world." She flashed her teeth in more of a grimace than a smile and drummed her fingernails on the table. "Is it interesting work?"

"It can be. There's a lot of travel involved, which I like."

"I like to travel, too." She stopped fidgeting and pressed her palms together. "Things will be a little different for me now, now that…"

"Your father died. Sorry for your loss."

"Thank you."

"He left you in charge?"

Her eyes narrowed and glittered. "You sound surprised."

"You sound defensive."

She puffed out a breath, blowing a strand of hair from her eyes. "Let's just say I'm dealing with a lot right now. Lots of unhappy people never expected Dad to put the reins of Breck Global Enterprises in the hands of his flighty daughter."

"You're his only child?" He knew that, of course, even if he didn't follow San Francisco society closely, except when he needed to for his clients. But he stubbornly wanted to pretend he knew nothing about her famous family.

"Only legitimate one." She rubbed her chin. "I do have a half brother. I'm sure my father would've preferred me as the bastard and Wade as the legitimate son. You have three brothers, right?"

He raised his brows but held his response as the waitress delivered their drinks and a bowl of peanuts.

The waitress asked, "Do you want anything to eat?"

"No, thanks." He tipped his chin at London. "You?"

"Not after all that rich food at the benefit."

He sipped the dark, malty beer through the thick head of foam and met London's purposeful look over the rim of the glass.

"Three brothers? I know one's a cop in the city, and then there's the one who was working with that writer."

"You seem to know a lot about my family."

"The Brody family is in the news almost as much as my family." Her lips puckered and she blew on the foam in her glass.

"For very different reasons." He shifted his gaze away from that kissable mouth. He'd let her make all the moves.

"While you're all busy delivering justice, the Brecks are delivering…money."

"Both equally necessary. Besides, I don't deliver justice. I just look out for pretty people and their pretty things."

He didn't believe in justice—not after losing his father when he was practically a baby and then his mother to drugs and alcohol. Sean had been a great big brother, but a sibling was no substitute for a mom and dad.

"Thank God for that." London clinked her mug with his.

The song on the jukebox had changed to a slow ballad all about how love hurt, and Judd took a swig of beer. Hell, love didn't hurt, not if you dropped it in its tracks.

London rapped her knuckles on the table between them. "You wanna dance?"

"You're kidding."

"There are some couples out there." She jerked her thumb over her shoulder at the postage-stamp dance floor.

"That doesn't mean we have to join them."

She tugged on his rolled-up sleeve. "Come on. I promise not to jump on the tabletop."

Her cool fingers brushed against his skin, causing a thudding ache in the middle of his belly. "Have you been known to do that? Jump on tabletops?"

Her fingernails dug into his forearm. "Don't pretend you don't know about me, Judd Brody."

Busted. He jumped from the booth. If this was some weird mating ritual she had, he'd play along.

When they hit the dance floor, he pulled her snug against his body. Who did she think she was toying with, some upper-crust rich boy? He didn't play games. If a woman signaled interest the way London was doing, he'd take her up on the offer every time.

Wrapping one arm around her slender waist, he reached up with his other hand to tuck her head against his shoulder. Her breath warmed his skin through the thin material of his shirt.

He rested his cheek against her bright hair, and the golden strands stuck to the stubble of his beard. Reaching between their bodies, he opened her leather jacket and drew her close, his chest pressing against her soft breasts beneath the silvery material of her dress.

She shifted and her soft lips touched the side of his neck.

He gritted his teeth to suppress the shudder threatening to engulf his body. Her expensive perfume enveloped them, and for the first time in a very long time and a very long line of women, he felt on the edge of losing control.

Then the door to the bar burst open and Theodore, bloodied and battered, staggered into the room and dropped to the floor.

Chapter Three

London screamed at the bloody mess that was Theodore's face and twisted out of the comfort of Judd's embrace, pitching forward. Judd curled one muscular arm around her waist to steady her.

He tucked her behind his large frame and strode toward Theodore, who had collapsed in a heap.

She made a grab for Judd's belt and hooked two fingers through the loop, following him as people cleared a path to Theodore's inert form.

Judd yelled over his shoulder at the bartender, "Call nine-one-one. Now!"

He crouched beside Theodore, feeling for his pulse. "Towels, I need some clean towels to stop this bleeding."

"I-is he still alive? Has he been shot?" London had never seen so much blood. She unbuttoned Theodore's shirt at the neck.

"He's still breathing, and I don't see any bullet wounds."

The waitress who had served them earlier rushed from behind the bar with a stack of white towels. "Is he okay?"

"He's lost consciousness."

One of the bartenders knelt beside Judd with a pitcher of water. "Ambulance is on the way. Do you need this?"

London dipped one of the towels in the water and dabbed

Theodore's split lip as Judd pressed another against the gaping wound on his head.

Taking Theodore's big hand in hers, London squeezed it and whispered, "You're going to be okay."

The wailing sirens scattered the crowd of people hovering over Theodore. When the EMTs rushed in, Judd talked to them as they worked on their patient.

Once the EMTs bundled Theodore into the ambulance, a police officer approached Judd. "Do you know the victim?"

Judd turned to London. "He's her driver."

"Black limo? License number—" the officer flipped open a notepad "—BGE21?"

London's heart fluttered in her chest. "That's right. What happened to Theodore? Where's the car?"

The officer tapped the pad of paper against his chin. "The car's registered to Spencer Breck and Breck Global Enterprises."

"That's me." London waved her hand. "I'm Breck Global Enterprises."

The cop's eyes widened for a second and then shifted to the diamond necklace around her throat. "Of course, Ms. Breck. The car—your car—was found idling at the curb by the park. The driver's-side door was open and it looks as if the car had rolled partially into the street and then was hit by another car."

Judd's head shot up. "Was there blood near the car? On the seat?"

"Exactly. It appears that someone pulled the driver from the car and beat him on the street. His plans to steal the car were probably thwarted when it rolled into the street and got hit." The officer's eyebrows met over his nose. "And you are?"

"Judd Brody."

"Brody…"

"He's my friend. Is that what you think this was? An attempted car theft? Of a limo?"

"Could've been kids looking for a joyride." He scratched his chin and eyed Judd. "Aren't you…?"

Judd sliced his hand through the air. "I don't think kids could've done that much damage to a big guy like Theodore."

Good to know she and Judd were on the same page. Wedging her hand on her hip, she said, "I don't think kids would be out to steal a distinctive limo, either."

"That might be just what they wanted. We don't have any witnesses. I'm amazed your driver made it this far in his condition. He should've just called the cops himself."

The officer asked them several more questions and told her where the ambulance had transported Theodore. He had a daughter in New York and one in Atlanta, and she intended to call both of them just as soon as she checked up on Theodore herself.

How could this happen? Theodore had never run into any trouble driving her father around. She couldn't even keep her employees safe. How was she supposed to run a company? Maybe she did need Roger's help.

She arranged for a tow service to take the limo back to her father's place, and Judd called a taxi.

London twisted her fingers into knots. "It's all my fault. I should've insisted that he take the car back instead of waiting around in this crappy neighborhood."

"The only people who deserve blame are the dirtbags who tried to jack Theodore." He brushed a wisp of hair from her cheek with the rough pad of his finger. "There's no way you were going to convince Theodore to leave you. He takes pride in a job well done."

"You're right, but we should've gone somewhere else." She shoved her hands in the pockets of her jacket. "I need to stop being the wild-child free spirit."

He wedged a finger beneath her chin and tilted her head back. "Who says?"

His soft touch and low voice caused tears to prick the backs of her eyes. How had he gone from sexy alpha male on the dance floor to this man with the understanding eyes? And why was she falling under his spell so quickly?

She jerked her head away and ducked to peer through the window. "I think our taxi's here."

They climbed into the backseat and she put her hand on his forearm, which tensed beneath her fingers. "Your jacket's in the back of the limo."

"Don't worry about it. I don't think I'll be needing it anytime soon."

"Where do you live?" She leaned forward in her seat.

"We'll have him drop you off first."

She gave the taxi driver her address and fell back against the seat. "I hope Theodore's going to be okay. Maybe we should follow the ambulance."

"And have you create a media circus? Not a great idea. Theodore lost a lot of blood, but I've seen guys a lot worse off than that after fights. I think he'll pull through."

"Thanks to you. Is all that first aid—" she waved her hand in the air "—part of your job?"

"Yeah. I spent several summers working as a lifeguard in Santa Cruz, so I had all that training, which comes in handy now."

She closed her eyes. Was there anything this man couldn't do?

Too quickly, the taxi pulled in front of her building.

Judd tapped the driver's shoulder. "Wait here. I'll be right back."

He took her hand to help her from the car and dropped it all too soon as they walked to the front door of her building. She entered the code to open the door and turned on the step. Under better circumstances she'd invite him up for a cocktail, see if his slow seduction on the dance floor would come to fruition.

Now she just wanted to wash her hands, still smudged with Theodore's blood.

"Thanks for everything tonight, Judd Brody."

"You're welcome, London Breck. Do you need me to walk you up to your place?"

She pointed inside the lobby at the security guard sitting at the desk watching TV monitors. "Twenty-four-hour security here. I'm not the only celebrity in the building."

"Good, but don't forget how the evening started, with you being attacked in an alley."

Judd didn't even know about the threatening note. "I guess Theodore and I both had targets on our backs tonight."

His brow furrowed. "Yeah, you did."

He obviously wasn't going to sweep her into his arms for a good-night kiss, no matter how much she needed the comfort, so she stuck out her hand. "Good night."

"Goodbye." He gave her hand a hard squeeze and then turned away.

Ouch. That had a ring of finality to it. Why shouldn't it? They were two strangers thrown together by two extraordinary events. They'd shared a little flirtation, but so what? A man like Judd Brody must have had many little flirtations to his credit…and many notches on his bedpost.

She had more important matters to think about anyway. She waved to the security guard as she crossed the marble-tiled lobby. She had to grow up and take charge of a multibillion-dollar enterprise—and Judd Brody couldn't help with that at all.

THE FOLLOWING DAY, London scooted the plastic chair closer to the bed and patted Theodore's arm. "I don't get why someone would want to carjack a limousine. And why did you go to the bar instead of calling the police?"

Theodore moved his head from side to side and groaned.

"Keep still." She reached for the plastic cup on the table beside his hospital bed and held the straw to his swollen lips.

He sipped some water and then waved it away. "Pulled me out of the car, and I lost my phone in the fight. I wouldn't let them…wouldn't let them take the car."

"That's just silly. Why are you protecting a heap of metal? You should've let them have the damn thing and saved yourself."

"Couldn't let them. Had to protect you."

"Me?" She folded the sheet under his side. "I wasn't even there. I was perfectly safe at the bar with—at the bar."

She'd fallen asleep thinking about Judd's arms wrapped around her on the dance floor, about the way the warm skin of his throat felt against her lips. Then she heard his goodbye. Curt. Final.

"If they got the car…they could get you."

Her gaze darted to his face and she flashed on the threatening note from last night. "What does that mean?"

But Theodore had closed his eyes, and his breathing deepened.

His nurse bustled into the room. "Is he sleeping? I gave him something for the pain."

"How much longer will he be here?"

"You'll have to ask him. You're not next of kin, and we can't reveal those details."

London rolled her eyes and rose from the chair. "His medical expenses are covered by an insurance policy with Breck Global. I have his medical card."

"If you can drop that off at the nurses' station, they'll take care of getting that to billing."

Ten minutes later, London retrieved her Mini from the

hospital's subterranean parking garage and decided to check out the limo, which the tow truck had brought to her father's place. Why had Theodore thought he was protecting her by not allowing the carjackers to take the car? Maybe he hadn't wanted them to get the keys or the car registration, but the registration listed the address of BGE, not her place in Nob Hill.

She maneuvered through the traffic on Van Ness and turned toward Lafayette Park, rolling through the well-ordered streets with their manicured lawns. The tow-truck driver must've used the remote control in the limo for the gate, because he'd parked the car in the driveway.

London opened the front gate to the mansion with her key. The couple who looked after the house was still living here. London didn't have the heart to turn them out any more than she could let Theodore go.

The limo sported a dent in the left front panel and a smashed window. The cops had tried to lift prints from the vehicle, but hadn't had any luck.

She opened the door and shivered at the sight of Theodore's blood on the leather seat. She'd get the car detailed at the same time she dropped it off for bodywork. Peering under the seats, she spotted Theodore's cell phone and pulled it out.

He had left the sliding partition between the front and back seats open and a heap of material caught her eye— Judd's dinner jacket. A thrill of excitement zipped up her spine. Now she had an excuse to call him. Then she remembered his abrupt goodbye. Victor at the house could earn his salary by returning Judd's jacket to him.

Grabbing the handle of the back door, she yanked it open. She fell across the seat and buried her face in the fine material of Judd's jacket, inhaling the masculine scent that clung to its folds.

"Ms. Breck?"

She recognized Anna, the housekeeper's, voice, and rolled to her back, hunching up on her elbows. "Hello, Anna."

"Are you okay?"

Anna's lips twitched with disapproval and London knew whatever response she made, Anna would never think she was okay. Anna had been around since before her mother died, had been around for all the craziness and the acting out and…all the other stuff.

"I'm fine. Victor told you what happened to Theodore, didn't he?"

"Foolish man." Her nostrils flared. "He should've let them have the car."

"That's what I told him, but he said he was protecting me."

Anna's face puckered as if she'd just sucked a lemon. "Are you going to get the car fixed?"

"Yes, I was just—" She plucked at Judd's jacket. "My friend left his jacket in the car."

Anna screwed her face up even more, leaving no doubt about what she thought London and her so-called friend had been doing in the backseat of the limo.

She should've been so lucky.

"Maybe Victor can return it to him."

"Of course. Are you staying, Ms. Breck?"

"No. I just wanted to get my friend's stuff." *And roll around in it while I think of his hard body.*

The old London would've voiced those exact words just to see Anna's face implode, but the new London, the CEO London, kept those thoughts to herself.

"You can give your friend's items and an address to Victor. He'll be happy to return them." Anna's rubber-soled shoes squelched on the damp flagstones as she went back to the house.

When London heard the front door shut, she collapsed

against the seat again, against Judd's jacket, her arm dangling to the floor of the car. Her fingers met the stiff cummerbund Judd had discarded and something else—something soft and fuzzy.

She closed her hand around it and held it above her face. She drew her brows together. It was a beanie, a watch cap. No, a ski mask.

A ski mask with a white zigzag down the front.

Chapter Four

Judd tossed his cell phone onto the desk and leaned back in his secondhand chair, which squeaked in protest. He wanted to find out how Theodore was doing, but he couldn't get anything out of the hospital and he didn't have any pull with the SFPD with his brother Sean still on a leave of absence.

He watched the pedestrians in the street from his small second-story office in North Beach. He had only one room with an old desk, two chairs, a bookshelf and a dying plant, but it kept his clients away from his apartment.

Yawning, he scratched the stubble on his chin. He'd had a cancellation and should be using the downtime to do some paperwork, but he hated paperwork. He needed an admin assistant, but didn't like people poking around his business, and there wasn't enough room in this office for a second person.

He grabbed his phone again and traced the edges with his fingertip. It would be easy enough to leave a message for London at the BGE offices. She did still have his dinner jacket from last night. He could use that as an excuse.

Smacking the phone against his palm, he swore. Why did he need an excuse? She wasn't the queen. He could call her if he wanted to call her.

He dropped the cell on his desk again. He knew damned well her wealth and power weren't deterring him from contacting her. It was the way she made him feel—and those feelings had *danger* written all over them.

He ran a hand through his hair. "Let it go, Brody."

"Let what go?"

He stared at the vision outlined by the open door of his office as if he'd conjured her from his mind. London had one hand on her hip and the other supporting her on the doorjamb. Faded denim encased her long legs and a pair of high-heeled boots hit just above her knee. A green sweater with a dipping neckline matched her eyes, and she'd pulled her silvery-blond hair into a ponytail that fell over one shoulder.

Danger.

"How'd you find me?"

"You're kidding, right?" She launched into the room, sweeping a bag from the floor on her way in. "I have BGE's formidable resources at the tips of my fingers."

"How's Theodore doing?"

"He's out of danger. I called his daughters this morning, and one is coming out in a few days."

"That's good."

Dropping the bag at her feet, London scanned the room. "This sort of reminds me of Philip Marlowe's office."

"Um, I don't have any palm trees swaying in the Santa Ana winds out my window."

She spun around, arms flung out to her sides. "You know what I mean—cramped quarters, battered old desk, piles of paper all over."

"You make it sound so…charming." He pointed to the bag on the floor. "Are those the rest of my clothes?"

"Yes." She folded her hands in front of her, an expectant look on her face.

She must've wanted to see him, or she would've sent one of her lackeys over here. Did she want him to ask her out? Continue their game of flirtation? Take her across his battered old desk?

He cleared his throat and wedged one motorcycle boot against the edge of the desk—just in case.

"I—I have a proposition for you."

A pulse thudded in his throat. He liked propositions from beautiful women. He could sweep all this junk off his desk in two seconds. "Yeah?"

"I want to…hire you."

He crashed to earth but kept his expression immobile. "To do what?"

"To do what you do." She flicked her fingers in the air. "To be my bodyguard."

He clenched his jaw. Bad idea. Instead of dating him, did she think she could keep him on a chain, yanking him this way and that, barking orders? He didn't roll that way.

"No." He let his foot drop heavily to the floor.

She blinked and then widened her eyes. "Why not? That's your profession, isn't it? If it's the money—"

He held up a hand. "I know you're good for it, but I don't do that type of bodyguarding."

"What type?" She tilted her head and her ponytail swung to the other shoulder.

"The general you-can-be-my-lapdog-and-carry-my-shopping-bags type." He pushed to his feet and folded his arms across his chest, flexing just in case she didn't get the message.

Her lips parted and a rosy flush spread across her cheeks. "I'm not—you're not—it's not like that."

"Really."

"I need a protector, not a lapdog." She reached into the bag, pulled out his dinner jacket and tossed it onto the desk. She threw the cummerbund over her shoulder onto the floor. Then she straightened to her full height, plus five-inch heels, clutching a black watch cap to her chest.

"I need protection from this." Pinching the cap between two fingers, she dangled it in front of him.

His eyes narrowed as he took in the ski mask with the white lightning bolt down the front of it. "Where'd you find that?"

"It was in the backseat of the limo." She jiggled it so that it danced between them. "One of the carjackers, because Theodore confirmed there were two, must've lost it in the struggle. The same ski mask he wore when he attacked me outside the hotel last night."

"Let me see it." He held out his hand and she dropped it onto his palm. He stretched it out and traced the white pattern. "It's definitely the same one."

"Someone attacked me last night and then followed the limo and for whatever reason tried to steal it from Theodore."

"Sure looks that way." He poked his fingers into the eyeholes of the mask. "Maybe he got a good look at your diamonds and decided to go for them again."

"Then there's the note."

"The note?" He jerked his head up as London plunged a hand into her purse.

She pulled out a white piece of paper and waved it at him. "I got it last night at the benefit. Someone dropped it onto a waiter's tray and he delivered it to me."

"Would you stop—" he snatched the note from her "—waving things in my face."

He unfolded the notepaper and read aloud. "'Your father was murdered. You could be next.'"

"Looks like they planned to make good on that threat last night." She hunched her shoulders and hugged her waist.

"Why didn't you tell me about this before?"

"The note? I honestly never connected it with the events of last night. I thought the first was an attempted robbery and the second a carjacking. It occurred to me briefly when

I saw Theodore in the hospital this morning and he said something about trying to protect me."

He flicked the paper with his finger. "The wording is weird. 'You *could* be next'? Why didn't he write 'you *are* next'? 'You could be next' implies a conditional situation. You could be next *if* you do this or that."

She snapped her fingers. "That's why I need you."

"The two events are definitely connected, but we don't know if they're related to this warning." He slid one corner of the note beneath the blotter on his desk. "Do you think your father was murdered?"

"I didn't before last night. He had heart disease and he'd already had bypass surgery, but he didn't take care of his health—drank too much, had too much stress and his exercise consisted of walking from his golf cart to the tee."

"Was an autopsy done?"

"For a man as wealthy as my father? Of course. Atherosclerosis—blocked arteries."

"The note could be some kind of scam."

"I thought of that."

"What would the motive be?"

"Money, always money." She hooked a thumb in one pocket of her tight jeans. "So do you accept my proposition? I'll make it worth your while."

He kicked the leg of the single chair opposite his desk. "Have a seat."

She perched on the edge of the wooden chair, clutching the arms. "Does this mean yes?"

"Uh-huh." He yanked open a desk drawer, pulled out a file stuffed with blank contracts and dropped it on the blotter. He raised an eyebrow at her stiff posture. "Relax. I just want to review my terms with you. I'm not gonna require your firstborn or anything."

A blush rushed up her throat, flooding her cheeks and turning her creamy complexion a mottled red.

He needed to tone down the teasing. She couldn't seem to handle it in her agitated state. He also needed to keep this as professional as possible to cool the attraction between them. He'd be no good as a bodyguard if he spent his time lusting after the body he needed to guard.

"Here's my standard contract." He flipped open the file and slid a stapled set of papers toward her. "If you want your attorney to review it…"

"I'm sure it's fine." She plucked it from the desk and flipped through the pages. "Since it's a boilerplate, can we make adjustments as needed? I have several events coming up—there may be some travel."

"Of course. There's a section of the contract that deals with that—page three. Once you review and sign it, I'll ask for a retainer and we can get started."

"How much?" She dipped her hand into her purse and pulled out a checkbook. "I want you to get started right now. I don't need to review the contract. I trust you. You already saved my life once, and you were there for Theodore."

He sat back in his squeaky chair and steepled his fingers. Finding that ski mask had really spooked her, or maybe the note had done the trick.

She didn't even blink an eye when he told her the amount for his retainer. She scribbled out the check and slid it in front of him. "Where do we start?"

"Before we get started, I have a question for you." He picked up the corner of the check and tapped the edge on the blotter. "I'm assuming Breck Global Enterprises has a security force."

"We do."

"Why not enlist their help? You could probably pluck a bodyguard from the staff—someone already vetted and polished up to the BGE standards."

She glanced over her shoulder at the closed door.

"They're not my people. I haven't been at the company that long."

"You don't trust them." This introduced a new twist to the plot. "Who's been running BGE since your father's death? I'm assuming you're still…getting up to speed."

She jumped from the chair and it spun out behind her and hit the wall. "I *am* still getting up to speed, but I'm a fast learner and I'll get there."

"Wow." He raised one eyebrow and settled his boots back on the desk. "You need to chill. If you act this defensive around all the muckety-mucks at BGE, they're going to seriously doubt your abilities even more than they apparently do now."

"Damn." She turned and hit the wall with her palm. "It's just that everywhere I turn, I have people questioning me. It's Dad's fault. He never groomed me to take over the company."

"Did he groom someone else? Another relative?"

She puffed out a breath and swung the chair back in place. "Not really. He acted like he was going to live forever, even after the bypass. My cousin Niles has an interest in the company, and my half brother works there. He's a numbers guy. To answer your previous question before I went ballistic on you, Richard Taylor has been running the show since Dad's death. He and…his son have been my constant companions lately."

He rubbed his knuckles against the stubble of his beard. This looked to be an easy job—expectant relatives or co-workers got their noses out of joint when the old man handed over the reins of his company to his inexperienced daughter, and they decided to use a few threats and scare tactics to get her to decline the responsibility and return to her partying ways.

Gripping the back of the chair, she leaned forward, her silky ponytail falling over her shoulder. She parted her luscious lips and the scent of her expensive perfume washed over him.

This *could* be an easy job, or it could be very, very hard.

"You think you can help me?"

"That's what you're paying me for." He picked up the check and dropped it into his desk drawer. "First things first. I want to have a look at your place, check out the security there. When's a good time for you?"

"Right now, but you saw my building. It's like Fort Knox."

He shoved out of his chair and hunched over his desk. "Are you going to let me do my job, Ms. Breck, or are you going to try to run the show?"

"London. Call me London. After all, we shared a beer and a dance and...other stuff."

It's the other stuff that had him worried. "You didn't answer my question, London."

"I have enough shows to run, Judd. You can have this one."

"You didn't drive over here, did you?"

She snorted. "I didn't want to draw the attention of the paparazzi. So I snuck out and took a taxi."

"Are you okay riding on the back of a bike?"

Her gaze dropped to his boots. "A motorcycle?"

"Yeah."

"I've spent my share of time on the back of motorcycles."

I'll bet you have.

"I'll take you back to your place and have a look around, check out your security and make some notes."

"Sounds good to me."

He locked up the office behind them and followed her downstairs to the street, her high heels clicking on the steps. When they got to his Harley, he unlocked the helmet from the side. "You can wear this. If I get pulled over for not

wearing a helmet, I can always have my brother Sean fix
the ticket for me."

"Ah, nice to have connections."

"Just kidding." He placed the helmet over her head and
buckled the strap beneath her chin. "My brother wouldn't
fix a ticket for me or anyone else. Take this, too." He swung
his jacket over her shoulders. The wind would blow right
through that low-cut sweater.

She shoved her arms through the sleeves and zipped
up the jacket.

He straddled the bike and tilted it to the side. "Hop on. I
have a backrest, but you might want to hold on while we're
going uphill so you don't shift back and forth."

Placing one hand on his shoulder, she climbed onto his
Harley. Her knees touched his thighs and she put her hands
on either side of his waist while sitting upright. That erect
posture wouldn't last long once they started going up and
down the hills of the city.

He revved the engine and took off from the curb. When
the bike jerked forward, her hands clutched his shirt.

As they idled at a red light, she yelled in his ear. "Do
you remember where my place is?"

He nodded once. How could he forget? She lived in one
of the most exclusive buildings in the city, in an area where
the old robber barons used to have their mansions before
the earthquake and fire destroyed most of them.

He climbed a hill with a picture-perfect view of the
Transamerica building, and London tightened her grip
around his waist as she slid back on the seat. As they rolled
down the next hill, her body slammed against his.

"Sorry!" The wind snatched her word and carried it
away.

As it should. He didn't need an apology for the pres-
sure of her soft body against his back, her arms wrapped

securely around him, the scent of her perfume drugging him. Even her legs tightened against his hips.

He'd have to find another hill to descend.

All too soon he pulled up to the curb in front of her building. He cranked his head over his shoulder. "I'll let you off here and park between those two cars."

He steadied the bike as she clambered off, and then he backed into the space.

She was still fussing with the strap on the helmet when he joined her on the sidewalk.

"Let me. It's a little tricky." He flicked open the catch with his thumb and pulled the helmet from her head.

She tossed her mane of silver hair, which had escaped from her ponytail, back from her flushed face. "Mr. Toad's Wild Ride. That was always my favorite."

"Was it?" A strand of hair clung to the gloss on her mouth and he brushed it aside, the tip of his finger skimming across the smooth skin of her cheek.

Her chest rose and fell as her tongue swept along her bottom lip. Her half-closed lashes fluttered.

If he ever saw an invitation to a kiss, this ranked right up there with the best of them. Did she taste expensive, too? Like Cristal champagne and succulent strawberries?

The cold, hard cash—or at least the cold, hard check she'd written to him that was waiting in his desk drawer—had him pivoting away from her charms. Planting one boot on the step to her building, he smacked the heavy door to the lobby with the palm of his hand. "This is the first line of defense?"

She blinked. "Uh-huh."

He tried the door handle and the solid door didn't budge.

"There's a code." She pointed to the silver keypad to the right of the door, which he'd seen her use last night to gain entry.

"Wait." He held up his hand and started randomly punching buttons on another keypad on the other side of the door.

After several tries, a voice came over the speaker. "Yeah?"

Judd leaned forward. "Forgot my code."

The door clicked and Judd shook his head at London. "Fail."

As they stepped into the marble lobby, she pointed to the security guard at the front desk in front of his monitors. "Backup."

The guard looked up from his magazine and pushed his hat back from his graying hair. "Hello, London."

"Hey, Griff." She wedged her hip against the desk. "Griff, this is Judd Brody. I hired him for some extra security, so you'll be seeing his face around here for a while. Judd, this is Gene Griffin, but we all call him Griff."

The older man didn't even rise from his chair, and Judd leaned over to shake his hand. "Retired cop?"

Griff grinned. "That obvious?"

Obvious he'd found himself a cushy job while collecting his pension. "I have a couple of brothers who are cops—it's just the look."

He walked behind Griff and hovered over his shoulder. "Why is that monitor dark?"

"Couldn't tell you. I'm not the tech guy. It's been reported and someone's going to come out to work on it."

"Which area does it cover?"

"The garage, I think." He slapped his magazine down on the desk and tapped a few keys on the keyboard, which did nothing at all. "Yeah, that's the garage."

"What are your shifts here?"

Griff shot a look beneath shaggy eyebrows at London, who lifted one shoulder. "Eight to four, four to midnight, and midnight to eight. It's twenty-four-hour coverage."

"Do you ever leave the desk?"

The guard picked up his celebrity magazine and shook it out. "When nature calls, buddy."

"Lunch? Patrols around the building?"

"Yep."

"Any coverage when that happens?"

"Nope."

Judd rapped on the desk with his knuckles. "Thanks for the info, Griff."

He hadn't meant to piss off the old guy, but some people took his tone the wrong way. Hell, London had hired him to protect her, not make nice with lazy security guards. The guys on the night shifts had to be better.

As he followed London across the lobby to the elevators, he glanced up at the cameras in the corners—visible and easy to dismantle or block.

London stabbed at the elevator call button and hissed, "Why were you interrogating Griff like that? He's a good guy."

"He's a retired cop who found himself an easy gig where he can sit on his ass and read celebrity rags."

"Shh." She put a finger to her lips, her sculpted eyebrows colliding over her nose.

The elevator doors whispered open and he stepped into the mirrored car after London. "Just calling it like it is. I'm here to assess the risks to your security and I just found two of them. You don't let random strangers into the building just because they buzz your place, do you?"

"No, sir." She trailed a finger across her left breast. "Cross my heart."

He dragged his gaze away from her cleavage and backed up against one mirrored wall. "Good, because that's just stupid. What's the point of having a coded key entry?"

"No point at all."

"Are you making fun of me? Because this is serious. This is your security."

Her smile twitched at one corner. "It's just that you got all stern on me and poor Griff."

God, he must've come across like his brothers. He folded his arms across his chest. "Just doing my job, ma'am."

"And I appreciate that."

The elevator dinged to a stop and the doors slid open onto a quiet hallway. The shiny marble from the lobby had been replaced by carpet so thick his boot would probably leave a crater in the pile.

"How many places up here?" He glanced down the hallway. Technically she had the penthouse, since her place occupied the top floor of the building, but it looked as if she shared the space with at least one other unit.

"Two." She had her keys in her hand.

"Who's your neighbor?"

"I don't have one."

"Is the other place for sale?"

"No." She spun around at her door. "I own the other place. I bought it when the previous owner gave it up."

He held up his hands at her defensive tone. "Hey, I'd do the same."

She shoved her key into the dead bolt and froze. "Judd."

"What?"

"I always lock my dead bolt, and it's not locked."

Adrenaline shot through his system and he reached for the weapon in his gun bag. "Step back, London. Let me go through first."

She unlocked the door handle and he twisted it. He raised his gun, easing the door open.

He took in the scene before him. Either London Breck was one messy heiress or her place had been tossed.

She gasped behind him and let loose with a string of profanities.

Her place had been tossed.

Chapter Five

London pushed past Judd's solid frame, but he grabbed her around the waist before she hit the foyer, nearly lifting her off her feet.

"Hold on. We have no idea if the perpetrator is still here or not."

"Perpetrator?" Her blood simmered and she felt like putting her fist through the wall. "I've got a few other choice names for him."

"Yeah, you just screamed them in my ear." He tugged on his earlobe and tilted his head back. "How big is this place?"

"Big."

Judd kept his gun in front of him, and she almost wished the SOB was still here so he could get a load of that.

"Okay, stay with me and we'll do a sweep of the place, unless you want to leave now and call the cops."

"I'm hoping we catch him in the act. I'm not waiting for the cops."

"All right, Calamity Jane, just stay behind me in case he is."

She stayed close to Judd as she directed him through the rooms of the condo, each one ransacked and upended. They even looked in the closets and under the beds, but the slimeball had done his dirty work and escaped.

He replaced his gun in what she assumed was an out-of-character fanny pack and hooked a thumb in one belt loop. "Now that we know he's not here, do you want to see what's missing? I'll get on the phone and call the cops."

Crooking her finger at him, she marched across the great room and through the double doors to the library. She placed both hands against a bookshelf and shoved. It turned into the wall, exposing a cavity with a squat metal safe in the center.

Judd whistled. "That's some James Bond stuff right there."

She aimed the pointed toe of her boot at the safe. "All my important papers and real jewelry are in there, except for the important papers and real jewelry in some safe-deposit boxes."

"Check it just to make sure."

She crouched in front of the safe and he turned away while she spun the dial on the combination lock. He *did* take his job seriously.

The safe opened with a heavy click and she pulled open the door. "You can peek now."

He squatted on the floor beside her, his hands braced on his muscled thighs, his shoulder brushing hers. They were almost as close as they'd been on that motorcycle. Every time he'd gone downhill, which had seemed to happen a lot, the decline had thrown her against his back. She'd fought mightily against resting her head against his shoulder and exploring beneath his shirt with her hands.

That ride, with him between her legs and the monster machine buzzing beneath her, had been about the most sensuous journey she'd ever experienced.

Only to come to a screeching halt when they reached her ransacked apartment.

He cocked his head, and his long black hair tickled her cheek. "Well?"

She plunged her hands into the recesses of the safe and grabbed stacks of paper bonds, bringing them into the light. She tossed them back inside and her fingers curled around a velvet box, which she pulled out and dropped to the floor. She flicked the latch and the jewels inside glittered in the muted light.

"Did you get those from the queen of England or something?" He reached into the box and hooked a finger around a necklace of rubies with pink diamonds clustered around each one.

"My father bought that for my mother. I have no idea where he got it." She wrinkled her nose. "It's not my style."

He dropped it. "Not mine, either. I guess your taste runs more toward three-hundred-carat yellow diamonds."

She sucked in a breath. So he *did* know all about her. Well, not everything. "Sheikh al Sayid gave that diamond to me. Of course he was going to deny it when his wife found out—*one* of his wives, I may add."

"The question is, what did you do to earn it?"

"You have a dirty mind." She punched him in the shoulder and then shook her fist. Was the man hard all over?

He wasn't the only one with a dirty mind.

"Any other treasures in there?"

There were, but a few she'd keep to herself.

"There's nothing missing from this safe." She slammed the door shut and fell to her backside. "Whatever else he might've taken—cameras, computers, gadgets—he's welcome to them."

"Computers? If he has your computers, you could be in for a lot of trouble."

"All company information and financials are stored on computers at the office. I don't do any of that at home, not even on a laptop. I have a backup service, so I'm not going to lose any music or pictures." She covered her mouth with her hand. There were pictures she didn't want anyone to see—not even some junkie thief.

"What is it?"

Judd had moved closer, his knees bumping hers.

She looked into his eyes, the darkness of the room casting them the color of a deep ocean-blue. She probably should tell him everything, come clean about everything. No. Maddie had nothing to do with any of this, and she didn't need Judd Brody thinking of her as any more flighty than he already did, or worse, as someone heartless and selfish.

"Getting all those files restored would be a major pain."

Pushing to his feet, he extended his hand. "Then let's go see what's missing, and I'll call the cops." He circled his finger around the safe room. "I wouldn't mention this, though—to anyone."

"Nobody knows about it except me and you. My father had it put in when I bought this place."

She grasped his hand and he pulled her up. The small room had them inches apart and she breathed in the scent of him—soapy with a hint of mint from his warm breath—and something else. Something she couldn't identify, but that made her think of tousled sheets and bare skin and bruised lips.

Must be all the heightened tension of the break-in, but he could take her right here and she wouldn't complain one bit. She'd make it a point to be the best he ever had—and from his looks and manner, he'd had more than his share.

He kicked the door of the safe closed with a bang and she jumped. "The rest of your stuff?"

His harsh tone brought her back to reality. He'd made it pretty clear he didn't want to take her here or anywhere. Not that he didn't enjoy the sparks between them—she could read a man as well as the next girl—but he had no intention of lighting that fuse.

She bent forward and it was his turn to jump back. She flattened out her smile as she twirled the dial of the safe. "Just locking up."

Squeezing past her, he backed out of the room, his thigh brushing against her bum.

"Claustrophobic in there." He let out a long breath and raked his fingers through his long hair.

He helped her swing the bookcase back into place, and she turned to survey the rest of the library. The monitor for the desktop computer was askew, and she looked beneath the desk for the CPU.

"One computer gone."

"I suppose he had to take something to make it look good."

"What are you saying?" She placed her hand on his forearm, her nails digging into the ink of his tattoos.

"London, this is obviously linked to the previous threats. Someone is trying to spook you or warn you. This is not some garden-variety break-in. I thought you'd figured that out the minute we walked into the condo."

"I guess I did." She twisted a strand of hair around one finger. She hadn't really thought about who was responsible and why. That white-hot anger thumping through her veins had blotted out everything else, but it made sense.

"So you don't think whoever broke in is really interested in what's on my computer?"

"I can't know for sure, but this seems like another scare tactic—he can get to you."

"Where's the demand? If he wants me to do or not do something, how am I supposed to know what that is?"

"Maybe he figures you'll get so stressed out, you'll drop the whole idea of running BGE."

It must be someone who knew her well, then, because that was exactly what she would've done in the past. When the going got tough, London Breck threw up her hands and took a vacation. The *old* London Breck.

"I don't know, Judd." She left the library and checked the kitchen table, where she usually kept her laptop. "My laptop's gone, too."

A little fizz of fear made its way up her spine. Whoever had that laptop could make some interesting deductions from the pictures she kept on there.

She poked around and discovered other items missing—small electronics, some costume jewelry, three designer handbags—little stuff. Personal effects that would indicate a quickie burglary by someone who needed cash.

Slumping on the couch, she tilted her head back against the cushion and closed her eyes. "Are the cops on their way?"

"Eventually. I'm going to have a talk with Griff before they get here."

"Great. He'll probably never speak to me again."

"He should lose his job. It happened on his so-called watch."

"Please." She opened one eye. "Do not get him fired."

"Afraid of being labeled Ms. Scrooge? I'm sure the other tenants in this building are going to want to know about this." He sat on the arm of the couch. "I wouldn't worry too much about old Griff. He's collecting a nice pension. He's not going to starve in the streets."

"I'm not going to be responsible for anyone losing a job."

"Oh, boy." He flicked her earlobe. "How are you going to run a multibillion-dollar global company?"

"I haven't figured that out yet. Any ideas?"

"Me? I don't even have a filing system down for my business."

She trudged after Judd through the lobby, keeping her focus on his nice backside to avoid thinking about the conversation ahead and everything else going wrong in her life right now. If he didn't want her jumping his bones, why did he wear jeans like that? Why did his blue eyes smolder when he looked at her? Why did his long hair brush his collar, asking to be smoothed away?

"Griff, we have a problem."

Griff peeked over the top of his magazine. "You again."

"Someone broke into Ms. Breck's condo, ransacked the place and stole some items."

Griff's eyes bugged out from their sockets and his magazine dropped to the floor. "Th-that's not possible."

"It's not only possible—" Judd hunched over the table, the muscles in his arms flexing, his tattoos dancing "—it's a fact. What time did you vacate your station after Ms. Breck left this morning?"

"Vacate?" His previously bulging eyes narrowed. "You make it sound like I did something on purpose."

Judd straightened up to his full height and crossed his arms over his formidable chest. "Why would you say something like that? *Did* you do something on purpose?"

"I don't know what the hell you're talking about." He shook his finger at Judd. "Don't think I don't know who you are. Brody."

He practically spit out the name, and Judd's posture grew more rigid. Danger shimmered from him in waves.

London's quick glance at Griff confirmed that he felt it, too. His face reddened and the muscles seemed to go slack, but he carried on.

"Your brother and that true-crime writer might've exonerated Joey Brody, but I don't believe it. If he didn't do all those people as the Phone Book Killer, why'd he off himself, huh? Why'd he take a dive off the Golden Gate?"

A muscle in Judd's jaw twitched, and London raised a shaky hand—as if she could stop a panther once he went into attack mode.

A pounding on the front door made them all stop and

turn around. Two uniformed officers cupped their hands on the glass and peered into the lobby.

Griff couldn't open the door fast enough. He fumbled for the button beneath his desk and the doors clicked.

The cops strolled in and the older one asked, "Are you London Breck? Your place was robbed?"

"That's right." She approached them, extending her hand. "We were just—ah—talking to the security guard to find out if he noticed anything."

The officer shook her hand. "I'm Officer Jessup and this is Officer Spann."

Judd broke away from the desk. "I'm Judd Brody. I'm working security for Ms. Breck."

Jessup coughed. "That's a coincidence. Have you had previous break-ins, Ms. Breck? Is that the reason for hiring a P.I.?"

She didn't even bother to ask how he knew Judd was a private investigator and not just a security guard. It seemed as if the entire law enforcement community knew about the Brody brothers.

"Not a break-in, but I've been having some issues ever since my father passed away."

"Of course. Sorry for your loss, ma'am. Your father was a big supporter of the SFPD. We'll miss him."

"Thank you."

Officer Spann had parked himself in front of the security desk and a visibly shaken Griff. "Did you notice anything?"

"No. I did my rounds, as usual. Took a few breaks." He shot a glance at Judd. "Which is allowed."

The cop tapped the top of one of the monitors. "You have security cameras and footage, right?"

"Yeah, when they work." He jerked his thumb at the dark screen. "This one's been on the fritz."

"Can we have a look at those right now?"

While Officer Spann hung over Griff's shoulder at the

security desk, Officer Jessup pulled a notepad from his pocket. "What did he take, Ms. Breck?"

"A couple of computers, some costume jewelry, a camcorder." She held up her hand, ticking the items off on each finger. "I can get you a list, the same one I'm sending to my insurance company."

He turned to Judd. "Any sign of forced entry?"

"No. He picked the lock or had a key." His gaze wandered toward Griff, who was tapping the keyboard and jabbing his finger at the monitors.

Judd really had it in for Griff, especially now after that jab at his father. Judd had told her he'd put the past behind him, that it didn't matter, but his reaction told another story.

She cleared her throat. "I doubt he had a key, or he would've locked the dead bolt behind him, and he didn't do that."

"Or maybe he didn't lock the dead bolt because he didn't want you know he had a key."

"We'll come up and have a look." Jessup tilted his head back to take in the high ceiling of the lobby. "If you're on the top floor of this building, he didn't climb through the window."

"Jessup, you gotta see this." Spann looked up from the security desk, over Griff's red face.

London's pulse jumped. "Is he on the video?"

"Not only is he not on it, nobody's on it. The lobby camera hasn't been recording anything all morning."

London stamped her foot. "That figures. What is the point of having cameras when they're always breaking down?"

"Exactly." Judd's eyes glittered like chips of agate.

Griff's Adam's apple bobbed in his flushed throat.

Tugging on Judd's sleeve, London said, "Let's show the cops my place. Maybe they can get some fingerprints."

The officers checked the door and surveyed the mess,

but they couldn't get fingerprints or tell her anything more about the break-in. She promised them the complete list of stolen items, but had no hope of getting any of them back.

When the cops left, London collapsed on the couch. "They'll never see my stuff in a pawnshop, will they? That's not why the thief or thieves stole it."

"You're catching on." Judd paced in front of her. "They wanted it to look like a burglary, but we both know they just wanted to scare you."

She kicked her feet up onto the coffee table. "They're going to have to do more than that to get me to give up control of BGE."

"That's what worries me, London. If I don't find these guys now, what else do they have planned for you?"

"They'll slip up—maybe next time."

"I don't want there to be a next time. I need to find them now." He punched his fist into his palm. "And I know a good place to start."

He turned toward the door and she jumped up. "You're not going to harass Griff again, are you?"

His eyebrows spiked. "Harass? He knows something, London. Do you think it's just a coincidence that the cameras failed this morning at precisely the time someone gained entry to the building to break into your place?"

"Wait. You're telling me he's working with these guys?"

"Why is that so hard to believe? The guy has a good pension and benefits from the city and he's still working as a security guard? He obviously needs money."

He swung open the door and she rushed to follow him. "I'm coming with you so someone doesn't wind up in the emergency room."

When Judd burst onto the lobby floor, Griff's mouth gaped open.

"What do you want? I told everything to the cops and I'm not saying any more, especially to you."

Judd lunged over the security desk and grabbed the front of the man's shirt. He pulled him from his chair. "You are going to talk to me—right now."

Griff choked and coughed. "Let me go."

Judd shook him like a rag doll and then dropped him in his chair. "Why did you turn that camera off? Who did you let in here? Who paid you?"

Griff scooted his chair back. "You're crazy, violent, just like your old man."

Wrong thing to say. Griff was either brave or stupid. London held her breath.

That stillness fell over Judd again, and then he whipped around the desk with a quickness and agility that didn't match his size.

He yanked Griff out of his chair again and slammed him against the wall.

Mrs. Schrader and a friend came through the lobby doors and tripped to a stop.

"Everything okay, London?"

"Uh, my place was broken into this morning. The cops are just trying to get some answers from Griff."

If Mrs. Schrader and her friend wondered at this so-called cop's methods, they didn't seem to want to inquire further. They scurried toward the elevator without a backward glance.

Judd dug his hand into the front pocket of Griff's pants and pulled out a thick envelope. He tossed it onto the desk— a few bills peeked from it.

"Where'd you get that, huh?"

Griff slumped against the wall. "I didn't know they were going to break into your place, London. I swear."

"What? Someone paid you to let them in the building and then mess with the lobby camera?"

"Yeah." Griff sank to his chair. "It wasn't the first time, and nothing like a robbery ever happened before."

"You've done this before?" Judd stepped to the other side of the desk, flexing his fingers.

"Yeah."

"Why?" London felt like sitting down herself.

He prodded the envelope with his finger. "Money. It's only the paps. That's who I thought it was this time. That's what they told me."

"The paps?" Judd's eyebrows collided over his nose. "The paparazzi?"

The color rushed into Griff's face again. "They pay good money to get into places like this. Sorry, London. I didn't think there was any harm. They usually just want a few pictures, maybe to dig around your trash. I've worked with Ray Lopez before, and he's a good guy."

"My trash?" She felt as if she needed a shower.

"It's not just you, London. There are a few others in this building they want. You know who."

Judd landed his fist on the desk. "This time they wanted to break into her place. What if they wanted to kill someone? Would you be okay with that, too?"

"Kill someone?" He shook his head back and forth. "They just want information, a scoop. You know, like Ray Lopez."

"The men who broke into London's place weren't paparazzi, you idiot."

Griff's eyes popped open. "Of course they were. They told me they were."

"How long were you a cop?" Judd ran a hand through his hair.

"I've done this kind of thing before and never had a problem."

Judd propped up the wall with his shoulder as if to box Griff in. "What did they look like, these two paparazzi?"

"I—I don't know."

"What?"

Griff folded his arms over his paunch. "They were wearing disguises. You know, caps, sunglasses, facial hair."

Judd's mouth fell open. "And you didn't think that was weird?"

"Naw. They do that all the time." Griff smacked his magazine. "They have to go to extremes to get the good pics."

"Can you at least write down their height, build, accent… disguises?"

Griff pulled a piece of paper in front of him and started writing.

When he handed the descriptions over, Judd shoved the paper in his pocket and asked, "Did they at least give you back the key?"

"I didn't give them any key." Griff spread his hands. "I swear, London. They just asked for the number of your place and floor."

She turned to Judd. "Then they picked the locks?"

"Probably." Judd hunched over the desk. "Did you see them leave?"

"That was part of the deal. I made myself scarce." Griff chewed on the side of his thumb. "Do you have to report this to management, London?"

"Griff, it's completely out of my control. The management company has to know there was a burglary in the building and why."

He heaved a heavy sigh and leaned back in his chair. "Guess I'll be looking for another gig."

Judd took her arm. "Let's go back up. I have one more thing I want to check."

This time when she put the key in the dead bolt, it clicked. "At least they didn't sneak back in while we were downstairs." She surveyed the mess. "I'll start cleaning up. What else did you need?"

Prowling around the room, checking lamp shades and pictures, Judd answered, "I'm doing a cursory check for bugs—audio and visual. I have equipment that can do a more thorough job, and I'll be bringing that over."

"Ugh." London shivered. "That's a creepy thought."

"I think they broke in today just to give you another scare, make you think twice about stepping into your father's shoes. But if you don't give up, spying on you could be an effective weapon in their arsenal against you. I've dealt with corporate spying before—it's not unusual."

London dipped her head. If the burglars got a load of the pictures on her laptop, they just might have another weapon in their arsenal against her.

She replaced cushions and reshelved books while Judd continued his search for bugs—much scarier ones than spiders.

When he finished, he stood in the middle of the great room. "I didn't find anything, but I'm going to come back tomorrow with my equipment for a more thorough check."

Sounded as though he planned to leave—not that she believed she could keep him here forever. "I should be around in the afternoon."

"Get the locks changed tomorrow as a precaution and leave a new key for me with security."

"Right. Come whenever you like." She waved her arms around the room. "I'll keep putting things together tonight."

"Let me know if you discover anything else missing—or anything out of order."

"I will. Thanks for everything, Judd. Without your perseverance, we never would've gotten the truth out of Griff."

"Glad you see it that way." He scooped up his jacket and helmet. "I'll be in touch tomorrow."

She closed the door behind him and locked it. If he hadn't been with her today, she would've freaked out walking in on this mess alone. In hiring Judd Brody to have her back, she'd made the first in what she planned to be a long line of good decisions.

London spent the rest of the afternoon cleaning up without discovering any other missing items—or bugs.

When her stomach growled for about the hundredth time, she realized she'd completely skipped lunch. She should've invited Judd out for lunch, but she hadn't wanted to be too forward or cross the line with him.

He seemed hung up on their working relationship and she should be hung up on it, too. Professional people knew the line between business and pleasure and adhered to it. If she wanted to step up as the CEO of BGE, she'd better start acting like a professional.

If Judd Brody could keep his lust zipped up while they worked together, so could she.

Her cell phone buzzed and she swept it off the counter, checking the display. "Hi, April."

"Hi, just checking to see if you're still going to that new club with us tonight."

London opened the sliding doors to the balcony and stepped outside. "I'm going to pass."

April wailed, "You're turning into a drudge, London. Gemma's cousin is in from Monte Carlo, and he's really interested in meeting you."

"Is this the gambler? I bet he's really interested in meeting me."

"Oh, stop. He has money of his own. Not every man is after your big bucks. Do not tell me you're seriously considering Roger Taylor's proposal. Just because he's über-rich, that doesn't make him a perfect match for you."

A flash of blue eyes and the revving engine of a Harley made it clear that Roger could never be her perfect match. "Don't worry. I'm not that much of a drudge. Someone broke into my place today and I've spent all afternoon cleaning up—not the best prelude to a night out."

April gasped. "What did he take?"

"Nothing of importance." Except that laptop. "But I'm not in any mood to go clubbing."

"I hear ya. I'll tell you all about the new place and the new man."

"Have fun, April." London cradled the phone in her hands and gazed at the lights blinking on in the city. She still needed to eat, but she didn't feel like venturing out and she didn't want to cook. She punched in the number for the local pizza place and ordered a large vegetarian pizza.

By the time the pizza had arrived, she'd taken a quick shower and changed into yoga pants and a light hoodie. She spoke into the intercom. "I'll be right down."

She grabbed some bills from her purse, locked the door behind her and headed down to the lobby in the elevator.

Jerome, the night security guard, had his eye on the delivery guy as if half expecting him to pull a gun out of the pizza box.

London exchanged the cash for the pizza and thanked the delivery boy.

When he left, she placed the pizza on top of the security desk. "I suppose you heard what happened this morning."

Jerome shook his head. "I always thought Griff was trouble—him and those celebrity rags. Shoulda figured he'd be one of those guys selling stories and stuff."

"Do you know if he's been fired?"

"Not sure. I guess we'll find out come eight o'clock tomorrow morning." Jerome straightened his shoulders. "I hope you know I'd never do anything like that, Ms. Breck."

"I know that. It's just crazy Griff didn't think about the consequences."

He pointed to the pizza box. "No fancy shindig tonight, huh?"

"I don't know, Jerome." She wrapped her fingers around the edges of the pizza box. "I think my fancy shindig days are over."

She carried the pizza up to her place and settled it on the kitchen counter. She had a few files to go over before tomorrow's shareholder meeting and would try not to get tomato sauce on them.

A few hours later, she put the leftover pizza into the fridge and scrunched her paper plate in the trash.

Her phone buzzed again, once. If April thought she could talk her into going out, she had it all wrong, even if the man from Monte Carlo had turned out to be a winner.

She washed her hands and retrieved her phone to check the text message. Take out the trash.

Her brow furrowed. Who had sent that? She squinted at the display—blocked. Must be a wrong number.

The text indicator buzzed again and she smirked. Some husband was going to be in big trouble tonight for not taking out the trash.

Yawning, she slipped the phone into the front pouch of her hoodie. It buzzed again, tickling her tummy.

She pulled it out and typed in a reply—wrong number.

As she wiped the crumbs from the counter, another text came through. She tossed the dish towel into the sink and dragged out the phone again.

She froze. Take out the trash, LONDON.

Was this some kind of joke? Had April had one of her fellow club hoppers text her? But what did it mean?

The phone continued to buzz in her hand as the text came through over and over. Take out the trash? She glanced at the empty pizza box. She had to take out the trash anyway.

She tucked the pizza box beneath one arm and grabbed her key. With the text message indicator still buzzing, she locked her door behind her and trudged to the end of the hallway to the little room that contained the trash chute.

She licked her lips and shoved open the door. The silver lid of the trash chute gleamed in the dim closet. She lifted the lid with two fingers and the smell of garbage wafted into the small space. Wrinkling her nose, she dropped the pizza box down the black hole and let the lid fall back into place.

The clang resounded in the closet.

She pulled out her phone and spoke to it. "There, are you happy?"

It must be April playing some kind of joke. Maybe she'd meant take out the trash and make room for a new man? It had to be April.

When London got back to her condo, she tapped April's name in her contact list with a less-than-steady finger.

April answered with a breathless voice. "Change your mind?"

"No. Who's sending me texts about the trash?" She held her breath, hoping for April's laughing admission of guilt.

"What?"

"Are you having someone text me messages about taking out the trash?"

"London, what are you talking about? Look, I'm in a taxi on my way to the Bay Club for cocktails. Then it's off to the new place. If you've changed your mind, meet us there."

"You didn't put someone up to texting me?" Her voice rose to an unnatural high note.

"About trash? No. You're losing it."

She just might be. While she'd been on the phone to April, the text had come through five more times.

What trash? Was her stolen stuff in the trash? Had the burglars had second thoughts? Maybe they'd seen the police here. How the hell had they gotten her number?

All the trash chutes on this side of the building led to a larger bin in a room off the lobby. Was that the trash she should check? She didn't want to do it alone.

Jerome was downstairs. He could come with her.

Once again, she pocketed her still-buzzing phone and

left her condo. A couple got into the elevator with her on the third floor and she nodded at them.

The woman jabbed the button for the lobby. "Did someone break into your place today?"

"Yeah. Turns out Griff was giving the paparazzi access to our building."

The woman's nostrils flared and she sniffed. "That's very unfortunate. I hope he's gone."

"I think he is." Thanks to Judd.

The elevator opened onto the lobby, and the couple continued out the front door, where a town car waited for them.

Jerome looked up from the monitor. "More pizza, London?"

"No, I keep getting a weird text from some unknown person telling me to check the trash. I looked into the chute upstairs, but there's nothing there."

He raised his eyebrows. "Just because you get a text from someone doesn't mean you have to do what it says."

"I know." She placed a shaky hand over the buzzing phone in her pocket. "I just have a feeling—maybe my missing stuff is in the trash bin down here. Can you check it out with me?"

His gaze darted between the empty lobby and the working monitors on the security desk. "I don't want to leave my post, especially since Griff basically broke the camera down here and there's no coverage on the lobby, and there's still no coverage on the garage."

She turned toward the door that led to the trash room and crossed her arms. "I'm still a little on edge after the break-in."

"Tell you what—" Jerome reached under the security desk and held up two slanted blocks of wood "—prop the doors open with these. I can sort of see into the hallway."

"That'll work." She took the doorstops from him and

marched toward the first door. She shoved open the door and kicked one piece of wood beneath it to hold it open.

The chill from the cement floor in the hallway caused a rash of goose bumps to spread across her arms. She eyed the metal door at the end of the hallway. "The trash room is that door at the end, right?"

"Yeah. Prop that one open, too, when you get there."

"Sure thing." Her voice rang out brighter than she felt. Maybe she should just turn off her phone, forget the whole thing tonight and have Judd trace the call tomorrow.

The phone buzzed again with the same message, as if taunting her. If she planned to hold on to her job and execute her responsibilities at BGE, she'd have to show these goons they didn't scare her.

"Okay, I'm heading down the hallway. Maybe management should put a camera over here, too."

Jerome called back from the lobby, sounding very far away. "I'll suggest it. There's nothing out there or in the alley where the garbage trucks pull up."

London threw back her shoulders and proceeded down the corridor, her flip-flops smacking the cement. She grabbed the handle and pressed down, nudging the door with her hip. It opened with a creak.

"This door needs oil." She cocked her head. "Jerome?"

"I hear ya. Maybe I'll suggest that, too. You see anything in there?"

"Just a couple of big trash bins." She pinched her nose.

A soft, rhythmic tapping sound had her stumbling backward. "Are there rats out here?"

"I hope not, or that's another suggestion."

Crouching down, she shoved the doorstop in place and rose slowly, brushing her fingers against her yoga pants.

A bag of trash hurtled down the chute and London pressed a hand against her heart. "Scared me."

"What?"

"Nothing, just some trash coming down."

"It *is* the trash room."

She grabbed the edge of the bin and found a foothold on the edge, peering inside. Yep, trash. No computers, no camcorders, no jewelry.

Someone had decided to yank her chain with those texts—maybe the burglars, maybe not.

The tapping noise started again and she jumped off the bin. Her gaze wandered to the other door in the room. "Jerome?"

"You done in there?"

"Yeah…no." She took a step toward the metal door. The tapping had turned into a soft scraping sound coming from the other side of that door.

"What's this door in here?"

"Leads to the alley, same as the sliding door. We roll up the sliding door on garbage day so the trash collectors can pick up the bin and empty it.

She hadn't noticed the warehouse-style corrugated metal door behind the bin.

"I-is it locked?"

"Just from the inside, but what do you want to go outside for?"

"There's a noise out there."

"Probably cats."

"Probably." She edged toward the door and placed her hand on the cold handle. She swallowed and pushed it open.

The door hit something hanging from above. Looking up, she peered around the edge of the door and then wished she hadn't.

A man's lifeless body hung from the awning above the door—a celebrity magazine sticking out of his pocket.

Chapter Six

Judd rubbed circles on London's back as she rocked back and forth. Every once in a while, she'd stop rocking and a tremble would roll through her body. When that happened, her teeth would chatter and she'd hunch her shoulders, giving him the urge to take her lithe form in his arms.

He resisted the urge.

The SFPD homicide detective, one of his brother's colleagues, tapped the plastic bag containing London's phone. "We can trace the texts, but most likely it'll come back to a throwaway phone. People who commit murder do not leave messages from traceable phones."

Judd's hand paused on London's back. "You're probably right, but it's worth a try. You might get lucky."

Unlike Griff. The SOB had gotten involved with the wrong people. He thought he'd hit the jackpot and picked up some extra cash. Now the crime-scene techs were downstairs and the coroner was probably on his way.

Detective Curtis planted his hands on his knees and pushed to his feet. "Thanks for the info, Judd. Why someone, especially a former cop, would allow a couple of guys wearing obvious disguises into an exclusive building like this one is beyond me."

Judd got to his feet and shook Curtis's hand. "I guess your pensions aren't big enough. Griff did it for the money."

"You said he had an envelope stuffed with bills?"

"Yeah, payment from the burglars."

"Well, whoever killed him took that off him, too."

London raised a pair of wide eyes, peering at them through a veil of hair. "Griff didn't have a family, did he? He never mentioned a wife and kids to me."

"I'm not sure, Ms. Breck. We've contacted his employer for next of kin, although the other security guard said Griff had been divorced for a while."

Judd saw Curtis to London's front door since she'd retreated behind her hair and the blanket he'd draped around her shoulders.

"You take care, Ms. Breck. I called Captain Williams at home to let him know what happened, and he was glad I did. We'll notify you if anything breaks. In the meantime, I'm leaving you in good hands."

Judd thanked Curtis and returned to London's side. "How about a glass of wine? Some tea? Water?"

Her head jerked up. "I didn't hear your conversation with Detective Curtis earlier. Was Griff dead before they strung him up or d-did they hang him?"

"You didn't hear that conversation for a reason. Do you really need to know that?" She needed wine, and he wandered into her vast kitchen to look for a bottle.

"Yes." She knotted her fingers and he could see how unsettled she was. "I need to know everything."

He banged open a few cupboards. "Wine?"

"In the wine cellar."

Oh, yeah, he vaguely remembered a step-down room, dark and oaky, filled with racks upon racks of bottles.

She must've noticed the confusion crossing his face, because she flicked her fingers toward the kitchen. "There's a top-rated *Wine Spectator* pinot grigio open in the fridge."

Of course, pinot grigio in the fridge. Who didn't have a

Wine Spectator top-rated pinot grigio in the fridge? What-ever the hell that meant.

He pulled open the door, grabbed the bottle of wine off the top shelf and snagged himself a top-rated Judd Brody bottle of beer in the process. She could open a bar with the stock she had on hand, and a coffee shop with all the coffee gadgets littering the kitchen, and probably a flower shop to top it off.

He lifted a glass from the cupboard, poured in the wine and twisted off the beer bottle's cap. He needed a drink after his epic fail. He'd figured the intruders had broken in as another scare tactic, but they'd just added murder to their repertoire—and they'd wanted to make sure London found the body.

Why?

Were they really threatening her life if she didn't give up control of BGE? He'd have to take a look at the players in that corporation, although it could be someone outside the corporation—a competitor or disgruntled former employee.

He sat down next to London and placed her glass on the coffee table in front of her. She deserved to know what she was facing.

"They killed Griff before they hanged him. They choked him, probably with a garrote."

She took a gulp of wine and pressed the back of her hand to her lips. "Why?"

"So he wouldn't identify them, because he talked to the cops, or maybe just to get rid of him and tie up loose ends."

"Do you think Griff was telling the truth about the dis-guises? Maybe they didn't have hats and beards. Maybe they'd just warned Griff to keep quiet and he had no inten-tion of telling us anything about them."

"If so, he misplaced his loyalties." He rolled the damp beer bottle between his palms. "Who's Captain Williams? The name sounds familiar."

"He's a captain in homicide. Your brother probably knows him. He and my father go way back, and he's been trying to get the chief's position for years."

"Williams, yeah." He took a sip of beer. "You need to replace your phone, get a new phone number."

"I'll do that tomorrow."

"Today." He tapped his watch. "It's after midnight."

She ran her fingertip around the rim of her glass. "I'm used to the general trouble fame causes—paparazzi, media, gossip. But this…it's serious."

"Damn straight it is. It was serious when they beat Theodore to a pulp, and now it's deadly serious."

"I don't understand what they want. Why don't they, whoever they are, give me some demands?"

"Maybe they don't have any demands."

"You mean they just want to kill me?" She threw back another gulp of wine.

"I don't think so. It's not as though they didn't have their chances to do that—in the hotel alley, here in your place or down in that trash room—an idiotic move on your part, by the way. Why would you go down there on your own after what's been happening?"

He saw the color rise in her face when he called her actions idiotic. "I planned to take Jerome with me, and he was right in the next room."

"Not close enough." He chugged the rest of his beer and stretched. "I'm staying here tonight."

Her wine sloshed over the rim of the glass. "I beg your pardon?"

"I'm going to camp out—" he bounced his fist on the cushion next to him "—right here."

"Do I have to pay extra for that service?"

"You'll see it on my bill."

"If I'm going to be charged for the twenty-four-hour

coverage, you might as well stay in style. I have several guest rooms, beds already made up."

"I think I need to stay right here. Unless, of course, this is a top-rated *Couch Spectator* couch."

Even though the strain of the evening still clouded her eyes, the corner of her mouth lifted in a smile. "You don't want to know how much that couch cost, but you're welcome to it—as long as you remove your motorcycle boots."

"I'll remove more than my motorcycle boots."

He ignored the look from her narrowed eyes and pushed up from the couch with his empty beer bottle in one hand. "If you're going to be ready for your meeting tomorrow morning, you'd better get a good night's sleep. And since I'm going with you to the office, I'm going to hit the sack, too."

She reached for her glass, almost knocking it over, but swooped in before it hit the table. "Y-you're coming with me?"

"Yep."

"In what capacity?"

"Bodyguard."

"Should I introduce you as my bodyguard?"

"Sweetheart, you can introduce me as whatever you want or don't introduce me at all, but you should keep mum about the activities of the past few days."

"I'm probably not going to be able to hide the fact that a security guard was murdered in my building and I found him."

"So? Your involvement ends there. Don't you ever keep secrets?"

"Sure." She jumped from the couch and turned toward the kitchen. "I'll get you a blanket and pillow for the couch."

She rinsed her glass in the sink and then disappeared upstairs.

True to his promise, Judd sat down and pulled off his boots. He stuffed his socks inside and placed them beside the couch. Then he chucked a few throw pillows onto the floor to make some room. The couch had to be six feet long, but that still wouldn't accommodate him from head to toe.

No doubt he'd find more comfort in one of London's guest rooms, but he could keep better watch down here by the front door, and he didn't want to be in some soft, comfortable bed with London in her soft, comfortable bed somewhere down the hall. He didn't need the distraction.

"I brought a sheet to tuck in around the couch and a blanket and pillow. Do you think you'll need another blanket?"

"You keep the temperature warm in here. I'm good."

She shook out the sheet and handed him one corner. "I'll help you."

The sheet billowed as they each grabbed an end, and some flowery scent wafted into the air. They secured it around the edges of the couch and Judd tossed the pillow onto one end.

"Perfect." He poked a few buttons on his watch. "What time is your meeting tomorrow morning? I'll need to go home first and change, and then I'll meet you in the lobby of your office building."

"Do you know where it's located?"

"I did some research on you after I left today."

Her eyebrows jumped. "Did you discover anything interesting?"

"Let's see." He raised his eyes to the ceiling. "Lots of crazy parties, wild friends, escape from boarding school, a few arrests, exotic travel. Typical life of an idle rich girl."

"Ouch." She clamped her hands over her stomach as if he'd stabbed her.

"Hey, no judgment here." He turned off the lamp beside the couch. "Get some sleep, London."

She crept away in the darkness and turned at the bottom of the stairs. Her whisper floated across the room. "I'm changing all that."

Before he could reply that it didn't concern him one way or the other, she'd jogged upstairs, and a door slammed in the recesses of the condo.

Probably a good thing he hadn't had time to answer. She seemed sensitive about her wild-child image. And besides, he would've been lying—it did concern him.

Everything about London Breck concerned him.

JUDD ROLLED UP his motorcycle jacket and stuffed it into one of his bike's saddlebags. Leaning forward, he ran one hand through his helmet hair and then tugged on the lapels of his suit jacket.

Sean had helped him pick out the suit. As fastidious about his clothes as he was about everything else in his life, his brother knew a good suit and a good tailor. Judd felt at ease that he'd fit in with any of these financial types at Breck Global Enterprises.

He ambled from the parking garage into the lobby of the building where BGE occupied the top four floors. He parked himself next to a potted plant and watched the twirling glass doors from the street to the lobby.

A tall, cool blonde with her hair in a loose bun sailed through the doors. London shoved her sunglasses on top of her head and hoisted the soft-sided black briefcase over her shoulder.

When Judd stepped into her path, a hitch hampered her long stride but didn't stop her. He matched her step for step on the way to the elevator.

She pressed the button and cranked her head to the side,

her gaze scanning him head to toe. "Nice suit. You look like Secret Service with those sunglasses."

He took them off and slipped them into his front pocket. "Better?"

"How'd you sleep last night? I didn't think you'd be gone when I got up."

His pulse quickened. "Everything okay this morning?"

"Fine." She stabbed the button again. "So were the accommodations satisfactory?"

"Fine." He'd slept lightly. A few bumps in the night had had him bolting upright, but he'd put them down to the settling of the building.

A few other people joined them in the elevator.

London shifted toward him, close enough for him to see the sparkle from the dusting of powder across her nose.

"Here's the agenda for the morning. I'll look over my email and return any calls. The meeting starts at nine o'clock. I'll try to point out all the players to you beforehand, and maybe you can hang out in my office during the meeting and go through some company files."

"Sounds good."

The doors to the elevator swished open, and Judd stepped back and held the door for the others. Silence reigned as the car delivered the other three to their destinations.

When the doors closed behind the last person, London turned to him. "If anyone asks, you're just additional security."

"Got it." He saluted. "Nice to meet you, I'm additional security."

She drummed her fingers against his biceps. "Very funny. Did you hear anything more about Griff? Is it in the paper?"

"I haven't heard anything, and I didn't see it in the newspaper, but it's probably online."

"I know nothing." She traced her fingertip along the seam of her lips.

Sleeping downstairs last night had been the best move he could've made. This woman, with her hard shell on the outside and squishy, soft insides, had gotten under his skin. Her reputation as a hot party chick had hooked him, but her wit and self-deprecating humor were reeling him in.

The elevator took them to the very top of the building and spit them out onto plush carpet, facing a glass-block wall with the BGE logo shimmering on it.

London exited to the right and he followed her to a reception area adorned with fine art, a couple of chairs, a few exotic plants and an even more exotic receptionist behind a mahogany desk.

"Good morning, Arianna." London flashed a smile at the receptionist, who could moonlight as a model.

"Good morning, London." Her dark eyes flicked to Judd.

"This is Judd Brody. He's going to be providing some extra personal security for me in the next few months."

Months? He had to maintain a professional demeanor with this woman for months?

He nodded toward Arianna, who smiled serenely, as if a personal bodyguard was the most common accoutrement in the world.

London continued to the back of the building, where individual offices lined the walls and buzzing office staffers guarded their ground.

London nodded and waved her way through the maze until she reached the back office. Another impeccably coiffed and dressed woman sat with perfect posture behind a desk.

"Good morning, London."

"Good morning, Celine. Everything ready for the meeting this morning?"

Celine's gaze darted toward Judd and back to London's face. "All on your desk. Roger has already been by this morning."

"Thanks." She tilted her chin at him. "This is Judd Brody. He's…uh, with security."

Celine smiled brightly. "Good morning. Would either of you like some coffee?"

"I would. Judd?"

"Black."

Celine scooted back from her chair and scurried out the door.

An older gentleman—silver hair, impeccable suit, moneyed ease—strolled into the outer office. "Nice to see you here, London. Are you ready for the meeting?"

"I am."

"I'll be seated to your right, and I can guide you through anything that throws you for a loop."

"Thanks, Richard." She made a half turn toward Judd. "Richard, this is Judd Brody. He'll be providing some additional personal security for me. Judd, Richard Taylor, executive vice president of BGE."

Richard nodded, a tight smile on his patrician face. "Welcome aboard."

Richard must have thought Judd was a new BGE employee or something, but if London didn't see fit to correct him, far be it from Judd to do so. He nodded back.

Did the vice president have a hankering to be CEO?

"I'll see you at the meeting, London—nine sharp." He pivoted out of the room, almost colliding with Celine carrying two cups of coffee.

"Sorry, Mr. Taylor." Celine rolled her eyes at London and handed them the coffee.

London waved Judd through another door. "My office." She shut the door behind them and sighed. "You don't know how much I hate walking through that gauntlet of employees."

"Why?"

"I don't know. They all work for me. Their livelihoods depend on me and my decisions. I feel like they're out there sizing me up."

"They probably are." He perched on the edge of her desk and folded his arms. "Why does my job title keep changing for every person I meet?"

"They're all the same, aren't they?" She dropped her briefcase on the floor by her chair.

"It all sounds vague."

"I don't know." She eased into the big leather chair behind the desk. "You want me to keep quiet about the threats, and I don't want to come across as paranoid."

"What's the saying? If someone really is trying to get you, it's not paranoia."

Tapping the keyboard of her desktop computer, she said, "I thought I wasn't giving anyone the full scoop."

"Might be fun just to see their reactions. I wonder if anything could break the mask that Richard Taylor wears. He's one smooth SOB, isn't he?"

"Always has been. Do you want to meet the rest of the likely suspects?" She twisted her monitor to one side. "I've got the rogues' gallery right here."

He stepped around to the other side of the desk and leaned over her shoulder, taking in a webpage with an org chart and photos. He tapped a finger on the top picture—Spencer Breck. "Looks like it needs to be updated."

"Putting my picture up there will make it seem so final." She scooted her chair to the side. "Have a seat."

He pulled a heavy chair as close to the desk as he could get it and hunched over.

She rattled off names and positions. He'd have to print out this chart and study it more closely, maybe do a little background on these people.

He held up his hand when she got to her cousin Niles. "Tell me about him."

"He's not much for business but loves the trappings. My father and his had their issues, and Dad never much liked Niles. Left him some money and property in his trust, but not much responsibility at BGE."

"Is Niles an only child, too?"

"Too?"

"Like you."

"I thought I told you at the bar, I'm not an only child." Her finger drew a circle around the picture of a serious-looking dark-haired man in his mid-thirties. "That's my half brother, Wade."

"You did mention a half brother." Judd squinted at the name beneath the picture. "Wade Vickers. He's not a Breck?"

"Vickers is his mother's name. He never took the Breck name."

"Bad blood between his mother and your father?"

"You could say that. Wade was born before my parents married, so my father could've married Wade's mother. He didn't."

"But your father still gave him a place in the company."

"No reason not to." She shrugged. "He's smart, has a good head for business and likes this stuff a lot more than I do."

"Your father still left you in charge."

"Go figure."

Wedging a knuckle beneath her chin, he turned her face toward his. "Why are you here, London?"

"Because my father left me in charge, and I have something to prove." Her bottom lip trembled. "It was his last ditch effort to…to…"

"Turn you into him?" He waved his hand around the

office with its gleaming surfaces and dark leather. "This is him, not you."

She wrinkled her nose as she glanced around the room. "I plan to redecorate."

"I'm not talking about the decor. I mean all of it—the corporate world, shareholder meetings, the bottom line."

"This *is* me." She jumped up from her chair and smacked her palms on the desk. "I can do this. You don't know anything. You don't know me, Judd Brody. I'm not that girl in the tabloids. Not anymore."

She was right. What made him think he could give her advice, judge her? And why did he care?

"Okay, okay." He shrugged his shoulders. "Maybe this is you. What the hell do I know?"

"Let's get back to what you do know. Anything about any of these guys that jumps out at you? Honestly, I can't imagine any of them going to such lengths to threaten me. A few of them have told me straight up I'm in over my head and to give it up—sort of like you."

"Wait a minute. I never said that. You can probably do whatever you set your mind to. I just didn't think the corporate world was a good fit for you, but you set me straight." He steepled his fingers. "Any one of them has motive enough for getting rid of you, I suppose. How do you and your brother get along?"

Walking to the front of her desk, she smoothed back a piece of hair that had slipped out of the bun—another affectation. The bun didn't suit her, either.

"Wade is more like my father than I am. He's almost ten years older than I am—wife, couple of kids. He's a good guy, if a little dull."

He took in the four walls of the office. This environment could make anyone dull. "You two are on friendly terms?"

"I'd say so."

"Did your father take care of him in his will? Is your brother satisfied working for you?"

"Wade is very comfortable, thanks to Dad, and he's happy with his numbers." She sighed and perched on the edge of the desk. "I wish there was one villain to point to, but BGE has no villains."

The door to her office burst open and a stocky man with dark hair charged through, with Celine on his heels. "I asked him to wait, London."

The guy bounded across the room, landed in front of London, grabbed her shoulders and planted a kiss on her mouth. "La-La, I missed you so much. I came straight here from the airport."

Judd rose from his chair, his hands curling into fists. Who was this guy and who the hell was La-La?

"London?"

She turned a flushed face toward Judd, her hands against the man's chest.

The intruder glanced at Judd as if seeing him for the first time and raised one eyebrow. "Who's this?"

Judd expanded his chest and took one step forward. "Who the hell are you?"

The man finally dropped his hands from London's shoulders and turned to face Judd fully. "I'm London's fiancé."

Chapter Seven

London rolled her eyes. *Here we go again.*

She'd better say something, since Judd looked about ready to use Roger for a punching bag and Roger looked about ready to slap Judd across the face with a glove.

She sliced a hand between the two men. "Not exactly, Roger."

"You mean, not yet." He chucked her under the chin with his knuckle, a gesture similar to one Judd had used on her just a moment ago. Only when Roger did it, she felt about two years old.

"Roger, this is Judd Brody. I hired him for some additional personal security. Judd, this is Roger Taylor, CFO of Breck Global and Richard's son."

Judd thrust out his hand. "Sorry about the earlier antagonism. Ms. Breck never mentioned her engagement to me, so when a strange man burst in here and grabbed her, my adrenaline started to pump."

Roger eyed the tattoos peeking from the sleeve of Judd's jacket. "No worries. London could use a little extra security, but you're not from BGE, are you? Unless you joined the staff while I was out of the country."

"He did." She met Judd's gaze over Roger's shoulder and put a finger to her lips. It would make her life easier if Roger didn't know she didn't trust BGE security—at least not with her life. She just needed to stick with the same story for everyone.

Judd dipped his head. "New hire."

London let out a measured breath. "I'll see you in the boardroom, Roger. Judd and I have a few things to review."

Roger reached for her again, but this time she sidestepped him. She didn't want him mauling her, especially under Judd's watchful glare.

Roger winked and turned his fingers into a gun, pointing at her. "Don't you worry about a thing, London. I'll be right there beside you in the boardroom."

She pasted a smile on her face and nodded.

Roger exited the office, calling out to Celine, "Grab me a coffee."

London snapped the door closed and rested her forehead against the heavy wood. "Now I have to smooth Celine's feathers since she absolutely hates it when Roger orders her around. He has his own executive assistant."

"Fiancé?"

"No." She turned, putting her hands behind her back and pressing them against the door. "He likes to think we have some understanding, but we don't. I don't. We dated a few times over the years, but we are not compatible in any way."

"I can't imagine how a guy like that with a stick up his... back could ever think he'd be happy with a woman with your wild ways."

She opened her mouth and Judd held up his hand. "Former wild ways."

"That's just it." She blew a strand of hair from her face for about the hundredth time that morning. "He loves my former wild ways. He used to pretend my antics frustrated him, but that was an act. My mishaps allowed him to be paternal toward me, correcting and chastising me."

"That sounds like a seriously creepy dynamic."

"Part of it has to do with all this." She spread her arms

wide. "If I keep screwing up, it gives him greater control over me and BGE—at least he thinks so."

"Does he want it enough to kill for it?"

"Roger? I don't see him as a killer, but he wants it enough to marry me for it."

Judd's blue eyes glittered, almost slicing through her. "And that would be a great hardship for him?"

The warmth started in her belly and made a fast approach to her face. She snorted and made a beeline to her desk, ducking into one of the drawers. "For him, I think it would be, but I'm going to spare him the sacrifice."

She retrieved a pad of paper from the drawer and smacked it on the desk. "You can work in here while I attend the meeting."

"How long will you be?"

"About two hours." She couldn't stop the grimace that twisted her lips. "Then I'm going to stop by the hospital and visit Theodore. Do you want to come along?"

"Absolutely. I'm your bodyguard, remember?"

When he looked the way he did now, his raw power barely contained by his suit and his eyes hard and... possessive, she didn't want to forget.

She'd hardly gotten one wink of sleep last night with him downstairs on her couch. She could understand he wanted to keep their relationship professional. He must have all his female clients throwing themselves at him, and he couldn't accept every offer.

Hell, if he made good on the promise in his eyes, she'd be wondering if he bodyguarded everyone the same way.

Celine's tap on the door broke the spell between them. "C'mon in."

"Meeting in ten minutes. You probably want to be one of the first people there."

"Thanks, Celine. Sorry about Roger."

"He's so annoying."

"I know. I'll talk to him again." She gestured to Judd, who had removed his suit jacket and draped it over the back of a chair. "Judd's going to be working in my office while I'm in the meeting. After the meeting, I'm leaving for the rest of the day."

Celine's eyes widened behind her trendy glasses as she took in the view of Judd stretching, his muscles shifting beneath his crisp white shirt. She swallowed. "Okay. Let me know if you need anything, Judd—more coffee, water, supplies."

A back rub. A soft place to rest your head. A mother for your children.

The thoughts marching across Celine's face could be London's own.

London dipped behind the desk and grabbed her brief-case. Might as well look as though she knew what she was doing, even if she was clueless.

Judd looked up, oblivious to the drooling females before him. "Knock 'em dead."

London reached back, plucking the pins from her hair and shaking it free from the bun. "I will."

JUDD RUBBED HIS eyes and shifted his chair to take in the view out the window. Spectacular. It still couldn't make up for being ensconced in an office in a suit all morning.

The job of CEO of an international corporation did not suit London—and it had nothing to do with her intelligence, her ability or her crazy ways. Maybe a little to do with her crazy ways. She struck him as a free spirit. This job might as well have *free spirits need not apply* stamped across its letterhead.

What had a hardheaded businessman like Spencer Breck been thinking when he'd left control of the company to her? Maybe he'd done it for spite.

Maybe father and daughter never got along. She hadn't

seemed all that broken up over his death. Of course, what gave him any idea that he could adequately judge grief? He'd stuffed his away for years.

His brothers had been stoked when the real Phone Book Killer had revealed himself, but the news had left him empty—as usual. His old man had still offed himself. What kind of man did that to his family?

From all accounts, his father had been a good detective. When the Phone Book Killer had started his killing spree, the killer had begun sending messages to Detective Joseph Brody. The SFPD brass had become suspicious about the messages, and then evidence linking his father to the crimes turned up. His father was innocent, so why didn't he stick around and fight for justice instead of ending it all with a jump from the Golden Gate Bridge?

Celine knocked on the door for the tenth time in an hour, and he invited her in. This time she had company.

"Judd? Sorry to bother you again, but we need to leave something on London's desk."

The older woman with Celine scowled at him over her glasses, her gray eyebrows meeting over her nose. "Who are you?"

Celine's cheeks sported two red circles. "I told you, Mary. He's working for London."

Mary's gaze traveled from Judd's face to his arms, which were bared to the elbow. "As what?"

Celine giggled and rolled her eyes. "He's in security."

The woman turned, blocking Celine's entrance. "That's all, Celine. I'll take it from here."

Shooting him a glance over the ogre's shoulder, Celine backed out of the room.

When the door closed, Mary broadened her stance and crossed her arms over her ample bosom. "BGE security working alone in the boss's office?"

Judd kicked his feet on top of London's desk and crossed

his arms behind his head. "Celine forgot her manners. Who are you and what do you want to leave for London?"

"You're a smooth operator, aren't you?" She pulled back her shoulders and Judd feared the buttons on her high-necked white blouse would pop. "My name is Mary Kowalski, and I was Mr. Breck's secretary for forty years. None of this administrative assistant nonsense. I wasn't Mr. Breck's assistant. I was his secretary—I took shorthand, typed one hundred words a minute and, yes, I got him coffee and picked up his dry cleaning, because that's what we did back when I was first hired, and I was grateful for the job. I maintained the same level of service until the day I retired."

Judd's eyebrows had been rising with each of Mary's words, so they were probably somewhere on the back of his skull by now.

He removed his feet from the desk and rose, Mary's eyes following his ascent. "Nice to meet you, ma'am. I'm Judd Brody, and Ms. Breck hired me as her personal bodyguard."

"You're a big 'un, aren't you? That's handy in a bodyguard." She reached into her enormous handbag and drew out a white envelope. She shook it at him. "You're one of those Brody boys. I followed your father's case closely. He'd been a good cop for years. I knew Detective Brody was no killer."

"That I am, ma'am."

"You can stop with the *ma'am* nonsense. Call me Mary and I'll call you Judd." She settled herself in the chair facing the desk. "How's our girl doing?"

"Our girl?"

"London." She chuckled. "Is she stepping in it yet with those ridiculous heels she favors?"

"Stepping in it?"

"Are you a P.I. or a parrot?"

He choked and took a swig of water. "I think she's doing just fine."

"Nonsense. She's not cut out for this. I don't know what Mr. Breck was thinking."

Since that was exactly what he'd been wondering, he warmed up to Mary even more, although she reminded him of his first-grade teacher, Mrs. K. Treated him like Mrs. K. had treated him, too.

"She's a grown woman. I suppose she can make her own decisions. I'm just here to—" he closed the website on the monitor "—make sure she's safe."

"All kinds of ways to make sure someone's safe. I heard someone beat up Theodore two nights ago."

She must not have heard about Griff. "He's in the hospital."

She scowled and placed the envelope she'd had in her lap between a pencil holder and a framed photograph—one of Spencer Breck shaking the hand of some guy in a uniform as he got an award.

"Then London did the right thing hiring you. The first sensible thing she's done since her father died."

"Were London and her father close?"

She smoothed her hands over her skirt. "She wouldn't say so, but he loved and admired his girl."

"Admired?" That seemed to be an odd sentiment for a father to have about his daughter. Should be the other way around. Not that he admired his father—not at all.

Mary shifted her eyes from his face to just over his shoulder. "He admired her honesty and that she had the guts to do just what she wanted to do. It's only when she tries to please someone else that she gets confused." Her eyes found his again. "Like now."

He couldn't agree more, but he didn't think anyone could dissuade London from taking control of BGE—not even a killer.

Glancing at his watch, he said, "She should be back soon. Do you want to wait for her?"

"No." She struggled to her feet from the deep leather chair, and Judd rushed around the desk to help her. She tapped the edge of the envelope with her finger. "I just came to bring her that."

"Will she know what it is?"

"I don't even know what it is." She kept hold of his arm with one hand while she tugged at her skirt with the other. "It's from her father. He gave it to me two years ago and asked me to deliver it to London a few months after his death."

"Maybe it's the reprieve she's been looking for, and he's rescinding his offer of the company."

"I wish." Mary drummed her chin with her fingertips. "Anyway, when I retired last year, I asked Mr. Breck if he still wanted me to hang on to the envelope, and he did. Same instructions. If I'd passed away first, I assumed he would've given the same instructions to someone else."

"Mary!" London barreled into the room and practically tackled the older woman. She wrapped her in a bear hug. "What are you doing here? Can I convince you to come out of retirement and come back to work?"

Mary smiled for the first time since entering the office as she stroked London's hair back from her face. "You look good, a little tired."

"The past few days have been crazy." She raised an eyebrow at Judd. "Have you met Judd Brody?"

"We were discussing you." She broke away from London and grabbed his biceps, giving it a squeeze. "You let this man look out for you. I get a good feeling from this one."

"That's what he's doing here, but what about you? What brings you to BGE?"

"I brought you something." Mary pointed to the envelope on the desk. "From your father."

"More forms?"

"I don't know what it is, London. He gave it to me a

few years ago with instructions to hand it off to you after he passed."

"That sounds mysterious. Why wouldn't he just give it to his attorney?"

Mary clicked her tongue. "You know I never asked your father questions. Not my place."

London reached for the envelope, and Mary crossed two fingers in front of her. "Don't open it while I'm here. It's a private matter and you need to keep it private."

London dropped the envelope. "I'll wait. Can I buy you lunch?"

"Does it look like I need lunch?" Mary patted her belly. "I'm meeting my walking group at the wharf today."

"That's great, Mary."

"It's not so great, but it keeps my doctor happy." She leveled a finger at Judd. "You take care of her, Judd Brody. She deserves the moon and the stars."

London walked Mary out of the office into the outer area, where it looked as if Mary was giving Celine a few parting instructions.

London returned to the office laughing; that little vertical line that had been in place when she'd returned from the meeting had disappeared. "Mary is a character. Did she scare you?"

"Took me back to first grade."

She tilted her head to one side. "I can't see you as a first grader. Shy loner?"

"Close—class clown." He kicked out the chair Mary had just vacated. "How'd the meeting go?"

"Boring and largely incomprehensible." She sank into the chair and then straightened her spine. "But really informative. I learned a lot."

He flicked the envelope with his fingers. "Are you going to open this message from your father?"

"I thought the old man was dead."

Judd glanced up at the open door to see London's cousin gripping the doorjamb.

London twisted in her chair. "Something more from the meeting, Niles?"

"No. Just heard the scuttlebutt about your new body-guard and came to see for myself."

"This is Judd Brody. Judd, this is my cousin, Niles Breck."

Judd nodded but didn't rise. London didn't have to introduce him around as if he was her date.

"I'm glad you're watching my feckless cousin, but why do you need more security, London? Bunny told me what happened to you in the alley. I've told you before to use the front entrances and brave the paparazzi. At least they're not out to snatch your priceless jewels."

"There have been a couple of incidents. Anyway, his salary is not coming out of your pocket, so don't worry about it."

"What did I hear when I walked in? You got a message from your father? How did he manage that?"

A tall man came up behind Niles and tapped him on the shoulder. "Do you have those figures for me?"

"Did you come to check out the new guy in security, too, Wade?"

London's brother, tall and thin like his cousins, pursed his lips. "I did not, although I don't think it's a bad idea."

"Brody." Niles snapped his fingers. "Your brother is a homicide detective and your father—"

"That's right." Judd crossed his arms.

Wade's detached demeanor sharpened at Niles's announcement, but he backed out of the office, nudging Niles. "Those figures?"

"Duty calls." He tugged at the narrow lapels of his suit. "I'll leave you with that message from beyond the grave."

The door closed behind the two men and Judd let out a breath.

"You did call it a message." She lunged for the envelope. "I just figured it was another form or document that I have to sign—one in a tall stack of many."

"I don't know what it is, London. I can hit the men's room if you want to read it in privacy."

"Oh." She fanned herself with the envelope. "If you think it's some sentimental missive from dear old Dad, you can relax. He did not roll that way."

"Okay, then, I'm going to close out of this stuff I was going through, and we can get going—unless you need to handle anything from the meeting."

"Nope. It's all being handled by other people. Other people can do this. Other people can do that." She slipped her finger into the fold of the envelope and ripped across.

Judd hunched over the computer and closed some files. London had been chattering, and then she fell silent.

He looked up. Her eyes were huge glassy pools in her pale face.

"What's wrong?" He almost leaped across the desk, but her accusing tone stopped him.

"Is this some kind of joke?"

His fingers, wedged against the desk, curled into the wood. "What are you talking about?"

"This." She waved a single sheet of paper at him. "Is this your idea of a joke?"

"London, I don't know what you're talking about."

She flung the paper at him; it settled on the keyboard.

He picked it up by one corner and read it aloud. "'Detective Joseph Brody is innocent of murder. At least tell his sons that. They deserve to know.'"

The paper slipped from his fingers, and the room tilted.

What the hell did his father have to do with Spencer Breck?

Chapter Eight

London blinked. Judd looked as dazed as she felt.

What did it mean? Why was her father's last communication to her about Joseph Brody? And what were the odds that one of Joseph Brody's sons would be standing right across from her while she received it?

"Y-you don't know anything about this?"

He fell heavily into the chair and plowed his fingers through his thick hair. "What do you mean? Know anything about it as if I wrote it and sent it? Is that what you think? Mary brought it. I never saw this note before in my life and I don't have a clue what your father knows about my father and why he'd tell you anything about it."

"This is crazy." She massaged her temples. "Why would he send me this note about your father after his death?"

"Could it be someone else playing a joke?"

"What kind of joke is this?"

"You tell me, since you just accused me of playing it on you."

"Why would my father want to tell me this? And why didn't he just tell me while he was alive?"

"Did he ever mention the Phone Book Killer case or my father?"

"Not that I recall. Maybe he had some contact with your brother? The detective? He was a big supporter of the SFPD.

He was close to Captain Williams. He was even on the police commission at one time."

Judd leaned over in his chair and plucked the piece of paper up from the carpet where it had drifted. He smoothed it out on the desk. "I have no idea if he ever contacted Sean, but I intend to ask him."

"My dad died before your other brother, Eric, uncovered the truth about the Phone Book Killer. Maybe if he had lived to see that day, he would've gotten rid of this note. But why write it in the first place? It's a crazy coincidence that I hired one of Joseph Brody's sons to protect me. Maybe Dad was guiding me the night of the benefit."

"Do you believe that kind of stuff? My future sister-in-law is…sensitive that way."

"Yes, I heard. She was involved in catching that occult serial killer after he kidnapped her daughter." She gripped her upper arms and shivered.

"How far back was your father involved with the department?"

"Way far back, when my mother was still alive. There are some pictures at his house showing him and my mother at some police functions." She snatched the picture on the desk and tapped it. "This is my father and Captain Williams."

"Did the support start over twenty years ago?"

"Definitely. Is that when your father—"

"Yeah." The line of his jaw hardened. "The note exonerates my father as the Phone Book Killer, but it doesn't explain why he jumped from the bridge."

It always came back to that for Judd. He'd never be able to forgive his father. They had that in common.

"This is one of those freaky coincidences, or maybe your FBI sister-in-law is right—there are mysterious forces at work in the universe."

"Those mysterious forces still don't explain how your

father knew mine was innocent, and why he thought it was so important for you to impart this info to me and my brothers."

"Maybe Mary knows." She snapped her fingers. "Maybe Theodore knows. He was with my father almost as long as Mary was."

"Then let's pay a visit to Theodore."

A half an hour later, London tapped the toe of her shoe on the sidewalk as she watched Judd climb off his bike and secure his helmet to the side. The incongruity of the suit and the Harley only made Judd look hotter. If she hadn't been wearing this straight skirt, she would've climbed on the back again.

That had been the best part of these past few days—riding on the back of Judd's Harley. Actually, Judd had been the best part of these past few days—the past few months.

After reading her father's note, she had to believe the stars had fated her meeting with Judd the other night. He'd been with her when Theodore was attacked and when she'd discovered her ransacked home. He ran a hand through his hair and straightened his suit jacket. He didn't look much like a guardian angel, but he'd come through for her twice.

"How'd your taxi get here so fast?" The hospital doors slid open and Judd waved her through first.

"I think he figured the faster he went the better tip he'd get."

"Did it work?"

"I'm a big tipper anyway. Last thing you want as a rich person is to get the reputation of a cheap tipper."

"I'll remember that about rich people."

"Some of them don't care. There are plenty of chintzy tippers among the rich."

"I'll remember that, too." He stabbed the elevator button. "You're giving me a lot of good information about rich people."

"Ha." She smacked the button for good measure. "I have a feeling you've been in contact with a lot of rich people in your line of work."

"Yeah, but none have ever divulged the secrets of the rich to me before."

The elevator doors opened and she stepped into the car. "I know. I talk too much."

"You're the most normal rich person I've ever met. So there's that."

She tossed back her hair and laughed. "Yeah, we're a strange bunch."

"Nice to hear you laugh." He cocked his head. "Does that mean you've dismissed the idea that I somehow engineered that note from your father?"

"I didn't think that."

"Yeah, you did. You said it with your eyes and the tone of your voice. You thought I'd tricked you in some way."

She smoothed her hand across her warm cheek. "The note surprised me, shocked me."

"That's another thing about most rich people."

"What's that?"

The doors opened and Judd smacked his hand against one side. "You always have to worry about people using you."

She walked past him quickly, tears stinging the backs of her eyes. She'd exposed her weaknesses to him and must seem pathetic in his eyes. She shrugged. "Poor little rich girl should walk a mile in someone else's shoes, where the fear of feeding your family trumps the fear of being used for your money."

"Hey." Judd grabbed her arm. "I never said that. We all have our problems—rich and poor."

Now he felt he had to make her feel better? She stopped in front of Theodore's room. "And Theodore has his problems."

When they pushed through the door, a young woman

sprang up from the chair beside Theodore's bed. "You must be London Breck."

"And you must be Shannon." She reached out and took Theodore's daughter's hand. "I'm so sorry this happened to your dad."

"Dad's an ex-marine. He had no intention of backing off when those men tried to steal the car."

Theodore grunted. "Those fellas messed with the wrong driver."

London studied Theodore's bruised face. "You're looking a little better."

Theodore grunted again. "Time to get out of this place. The food alone will kill you."

London made a half turn toward Judd. "Shannon, this is Judd Brody."

Shannon grabbed Judd's hand in both of hers. "Thank you so much. Dad told me you probably saved his life when you attended to him in that bar."

"I wouldn't go that far. The paramedics got there fast."

"I owe you one, Brody." Theodore winced and sank against his pillows.

"And I owe you, London." Shannon flung her arm to the side. "Dad's insurance doesn't cover this private room or the extra day he's been in here. The nurses' station out front said it had been taken care of, and I'm sure that means you."

"Your father works for BGE and he's been a family friend for years." London gripped the back of the plastic chair and leaned over it.

"Well, I appreciate it, and my sister and I appreciate that you called us right away."

"I'm just glad you could come on such short notice. That's another thing, and I don't want any arguments. I'm paying your expenses."

Shannon opened her mouth, but London stopped her with an upheld hand. If she couldn't do stuff like this with all the money she had, what was the point in having it? "It's done. Now, why don't you go get something to eat while I talk to your dad?"

Shannon's gaze traveled to Theodore, who waved his hand. "Go on, girl. I'm mighty tired of your fussing."

Shannon wedged her hands on her hips. "You can have him, London."

When Shannon closed the door, London skirted the chair and sat down. "Are you feeling better, Theodore?"

"Don't you start. I feel fine."

"Good." She pulled the envelope from her purse. "I have something to ask you about Dad."

His eyes dropped to the envelope. "Fire away."

"Did Dad ever say anything to you about Joseph Brody and the Phone Book Killer case?" If she expected surprise on Theodore's face, he didn't deliver. Her pulse ticked up a notch. "Did he?"

Theodore looked at Judd. "He knew about it—everyone did. He was even on the police commission at the time."

"He was?" She scooted her chair closer. "What did he say about it then?"

"When some of that evidence came out against Brody—" Theodore's eyes shifted to Judd again "—he was surprised, like everyone else. Thought it was…unfortunate that a good detective had fooled everyone. Thought it was an embarrassment for the department."

Judd braced one shoulder against the wall. "He believed in my father's guilt?"

"At the time I think he got caught up in it, but it turned out that first victim's husband was just trying to cover his tracks."

London twisted the edge of the bedsheets. "We know that now, but are you telling us that Dad believed Joseph Brody was the Phone Book Killer?"

"He did. Sorry, man."

Judd pushed off the wall. "No offense taken. A lot of people thought he was guilty. He killed himself—that sort of screams guilt."

"That's weird." She pulled the note from the envelope. "At one point, did Dad change his mind, and why?" She shook out the note and handed it to Theodore. "Looks as though he felt bad about it and wanted to somehow set the record straight."

Theodore reached for his glasses on the bedside cart and put them on. He held up the note and scanned it. "Where'd you find this?"

"That's what's so strange. Mary Kowalski hand delivered it to me. Said Dad asked her to keep it and give it to me after he died."

Theodore's forehead furrowed. "That doesn't make any sense."

"Exactly. I thought you might be able to shed some light on it, but you've only added to the mystery."

"Not really." Judd shoved off the wall and loomed over Theodore's bed. "You said he was on the police commission at the time. Who else was on the commission?"

"Couldn't tell you that, but I'm sure you could find out. What are you aiming at?"

"I'm not sure. If he knew my father was innocent, maybe others on the commission knew it, too." Judd blew out a breath and stepped back. "You know what? It doesn't really matter, does it? The real killer confessed to my brother, and my father's name has been cleared. How or why your father knew about it isn't an issue at this point, is it?"

London narrowed her eyes. For a minute there, Judd had dropped the pretense of not giving a hoot about his father's reputation, but he'd recovered himself nicely—back to the aloof, slightly sardonic, devil-may-care P.I.

"I just think it's weird that my father left me a note from the grave about this. Why not some warm words for me or remembrances of my mother? It's clearly something that bothered him."

"Now your father's dead, my father's dead and his name has been cleared." Judd's heavy lids fell over his eyes. "Doesn't matter."

Theodore nodded. "I agree, London."

"I guess I've been overruled here." She snatched the letter from Theodore's lap and stuffed it back in the envelope. "Are you going back to Atlanta to see your other daughter when you get out of here? I know you have another grandson you haven't seen yet."

"I know that tone of voice." He rolled his eyes at Judd and winked. "Boss's orders?"

"Boss's orders." London's lips twitched. Sometimes it was good to be the boss. "Let me know before you leave town. Call me at the office—something happened to my phone."

She heard Judd's intake of breath but ignored him. She didn't want to tell Theodore about the break-in at her place or Griff's murder. He might get it into his head to stick around.

She had all the bodyguard she needed.

"I'll do that. If they let me out of here tomorrow, I'll probably take a few days to make arrangements before leaving."

"Make sure you put all expenses on your BGE credit card—airfare, everything. I mean it."

"Yes, ma'am."

They waited until Shannon returned before leaving Theodore.

Judd turned to her at the elevator. "You didn't want to tell him what happened at your place?"

"I didn't want to worry him."

"I agree. Nothing he could do about it anyway."

They reached the lobby and Judd hesitated at the door. "Are you going straight back to your place?"

"Yeah." She patted her stomach. "We never did have lunch."

"I could use something to eat. I was going to stop by my office and get that equipment I mentioned yesterday. I still want to do a clean sweep for bugs at your place."

"Why don't you do that, and we'll meet at a restaurant near your office for lunch. I can grab a taxi over."

"There's a decent Italian place down the block from my place—Napoli's."

"I know it. I'll get us a table."

She snagged a taxi near the emergency room entrance as Judd took off on his bike. She gave the driver her location and collapsed in the backseat. Both Theodore and Judd had been quick to dismiss her father's note, but she couldn't do it. She and her father hadn't always gotten along, but she knew him. For him to leave a note with Mary to give to her after his death, it had to be something of great importance.

Why hadn't he told her this when he was alive? Better yet, why not tell the Brodys? If he felt so bad about it, why not tell the people it affected the most?

The police commission. It had to be related to his time on the commission. It coincided with the events of Detective Brody's downfall. Maybe unraveling this mystery would help reveal the reason behind Brody's suicide.

That alone should motivate Judd. The fact that his father had taken his life bothered him more than the suspicions surrounding Joseph Brody. Maybe she could use her pull to give Judd some closure on the issue. That would be worth more than any retainer she could pay him.

"Excuse me." She leaned forward in her seat. "I need to make a stop first. Take me to the financial district."

The taxi driver nodded and took the next turn.

When he pulled up in front of the building, she said,

"Wait here. I'll be about ten minutes." She dashed into the building and back up to the BGE offices.

When she saw London, Celine reddened up to the roots of her hair and jumped off the edge of her desk, where she'd been flirting with one of the guys from marketing. "Did you forget something, London?"

"Yeah, in my office." She brushed her fingers in Celine's direction as she started for the office. "I'll get it."

London closed the door behind her and pressed a button to drop the blinds over the windows. She moved behind the desk and extended her foot beneath it to feel for the lump beneath the carpet. When she located it, she pressed down with her foot.

She ducked under the desk and lifted a piece of carpet. Then she slid a panel of the floor to the side and reached in for her father's laptop.

When he'd showed her this hiding place, he'd told her that nobody knew about it, not even Mary.

She'd seen him put this laptop in here before and hadn't thought about it when he'd passed away, since all the main BGE business resided on the desktop computer in this office. But this had been his private laptop, and if her father had had any secrets they would be on this computer.

Just like she'd kept her secrets on her laptop—the one that had been stolen from her place yesterday morning.

Maybe her father had had the right idea with a secret hiding place.

She replaced the panel and carpet and then smoothed it with her hand. She shoved the laptop into her briefcase.

Leaving the blinds closed, she swung the door open.

Celine had returned to her chair and was typing away on her keyboard. "Did you find everything okay?"

"I did, thanks." She slowed her gait. "I forgot to mention that I'm going to get a new phone. I don't have mine anymore."

Celine stopped typing and shoved her glasses onto her nose. "London, is it true that a security guard at your building was murdered last night and that you found his body?"

London stumbled to a stop. Did everyone know the rest of the story? "Yes, I did. The police don't want me to say anything about it right now."

"That's so creepy. Is that why you have tall, dark and gorgeous looking out for you?"

"A little extra security never hurt anyone."

"Especially extra security like Judd Brody. He can guard my body anytime."

London had no idea what kind of expression just crossed her face, but it had Celine backpedaling. "I—I mean, I'm sure he's professional and all and you don't see him like that. And I don't see him like—or I wouldn't see him like that if he was guarding my body…I mean, if he was my bodyguard."

London tried a stiff smile. "I know what you mean. He's a good-looking man."

"Well, have a great day." Celine waved and dipped her head toward her monitor again.

London traipsed toward the elevator, the added weight of the laptop causing her briefcase to bang against her hip. She'd probably just confirmed to Celine that she thought of Judd as much more than a bodyguard. Maybe she never should've invited Celine to call her London. Mary still called her father Mr. Breck, even after his death.

She could be a different kind of CEO than her father and still be successful, couldn't she? Of course, she didn't even know what a successful CEO looked like. Did it mean having everyone around you address you by your surname?

Too bad her father hadn't left her a rule book—*Being a CEO for Dummies.*

She scrambled back into the taxi. "Okay, on to Napoli's."

She still beat Judd to the restaurant. She got a table for

two by the window and watched out for his arrival. She heard him before she saw him—the distinctive growl of the Harley's engine.

He rolled the back wheel to the curb and lifted the helmet from his head. Sliding from the bike, he tucked the helmet beneath one arm and strode into the restaurant.

Worn denim encased his long legs and his boots clumped across the wood floor of the restaurant. He pulled out the chair across from her. "Waiting long?"

Actually, she'd just arrived, but he didn't need to know she'd made a stop. "Not too long. You changed."

"I couldn't keep running around in a suit all day."

"I hear you." She tugged at the lapels of her jacket. "Did you get everything you need for my place?"

"I packed a bag. I'll pick it up after lunch." He tapped the table. "The service isn't usually this slow here. You don't even have a drink."

"I, uh, waited."

Two minutes later Judd had an iced tea in front of him and she had a sparkling water. Fortunately the waitstaff hadn't recognized her, or if they had, they didn't let on.

"Nothing from the police yet about Griff or my phone?"

He crunched a piece of ice and held up his finger. "Got a call from Detective Curtis. As we figured, the texts sent to your phone came from a disposable phone that can't even be pinged. It must've been destroyed already."

"Great." She squeezed the slice of lemon into her water. "I suppose I can understand why the burglars murdered Griff. He saw them and they wanted to keep him quiet. But why involve me? Even if I hadn't discovered the body, I would've found out about the murder."

"Scare tactic."

"But why? They already broke into my place. All this would make more sense if they sent me some kind of message. Are they trying to scare me into doing something or not doing something? How can I comply when I don't know what they want?"

"You're attributing way too much logic to a couple of thieves and murderers. Maybe one's a psychopath and likes playing mind games."

She slumped in her seat. "That makes me feel a lot better."

His hand shot out and covered hers for a brief moment. "I'm sorry. You didn't strike me as the type of client who wants me to hide things. You asked how Griff died yesterday, and I told you because you deserve the truth. But maybe you don't want that truth."

"Just give it to me." She sucked the lemon juice from her fingers and her mouth puckered.

Judd's blue eyes deepened in color and intensity. She had not calculated her actions to get a response from him, but it seemed to happen naturally.

If they'd met in a bar or at a party, they'd be in bed by now. Or maybe the old London would've headed down that path. The CEO London would shake his hand and leave him her card.

"I promise to always tell you the truth." He held up two fingers like a Boy Scout.

He'd tell her the truth but deny the attraction that sizzled between them.

It gave her an excuse to keep her secrets, too.

Over lunch, they seemed to come to an unspoken agreement to keep it light. He told her funny stories about his jobs, never once revealing the names of his clients. She shared the details of her mishap in Qatar.

"The sheikh must've been furious to discover you'd taken the diamond without actually joining his harem."

She dabbed her eyes with her napkin, struggling to control her laughter. "I kept telling him it would never happen. It's not my fault he believed that diamond would seal the deal."

"I suppose it had nothing to do with the fact that you'd been admiring it, leading him to believe he'd found the key to your heart."

"It wasn't my heart he wanted to unlock." She set the napkin back in her lap.

"Didn't he have you arrested? How'd you get out of that?"

She rubbed her fingers together. "Connections and pay-offs. It's the way the world works."

"I suppose you learned that at an early age."

"We all get our life lessons." She shoved her plate away from her. "What about you? What life lessons did you learn?"

"Shoot first, ask questions later."

"At five? You learned that lesson at five years old?"

He raised his eyes to the ceiling. "Maybe four."

"You're lying."

"Are you done picking at that salad?"

"Why, do you want the rest?"

"I have work to do." His tone was hard. He caught the waiter's eye. "You're not paying me to sit around eating lunch."

"But I am paying for lunch." She made a grab for the check when the waiter left it on the table, but Judd beat her to it.

"I wouldn't call this a working lunch."

"Sure it was." Her lashes fluttered despite her best efforts to keep a poker face. "What would you call it?"

He pulled his wallet out of his back pocket. "We didn't discuss business."

So he wouldn't call it a date even though that was what it had felt like to her. "We got to know each other a little better, and that's business. How are you going to do your job if you don't know your client?"

"You think I knew that pop singer I worked for over in Hawaii?"

"I think this is a little different. You were protecting her from hormonal teenagers. We have no idea yet what you're protecting me from. Don't you think getting to know me better will help you figure out where the threat's coming from?"

"Are you telling me that sheikh from Qatar is out for revenge?"

"I did give the diamond back." She folded her hands on the table and pursed her lips.

"So we can cross him off the list."

"Anyone else you've crossed off the list?"

"Nope. I'm glad I got to meet a lot of the players at your office today—your cousin, your half brother, your fiancé, your fiancé's father."

"Roger is *not* my fiancé." She flicked her fingers against his forearm.

"Will I get a chance to see them again? Most of them viewed me as the hired help, which works."

"There's something coming up this weekend, a social event."

"Argh." He sank his head in his hands and grasped his hair. "Another suit? I've worn more suits and tuxes this week than I have all year."

"What are you worried about? You certainly do them justice." Her gaze meandered across his wide shoulders. He looked better in a tux than any man she'd ever seen. It had to be because it looked as if he could burst out of it at any moment.

"They're uncomfortable." He ran his finger along the neckline of his T-shirt as if just thinking about a shirt and tie was choking him.

"Are you going to suck it up for the sake of getting close to my adversaries?"

"I will suck it up." He pushed back from the table and picked up his helmet. "But right now I'm going to scan your place for bugs."

"Can I borrow your phone?"

"What for?" He dragged it out of the pocket of his jacket.

"I need to call another taxi."

"Hop on the back of my bike."

She plucked her pencil skirt away from her thigh. "In this?"

"Can't you just suck it up so I don't have to wait for you?" He pointed to her legs. "If you're that modest—and I've heard otherwise—you can always put my jacket around your waist."

"Oh, hell, why not?" She slung her briefcase across her body. "It's not as if I'm not wearing underwear."

"I think you'll discover most CEOs do, but then, what do I know?"

Once outside, Judd grabbed the handlebars of his bike and flipped up the kickstand as she fished her sunglasses out of her purse.

"What's this?" Judd swiped a piece of paper from the seat of his bike.

"A ticket?" London shoved her glasses on top of her head.

Judd hung his helmet on one handlebar and snapped the paper open with both hands. "It's a newspaper article."

"Maybe it's trash that blew onto your bike. The wind picked up this afternoon." She slipped the helmet from the bike and fiddled with the strap.

"London."

Judd's tone of voice stilled her fingers. "What is it?"

"It's an old newspaper article about the SFPD police commission—and your father."

Chapter Nine

London's stomach dipped as her gaze scanned the sidewalk for the messenger. Were they being followed? "You're kidding."

He waved the neatly clipped article in her face. "No."

"Does it have a date?" She held out her hand, wiggling her fingers.

He handed the article to her. "No date, but it names your father on the commission, so what year was that?"

She scanned the words of the article. "Theodore didn't say, did he? But he mentioned it was at the time of the Phone Book Killer. Wait, the article even mentions the Phone Book Killer."

"Who put this on my bike and why?"

Her father's laptop burned a hole in her briefcase. She shouldn't have any secrets from him. Well, almost none.

"I think we need to get to the bottom of this, Judd. It all means something. No way would my father leave me a note about your father if it weren't important, if he didn't know something or wasn't involved in some way. My father wouldn't randomly feel sorry for your family. I wouldn't call him a cold man, but he wasn't overly sentimental, either."

"I guess we can do some research on the commission at that time, but I don't see how that's helping you with your safety, especially if someone is following you."

She shrugged. "Let's change the contract. You're a P.I. in addition to a bodyguard. I'm making an amendment to our arrangements. I want you to help me with this mystery, the purpose behind my father's note. I'll up your retainer."

"No need. You're paying me plenty to cover a few searches on the internet."

"We can do more than that." She patted her briefcase. "I have something to show you when we get back to my place."

"Related to that newspaper article?"

"Related to all of it."

"Then let's get going. I need to pick up my equipment at the office first."

He straddled his Harley as she creased the article and dropped it into her purse.

He tilted the bike to the side and she hiked up her skirt almost to her hips and climbed on. Once seated, she wrapped the arms of his jacket around her waist, draping the soft leather over her thighs.

He revved the engine, and they zoomed away from the curb. After darting in and out of traffic, he rolled to a stop in front of the building that housed his professional digs.

While he jogged up to his office, she stayed seated on the bike, not wanting to rearrange her skirt again.

He returned with a black bag and tapped her leg. "I need to put this in the saddlebag."

She shifted and curled back her leg as Judd opened the saddlebag and stuffed the black bag inside. His hand brushed her bare calf, and then he cinched her ankle and placed her foot back on the footrest.

"Don't want you falling off."

This time London held on to Judd for dear life—not because he took the turns any faster than last time or sped up and down the hills any faster, but because she didn't want to pretend anymore that this attraction didn't exist between them.

In Judd, she'd found a kindred free spirit. He didn't pass judgment on her past actions. He was down-to-earth and had no pretensions and treated her like a normal person.

That lunch had felt too much like a date, and she felt too connected to him now to return to some kind of professional relationship, which they'd never really had to begin with.

So she snuggled against his back, as close as the helmet would allow, and gripped his hips with her knees.

Judd pulled up to her building. With the motorcycle idling at the curb, London scrambled off, tugging at her skirt beneath the leather jacket around her waist. She pulled off the helmet and handed it to Judd when he climbed off the bike.

A new security guard greeted them in the lobby, and London crossed the marble floor to introduce herself. "I'm London Breck. You're the new guy?"

He stood up, holding himself as stiffly as a military man. "Yes, ma'am. I'm Paul Madden."

"Nice to meet you, Paul. This is Judd Brody. He's my… bodyguard."

If Paul found it odd she had a bodyguard, he didn't let it show on his stern face. He shook Judd's hand. "Sir, if you need anything from me, I'm at your disposal."

When they got to the elevator, Judd dipped his head and whispered in her ear, "He's a far cry from Griff."

"Too bad management didn't have him in place yesterday. Those thugs never would've gotten into my home."

Judd tensed beside her when she unlocked her door, but this time not a magazine was out of place.

As soon as the door shut, he dug into his bag and said, "I'm going to do a quick sweep of this room before we check out the computer, and then you can show me what you got."

While Judd scanned the great room, she dropped her briefcase and got some water. Watching him do his thing, she pulled the laptop from the case and settled it on the coffee table.

When he was done, he stuffed his instruments back into his bag and sat next to her. "Are you ready?"

She flipped open the computer and said, "It's in here. It's my father's laptop."

"You took it from the office?"

"Yes." He didn't have to know where, exactly.

"I'm confused. Haven't you already been working on your father's computer? How could you take over his duties without all his files and data at your fingertips?"

"Not—" she tapped the keyboard to wake it up and entered the password "—this one."

"Is that his personal computer?" In two long steps, he was at her side.

"It's personal and business. He used it to back up important files from his work computer, but I know he kept other information on it."

"Who else had access to it since his death?" He leaned over her shoulder, his hair tickling her cheek.

He had one lock of hair that always curled into his eye, and her fingers tingled with the thought of brushing it back from his forehead.

She clicked a few more keys, launching some folders. "Nobody. My father locked up this laptop. I'm not sure anyone knew of its existence except me, and maybe Mary. But even Mary didn't know where he hid it."

"Okay. Let's get searching." He patted the cushion of the couch and she sat down. He sat next to her and she dipped toward him, her shoulder brushing his.

Her bare thigh pressed against the rough denim of his

jeans, but this time he didn't move away from her. Progress. Maybe the lunch had changed the direction of his feelings, too.

She blew out a breath. "As you may know, my father and I weren't that close."

He leaned back against the couch and rested one booted foot on his knee. "From all the news stories about you over the years, I figured you were Daddy's little princess."

"Why would you think that?"

"I don't know. You pretty much did as you pleased, and he'd always rescue you. Didn't it work like that?"

"I suppose so, but he didn't consider me his princess— more like a thorn in his side. I often think he left me in charge of the company to get back at me for all those years of hell I put him through."

"And if he did?"

"I deserve it. I did put him through hell."

"You were a little girl without a mom."

Her nose tingled and the memory of rose-scented hugs feathered across her senses. She stretched her lips into a smile. "I don't know if I can blame all my craziness on being motherless."

"Sure you can." He traced the line of her jaw with the rough pad of his finger.

"Do you?"

His finger froze at the end of her chin and he sucked in a breath. "I had a mother."

"Yes, yes, your mother, but you missed your father." She dabbled her fingers down his forearm. "Is that what made you the tatted-up, Harley-riding badass?"

His chest rose and fell with a deep breath, and London held hers, wondering if she'd gone too far with him.

His thick, dark lashes fell halfway over his eyes and his mouth lifted at one corner. "Naw, I'm just naturally a badass."

She punched him in the arm to break the tension that had built up between them. She'd rather plant a kiss on his sexy mouth, but she knew Judd Brody wanted to be the hunter and not the prey.

He rose to his feet, stomping his boots. "I will leave you to deciphering your father's secret computer while I continue searching the rest of your place." She let him go, watching him from the corner of her eye as he pawed through his bag, pulling out unidentifiable bits and pieces.

"I'll start upstairs and work my way down."

She waved her hand. "Be my guest."

He pointed to his motorcycle boots. "Should I take these off? I should've asked you that before."

"I'm not that picky. Take them off if you want to."

"Since I may need to climb on top of some chairs, maybe I should." He pulled off his boots and lined them up at the fireplace.

The masculine shoes looked incongruous in her decidedly feminine place, but she liked them there.

After she watched him disappear up the stairs, she turned her attention back to her father's computer. She tried searching for the words *police, commission, Brody, Phone Book*. Nothing.

She reread the article that had been left on Judd's bike. It discussed her father's appointment to the police commission. Richard Taylor had also been on the commission at that time. Had he left the article for Judd? Why?

Had it come from Mary? Somehow she couldn't picture her father's secretary skulking around the streets of North Beach looking for Judd's motorcycle.

Who had left it for him and why? Or maybe it was intended for her? If someone knew she had Judd on her payroll, maybe he figured Judd would turn the article over to her.

It could be same person who'd texted her. She let the article drift to the coffee table. How had that thought crept into her head? Her father's note about Joseph Brody's innocence had nothing to do with the current threats against her. In fact, she'd been using Spencer's note to escape the realities of the break-in, Theodore's beating and Griff's murder.

She typed in another search, and while scanning the results, realized she'd been searching for files only. She entered *police* again and expanded the search to all items.

She blinked when several picture files appeared in the list. He'd kept pictures on this laptop?

She clicked through the pictures and discovered several of her father with the commission. He must've scanned those onto this computer.

She dragged them all into another folder and printed them out. Then she clicked on the pictures icon.

She gasped and the hand hovering over the directional mouse trembled when she saw the picture folder called "Madeline."

He couldn't. He didn't.

Lodging her tongue in the corner of her mouth, she double clicked on the folder. Neat yellow folders organized by date populated the monitor. She clicked on the first chronological folder.

Her eyes flooded with tears and she covered her mouth with one hand as her gaze locked on the blond-haired tot in the sandbox. Her heart thumped painfully in her chest as she launched each picture in succession. Each image sucked more air out of her lungs until she felt suffocated.

Where had he gotten these? Why?

A heavy step on the stair had her snapping the laptop closed on the bright-eyed girl with the happy grin.

She pressed the heels of her hands to her eyes and then wiped her hand across her nose. She coughed. "All clear?"

"Haven't found anything yet. Have you?"

Oh, yeah. She'd found more than she'd bargained for.

"Some pictures." She opened the laptop and closed the Madeline folder. "One of my father and the rest of the police commission the year he was appointed."

"Well, that's something. He must've taken the trouble to scan those in, since I don't think digital cameras were all that common twenty years ago."

He aimed some device at the wall and moved it across the area.

"I was thinking the same thing. It must mean something for him to have taken that trouble."

Judd held something that looked like a microphone up to the four corners of the room.

London ran her hands over her warm face and scooped her hair into a ponytail. "Is that thing supposed to beep or something if it finds anything?"

"Sort of. I can't detect any evidence of bugs in your place. It's lookin' good."

"That's a relief. Maybe it's over, Judd."

"What do you mean?"

"Someone tried to ruffle my feathers, but it's not working. Maybe they're done now. I attended the board meeting today as CEO."

"I'd feel better about that theory if Griff's body hadn't been hanging outside the trash room of your building. That's more than ruffled feathers, wouldn't you say?"

"Of course. I didn't mean to make light of Griff's death at all. Maybe that part of it was a big mistake."

"And the text messages leading you to his body? Those were a mistake, too? Somebody wants to do more than ruffle your feathers, London."

She jumped up, tossing her hair over one shoulder. "If someone wants to kill me, why doesn't he just take his best shot?"

"Hey." He dropped his microphone and took her by the

shoulders. "Don't say that. Nobody's going to hurt you. Not while I'm on the job."

She didn't break away from him and he didn't let go. Instead she stared into those fierce blue eyes—ferocity on her behalf.

"Judd, do you think it's all connected?"

"What?"

"The threats, the note, the article, your father, my father—us."

His grip on her shoulders softened into a caress. "How?"

"I'm not sure. It occurred to me when I was looking through the pictures on my father's laptop. Why now? Why did Mary deliver the note? Who put the article on your bike? Someone's tracking our movements—yours and mine."

"Maybe it's all one big coincidence, London."

She ran her thumb between his eyebrows, smoothing out the crease there. "You don't really believe that. Stop trying to make me feel better. We both know none of this is coincidence. How did you wind up taking that job for Bunny anyway?"

"I told you. A buddy of mine had the job and couldn't make it."

"Why not?"

"I don't know. I didn't ask. He called, said he had an easy gig with good pay and needed someone to cover for him."

"Had you ever covered for him before?"

"No, he always needs the money." His hands slid from her shoulders to her upper arms. "I'm glad I did cover for him."

"I am, too. It's almost like fate. Our pasts are tied together somehow."

He traced his finger along her jaw. "It's not just the past, is it?"

Her lips parted as she panted out a breath. Would he acknowledge the connection they had in the present? Should she? She needed to tread lightly. You didn't corner a man like Judd Brody.

"Whatever is in our pasts is affecting the present. Forces beyond our control are bringing us together, and those same forces are going to bring us resolution."

Judd threw back his head and laughed. Then he tapped her temple lightly. "I think you're getting carried away with all the fate stuff."

His laugh had broken the spell and brought her back to earth. "You're right. It's looking into the past, plus the time of day."

He glanced out the large window with the view of the city, lights twinkling in the office buildings. "The sun's going down and I'm just about finished."

He turned abruptly from the window and stopped. He swayed to one side and then the other.

"What's wrong?"

"A light. I saw a glimmer of light on that wall."

"That's wallpaper."

"I know." He crept across the room on silent feet. Extending his arms, he ran his hands across a portion of the wall. "London."

"What are you doing?" His manner and his voice had her heart tripping over itself in her chest.

He pressed his fingers against a spot on the wall. "Turn on the lights."

She stumbled toward the lamp next to the couch and turned the switch. "What do you see? Is it a bug? I thought your secret-agent equipment didn't detect any of those."

"It's not—" he scratched his fingernails against the wallpaper "—a bug."

"I don't get it." She swallowed, her throat dry.

He landed his fist against the wall. "What's on the other side of this wall?"

"It's the other unit, the one I bought to have the floor to myself." She inched toward him and the…thing on her wall.

"What's in that other unit?"

"Nothing. It's empty. Are you going to tell me what's going on? What did you find?"

He stepped back and tapped the wallpaper. "Look."

Licking her lips, she leaned forward. A round piece of glass or clear plastic caught the light. "What is that?"

"It's a simple device that's allowing someone to see into your place."

"Th-that's crazy. There's nothing next door. There's nobody there."

"Do you have the key? We're going over there right now."

She headed for the kitchen, glancing over her shoulder at the wall. Judd had this all wrong. The walls in this building were too thick to allow something like that.

She opened a cabinet and lifted a key ring from the rack. She twirled it around her finger. "This is it."

He followed her into the hallway, and she jerked her thumb to the left. "The front door's that way."

When Judd reached for the weapon he'd shoved in his waistband, her heart started to gallop. She turned the key in the lock and Judd stepped forward, tucking her behind him.

It reminded her of the other night. What would they find this time?

He pushed the door open and walked into the entryway, leading with his gun.

The layout of the condo mimicked her own, and she followed Judd down the two steps into the unfurnished great room. She flicked on the switch to the chandelier that hung above the dining area, and her nostrils twitched as an unpleasant smell wafted toward them. "What is that smell?"

Judd lifted his nose to the air. "Smells like garbage…or something rotting."

"M-maybe a rat got in here and died."

"While eating take-out pizza?" He pointed to the large kitchen island that separated the kitchen from the dining area, littered with two pizza boxes.

"What the hell?" She stomped toward the boxes and flipped up a cardboard lid. Half-eaten pieces of pizza emitted a rank odor and she pinched her nose as she gagged.

"Looks as though someone has been making himself at home. Where's the common wall with your living room?"

"It's back this way. It's a downstairs office or bedroom. The whole place is unfurnished. With my father's death and taking over the company, I haven't had time to remodel yet."

She led the way and he followed close on her heels. She pushed open the door and pressed the light switch on the wall.

A bubble of fear rose in her throat as her gaze tripped over a pillow on the floor next to the wall.

"I—I didn't put that there."

Still gripping his gun, Judd squeezed past her into the room and headed for the pillow. "Your living room is on the other side of this wall." He pressed his hand against the wall's surface and a piece shifted and fell to the floor.

London jumped back. "What is that?"

"Someone sawed out a piece of the wall." He kicked it with his toe, then crouched down and stuck his head in the hollow of the wall. Then he cursed, his voice muffled. "London, you have to see this."

She willed her feet to move across the floor even though they felt like lead blocks. She knelt beside him, taking little comfort in his solid shoulder pressing against hers.

"Put your eye to that plastic circle embedded in the drywall."

He shifted to the side and she ducked her head, pressing her eye against the circle. She yelped at the panoramic view of her great room. "That's my place."

"Someone has been watching you, London. Watching you from this room."

Chapter Ten

London fell backward and he caught her in his arms, holding her against his chest.

Trembles passed through her body like waves and he rested his cheek against her hair. "Are you okay?

She turned her head to look into his face, her eyes huge and round. "I can't believe someone would do something like this. How in the hell did he even get in here?"

"It doesn't look like anyone's been here for a few days. Maybe he was worried that he'd be discovered after Griff's murder and left." He wrapped an arm around her waist and pulled her away from the wall. They both landed on the floor with her halfway in his lap.

She folded one leg beneath her and leaned against his thigh. "Do you think Griff let them up here? I can imagine they gave him some line about getting some stories on the people who live in this building. Griff told us he'd cooperated with the paparazzi before."

She seemed to have recovered some of her composure—but she stayed in his lap.

"That could be. He mentioned that he'd done it before without any bad consequences. I don't see how a stranger or maybe more than one stranger could make his way into this unit, cut a chunk out of the wall, order pizza and spy on you without someone in this building helping him out."

She gathered his T-shirt in her fists. "Maybe if we leave everything as is and pretend we never found his little squirrel hole, he'll come back and we can catch *him* in the act."

"I think the game is up for him. He literally destroyed his contact in this building by killing Griff. He's not going to try to buy off another security guard—especially that guy down there now."

She released his shirt and rubbed her eyes, her knuckles digging into her sockets. "Now I'm sitting here thinking about all the stuff I did in that room over the past few weeks. Who knows? Maybe even longer than that."

"None of that dancing naked on the tabletops?" He tugged the end of one blond lock of hair hanging over her shoulder.

She rewarded him with a shaky smile. "I thought I told you, all that stuff is behind me."

"Why?" He clinched the strand of hair and wound it around his finger. "Why are you trying so hard to run away from the old London? She sounds like a lot of fun."

"The old London made a lot mistakes."

"How many mistakes can a twentysomething make?"

Her green eyes clouded over, and she stared out the window over his shoulder. "You'd be surprised."

"Do you think London Breck the CEO isn't going to make mistakes? All you can do is be true to yourself."

"Do you follow your own advice, Judd Brody?"

"I try." He held her gaze even though the lie burned in his gut.

"Right." She fell back on the floor, crossing her arms behind her head and staring at the ceiling. "I have a new wrinkle to our contract."

"Oh?" He stretched out beside her, digging his elbow into the carpet and propping up his head. Was she going to put a moratorium on personal conversations?

She rolled her head to the side. "I want you to move in—here."

He blinked. Move in to a posh Nob Hill condo? Next door to London Breck? He could do that.

"Do you want me to watch you through that peephole?"

She flung her arm out to the side, smacking him in the belly. "No. If you don't mind roughing it, we can set up something for you to sleep on. I'd just feel safer having you close by."

"I'm not going anywhere." He took her hand, threaded his fingers through hers and pulled it back onto his stomach. "I'm going to figure out who's threatening you and why, and then I'm going to put a stop to it."

She squeezed his hand. "Judd, I think it has something to do with my father's death, and I think it has something to do with the note he left me, which means it has something to do with your father."

"I think you're right."

"Aren't you curious about why your father jumped from the bridge? Especially now that his name has been cleared of the Phone Book slayings?"

That familiar tightness crept into his neck and jaw. "He probably thought he was being set up and didn't see a way out. Or he'd already planned to kill himself and the situation offered the perfect excuse. Either way, he took the coward's way out."

She sat up, dragging her hand away from his. "You're right. It does seem as if he *was* set up to take the fall. Certain items were found in his personal belongings, items that didn't belong to him, right?"

His heart tapped out a staccato beat. "Yes."

"Someone must've put them there, planted them so that suspicion would fall on him."

"My brother Ryan figured it was the real Phone Book Killer, Russ Langford. The man was a psychopath who murdered his wife and then went on a killing spree to cover the deed. Ryan believed Langford set up my father, too."

"Did he admit to it?"

"No. He was killed by a police sniper before he did too much talking to Ryan."

"Did Ryan investigate any further?"

"It was a touchy situation. It turned out the writer who'd been helping him, Kacie Manning, was Russ Langford's daughter. She'd believed my father had killed her mother and then discovered it was her own father."

Her jaw dropped and she pressed her fingers against her lips. "And Ryan didn't want to look into it any further?"

"By the time they'd made the discovery, Ryan had fallen in love with Kacie. He took her back to Crestview with him, and his primary focus now is protecting Kacie and helping her heal from the revelations."

"That's sweet and all, but this is your father."

He didn't need London telling him that. "I think it's safe to say that Langford set him up."

She raised her brows. "If you were working that case for me, I'd fire you. Shouldn't a P.I. be curious about everything? You're leaving no stone unturned for me. Why not do the same for yourself?"

He rubbed a hand across his mouth. "It's different, London. Nobody's threatening me. My father's already been vindicated."

"Not really."

"Sure he has. Langford admitted to being the Phone Book Killer, the newspaper printed a big article, case closed."

"Except your father jumped from the Golden Gate Bridge for some inexplicable reason."

He opened his mouth, but she held up her hand. "And you can't forgive him for that."

His back stiffened, his repose no longer comfortable or relaxing. "I guess that's something for me to deal with."

He rolled to his stomach and army crawled back to the wall. Then he sat up, picking up the piece of drywall and fitting it back into place. "As soon as I bring the rest of my stuff here, I'm going to dig that spy device out of the wall and patch this up."

"Should we try to get fingerprints?"

"You can call the cops and tell them you had a squatter here. They'll dust the place, but I doubt you'll find anything. Someone is not going to go through all this trouble and then leave a set of prints."

"It's getting late." She rubbed her belly. "And I'm hungry despite the disgusting smell in the other room."

"If you want to change, I'll take you out to get something to eat and we can drop by my place to pick up my stuff." He tapped the wall. "Do you even have a car here in the city?"

"I do. It's in the garage downstairs, but I don't drive it much when I'm here. Since Dad's death, Theodore's been insisting on driving me around in that limo. But he keeps that at Dad's place in Pacific Heights. Besides—" she leaped to her feet like a ballerina "—I like riding on the back of that Harley."

And he liked her there, her arms wrapped around him, her body pressed against his. He could get used to that.

"Okay, let's lock up and get some food."

She tugged at her skirt. "I'll change first."

"I'll come with you, but let me get rid of some of this trash first."

After this discovery, he didn't want to leave London alone for a second. Maybe she had a stalker. Maybe it had nothing to do with her father—or his.

He studied her profile as she locked up the condo, her jaw still hard and her mouth still tight. The stress had her all wound up. She didn't need to hear his new theory right now.

She waited for him by her own door while he dumped the pizza boxes into the trash chute. When he joined her, she dangled the key out to him. "You can take this one. I'm going to slip into some motorcycle-riding clothes."

"I guess that means someplace casual for dinner."

"I attend enough galas and functions and benefits where I have to get all decked out. Casual is good."

While she changed, he wandered to the big window that took up the majority of her east-facing wall. She had a view that commanded the best of the city—this city full of secrets and lies. Since he'd opened up shop as a P.I., it seemed as if he'd been privy to half of those secrets and lies.

But he'd never taken a shot at why his old man had killed himself. Didn't want to. Had never wanted to dig that deeply. Never wanted to care that much.

He had to admit that he'd allowed events outside of his control to dictate his life, just as much as London had. Why did she want this CEO gig so badly when she hated it and was ill suited for it?

London jogged downstairs, a pair of black jeans stuffed into some boots and a powder-blue sweater that looked as soft as a cloud hugging her body. She made casual look decidedly upscale…and hot.

Judd tapped on the window. "That's the Bohemian Club."

She sidled next to him and leaned her forehead against the window. "Yeah, it's the old Fleck Mansion. Now that creepy men's club has it. My father was a member."

He mulled over the implication of her words, but before he had a chance to respond, she spun away from the window and called over her shoulder, "This time I'll wear my own motorcycle jacket."

"Is that the one you wore over that fancy dress the other night?"

"Yep." She pulled it from the closet in the foyer.

"Trying to make a statement?"

"I know I should've worn some tasteful stole or even, God forbid, a mink with that dress."

He opened the front door for her and narrowed his eyes. "You own mink?"

"No, I do not. Why? Would you throw red paint on me if I did?"

"I, uh—" he cleared his throat "—sort of have a thing for animals."

"Do you have any?"

"A fish tank."

She tilted her head as she took the helmet from his hands. "That's quite a commitment."

"I like animals. My brother Sean got me a mixed-breed mutt when I was a kid, and that dog, Prince, was my best friend." He secured the helmet on her head and buckled the chin strap, resisting the urge to flip up the visor and kiss her.

How did she manage to get this stuff out of him? He hadn't told anyone about Prince in years. When that dog died the year before he enlisted in the marines, it broke his heart. He didn't need to go that far and tell her *that*.

She tipped up the visor. "What happened to Prince?"

"Died of old age."

She studied his face for a few moments and then tipped the visor back down. "Where are we eating?"

"Do you like Indian food?"

"Sure. I know a place—"

He cut her off. "I know a place. It's on the edge of the Tenderloin, close to Union Square, so it's not too dicey."

He straddled the bike and tilted it to the side so she could climb on the back. "Hang on."

She obliged him, and his blood simmered as she tightened her arms around his waist. He could ride forever with London hanging on to him. He could use a long ride up the coast right now—take her away from all this, away from BGE, set her free.

Instead he wove through the city streets, stopping at signals as the transients shuffled in the crosswalks and the lights of the shops twinkled in Union Square beyond.

He pulled up to the curb in front of the restaurant. He shook his finger in her face as he loosened the strap on the helmet. "Don't get any ideas about slumming it in any bars down here."

"Don't worry." She pointed to the sidewalk. "This street is okay, but the one back there is sketchy."

"Funny how the good, the bad and the ugly exist side by side in this city, isn't it?"

"That's part of its charm."

"Would you live anywhere else?"

"No, would you?"

"Don't think so."

They stepped into the restaurant and the smells of curry and meats sizzling from the tandoori oven blasted him.

Judd requested and got a table by the window so he could watch his bike. He didn't want any more surprises—no newspaper articles pinned to his seat.

London stuck to the vegetarian dishes, and he stuck to drinking water.

He tapped her empty wineglass. "Feel free to have a drink. I never have even one while I'm riding my bike, but I don't mind if you do."

"I'm good. I hate drinking alone."

He tore off a piece of naan and dipped the bread in a green chutney. "Tell me about this fund-raiser you're dragging me to."

She huffed out a breath. "I'm not dragging you there. You want to see some of the players in action, right?"

"Sure I do. Where is it?"

"It's at the War Memorial Opera House."

He stopped chewing and took a gulp of water. "It's not the ballet. Tell me it's not the ballet."

"It's not the ballet…exactly."

"What does that mean?"

"My father was a big supporter of the arts in the city, and this is his annual fund-raiser for the ballet and the symphony. There are a few members of the ballet troupe who attend, and they usually perform—not a full-scale ballet or anything." She smirked. "Not a big fan of the ballet, I take it?"

"You could say that."

"It should be painless."

"Tux required?"

"Naturally."

He shook his head. "Never had to wear a tux for the pop princess."

They spent dinner covering dangerous ground again—sharing stories, feelings and more than a few laughs. He kept telling himself that London needed this break, that keeping her stress level down made his job easier.

That was what he told himself.

They finished dinner and on the sidewalk Judd handed London the helmet and grabbed his handlebars.

His phone buzzed in his pocket, and he leaned the bike back on its kickstand. "I have a call coming in."

London clamped the helmet between her arm and body. "Take it."

He pulled the phone out of his pocket and glanced at the display. "Unknown number. Hello?"

"Is this Judd Brody?"

"Yeah. Who's this?"

"Not important."

"I'd say it is, since you called me."

London tapped him on the arm, and he looked at her and shrugged.

"I have some information. Are you interested or not?"

"What kind of information?"

London kept tugging on his sleeve and he held a finger to his lips even though she hadn't said a word. Then he punched the speaker button for her.

"I'm not gonna say too much over the phone. I have the goods on how it all started."

London folded her arms around the helmet and hugged it to her chest while mouthing words he couldn't understand.

"How what all started? If this is legit, just tell me."

"Oh, it's legit, but I'm not staying on this phone long enough to give you the whole story. I'll meet you after that party tomorrow night, in the alley behind the symphony hall at midnight."

London sucked in a quick breath.

"How do you know about that?" Judd gripped the phone, his knuckles turning white.

"Stop asking so many questions and just be there…be there if you wanna find out what happened to Joey Brody."

Chapter Eleven

The line went dead and Judd stood on the curb staring at the phone.

London snatched it out of his hand and hit the redial button. The phone rang, but nobody picked it up.

He'd recovered from his stupor and shook his head back and forth, his shaggy hair brushing the collar of his leather jacket. "What the hell is going on?"

She pushed Redial again, her heart beating double-time. "It sounds to me as if the pieces are coming together."

"If someone wants to start passing on info about my father, that person would be better off giving it to my brother Sean. He's the cop. He spent most of his adult life trying to figure out what happened."

She disconnected the call again. "Sean's not working with me."

"What does that mean?" He grabbed the handlebars of his bike and kicked up the stand.

"My mystery, your mystery—they're linked. You have to see that now, Judd. Someone left that newspaper clipping about my father on your bike, not mine." She stuffed the helmet on her head and grabbed the straps with both hands. "Why now? Why you? I'll answer your questions. Now because your father has been cleared of the suspicions around him, and you because you're helping me."

"Hop on, and redial that number once more before I start the engine. We can try it again at the next light." He shoved the keys in the bike's ignition.

She punched the button again and the phone rang three times. Then a woman answered it.

"Who's this keeps calling? Jonny, baby. Is that you?"

London asked, "Who's this?"

"You called this phone. I ain't sayin' squat."

"Wait, wait. Someone called me from this phone. I'm just trying to figure out who it was. Is this your phone?"

"This is a pay phone, bitch, on one of my corners. You tryin' to shake your moneymaker in my territory?"

London choked. "Absolutely not, girlfriend. Some skank called my man from this phone, and I wanna know who it is."

The woman laughed. "Bitch, this is a working girls' corner, so if someone's calling your man from this phone, he's gettin' a little something-something on the side."

London screamed, "Where is it? Where is this corner?"

"It's at Sixteenth and Folsom in the Mission District, baby. And you can tell that skank Daisy sent you."

"Thanks, Daisy." London ended the call. "Did you hear all that?"

Judd twisted around in his seat with raised eyebrows and an open mouth. "Maybe you *would* make a good CEO after all."

Daisy's corner was a few miles south of them, and after convincing Judd he didn't need to take her home first, they rolled down Folsom Street, crossing underneath the freeway. The Mission didn't lack for nightlife, and a mixture of transients, hookers, partiers and clueless tourists milled around the streets.

When they idled at a red light, she tapped on Judd's shoulder and yelled in his ear, "It must be in that gas station."

He nodded once and when the light changed, he veered into the right lane and turned into the station.

A few ladies of the night gave Judd the once-over, watching him dismount from the bike. When London slid from the seat, took off the helmet and shook out her hair, the streetwalkers dispersed, on the prowl for likelier johns.

Judd ambled toward the phone booth, its glass scarred and cracked. "This must be it."

She held up her finger. "Hang on. I'm going to do a redial of the number to make sure."

He rested his hand on the receiver while she pressed the redial button on his cell phone. The shrill ring from the phone booth startled her, even though she was expecting it.

Judd picked up the receiver and spoke into the mouthpiece. "I'm amazed this thing still works."

"Well, it does, and this is the phone he used to call you. Turns out Daisy's no liar."

Replacing the phone in its cradle, Judd turned outward, facing the rest of the gas station and the street. "We verified the phone, but the caller didn't hang around to see if I could trace it."

"We could ask in there." She jerked her thumb over her shoulder at the cashier's window.

"The clerk's sitting behind bulletproof glass. I doubt he's going to give us anything."

"You're a P.I. You haven't greased a few palms in your day?"

He rolled his eyes. "If I did, I'm sure I didn't call it *greasing palms*."

"Oh, do they only say that in the movies?"

"Pretty much."

Judd hunched toward the window and rapped on the glass with one knuckle.

The clerk turned away from the TV he'd been glued to

and drew his bushy brows over his nose. "What do you want? I know you're not buying gas."

"I could." Judd tipped his chin toward the pay phone. "Who have you seen use that phone in the past half hour?"

"Nobody." The cashier turned back to the fight on TV.

Before London could reach for her purse, Judd dragged a bill from the front pocket of his jeans, wadded it up and rolled it into the tray beneath the window. "Past half hour? The man before the hooker answered the phone."

"There's no hooking around here." The cashier snatched up the bill.

"Of course not." Judd dug into his pocket again. "The man before that sweet girl was on the phone with her pastor?"

This time the man turned to face them. When he reached for the second bill in the cash tray, Judd plucked it away.

The cashier scratched his black stubble. "I might've seen a guy on the phone earlier. White guy, baseball cap. He might've even come up here to buy some smokes."

Judd dipped into his pocket again, and crumpled the money in his fist, which he rested on the metal ledge of the cashier's window. "Smoker, huh?"

"Ten gallons on number two!" a man yelled from the pumps.

The cashier flipped a couple of switches and returned his focus to Judd's face. "He was a hard-looking dude, prison tats on his neck, nose broken a few times. I'd guess ex-con. Middle-aged, around forty. Can't tell you much else. He was wearing sunglasses—at night—and he had that cap low on his face. Clean shaven. And I never told you nothin'."

"Nothing at all." Judd flicked the rolled-up bill into the tray and slipped a twenty in after. "And give me twenty bucks on number four."

London grabbed his arm as he strode back to his bike. "Ex-con. Do you believe him?"

"I believe the cashier thinks the man was an ex-con. Whether he was or not is another issue."

"But we're meeting him tomorrow, right?"

"We?"

"It's my function, it's my case and you're working for me."

"Ouch." He picked up the nozzle, squeezed a few times and replaced it in the pump. "I was wondering when you were going to play that card."

"What card?" She folded her arms, knowing damn well what card. "There is no card. I want in on this information. It's all part of the same investigation."

He climbed on the bike and tilted it for her to straddle the back. "You're getting kind of carried away with this P.I. stuff, aren't you? You're supposed to be a CEO. CEOs don't zoom around on Harleys meeting ex-cons."

Wrapping her arms around his waist, she slipped her hands beneath his T-shirt and dug her nails into his flat belly. "Now who's playing a card?"

"What card?" He tensed the muscles in his stomach so that it felt as though her nails were scraping granite.

"The CEO card. Do you think you can stop me from doing something by pointing out it's not something a CEO would do?"

He laughed and started his engine. "Thought it was worth a try."

"You know, I can always hire another P.I.—one who appreciates my efforts."

"No other P.I. can give you what I can give you. Now, can you get your claws out of me?"

She flattened her hands and rubbed her palms against the rigid muscles of his belly. Then he took off and she flew against the backrest.

The rumble of the Harley's engine didn't allow for any more conversation, but when it became clear Judd was heading back to Nob Hill and not his place, she shouted in his ear at the next stop sign, "Are you going to get your stuff?"

"Tomorrow." He revved the engine and continued.

Did that mean he wasn't going to spend the night in the empty unit? If so, she'd have to convince him otherwise. She needed him tonight, needed him close. The two of them were on the verge of a big discovery, one that involved both of their families.

On the next downhill, she fitted her body against his, resting her helmeted head against his back. For a fleeting second, she wished all the turmoil would just go away and she could ride off with Judd into the sunset.

Her lips curved into a smile. Where would they be without the turmoil? He craved it as much as she did. Judd Brody was an adrenaline junkie through and through.

When Judd pulled up to her building, she held her breath. Would he come up?

He cut the engine and twisted around in his seat. "Where can I park this thing for the night?"

She released a long breath, fogging up the visor. She flipped it up. "Let me off and I'll enter the code for the garage. You can park it next to my car."

"Do you have an extra toothbrush?"

"Of course. You can stay on my couch again tonight until we get things set up next door."

He steadied the bike for her and she climbed off. Removing the helmet, she approached the keypad for the garage door and entered the code.

The gate slid open and Judd rolled his bike down the driveway.

She waved him toward the parking space behind hers and he wheeled the bike into place.

When he got off, he pointed to her Mini. "You're kidding me. That's what you drive?"

"You know how it is driving in this city. Isn't that why you ride a Harley?"

"One of many reasons."

He stroked the handlebars of the bike, and she shivered. Oh, to be caressed by those hands like that.

He smacked his hand against the seat and she jumped. "Are we going up or are we just going to stand around an exhaust-filled garage admiring my bike?"

When they got to her door, he held up the key to the other unit, swinging it around his finger. "I'm going to do a sweep of the place next door. Do you have a big garbage bag? I'll at least get rid of some more of that junk and that pillow."

She gave him a plastic bag. When he left, she rummaged through the cabinet in the master bath for a new tooth-brush. She also folded a blanket on the edge of the couch and added the pillow he'd used the other night.

Before she dropped the pillow on the couch she buried her face in it, breathing in Judd's scent. She'd dated too many guys who went heavy on the cologne. Judd had a different essence—natural, manly. Even the smell of him made her feel safe and protected.

She unzipped her boots and pulled off her socks. She stopped short of changing into pajamas. How obvious did she want to make this seduction? Of course, there were pajamas and then there were *pajamas*. She could slip into some baggy flannels. The silk and lace would act as a sledgehammer.

The key scraped in her lock and Judd charged through her front door. He kicked it closed behind him, and before she could say one word or catch her breath, his long stride ate up the distance between them and he pulled her into his arms.

He cupped her chin with his large hand and took posses-sion of her lips. While devouring her, he wrapped one arm around her waist and yanked her close. He fitted his pelvis against hers and she felt his erection through his jeans, her jeans and the haze of desire that had engulfed her.

He pulled away and she blinked, touching her throbbing bottom lip with her fingertips.

"What just happened?"

"Do you want this, London? Do you want me?"

If he had to ask, she hadn't been as obvious as she imagined. She couldn't even form one word. She nodded and squeaked.

"I'll take that as a yes." This time he took her face in both of his hands and got serious. He slipped his tongue into her mouth, and his kisses were as spicy as the curry they'd just consumed.

She undulated against his erection and he dropped his hands to her derriere and squeezed.

He growled. "Uh, can you hold off on that right now?"

She pressed her lips against his jaw instead and whispered, "What happened over there?"

"Over there?" He stroked one hand down her back and she felt as treasured as his Harley.

"Next door. Were you peering through the peephole and witnessed me taking off my shoes and socks and got turned on?"

His laugh turned into a growl. "I've been turned on since the minute you ripped your dress off in the alley."

Her tongue darted into his ear. "I only ripped off the bottom of my dress, and did it really take you that long?"

"Long? That was the first time I saw you."

"How soon they forget." She planted her hands against his rock-hard chest and grabbed handfuls of his T-shirt. "I've been turned on since the moment I saw you across the room at the hotel that night, and when I bumped into you."

"You bumped into me?"

"I guess I wasn't that memorable."

He snapped his fingers. "That was you. The cold blonde awash in sparkles. Untouchable."

She pulled her sweater over her head and unhooked her bra. Then she took his hands and placed them over her bare breasts. "Clearly, that's not the case."

His spiky dark lashes dropped over his eyes as he cupped her breasts and brushed his thumbs across her nipples. He hissed through his teeth. "So soft and warm for an ice princess."

She dragged her fingernails along the ink on his arm. "So sensitive and protective for a badass biker."

His eyelids flew open and he tugged at the buttons of her jeans. When they gaped open at her hips, he yanked them down to her thighs and she stepped back to peel them off.

She crossed one leg over the other, standing like a stork, and rubbed her arms. "It's chilly in here."

Before she finished the last syllable, Judd's warm, rough hands skimmed down her back and thighs. Then he cupped her bottom and hoisted her up until she wrapped her legs around his hips.

He held her against his body, strong enough for the two of them, and kissed her silly.

She tugged on his earlobe and he released her lips. "Do you want to find a bed?"

"As long as it's yours."

She untangled her legs from around his body and clutched his arm as she swayed. "You took my breath away, Judd Brody, and not for the first time."

She turned toward the stairs and extended her hand behind her. He laced his fingers with hers and she led him to the staircase.

Halfway up, he yanked her back toward him, hooked an arm around her waist and nuzzled her neck. "I could take you right here."

She turned in his arms, and being one step above him, she could stare deeply into his blue eyes. "Why now?"

"Because I like a little variety. We can do it on my Harley, too." He kissed her nose and she tugged on the lock of hair that curled beneath his ear.

"You know that's not what I mean. You've been sort of holding me at arm's length. I get that you wanted to maintain a professional relationship."

His blue eyes darkened, and she wondered if she'd ruined the moment by reminding him of his professional code.

He slipped his hands inside her panties and caressed her flesh. "It's like you said before, there's something between us, something between our stories. When this is over, we'll go our separate ways. You'll be heading your international corporation, and I'll probably be off to the Greek isles to keep an eye on some shipping magnate's daughter. Why not—" he yanked down her panties so that they puddled around her ankles "—live for the moment?"

Before she could object to the part about going their separate ways and the Greek shipping magnate's daughter, Judd caught her in his arms again and eased her back against the steps.

The Persian runner that climbed up the center of the stairs did little to cushion the hard wood beneath. Then she forgot all about the wood and the shipping magnate's daughter as Judd knelt on the stairs below her and pressed his hands on the insides of her thighs, nudging them apart.

He buried his head between her legs, and when his tongue touched her most sensitive area, she gasped and threw her head back. He probed her with his tongue, and just when she thought she couldn't stand the pleasure anymore, he burrowed inside her, bringing her to unimagined heights.

She panted his name, and he answered by planting a row

of kisses down her thigh while his finger took the place of his tongue.

She closed around him, lifting her bottom from the step.

Putting his hands beneath her, he guided her back to his mouth. He added his lips and teeth to the exquisite torture he was performing, driving her toward a precipice whose descent would surely shatter her into pieces.

He obviously didn't care. He suckled her between his lips and the world exploded behind her tightly closed eyes. She thrust her pelvis forward and then back over and over as the warm surge melted her bones.

When her climax had drained every drop of energy from her body, she collapsed on the steps like a rag doll, used and forgotten.

But Judd had no intention of forgetting her—at least not now.

He scooped her up in his arms, and her legs went around his waist again in a natural fit. As he climbed the remaining steps to the second floor, the soft cotton of his T-shirt brushed her breasts, making her nipples tingle all over again. The rough denim of his jeans chafed her sensitive flesh, still throbbing with her release.

With her curled around his body, he kicked open the door of her bedroom. "Ah, here's your bed."

He dropped her on top of the bedspread and then stood back, crossing his arms, his stance wide.

When he'd tossed her onto the bed, the lethargy from her climax had prevented her from making a move. She lay splayed across the mattress, her hair fanning out behind her, one arm dangling over the edge.

His gaze roamed over her naked body, and a slight smile hovered on his lips.

"Why—" Her voice came out as a croak, and she cleared her throat. "Why are you still completely dressed, down to your boots, and I'm stark naked?"

He cocked his head. "I thought you liked being naked. That's what all the tabloid stories say. London Breck naked in fountains. London Breck naked at the beach. London Breck naked on a yacht."

She scrambled to her knees, reached up and pressed two fingers against his soft lips, the lips that had just rocked her world. "London Breck naked and Judd Brody naked. That's all I want now."

"Come and get it." He spread his arms wide.

She pointed to his feet. "Okay, you're going to have to take off those boots yourself. I draw the line there."

He whistled. "After all that work I just did on the stairs? You *are* a diva."

She swung her legs over the side of the bed. "If you want me to…"

"Just kidding." He chucked her under the chin. He sat on the edge of the bed next to her, crossing one ankle over his knee. He pulled off one boot and then the other, peeling off his socks in the process.

She placed her hands against his back. "Stand up again. I want to do this right and I want to enjoy the view while I'm doing it."

He stood in front of her and she rolled up his T-shirt, pulling it from his massive shoulders and over his head.

Sitting back on her heels, she blew out a long breath at the sculpted figure in front of her. If she looked up the definition of *built,* a picture of Judd Brody's body would be next to it. Thick muscles bunched across his shoulders and arms, and another tattoo spilled across the chiseled muscles of his chest.

"Are you just lookin' or are you going to help me out here?"

By helping him out, she had no doubt he was referring to the bulge in his jeans.

"I'll gladly help you and help myself." She fumbled with

the button at his fly, suddenly as nervous as a virgin on her wedding night. While she tugged at the button, he plowed his fingers through her hair and whispered, "Like a silver mane, capturing all the light."

Her fingers shook as she pulled down his zipper. He had mad skills with his mouth and tongue *and* he could spout poetic lines.

She got the zipper down and peeled his pants away from the black briefs that barely contained his straining erection.

Tugging down his briefs with one hand, she caressed his smooth, tight flesh with the other. His body bucked, and she reached around and dug her fingernails into the hard muscle of his buttocks.

He sealed his mouth over hers and she deepened her strokes as he deepened the kiss.

She whispered against his mouth, "Join me on the bed."

He stepped back from her and pulled the tangle of jeans and underwear from his body. Before discarding the jeans, he reached into a pocket and pulled out two foil packs. He tossed them onto the nightstand.

She fell back against the pillows, stretching her arms over her head. "How long have you been carrying those condoms around? Or do you always keep a couple of spares in your pocket?"

He joined her on the bed, lining up his body with hers. "I've been carrying those since the moment I saved you in the alley."

She kissed her fingertips and dabbled them across his scruffy chin. "You're lying, but I don't mind a bit."

Slipping his arms on either side of her, he twirled her around so that his chest pressed against her back. He lifted her hair from the back of her neck and kissed the nape.

She wriggled against him and he prodded between her legs.

She heard the foil of the condom wrapper crackle. Then

he toyed with one breast as he smoothed his thumb down her belly. His thumb continued its downward path, and he entered her from behind.

Her heart stopped for a second, the connection between them electric. He made love to her, filling up all the empty places in her soul and satisfying every desire.

They lay spent in each other's arms. She couldn't tell if the sweat that dampened her skin was hers or his. She couldn't even tell where her limbs ended and his began as they tangled in the sheets.

He yawned and nibbled the edge of her ear. "Toothbrush."

She wanted to drift off to sleep in his arms, but hygiene called. "I left it—"

A bright, white light started blinking in the corner of the room as a high-pitched whine shattered the air.

Judd bolted upright. "What the hell is going on?"

The acrid scent hit her and she scrambled from the bed, grabbing Judd's arm. "Fire!"

Chapter Twelve

Judd grabbed his jeans from the floor as London flung open her closet door and disappeared into the walk-in. She'd better not be picking out a coordinating outfit.

"London!"

She stumbled out of the closet, clutching some clothes to her chest. "I need to get my father's computer."

He buttoned his jeans and swept his shirt from the floor. He took her by the arm. "We need to get out of here now."

They hit the bottom of the stairs and she pushed him toward the dining area. "Grab the laptop while I put these clothes on."

He snagged the computer from the kitchen table and tucked it under his arm. By the time he returned to the foyer, London had on a pair of sweats and was pulling a sweatshirt over her head.

He stopped her from rushing out the front door, placing his palms against it first. Not feeling any heat, he cracked open the door and stuck his head into the hallway. Gray smoke rolled down the hall from the opposite direction of the stairwell. He stepped out the doorway and pulled London behind him. "Let's head for the stairwell. I have my phone. I'll call nine-one-one."

He yanked open the heavy fire door leading to the stairwell and let it slam behind them. Their bare feet slapped against the metal stairs as they jogged down.

When Judd got through to the emergency line, they informed him that the fire department was already on the way.

They joined other residents of the building in varying states of undress in the stairwell. Nobody seemed to know where the fire had started—but he had a good idea.

If he hadn't been so focused on bedding London, he would've done a better job of securing that unoccupied unit. In fact, he should've stayed there like he'd planned to... until London had curled her arms around him on the bike, pressing her sexy body against his in all the right places. He'd decided then and there he had to make good on the promise between them.

When they hit the lobby, the overnight security guard was already letting the firemen into the building.

One of the firefighters stepped into the middle of the lobby. "Did anyone see anything?"

Judd spoke up. "There's heavy smoke on the top floor of the building from unit 502. It's unoccupied."

The fire captain directed the firemen streaming through the front doors of the lobby. "Fifth floor, unoccupied unit. Everyone out of the building."

The residents shuffled through the doors and Judd kept hold of London's hand.

She pressed her shoulder against his. "Someone set fire to my place. How did they get in?"

"They got in because I was too busy satisfying my own pleasure instead of looking out for you."

She squeezed his hand. "That's ridiculous. It would've been worse if you'd been sleeping in there. Maybe you wouldn't have made it out alive."

"If I'd been sleeping in there instead of in your bed, the

other guy wouldn't have made it out alive. There's a reason why you keep business and pleasure separate."

Tucking her fingers into the waistband of his jeans, she tugged him close. "That's not possible for us and you know it. We're in this together, Judd, now more than ever."

He wrapped his arms around her and held her snug against his body, and that was all the confirmation she needed.

While the firefighters worked upstairs, the residents returned to the lobby, where groups huddled under blankets and sipped hot coffee provided by the security guard.

The fire captain took the elevator down to the lobby, and London pinched Judd's arm and pointed. "That's a good sign."

"Ladies and gentlemen. There was a small blaze in the unoccupied unit on the top floor caused by some faulty wiring in the kitchen. We have it contained, and there's no damage to any of the common areas. I understand the owner of the unit is here, so I may please speak to her? The rest of you can return to your homes."

Judd pushed up from the floor where they'd been curled up beneath a blanket and extended his hand to her.

She grabbed it and he pulled her to her feet, leading her to the fire captain.

"I'm London Breck. I own the unit."

"Ma'am, I'm afraid there's some extensive damage to the place, mostly from the smoke and the CO_2 we used, but we had to make sure it didn't spread to the rest of the building or even the rest of the floor."

"I understand. You said it was electrical?"

"Some wires in the kitchen. It's common, especially in vacant units. You really should think about renting it out and keeping it occupied once you repair it."

"Thanks for the tip."

Judd grabbed her elbow and steered her toward the stairwell. "Can you manage five flights of stairs or do you want to wait for all those people to go up the elevator?"

"I can do stairs." She stopped at the first step and grabbed his arm. "Just so we're clear, we both know that was no accidental electrical fire."

"We're clear."

When they got to her floor, the smell of smoke and flame retardant lingered in the air. They didn't even bother going back to bed. She knew she couldn't sleep. Instead she plopped on the couch, crossing her legs beneath her.

"What was he after this time? Do you think he's trying to kill me?"

"I hate to break it to you, but there are easier ways to do that than setting fire to the unit next to yours. He was trying to drive you out of your place or destroy it."

She smoothed her hands across her father's laptop, which Judd had placed on the coffee table. "Or destroy something in it."

"Back to the laptop?"

"Maybe it wasn't the laptop. Maybe it's something else he thinks I have."

Judd rubbed his eyes. "I want to catch this guy in the act just once. All I need is five minutes alone with him. I'd get some answers."

She ran her hands across the muscles of his shoulders and down his corded arms. "I have no doubt about that, but until then we can do our own investigative work."

"There's just one problem with that."

Was he going to cut her out now? She wouldn't be able to go back to the office and be a good little CEO if he did.

"What's the problem?" She sipped a small breath in and out.

"My temporary crib just got burned out. You don't expect me to bunk next door now, do you?"

She scooted close to him and cupped his bristly jaw with one hand. "You're going to stay here with me."

"After the night we just had?" He cinched her wrist with his fingers. "For a second there, when I smelled that smoke, I thought it was coming from the bed where we'd just sparked a raging inferno."

"It *was* hot."

He shook his head. "I should've been able to control myself. We're both too distracted. We need to be stronger."

"I don't see it like that." She flicked his cheek. "When we connected, I mean really connected, I felt invincible. You don't distract me, Judd Brody. You don't make me weaker. You complete me. You make me stronger."

He loosened his grip and pressed a warm kiss on the inside of her wrist, the pulse in his lower lip matching the beat of her own pulse.

"Let's go to bed and get some sleep. We have a big day ahead of us."

JUDD STUDIED LONDON'S face, illuminated by the late-morning sun he'd allowed to filter through the blinds.

Her words from last night about their connection and completing each other had him rethinking everything. He couldn't lead her on. She expected something from him, something he wasn't capable of giving.

He had a big, gaping hole where his heart was supposed to be. How could he ever give London what she desired? What she deserved?

He touched the edge of her long lashes with his finger-tip. They both might be better off if he backed out now and turned over this job to another professional—a true professional, one who wouldn't allow a pair of long legs and a flash of silver hair to interfere with his work.

She sighed in her sleep and her lush lips parted.

He couldn't leave her now. He'd get to the bottom of who

was threatening her and why, handle it and then convince London she was better off without him.

He could always play on her desire to be the big, important, serious CEO. No CEO worth her salt would be caught dead with a man more comfortable in jeans straddling a Harley than in a Savile Row suit commanding a boardroom.

She had to know she couldn't keep one high-heeled foot in both worlds. He had to convince her.

Her fingers trailed along his bare thigh. "Breakfast in bed? The yummy kind?"

"I'm fresh out of condoms, and we have a lot to do today. I'm going to set up some cameras around here, since the management of this building seems to be delinquent on that score. I need to bring some of my stuff over here, too, if I'm going to be your live-in bodyguard."

"I like the sound of that." Her light touch turned into a caress, and he had to use every ounce of his willpower to break away from her.

"I'm going to take a quick shower and get some errands done before the festivities tonight. Do you need to go into your office today?"

"Yep. I'll be there all day, and we can meet up here to get ready for the benefit."

"Sounds good. I may be in and out of your building today to change the locks next door and to work on the camera coverage."

"You first." She snuggled back under the covers. "There are clean towels in the cabinet in the master bath."

He crossed the room and scooped up his jeans and T-shirt from the chair when he'd tossed them last night. He stepped into the cavernous bathroom and poked his head into the cabinet, which was stocked with thick beige towels and smelled like some kind of flower—roses or lavender. Hell, he didn't know the difference—it smelled sweet.

He snatched a towel and hung it on the rack outside

the rectangular shower encased in glass. Cranking on the water, he stepped into the shower onto the tiles that looked like river rocks.

The warm water hit his chest and steam rose immediately, fogging up the glass. He sluiced water through his hair and lathered it up. Then he squirted some liquid soap into his hands and ran them across his chest, the friction creating fragrant suds. He hoped he didn't end up smelling like a rose after this shower.

A blast of cold air hit his back and he turned right into London's arms.

Running her hands across his chest, she said, "Looks like I'm just in time. Turn around."

What could he do? She was his boss.

He turned and wedged his palms against the tile as the water beat against his side.

His belly tightened as her smooth hands rubbed circles on his back. When she reached his backside and skimmed her fingernails against his skin, he forgot all about professionalism. Forgot about the black hole in his chest. Forgot about leaving her.

Several hours later and in need of another shower, Judd stepped back into the hallway of London's floor and waved his hand at the minuscule camera in the corner. It worked on a motion sensor, so he wouldn't have hours of blank video to stare at. If something moved in this hallway, that camera would pick it up.

He'd crawled around the kitchen of the vacant unit in the wake of the firefighters but hadn't found any evidence to indicate the fire had started from anything other than faulty wiring. Of course, that could be manipulated—and probably had been.

The elevator pinged and his muscles tensed, his hand hovering over the weapon in his shoulder holster.

London stepped off the elevator, the navy blue suit she'd

donned this morning after their steamy shower still crisp and fresh.

She dropped her briefcase and put her hands on her hips. "What a welcome sight you are after the day I just had."

His pulse ratcheted up a few notches. "Anything go wrong?"

"Yes." Her eyes widened and she took a step forward. "Not in that way. Nothing life threatening, unless you count being bored to death."

"More meetings?"

"I think so. I was half-asleep."

"Everyone going to the ballet benefit tonight?"

"Everyone will be there. Why don't we just lock them up in the opera house and question them under a bright light?"

"The ballerinas, too?"

"Can't hurt." She gestured around the hallway. "Did you get all your stuff done?"

"Cameras, check. New locks, check. Clean clothes, check."

"Are you going to wear the tux from the other night?"

"Uh, let me think about that." He wedged a finger on his chin and rolled his eyes to the ceiling. "Yeah, it's the only one I have."

"Okay." She picked up her briefcase and sauntered to her door, key chain ready.

"Why? Something wrong with it?"

"It's fine, just a little tight through the shoulders and back."

"Yeah, well, if I stick out a little tonight among the mon-eyed set, that's a good thing. Don't want any of them getting too comfortable."

She slid her key home and laughed. "That's how I first noticed you the night of the gala. You looked like an alien in that bunch."

He covered her hand as she closed it around the door handle. "I always will, London. I'll never fit in."

The smile died on her lips as she twisted the doorknob and shoved the door open. "I don't want you to."

She showered first, and he left her in peace, although visions of her sleek wet body kept him from concentrating on the TV news.

He showered next, but this time she kept her distance. He had laid out his tux on the bed, and the room was empty when he finished his shower and dressed.

"Are you decent?" She poked her head into the bedroom.

"A little late for that consideration, wouldn't you say?" He leaned into the mirror, his fingers fumbling with the bow tie.

London stepped into the room, tightening the sash on her pink terry-cloth robe, her damp hair streaming down her back. "Let me."

She stood on her tiptoes between him and the mirror and took the bow tie from him as he tilted his chin toward the ceiling. The black band looped around her slim fingers as she tied it into a bow.

"There." She patted her handiwork with two fingers.

"Thanks." He tapped the base of her throat. "Shouldn't you be getting ready, or are you always fashionably late?"

"It doesn't take me long to get ready. I just need to dry my hair, put on makeup and slip into—" she waved her hand at a bag hanging on the door of her closet "—that."

"I'll wait for you downstairs. Do you mind if I take a look at your father's computer?"

Her eyes flicked. "I actually brought it back to the office today. There's a top-notch safe in my father's office. Really, I won't be long. Have a drink or something. You might need it to get through tonight."

Shrugging, he swept his jacket from the bed. "I might just do that."

He draped the jacket over his arm and jogged downstairs, passing the spot where he'd taken her last night. He'd been crazy with desire and a need to possess her after exploring the unit next door. The thought of someone spying on her, watching her through that peephole, had driven him to march back over here and make her his own. As if making love to her could somehow put a force field of protection around her.

Then someone had started that fire.

He crossed over to the wet bar, lifted a few stoppers from some cut-crystal decanters and sniffed the contents. The stuff inside was probably more expensive than the container that held it. Just what he needed.

He picked up two tumblers from the shelf below and filled each one about half-full with the amber liquid from the fanciest decanter. He swirled the booze in his glass and took a sip.

The cognac felt like warm velvet against his tongue. He cupped it there for a second before swallowing it, savoring the smooth taste. His gaze wandered toward London's briefcase on the floor by the coffee table.

He'd thought she'd be gung ho about his suggestion of searching through her father's laptop. She should've left it here for him to take a look at it. He hadn't placed as much importance on the laptop as she had, and maybe she didn't want him to rain on her parade. He'd have to insist they look at it together.

A flash of green from across the room caught his attention, and his head jerked up. He clenched his jaw so it wouldn't fall open and make him look like the village idiot. Not much he could do about the erection he sported.

"You look amazing."

She twirled for him, the skirt of the green mermaid dress flaring at her ankles and the flash of green light around her neck ricocheting across the walls.

"Are you going to be able to walk in that, or do I have to carry you around all night—not that I mind doing that?" He eyed the dress that fit tightly over her slim hips and down her thighs.

"There's lots of wiggle room." She thrust her leg through a slit in the front of the dress.

He leveled a finger at the deep, plunging neckline that almost reached her belly button. "You'd better not wiggle too much."

"Everything's firmly in place."

She cupped her breasts through the silky material of the dress, giving him an even bigger reason not to step out from behind the wet bar.

"And what is that rock hanging between your…uh… assets, there?"

"This little bauble?" She slipped her finger along the chain and lifted the green stone surrounded by diamonds from her chest. "This is an emerald. It has some significance for tonight—a Russian prince gave this emerald to a prima ballerina. One of the ballet dancers tonight is reportedly a descendant of that Russian prince."

"Are you going to give it back to him?"

"Ah, no." She dropped the emerald back against her chest, where it could've cracked her breastbone.

"You're just going to dangle it in front of him?" He'd rather feast his eyes on the creamy breasts cradling the emerald than that cold stone.

Cold. He couldn't believe he'd once figured London Breck for a cold ice princess.

He cleared his throat and tapped the glass. "Cognac?"

"Drop a few ice cubes in there and I'll take a sip." She tilted her head and her hair fanned out over one shoulder. "I thought you were strictly a beer man?"

"Did I say that?" He rolled the glass between his hands. "I prefer it, but hell, if I'm going to hobnob with the fabulously wealthy, I might as well drink like them. Where's the ice?"

"I'll get it from the freezer in the kitchen."

"I'll get it." He stepped around her with the glass in his hand and went into the kitchen. He stuck the cognac beneath the ice dispenser and pressed the lever. Two ice cubes splashed into the liquid and a few droplets hit his wrist.

He sucked it off and handed her the glass. He returned to the wet bar and raised his own. "Here's to getting some answers tonight—either at the soiree or after it."

"I'll drink to that." She tipped her tumbler toward him.

Before they could finish their drinks, a low buzzing sound came from her intercom. She pushed the button and the security guard's voice came through the box. "Ms. Breck, your car's here."

"Thank you. We'll be right down."

Judd said, "Too bad Theodore's not in the driver's seat tonight."

"You got that right. I just hired a service."

"Coat?" He jerked his thumb toward the closet in the foyer.

"I don't have anything that matches this. You'll just have to keep me warm." She winked at him as she swept past him out the door.

Watching her swaying hips, he said, "It didn't stop you from pairing a sparkly black dress with a leather motorcycle jacket before."

"I didn't have you to keep me warm then."

The acrid smell from the fire still lingered in the hallway—a bleak reminder that he could keep London warm, but he'd better keep her safe.

The driver was waiting by the limo and jumped to open the door when he and London stepped onto the sidewalk.

London plucked up the skirt of her dress, fell onto the seat and shimmied to the middle.

Judd ducked into the car and joined her. "I think you'd be more comfortable in the water in that dress than on land."

"I do look like a mermaid, don't I?" She smoothed the material across her lap.

"That was the first thing that came to my mind, except you'd lose that emerald in the ocean."

She plucked it off her chest and cradled it in the palm of her hand. "It belonged to my mother. But let's not dwell on the past."

"I like your past. It's colorful. It's you. Beats mine."

She brushed the back of her hand across his cheek. "I can't imagine. Kids need stability. They need both of their parents."

Her voice quavered in the darkness and he looked at her sharply. She didn't seem as though she would be overly fond of children in general. Did she pity the child he'd been?

He grabbed her hand and kissed her palm. "Don't feel bad for me. My brothers were all right—not exactly a substitute for a mom and a dad, but Sean did the best he could. Eric, too. From all accounts, my old man was strict. With him around, I probably would've turned out completely different."

"So you believe nurture has as much to do with our personalities as nature?"

"I guess so. Look at you."

"Me?"

"You lost your mom at an early age. Maybe with a mother's influence, you wouldn't have been such a hell-raiser, but then, it could just be in your genes." He tugged on a lock of her silky hair. He preferred it like this rather than up in some bun on top of her head.

"People can change."

He rolled his eyes. "Yeah, I know that, Ms. CEO."

The limo rolled to a stop and seconds later, the driver

opened the door for them. "Will you text your departure, Ms. Breck, or do you want me to be here at a specific time?"

"Plan for around midnight, but if you're not here, Mr. Brody will text you."

Other limos and town cars jammed the street in front of the opera house, depositing passengers who glittered from head to toe with jewels.

Not one woman could compare with London.

She took his arm as they ascended the steps, more date than bodyguard. How would Roger react to his presence?

Her cousin Niles greeted them first at the top of the steps. "London, you've outdone yourself. That necklace is the perfect touch. Is that that Kaparov emerald?"

"It is." She squeezed Judd's arm. "Niles knows my mother's jewelry better than I do."

Did he know it and covet it?

"I don't know why you keep insisting on referring to those jewels as your mother's. She left them all to you when she died. They're yours, London."

"Can we talk about this another time, like never?" She waved to a couple, her scowl morphing to a smile. "Are the dancers here yet?"

"I have no clue. I just arrived." Niles arched a brow. "Do you enjoy the ballet, Judd?"

"No."

Niles put one hand into the pocket of his jacket and tipped his nose in the air. "I'm going to mingle. You kids have fun."

As they watched him walk away, Judd leaned close to London's ear. "He knows way too much about your family business."

"That's because he's family."

He nodded toward Wade with a pretty African-American woman. "Does your brother know as much?"

"No. He's on the business side of things only. Dad didn't

include him in the personal details of our lives. His existence was a source of pain for my mother."

"Does he resent that?"

"I doubt it." She tugged on his sleeve. "Come on. I'll introduce you to his wife, Stephanie. She's his polar opposite."

"Hi, Wade. Stephanie, I'm glad you could get away from the kids."

Stephanie smiled and winked at Judd. "You make it sound as if they're holding me captive or something."

Wade nodded curtly at Judd, but Stephanie grasped Judd's hand with both of hers. "Are you going to introduce me to your date, London?"

"This is Judd Brody. Judd, Stephanie Vickers."

Wade rested hand on his wife's shoulder. "I told you, Steph, Mr. Brody is London's bodyguard."

Stephanie's eyes widened. "You never told me London's bodyguard was Judd Brody. I've been following your family's story recently, Judd. Can I call you Judd?"

"Sure."

London leaned in toward her brother. "While we're on the subject, did Dad ever mention Joseph Brody to you, Wade?"

That was one way to get it out in the open. Judd studied Wade's face, but it showed nothing but indifference.

"No." His fingers curled into Stephanie's shoulder. "Steph, we need to say hello to Adam Cantor and his wife."

"If you say so." She kissed London's cheek. "Nice to see you, London, and that dress is fabulous."

"They seem mismatched," Judd said after they moved away.

"Oh, I don't know. It's a case of opposites attracting. She makes him more human."

"And what does he do for her?"

"He's stable, a good provider. He offers her a lifestyle

where she can stay home with their kids. That's important to her."

Judd narrowed his eyes and peered across the crowded lobby. "Looks like my friend got another gig."

"Who do you mean?" She waved and smiled at a few more clusters of people.

"My friend Rick. He's the one who was supposed to be working for Bunny that night." He raised his hand. "He's over there."

"Do you want to talk to him? There are a few rounds I need to make."

"Go ahead. You're staying in this area, right?"

"Yes. I see the dancers by the stairs. I'm going to talk to them."

He watched her join the group of dancers, who were already in costume. Great, he'd have to sit through dancers tiptoeing across the stage.

He shouldered his way through the throng of people to reach Rick and thrust out his hand. "So Bunny gave you another chance, or is it someone else tonight?"

"I'm looking after Bunny." Rick whistled. "I saw your arm candy tonight. Seems like you made out like a bandit."

"London Breck? I'm doing some personal security for her."

"I wouldn't mind doing a little personal security for her." Rick wiggled his eyebrows up and down. "Guess it all worked out for the best."

"What did?"

Bright red suffused Rick's face. "I sort of tricked you, dude."

"Tricked me? What the hell are you talking about?"

"That night I was supposed to work for Bunny? I hadn't really double booked. I got a strange call from a lady the day before the gig."

"Have you been hitting the open bar? What are you

talking about?" Judd's heart had started to thump hard, rattling his rib cage.

"Look, man, I wouldn't have done it, but it was a lady asking, so I didn't see any harm. If I sensed any danger, I never would've done it."

"Rick, dude, would you just spit it out? What are you talking about?"

"The day before that Breck benefit, a lady called me. She said she was a friend of London Breck's and she wanted you two to meet. The whole thing was a setup."

Chapter Thirteen

The blood was thundering against his temples, and his vision blurred. "She wanted me and London to meet?"

"That's what she told me, just a little fun. She offered me money if I would give up the job for Bunny to you."

"You did that?" Judd's hands curled into fists.

"Dude, she offered me a lot of money, and I didn't see the harm in it."

"Really?" Judd had taken a step closer to Rick and loomed over him. "What if it was a setup? What if someone wanted me there to take me out?"

"It was a lady, dude."

"Who was it? What was her name?"

"I don't know. She didn't tell me and we never met. Once I cleared the gig with you and let her know, she left an envelope of cash in my mailbox. End of story."

It was far from the end of the story. Their meeting hadn't been fate, but it had been someone's plan.

"I can't believe you did that, Rick. You compromised my safety."

"Dude—" his gaze tripped over Judd's shoulder "—I think I did you a favor."

Judd could smell London's perfume before she tapped him on the shoulder. "Is this your friend?"

"London, this is Rick Jacobs. Rick, London Breck."

They shook hands. "Good to meet you, London. If this surly SOB ever gets on your nerves, I'm available 24/7."

"But Rick is a careless SOB."

London drew her brows over her nose and looked from him to Rick. "What does that mean?"

"Rick gave up his job with Bunny to me because someone paid him to do so."

"Dude!"

"Really?" London grabbed Rick's hands. "I knew it was all connected."

Rick's eyebrows disappeared in his shock of dishwater-blond hair. "Now I'm confused."

"Good. You deserve to be confused for pulling a stunt like that. Do you have this woman's number?"

"I can probably get it off my cell unless I deleted it. I figured since I didn't hear about your untimely demise at that benefit, she was on the up-and-up." He saluted at Bunny across the room. "I have to get back to work, but I'll find you later and we'll go through my phone."

When the crowd swallowed up Rick, London turned to Judd. "We're more connected than we realized."

"Maybe what our ex-con has to tell me tonight about my father will shed some light on your situation."

"I know it will." Her green eyes sparkled as brilliantly as that emerald around her neck.

His stomach clenched. She wanted in on the meeting tonight and he hadn't figured out yet how he planned to dissuade her, other than tying her up. "London."

She put her finger to her lips. "Listen. The orchestra is tuning up. I'm going to watch the performance. Maybe Rick can check his phone while they're playing."

She slipped away through the crowd, a flash of green darting among a sea of black.

Judd scanned the people moving toward the staircases and elevators like a herd of cows—very well-dressed cows.

He spotted Bunny with enough jewels dripping from her small frame to topple her over sideways. His gaze shifted to Rick hovering behind her.

If Judd had to hazard a guess, he'd bet that Bunny had a greater interest in keeping attractive young men at her beck and call than she did in protecting the wealth of jewelry she sported around her wrists and neck and hanging from her earlobes.

He caught Rick's eye and jerked his thumb toward one of the bars set up in the lobby.

Rick ducked his head and whispered into Bunny's ear. She patted his hand and took the arm of an older gentleman heading into the elevator.

The mass of people had thinned, and Judd strode to the bar and ordered a club soda just as Rick joined him.

"Make that two." Rick pulled his phone from his jacket pocket. "I'm guessing you want that number about now. Do not identify yourself or tell her I told you anything. The money she gave me was supposed to ensure my silence."

"You made an unethical decision by accepting that money."

"Yeah, yeah, tell it to the pop princess and Saudi princes you get to accompany to Hawaii and the French Riviera. Some of us P.I.s are working stiffs who don't get the jobs you do, Brody."

"I am a working stiff."

"Yeah, that's why you're here tonight at this gala."

"As a bodyguard, just like you."

Rick snorted. "Yeah, right. I wish my clients hung on to me the way London Breck hangs on to you—well, if my clients were London Breck."

Judd slammed his glass on the bar. "Just get that number."

Rick skimmed his thumb up and down his phone's display. "Let's see. That would've been almost a week ago, the day before the benefit at the hotel. I got it."

"You're sure? It's a real number, not blocked?"

"I think this is it." He held the phone in Judd's face.

Judd whispered the number several times, and then turned to the woman sipping a pink cocktail next to him. "Ma'am, can I borrow your phone to make a quick call? My battery's dead."

"Of course." She placed her drink on the bar and slipped her hand into her evening bag, pulling out her phone.

When he reached for it, she pulled it back. "I hope you're not calling a friend like—" her gaze roamed up and down his body "—you. My husband is very jealous and likes to check the numbers on my cell."

"I'm calling a woman. It shouldn't cause you any problems." Hell, her husband might've hired him to spy on her in the past.

She dropped the phone in his hand and retrieved her drink, taking a careful sip from the wide rim.

Judd closed his eyes for a few seconds to recall the number and then tapped it into the woman's phone. It rang four times before an answering machine picked up. "Hello. You've reached Bay Realtors, the San Francisco Realtor for all your real estate needs. Our office is closed, but if you'd like to leave a message, please do so at the tone. If you are calling about one of our listings, please leave the address of the property and the name of the Realtor. Thank you and have a great San Francisco Bay day."

When the tone beeped, Judd swallowed and ended the call.

"Well?" Rick took a swig of his water.

"It's a Realtor's office, no individual name. The person who called you could've borrowed a phone there, or could be a customer. Not a lot of help."

"I tried, dude."

Judd slid the cell phone next to the woman's cocktail glass on the bar. "Thank you."

She fluttered her eyelashes. "No problem. Not a fan of ballet?"

"Not really."

"Me, either." She adjusted the bodice of her halter dress, where a diamond almost the size of London's emerald glittered between her ample bosoms. "There's a quiet little alcove downstairs where we could get to know each other better and discuss our mutual dislike of the ballet."

"No, thank you, ma'am." He pushed away from the bar, ignoring Rick's smirk. "I'm working tonight."

She called after him, "You can work for me anytime."

"Haven't lost the old Brody magnetism." Rick punched Judd's shoulder and whistled between his teeth. "That one's ripe for the picking."

"That one's trouble."

"Never stopped you before."

A few hot retorts sprang to his lips, but he swallowed them. Rick had it right. Courting trouble had never stopped him before—before meeting London. Of course, London represented a whole other level of trouble.

He and Rick parked outside the doors to the orchestra level, where he could hear the music swell and fall. A burst of applause erupted and an attendant flung open the doors.

"Short intermission. Do you want to take a seat now?"

"No, thanks." Judd spotted London's gleaming head bobbing as she talked to several people crowded around her. He'd let her do her thing and tell her about the call when she could break away.

As if sensing his scrutiny, she glanced up and met his eyes. She must've read something in his face because she started to shuffle down her row of seats.

Rick clapped him on the back. "Duty calls. I'll catch up with you later."

As Rick melted into the crowd, Judd turned to watch London's approach. She could barely move three feet without someone stopping her to say a word or two, touching her arm, giving her a hug.

She drew people to her. They gravitated toward her as if to bask in her light, but they didn't stand in awe of her. They acted so familiar with her. Each and every one saw her as a friend, a confidante. She had the knack of making a person feel important, noticed.

Interpersonal skills like that didn't belong in a boardroom, behind a desk. Couldn't she see that she had something so much more important than a head for business?

When she reached him, she hooked her arm in his. "Sorry that took so long. All those people knew my father. I hadn't seen most of them since the memorial service and funeral."

She tapped his glass of club soda. "Is that water? I could use one of those."

"It's club soda. Hold it for me and I'll get you one." Once he'd gotten her drink, he turned back, but he could barely see her through the clutch of people hovering around her, including her cousin and Richard Taylor.

He hung back. They couldn't discuss business with all those folks listening in.

"I heard you were working for London."

Judd jerked his head toward the man to his left, who looked familiar to him. A former client? "And you are?"

"I'm sorry. I thought you would've recognized me since we met once or twice." The man's dark eyes assessed Judd as he stuck out his hand. "I'm Captain Les Williams. I work with your brother Sean."

Judd transferred London's glass to his left hand and gripped the captain's hand. "Good to meet you."

"Do you know when Sean is returning? We need him—damned good detective. Runs in the family."

"I don't know when Sean's coming back."

The crowd around London had thinned, and she was signaling to him. "If you'll excuse me."

"Of course. Who wouldn't rather be talking to that young lady?"

Judd hadn't even reached her side, and she broke away from the few remaining people in the group, including her cousin, who glared at him.

She grabbed his hand and pulled him into a corner. "Did Rick still have the number on his phone?"

"He did and I called it."

Her eyes widened as she squeezed his hand. "And?"

"It went to a real estate office—Bay Realtors. Just a generic message, no specific agent." He handed her the glass. "Your club soda."

"Oh." She wrapped her hand around the glass and gave him his. "It could be anyone—a client, a Realtor's friend, even a stranger."

"My thoughts exactly."

She tossed her head, flicking her hair over her shoulder. "But we can always look up the office and visit it in person, ask around."

"We could do that." He jerked his thumb toward the opera house, where the orchestra was striking up a few chords. "Another round?"

"It's very brief. Did you get something to eat yet?"

"There's food?" His stomach rumbled at the thought.

"I thought the caterer was going to start setting up during the first performance. You should check downstairs and eat something before the hordes descend. Nothing more frightening than a bunch of rich people stampeding for free food."

He traced his finger around the rock resting against the smooth skin of her chest. "You act like you're not one of them."

"Oh, I'm one of them. The trick is not acting like one of them." She dropped her long lashes over her eyes, handed the glass back to him after one sip and grabbed the arm of a passing octogenarian. "Oscar, so glad you could come out tonight. I hope you plan to leave a big check before you leave."

The old man chuckled and patted London's hip. "Only if you sit with me, dear."

Judd shook his head, downed his drink and then hers. Then he jogged downstairs to get first dibs on the food.

Through the next dance performance, Judd did justice to the free food and nursed another club soda. London hadn't been kidding about the stampede. The line for the fancy grub snaked downstairs from the lobby of the opera house to the restaurant on the floor below. He watched London as she barely took a bite of food, weaving through the lines, smiling and glad-handing. She'd probably raised a half a mil for the arts in the past half hour alone.

Turning his wrist, he checked his watch—fifteen minutes to showtime. Maybe he could sneak out of here for the meeting while London continued her fund-raising.

"Are you sure you're doing your job, Brody?"

Judd turned slowly and shifted his gaze down slightly to meet the cold eyes of Richard Taylor.

"London and I can't be joined at the hip at a function like this. I'm keeping my eye on her…sir."

"Joined at the hip." He stroked his chin. "That's an interesting image. It's a common one, but when is any one of us really ever joined to the hip of another?"

"Sir?" Judd's brows collided over his nose. What the hell was this reptilian SOB going on about?

"I actually wasn't referring to this event, Brody. I heard about the fire on London's floor last night."

Judd set his jaw and stared at Taylor without blinking.

He wouldn't give him the satisfaction of asking him how he knew about the fire. Besides, he needed to get rid of him.

Taylor blinked and glanced down. "I know people in the building."

Judd still didn't make a response or move a muscle.

Taylor coughed. "Just want to make sure London's okay. Unlike some, I applauded her decision to hire a... bodyguard."

"Enjoying yourself, Richard?" London stepped between them as if sensing the tension. "Where's Roger tonight?"

"A little under the weather." He held up his index finger and clicked his tongue. "You could deliver the cure if you accepted his marriage proposal."

London playfully grabbed his finger. "You know that's not going to happen, Richard. We would be just awful together and you know it."

"I'd love to have you as my daughter, London."

"The two of us can play pretend father-daughter without the marriage." She released his finger. "Now, if you'll excuse us, Judd and I have a little business to discuss. Don't forget your contribution tonight."

"I thought the ticket *was* the contribution."

"You know me better than that, Richard." She nudged Judd in the back and he nodded at Taylor.

She whispered, "It's midnight already. People are going to start leaving once they've eaten their fill."

"Stay here, London. I can do this on my own."

"I know you can, but I want to be with you."

He ran a hand down her bare arm. "You don't have a coat. Who knows if the guy's even there. We might have to wait out in the cold for him."

"I can fix that." She stopped at the coat check and hunched over the counter. "I'm so sorry. I forgot my ticket, but I see my cloak right there, the black one."

"No problem." The woman handed over the cloak and London slipped her some cash.

"I hope you plan to return this." He snatched the cloak from her arm and draped it over her shoulders, pulling the neck closed over the sparkling emerald.

"Of course. Now let's blow this joint."

"Have you noticed that you start using what you believe is gangster slang whenever we're about to do a little investigating?"

She emitted a very ungangster-like giggle and tucked her hand in his pocket. "May as well get into the spirit of things."

He took her shoulders, spinning her around to face him. "This isn't a joke, London. It's not one of your madcap adventures. You've been the victim of some crazy stuff this past week, and a man was murdered and left for you to discover. You do exactly as I say. Got it?"

Her eyes had gotten bigger and bigger with every word of his tirade and she nodded. "I didn't mean to make a joke about it. I—I mean, I haven't forgotten Griff or Theodore. I know it's serious, Judd."

He kissed her forehead. "Let's be careful."

Taking her hand, he tucked her against his side, and the silk of the cloak rustled as it brushed against him.

The night air felt refreshing after the warmth of the opera house. He rubbed his eyes and took a deep breath of cool air. They crossed the street and circled around to the back of the symphony hall, London's heels clicking on the sidewalk beside him.

He leaned in close. "I have my gun in my shoulder holster. If anything funny happens, duck on my word."

"Got it." She whispered in his ear. "What word?"

"Duck."

They reached the corner of the building and he turned first, keeping London behind him. His nostrils flared at the smell of cigarette smoke wafting toward them. Then he spotted the pinpoint of red light in the darkness.

He took one step toward it and cupped his hand around his mouth. "It's Brody. Walk this way."

A dark shape shoved off the wall of the building and the cigarette sailed into the gutter.

The man strolled toward them, taking his time. Just as the gas station attendant had mentioned, the stranger had a cap pulled low on his face. He kept to the shadows of the building and stopped about five feet away from them. "You alone?"

Judd recognized the voice from the phone call. "I'm with a friend."

"Cops?" The man's body jerked.

"No cops." London stepped out from behind Judd. "Just me."

"London Breck." The man laughed until he started hacking.

London exchanged a look with Judd. "That's right. Is that okay?"

He waved a hand and then shoved it into his pocket, withdrawing a pack of cigarettes, crinkling the plastic that encased the box. He shook one out. "Smoke?"

"No, thanks." Judd shifted his weight to his other foot since the leg felt heavy—too much standing around. "Get to the point."

"You know your old man's partner was killed in a shoot-out, right?"

Judd hunched his shoulders. "Yeah—a meeting a snitch set up that went south."

"That snitch didn't kill Rigoletto."

"He was tried and convicted."

"He was set up—sort of."

"How is someone sort of set up?" Judd blinked his dry eyes. That cigarette smoke was getting to him.

The man tapped his cigarette on his wrist and stuck it between his lips. "He agreed to the setup."

London's cloak rustled beside Judd, and he pressed his hand against the small of her back.

"Why would he do that?"

"Lots of reasons that aren't important now. Don't you want to know *why* he was set up? That's the important stuff."

"Okay, shoot."

The man held up his hands. "I ain't armed, boss."

"Go on."

"The cop that was gunned down, Rigoletto? He knew somethin', him and your old man."

Judd's heart thudded against the holster strapped across his chest. "What did they know?"

"That—" the man spit out grains of tobacco "—I can't tell you."

"How do you know the shoot-out was a setup?"

"I shared a cell with Otis Branch—the snitch. He told me someone hired him to take out both cops, but he only got one."

Judd sucked in a breath, which only made his mouth drier. "There was a hit put out on my father and his partner?"

"That's right, but Otis missed Brody. When he saw what went down with Brody about six months later, he figured they'd gotten him another way."

Judd's head pounded, and each thud let loose an explosion of pain. He rubbed his heavy eyes.

London gave him a sharp glance and spoke up. "It couldn't have been Russell Langford, the real Phone Book Killer, who set up Detective Brody. Why would he have any interest in Joe Rigoletto?"

The man clicked a lighter and the flame illuminated his face from below, giving him a ghoulish look.

Judd almost laughed but felt London's piercing stare. He reached out and held up the wall of the symphony hall with his hand.

The man lit his cigarette and took a long drag.

The smoke made Judd dizzy, and he propped a shoulder against the building.

"That's the point. Russ Langford was the Phone Book Killer, but someone besides Langford was setting up Brody. That whole sideshow was just a gift to Langford."

London squeezed his arm through his jacket and it felt so good. Lead weights tugged at his eyelids. He just wanted to find a warm, comfortable bed with London curled up next to him.

"Did Otis ever tell you who hired him?"

"Said he didn't know, but they paid him a lot of money, which he stashed away for his wife and daughter."

London looked at him with raised eyebrows. Was she expecting something from him?

She sighed and asked, "Why didn't he say anything when he was arrested? He just took the fall."

"That's what he got paid to do. He figured if these people could arrange the execution of a cop, they'd have no problem taking him out, or his family. He did his time and his wife got the dough. It's not as if Otis was any stranger to life in the big house."

The man's words rushed through Judd's head. He tried to make sense of them, but they tumbled one after the other.

"That's all I gotta say." He shrugged off the wall. "Thought Brody here would wanna know."

He hesitated and took a pull on his smoke.

Interesting. Or it would be interesting if he weren't so damned tired.

London broke away from his side and fished in her evening bag. She took several steps toward the man, and Judd tried to lift his arm to stop her. She shouldn't get so close.

But his arm wouldn't obey the command from his brain.

London murmured something to the man and he turned and sauntered down the street, his lit cigarette swinging at his side, before disappearing behind the building.

"Judd!" Her fingers dug into his shoulders and she shook him. "Are you okay? You just stopped talking and you look like you're about to topple over."

"Sick." His tongue felt five sizes too big for his dry mouth.

She took his arm. "Our car should be waiting in front of the opera house. If not, I'll text our driver. Just hang on to me."

He laid an arm heavily across her shoulders, but didn't want to lean on her. What if they both fell down? He could fall on top of her—in a fountain. Naked. The laugh that clawed its way up his throat sounded more like a bark.

She stumbled beneath his weight as they made it back to the front of the opera house. A few people littered the steps of the building and the sidewalk, but he couldn't think of anything to say to them.

"Your car, Ms. Breck."

"Thank you. Please hurry. Mr. Brody is ill."

Was he? When did that happen? He couldn't be ill. He was on a job. He had to protect London.

Rough hands grabbed him and bundled him into the back of the limo, and he slumped against London, who was already sitting on the leather seat.

"Hey, be careful. He's not well." She pressed her cool hand against his forehead as the door slammed after them.

He licked his lips. "Water. Give me water."

The car roared to life, throwing him to the other side of the backseat, his head hitting the window. A crack of pain splintered his skull and he blinked. "Water."

He heard the crack of a plastic lid on a bottle, and then

London held it to his mouth. He sealed his lips around the rim and chugged it so fast it ran down his chin.

"Judd!"

He sat up. "More water."

The fog in his head loosened, and he tensed every one of his muscles. He knew how to get out of this. He had to get out of this.

London turned toward him, another bottle of water clutched in her hand. This time he took it from her and downed it.

"Why are you so thirsty?" Her wide eyes glimmered in the darkness of the car. "What's wrong?"

"I've been drugged."

Chapter Fourteen

London's heart flip-flopped, and she stretched out her hand for the call button.

"Don't." Judd circled his fingers around her wrist and jerked her arm down.

"If you've been drugged, you need to go to the emergency room."

He crouched down in the seat and shook his head while reaching inside his jacket. He mumbled a curse. "He took my weapon."

Adrenaline spiked through her body, and she grabbed the seat, her fingernails digging into the soft leather. "Who? The driver?"

"Yeah. It's going to be okay. I didn't finish the last club soda—it tasted funny." He tossed the empty bottle to the floor of the car. "Another water."

Her hand shook as she offered him another plastic bottle. "Why would someone drug you?"

"To get to you."

Her eyes darted to the dark privacy glass that shielded them from the driver. "What are we going to do?"

"Since I don't have my weapon or any way to get to the driver, we're going to have to exit this car."

She swallowed, pulling the borrowed cloak up to her chin. "While it's moving?"

"Do you prefer we wait until he takes us to some location not of our choosing and delivers us to the person who planned this abduction?"

"Abduction?"

"That's what this is, London. Whether they plan to kill me first before we arrive or off me once we get there, they want you." He tipped the rest of the water down his throat and wiped his mouth with the back of his hand.

"You're in no condition to jump from a moving car."

"On the plus side, I probably won't feel a thing when I land. There's a reason drunk drivers never seem to get badly injured in accidents—their bones are like rubber, and that's how I feel."

"I wondered what was going on with you when we were talking to our informant. He said some pretty explosive things that barely got a reaction from you."

"First things first. We need to get out of this car the minute it slows down—while we're still in the city, while there are still traffic signals." His fingers curled around the door handle.

"What if he locked us in back here?" Her teeth chattered and she covered her mouth with one hand.

"I don't think so. He figures I'm going to be knocked out in several minutes, and you're more likely to ask him to take me to the emergency room than to catapult from the car and leave me." He narrowed his eyes at her. "Would you?"

She smiled behind her hand. "What would be the fun in that?"

"Keep this cloak wrapped around you." He tweaked the material with his thumb and forefinger. "It'll restrict your movement, but you don't have much mobility in that dress anyway, and the cloak will protect you if he takes off and you fall out of the car."

"We need your motorcycle helmet."

"We need a lot of things." He squeezed her knee. "Hang

on to me when I give the word. I can break your fall if I have to."

"Judd."

"Yeah?"

"I'm scared."

"Piece of cake. The driver's already hit a few red lights. Now that we're ready, we're going to take advantage of those. If he sees the alert for the open door, he might try to take off. Don't let that deter you. Jump and clear the car—moving or not."

She dipped her chin. "Got it."

London held her breath. She scooted even closer to Judd, pressing her thigh against his, clutching his arm with one hand.

The heavy tint on the windows obscured their location, but the car still trundled along surface streets. Once they hit the freeway, if that was where he was headed, they wouldn't have a chance.

The limo slowed, and Judd poked her leg. The car idled.

"Now!" Judd threw himself against the door, pulling her with him.

As predicted, the driver stomped on the gas and the car lurched forward with one of her legs still inside.

Judd yanked her free and they both stumbled into the street.

Headlights blinded her. A horn blared. A set of brakes squealed.

"He's stopping." Judd grabbed her hand and headed down the street, threading his way through traffic as drivers yelled and honked at them.

He shouted above the din, "We want to stay in public view so he won't take a shot at us or try to run us down."

London stole a peek over her shoulder. "He's on the phone."

"Probably giving his boss the bad news. Keep walking."

They escaped the traffic in one piece and turned down a side street, where a few bars bustled with business.

He pulled her through the first door. "We're going to get a taxi back to Nob Hill."

Fifteen minutes later, London closed her eyes in the backseat of a taxi heading home. "I don't understand what just happened."

Judd put a finger to his lips and then pressed it against hers.

They didn't utter another word until she shut the door to her place and locked it. She stood with her back pressed against the door. Then her knees weakened and she folded at the waist.

Judd was beside her in a heartbeat, catching her in his arms. He scooped her up and cradled her against his chest as if she were a kitten instead of a five-foot-ten-inch woman with gangly arms and legs.

He carried her into the great room and settled her before the fireplace. He dragged an ottoman to her back and she leaned against it while he hunched forward and started the gas to light the logs in the fireplace.

"Do you want another cognac? Just sip it for your nerves."

"Sure." She drew her knees to her chest and wrapped her arms around her legs. "Are you all right? Shouldn't you go to the emergency room?"

He poured from the decanter they'd sampled earlier in the evening. "I think it was a little codeine, that's it. I recognized the effects, and once I realized what had happened I was able to deal with it."

"It was someone in the opera house, someone at the gala."

"Someone you know."

She stretched her chilled fingers to the dancing flames. "Do you think whoever it was knew about our meeting?"

"I don't think so, and that's probably what saved me. If I'd been drugged and then packaged into that limo right away, I probably would've passed out before I knew what hit me. Instead we walked outside. The cool air combated some of the effects of the drug."

"If you hadn't acted so quickly, who knows where I'd be right now? Who knows where you'd be?"

"I should've realized something was up when that club soda left a funny taste in my mouth." He loosened the cloak at her throat. "Distracted. I'm too damned distracted to do my job."

"Stop." She slapped at his hands. "You saved me again. If that's you distracted, then I'm not sure I could handle your intensity undistracted."

He opened the cloak and she shrugged out of it. He draped it over the arm of the couch. "Is that poor woman ever going to get her cape back?"

"After I dry-clean it." She flicked the straps of her dress off her shoulders. "Are we going to call the police and report the limo driver?"

"Did you get his name? License number of the car? What exactly are we going to report? He picked us up and was driving us home."

"Y-you were drugged?"

"And how do I prove that? I'm telling you, it was codeine, a common enough drug."

Sighing, she hooked her little finger in the strap of her shoe and pulled it off her foot. "Were you clearheaded enough to hear what our ex-con had to say?"

"I heard, I comprehended the words, but I haven't been able to get my head around them yet."

"He said the shooting of your father's partner was planned, and someone intended the same fate for your dad, too."

"But Otis missed, so someone set my father up to take

the fall for those murders to get him out of the way or shut him up."

"That's the gist of it—and it worked."

"But shut him up about what? Did the guy mention that?"

"He didn't know. Otis didn't know, but when all that stuff started coming down on Joey Brody, Otis figured it was part of the same plan he'd been involved with."

"It's crazy." Judd pinched the bridge of his nose, closing his eyes. "I need to tell my brothers."

"My father knew."

Judd opened one eye. "Knew what?"

"He knew about the setup of your father and his partner. That's how he knew Joey Brody was innocent."

"Do you know what you're saying?"

"My father was a tough businessman. As far as I know, he was an ethical one, but somehow, some way, he had knowledge of what went down twenty years ago."

"And someone doesn't want you to find out what that was."

"That's it, Judd." She sat up, curling her legs beneath her. "There's someone worried about exposure—the murder of a cop, the obstruction of a police investigation of a serial killer, the planting of evidence."

"Driving of another cop to suicide."

"Do you think he knew? Do you think your father realized what was going on?"

"If he did, why didn't he just expose the perpetrators? Why jump off a bridge?" He smacked a fist into his palm.

"I don't know, but maybe once we find the proof, you can get some answers. Someone is trying very hard to protect the lies of the past."

"Who has the most to lose? Richard Taylor has been with your father from the beginning, hasn't he?"

"Pretty much."

"I'd like to have a look at your father's computer. If he went to such great lengths to hide it, there has to be a good reason." Judd peeled off his jacket and dropped it onto the chair.

London sucked in her bottom lip. Her father hadn't hid his laptop because of those pictures, unless he'd wanted to hide the pictures from her. No. He'd told her the location of the laptop, showed her how to get to it.

Through half-closed eyes, she watched Judd strip down to his undershirt and slacks. She didn't need to keep secrets from him. Showing him the pictures on her father's laptop might be the perfect way to tell him. If he judged her and she lost him…well, she'd never had him anyway.

Nobody owned Judd Brody and nobody ever would. He'd do as he pleased. Even now he preferred to call in his brothers rather than put forth an effort for a father he'd dismissed as weak.

Would he dismiss her as weak, too?

"Yeah, we'll look at his computer tomorrow. Like I said, I brought it back to the office, thought it might be safer there with all the stuff going on in this building."

He slid behind her, pulling her back between his legs. Then he kissed her neck. "We'll hit the real estate office first, and then go to your office for the laptop."

The warmth from the fire on her face and the warmth from his kisses on the nape of her neck soaked through the rest her body, and she felt as drugged as if someone had spiked her drink, too.

She curled her arms around his legs and rubbed her hands along the insides of his thighs, crumpling the smooth material of his slacks.

His legs tightened around her and his hands slipped beneath her low-cut dress to cup her breasts. When his thumbs toyed with her nipples, she melted against him.

And then he took her, and the fear and tension of the

evening drifted away. Maybe nobody would ever own Judd Brody, but Judd Brody owned her—mind, body and soul.

THE NEXT MORNING, London climbed on the back of the Harley in her pantsuit, feeling right at home. Judd hadn't bothered to exchange his jeans for a suit today, and he'd replaced the weapon the limo driver had taken from him last with another gun from his small arsenal.

They careened through the streets, leaving Nob Hill for the Sunset where Bay Realtors had an office—the same office that Judd had called last night.

When they reached the realty office, London slid from the bike and Judd slotted it into a parking space. He locked the helmet on the side of the bike and slicked back his hair.

She put a hand on his arm as they crossed the street. "Remember. We're not going to barge in there demanding answers. We play it by ear."

"I do this for a living, lady, and sometimes demanding answers is the way to go."

A bell jingled on the door when they entered the realty office and a man and a woman with their heads together, huddled over a desk, both glanced up.

The small office gave London hope. This didn't look like the type of office where strangers roamed in and out using the telephone. Of course, the caller could've been a client.

The two Realtors kept talking, and Judd whispered in her ear, "Doesn't look like either one of them recognizes us or is surprised to see us."

The man straightened up first and put on his best Realtor's smile. "Good morning. What can I do for you?"

Showtime. London cleared her throat. "We're interested in this area and were wondering if you have any listings."

The man made a detour to a desk and swiped a binder from the corner of it before approaching them. "Certainly. I'm Jonathan Quick, and you are?"

"I'm Connie and this is my husband, J-Jim." They hadn't decided on pseudonyms, but Constance was her middle name and Jim had a nice, generic ring to it. And of course, they had to be husband and wife. After the lovemaking they'd shared last night, anything else would be indecent.

"Connie, Jim." Jonathan shook her hand, but Judd had turned away and was strolling toward a rack of flyers.

"We have all our listings over there, but I have the Sunset ones in this book." He patted the white three-ring binder in his hand. "House? Town house? Condo? The Sunset has them all and parking to boot."

"We're looking for a detached single-family home."

"We have several of those." Jonathan placed the binder on a table and flipped it open. He shifted his gaze to Judd, now standing back and staring at some banner on the wall. "Sir, would you like to have a look with your wife? If anything interests you, I'd be happy to take you out for a showing."

Judd pointed to a sign hanging above a desk, crepe-paper streamers on either side of it. "Who's Cynthia?"

"What?" Jonathan's brow wrinkled and he darted a glance at London.

"Cynthia." Judd leaned forward and tapped the sign so that it swayed over the desk. "It says, 'Welcome back, Cynthia.' Is she an agent here?"

"Uh, yes. Cynthia Phelps. Do you know her?"

London took a few steps toward Judd and could feel the tension vibrating from his tightly coiled body. What was he getting at? Was he just fishing?

"I know someone who knows her. She just got out of the hospital, didn't she?"

London's breath quickened. Did Judd know something?

Jonathan joined them, the binder held open in his hands. "She did."

Judd turned, a fake smile on his face. "Is she here?"

Jonathan's shoulders sagged with the realization he might be losing some customers to Cynthia. "She's not here. Actually, she's taking some time off. She left town. Didn't Cynthia leave town, Lori?"

The woman called from her desk. "Yes. She's taking a break for a while."

Jonathan blew out a breath and hugged his binder. "She'll be gone for some time."

"But she was here." Judd flicked the welcome-back banner with his finger. "She came back to the office."

"Yes." Jonathan cocked his head. "We had a little homecoming party for her when she got out of the hospital. Did you speak with Cynthia before? Had she shown you any properties? Because I can pick up where she left off."

"Was she in the office last week?"

"Sir." Jonathan placed the binder back on the edge of the desk and folded his hands in front of him. "Cynthia is not here, but I can help you with your needs."

"She was here last week, wasn't she?"

The question sounded innocent enough, and Judd's voice, low and smooth, didn't contain a hint of a threat or violence, yet Jonathan's eyes bulged from their sockets and he stammered.

"I—I'm going to have to call the police if you don't leave."

"The police?" London stepped between the two men. "There's no need for that. My husband knows Cynthia and thought we could work with her. That's all."

Lori had risen from her desk, clutching her phone. "Why are you asking about Cynthia? She's been through enough."

Judd held up his hands. "I know. I know she has. My brother told me what happened to her. Ryan Brody's my brother, the guy who found her that day and helped her. I'm sorry. I didn't realize she worked here, and when I saw her name it sort of jogged my memory. My brother would want to know that Cynthia's okay. That's all."

London looked from Judd to the two Realtors, not knowing what to believe. Where had this all come from?

Jonathan leaned against the desk and licked his lips. "She's okay. That's all we can tell you."

"Fair enough. I'll let my brother know." He took London's arm and steered her out of the office with two pairs of eyes burning into their backs.

Judd marched her across the street, and when they hit the sidewalk, she jerked her arm away from his hold. "What the hell was that all about? Who is Cynthia? Was all that true about Ryan? What happened to her?"

Looking up and down the street, Judd said, "We need to find a place to talk."

"Coffee place around the corner. I saw it when we rode up."

They found the coffeehouse and grabbed a table by the window after placing an order.

"This is crazy." Judd ran his hands through his hair.

She snapped her fingers in front of his face. "Let me in on the crazy."

"Cynthia Phelps, aka Cookie Crumb, was a hooker who knew my father twenty years ago."

London widened her eyes.

"Not that way. He'd arrested her pimp or something. Anyway, Cookie was the last person to see my father alive. She saw him jump from the Golden Gate Bridge."

"What?"

"Ryan looked her up when he and Kacie Manning were working on that book together. They talked to her once, and when they went back to see her, someone had beaten her to a pulp. She went into a coma."

"And you think Cynthia's the one who called Rick and bribed him to give that job with Bunny to you?"

"It's obvious, isn't it? Bay Realtors didn't ring a bell with me, but Ryan told me Cynthia was a Realtor and she'd been attacked at a house she was showing in the Sunset. When I saw that sign with her name, it clicked."

"Why would Cynthia do that?"

"Ryan felt that Cynthia knew something. She was too afraid to talk to him and Kacie, and then someone made sure she couldn't talk to them."

"Did she contact Ryan when she came out of her coma?"

"No. Ryan kept calling the hospital until one day he called and they told him she'd been released. The police had spoken to her, but she claimed she couldn't identify her assailant."

The barista called out their names and Judd jumped up to get their drinks.

London took a sip of her coffee and then traced around the edge of the lid. "Instead of telling you what she knows about your father, she arranged to throw us together. That way nobody needs to know she talked to you…or me."

"Dr. Patrick, Cynthia Phelps, Marie Giardano—anyone who knows anything about what happened twenty years ago is a target."

"Who are Dr. Patrick and Marie Giardano?"

"Dr. Patrick was the department psychologist who saw my father after his partner was killed, which we now know was a setup. Before Sean had an opportunity to question him, he had a heart attack and died."

London gasped. "These people are serious. And Marie?"

"She's the longtime records clerk at the department, friends with both my mom and dad back in the day. Any time any of my brothers came around to request the old files to look into the case, she got very nervous, until she just disappeared a few months ago."

"Is she…?"

He lifted his shoulders. "We don't know. She took off

with her purse and passport, packed a bag, and disappeared. I hope to God she's okay and just keeping a low profile until this business all blows over."

"When will that be?" London bit the tip of her fingernail, holding her breath.

"When we solve the mystery and find out what happened twenty years ago. You're not going to be safe until that time, either. Someone out there is always going to be worried about what your father told you or what he left for you to discover."

"He should've just come clean instead of leaving me cryptic notes from the grave."

"He had to have known that he was putting you in danger."

"Wouldn't be the first time my father failed me."

"Join the club."

She covered his hand. "Your father didn't fail you, Judd. He got caught up in something that spiraled out of his control. His partner was murdered, he was being set up as a serial killer—maybe he thought he'd spend the rest of his life in prison for crimes he never committed."

"So you kill yourself? You give up?" He rubbed the hard line of his jaw. "It can't be that easy to set someone up for crimes he didn't commit, unless…"

"Unless what?"

"Unless you're privy to information and resources that would allow you to do something like that."

"Like the police?"

Their eyes met and London's heart hammered so hard she thought it might jump out of her chest onto the table.

Judd nodded. "And the police commission."

"We need to go through my father's files on the laptop, and, Judd—" she tapped the back of his hand with her fingertips "—we're not alone."

"What does that mean?"

"Think about it. Cynthia successfully engineered a meeting between us and someone left that newspaper clipping on your bike. Someone in the know wants us to find the truth. That ex-con stepped forward. Even my father is trying to speak out."

"Then let's go search that laptop."

London hugged Judd around the waist all the way back to the financial district. Whatever happened between them once this was all over, she'd have no regrets. She loved Judd, but she recognized a fellow free spirit when she encountered one. If he went his own way in the end, she could live with it. She'd loved and lost before. It had left a gouge in her heart, but she'd survived it.

He parked in front of the building and they took the elevator up to the BGE offices. London waved at Celine in the outer office.

"I wasn't sure you'd be in today, London. Do you want me to schedule any meetings for you while you're here?"

"No. Judd and I are going to do some work in my office for a while."

"Should I hold your calls? Someone's been trying to reach you all morning, some guy from the Global Giving Foundation."

"You don't have to hold my calls. Put him through when he calls again. That's one of my favorite charities."

"I will. He's been trying just about every hour."

Judd mumbled, "He must really want your money."

"Thanks, Celine." London snapped the door to the office closed. "I don't mind. It's one of the good charities—low overhead, very few administrators, does a lot for kids around the world. It's easy to get people to donate to a cause like that."

"You—" he kissed her on the tip of her nose "—could get people to donate money for snowboards in the Sahara Desert."

"It's easy to get other people's money for causes. Besides, you never know when you might need a snowboard in the desert." She rolled the leather chair to the side and ducked under the desk.

"What are you doing under there?"

"There's a floor safe under the desk. That's where my dad stashed his laptop."

"There's gotta be something more on there than company financials if he went to that much trouble to conceal it."

"That's what I think. That's what I've been telling you." She pulled out the laptop and stationed it on the desk. She slid a glance toward Judd as he pulled up a chair. She could show him the pictures after they went through the rest of her father's files.

She attached a mouse to the side of the laptop and powered on the computer. "I already searched for *Brody, police commission, Phone Book Killer.*"

"Let me have a look at some of the folders and see if anything jumps out at me. Also, if the file or folder doesn't have that specific name, the search may not find those terms in the text. There's a program you can install to block that kind of text search."

"You see? That's why I need your help with this."

They worked side by side, heads huddled together over the laptop. A lot of the files they went through were duplicates of the ones on her father's desktop work computer.

"I don't know." She massaged her temples. "Maybe he just used this as a backup in case the other one went down."

"You already have an automatic backup on the desktop computer. I checked that out when you were in the board meeting."

The telephone on the desk buzzed, and London pressed a button. "Yes?"

"It's that man again from Global Giving."

"I'll take it. I could use a break anyway." The line clicked once and London punched the speaker button while she drew her hands across her face. "Hello? This is London Breck."

An electronically altered voice intoned over the line, "And this is your guardian angel."

She dropped her hands. "Excuse me? Are you calling from Global Giving?"

"I'm calling to give you a piece of advice, London."

Judd's entire frame went rigid beside her.

"Who is this? What are you talking about?"

"I think you know what I'm talking about. I've been trying to get this message to you ever since your father died."

"What do you want? Just come out with it. What is it you want from me?"

"I want you to keep your mouth shut, go about your business and spend your billions of dollars on shoes and trips to the French Riviera."

"You don't want me taking over as CEO of Breck Global Enterprises?"

"I don't give a damn what you do, just stop looking into the Brody case. Everyone knows Brody's innocent now, so drop it."

"Why was he set up? Why was his partner murdered?"

The man on the phone whistled and it sounded like a buzz saw. "You know a lot, don't you? That's why it's time to stop looking for Operation Phoenix. Is Brody with you now?"

She glanced at Judd and he shook his head.

"No."

The man chuckled. "We could've settled this with you a long time ago if my guys had been able to get close to you, but Brody prevented that from happening. Relentless—just like his old man. You never should've hired Judd Brody.

You hired him to protect you, and he ended up putting you in more danger."

Judd's hand jerked and the mouse slipped from the desk.

"Well, I did hire him, and he's going to continue to protect me from your goons, and we're not going to stop. We're not going to stop until we find out what happened twenty years ago."

Judd had retrieved the mouse and was busy tapping the keyboard and clicking through files.

The man's voice sliced through the line like a cold blade. "Oh, but you are going to stop, London, or you're going to be very sorry."

"Let's see, you tried to snatch me twice, broke into my place, set fire to the unit next door, beat up my driver and killed a security guard at my building. I'm not quitting."

"Maybe we can't get to you as long as Brody is in the picture, but we can get to others."

A chill snaked up her spine. "What others?"

"Check your cell phone, London."

She scrambled for her purse and pulled out her phone. A text message with an attachment had come through. Judd hovered over her shoulder, and with trembling fingers she tapped the message to open it, and then tapped the picture attached to the message.

Maddie's face filled the screen. They had her daughter.

"Just one other, London, and we've already done it. We have your daughter, and we're prepared to do whatever it takes to stop you."

Chapter Fifteen

London choked and lunged for the phone. "What have you done with my daughter? Where is she?"

The line had gone dead, and Judd raked a hand through his hair as if to clear the confusion in his brain. A daughter? London had a daughter?

Once she realized her tormenter had hung up, she grabbed the phone and threw it off the desk. She screamed and pushed the laptop, but Judd collected her hands in his.

"Shh. It's going to be okay."

"Is everything okay, London?" Celine tapped on the door.

She called out in a clear voice, "Nothing serious."

Then she turned a tear-streaked face ravaged by grief toward him. "It won't be okay. It can't. He has my daughter."

He cupped her face with his hands. "Tell me. Tell me about your daughter and we'll get her back."

She drew in a shuddering breath that racked her entire body. "She's eight. I had her when I was a teenager. My father forced me to give her up—no…I gave her up willingly. He didn't have to force me. She was an inconvenience to me at that age. I got pregnant in Italy. Maddie's father was a race-car driver. He—he died in an accident, and my father instructed me to leave the country without telling Paulo's family."

She started sobbing and couldn't continue.

He swept away her stream of tears with this thumbs. "So you did the right thing and adopted her out to a loving family. Is she here in the city?"

"Yes, but you heard him. They have her. They must've found out about her from my laptop, the laptop they stole from my condo. I had pictures of her on that computer." She turned her father's laptop toward her. "And here. My father had pictures of her, too. I couldn't believe it when I saw them. He must've had someone taking pictures of her all along, but he never showed them to me. He must've figured I didn't care."

"Maybe he didn't want to upset you." He rubbed a hand down her arm, wishing like hell he could take away the pain etched into grooves on her face.

"Can you verify her…kidnapping with her parents?"

"I'm not in touch with them. If I tell them now this is all my fault, that they lost their daughter because of me, they'll hate me. Besides, you saw her picture. She was holding a copy of today's newspaper. They have her."

He pulled her head against his chest. "You didn't do anything wrong, London. He's not going to hurt Maddie. If he did, he'd have no leverage over you. He's just showing you that he can get to her."

Judd stopped stroking her hair, and a deep worry permeated his bones.

London looked up at him. "What's wrong? If I don't pursue this anymore, they'll leave her alone, right?"

He brushed her hair from her damp face and stared out the window. "Twenty years ago, when my father was going through hell, my brother Eric was kidnapped."

London sniffed. "He survived."

"He did. At the time, people said it was a sympathy ploy and a diversion for my father. They believed he planned the kidnapping himself."

"No parent would do that."

"It was the same as your daughter, London. They were proving to my father that they could get to his family. He knew. He knew he was being set up and he knew who was responsible. That's why he never said anything. They threatened us. They threatened his family. It's the same despicable bunch now."

Her hands fisted in her lap. "How are we going to get her back? How are we going to stop them?"

"We've got to put an end to this right now." He wiped her face with his T-shirt. "He made a mistake. He gave something away—Operation Phoenix."

"What is that?"

"Look." He tapped the laptop, bringing it to life. "I searched for Operation Phoenix while he was talking to you and got some hits."

London trapped her hands between her knees. "I'm afraid to know."

"No, you're not." He rubbed her back. "I know you want to get that little girl back to her family."

She squeezed her eyes shut and drew in a deep breath as if she were drawing upon some well of strength to face her fears.

He started opening the files and folders, and they began to piece together the story of Operation Phoenix.

"These figures are bad." She poked at the monitor. "BGE was facing some lean times twenty-five years ago, and then like magic our fortunes turned around."

"Look at these shipments." He ran his finger down the columns of a spreadsheet. "Pharmaceuticals, methylene."

She leaned closer. "BGE hasn't been in pharma for years."

"It looks as if this is where it started, London, but there doesn't seem to be any target location for these shipments."

"So where did all that methylene go?"

It took them skimming through a few more files, but Judd found what he was looking for. "Bogus companies, bogus addresses. All this methylene was ending up on the street as crystal."

"Meth?" She folded her arms across her stomach. "You mean BGE was supplying drug dealers. We made hundreds of millions of dollars from these shipments."

"That's what it looks like. My father and his partner must've suspected something when this stuff started showing up on the streets."

"I think I'm going to be sick." She cupped her hands over her mouth and nose and took deep breaths in and out. "I can't believe my father would do this."

"He may not have known." He flicked his finger at the monitor. "Look at all these scanned invoices. That's not your father's name, unless he used his middle name or something for signing off."

She squinted at the screen. "That's my uncle Jay's signature."

"Is that Niles's father?"

"Yes." She gripped the edge of the desk. "Are you trying to tell me my uncle Jay engineered the setup of your father and his partner because they found out about his side business? My uncle died years ago, after my father pushed him out of the company. So who's been stirring up trouble since then? Who's been trying to keep your brothers from discovering the truth? And who has Maddie?"

"Niles is the obvious suspect. And if that's the case, I don't believe he's working alone." He tapped the desk with the end of a pen. "He's a member of the Bohemian Club up on Nob Hill, isn't he?"

"Y-yes. I just told you the other day that my father was a member, too, and Uncle Jay."

"I've had clients who were members. One tried to blindfold me when he took me there, but I pointed out I wouldn't be able to do my job blindfolded."

"So they allowed a nonmember into the club? Did you witness any of their silly rituals?"

"He invited me in as a guest, which is allowed, and there were no rituals that night. But I did get an eyeful."

"Is it true there are nude, masked women lounging around the club?"

"Not that night, but I did see a few city movers and shakers, including a couple of high-ranking police officials. Anyone else may not have recognized them, but since my brother is a detective I knew who they were."

"What are you implying, Judd?"

"I'm connecting the dots. Your father's company was involved in illegal activities, whether he knew about those activities or not, and there had to be a lot of cover-up of those activities. Your father was also a big supporter of law enforcement. He was on the police commission."

"It's like we said before—who else but the police would be able to plant that evidence on your father? Who else could get to so many people so easily? But who do you think is involved? It can't be the chief of police. He's relatively new to the city."

"But there are others. Others who were around then and are around today. Others who don't want any of this to come out, any more than Niles does."

He reached for his cell phone. "I'm calling my brother Sean. He's been on his leave of absence long enough. We need his help."

"And what about Eric? You said he worked on the FBI's child-abduction task force. He was abducted himself—probably by these same people."

"I think Eric's in D.C., but he'll come out for this." He snapped his fingers. "And Ryan. I'm calling him down here from Crestview. He knows Cynthia. He spoke to the real

Phone Book Killer. We're going to put this together, and we're going to get Maddie safely home to her family and ensure her future security and yours."

She grabbed his hand and squeezed it so hard he heard his bones crack. "I gave her up to give her a secure life. As her birth mother, I owe her that."

"They won't hurt her. If they do, they know there's nothing stopping you from spilling everything you've discovered. They won't risk that."

"But once they find out we know it all, every sickening detail, they'll have nothing to lose by hurting her."

"Look at me." He took her chin between his fingers and stared into her green eyes, glassy with fear. "Nothing is going to happen to you or Maddie, not as long as I have breath in my body."

"When do you think he's going to call back?"

"When he's good and ready. That's the point, to show his strength and power. But we have work to do in the meantime."

LATER THAT NIGHT, back at her place, London paced the floor, cupping her phone in her hands. Judd's two brothers in California, Sean and Ryan, were already on their way to the city. Ryan might have already arrived. And Eric was taking the first flight out of D.C. Judd's plan had to work. She hadn't given up her baby all those years ago only to put her in mortal danger now.

The company she'd been trying so hard to be worthy of now sickened her. She wanted to believe it was all Uncle Jay's doing. It hadn't been too long after Joseph Brody's suicide that Spencer had pushed Jay out of BGE. If her father had been completely complicit in the illegal activities, he wouldn't have been able to do that. Jay wouldn't have allowed it. Her uncle probably would've used her father's involvement to gain a bigger foothold in the company—for himself and his son.

She had to hang on to that.

The phone vibrated in her hand and she checked the display. She nodded at Judd and put the phone on speaker.

"Hi, Niles. Thanks for getting back to me."

"Of course. You piqued my curiosity."

"I want you to come to my place so I can talk to you face-to-face and give you some paperwork, but the upshot is I want to step down as CEO of BGE."

He sucked in his breath, and his excitement was palpable over the phone. "I'm having dinner near Union Square. I can be there in a jiffy."

She ended the call and pocketed the phone. "So he's on his way."

"He's gonna wish he'd stayed in Union Square." Judd's eyes narrowed and the menace rolled off him in waves.

They finalized their plans and Judd relocated to the burned-out unit next door while she waited for Niles's arrival.

London paced the room until the buzzer on her intercom filled the room. "Yes?"

"What do you mean, yes? It's Niles."

"Okay, I'm letting you in, but you still need to check in with the security guard in the lobby—new policy."

She waited a few seconds and slipped out of her place. She jogged down the hallway and tapped once on the door to the empty unit.

Judd let her in. "Are you ready?"

"As ready as I'll ever be to detain and torture my cousin."

"Nobody's getting tortured." He placed his hand at the back of her neck and massaged the base of her skull with his thumb. "Just remember what he's been doing."

"Allegedly."

"Are you chickening out now?"

The sound of the elevator opening gave her renewed resolve.

"No."

She poked her head out the door. "I'm down here, Niles. Had to take care of a few things."

His gait faltered but he continued. "Can I just wait in your place?"

"It's locked up. We'll just talk here for a bit and then we'll go to my place, have a little wine and celebrate."

He brushed a lock of blond hair back from his high forehead. "I have allergies, you know. I may not be able to last too long in there."

"It won't be long, Niles." *Just until Maddie is back home safely.* She widened the door and stepped back.

He walked in, his nose wrinkling. "What are you doing in here anyway?"

Judd wasted no time. From his hiding place behind the door, he lunged at Niles and immobilized him. Then he forced him into the waiting straight-backed chair and tied him up before Niles recovered from the first assault.

Struggling against his restraints, Niles shook his head. "What is going on? Is this some kind of joke, London? This is too much, even for you."

Judd stepped in front of him, and Niles's eyes bugged out. "Wh-what are you doing here? What is this, London?"

"This—" Judd drew up another chair, facing Niles "—is an interrogation."

Niles sputtered. "This is an outrage. I'll have you arrested. I'll have your license. I know people."

"Funny you should mention those people now, because we're interested in those very people."

Niles's face drained of what little color it had. "Is this a joke, London?"

"Where's Maddie?"

"Who?" Niles ran his tongue around the outside of his mouth.

"My daughter."

Niles laughed, but it came out a croak. "You're crazy. You don't have a daughter."

"You know all about Maddie, the baby I gave up for adoption when I was a teenager. You saw her pictures on the laptop you had stolen from my condo. Did you know the men you'd hired for that job were killers?"

Niles's mouth gaped open like a fish on a line. "You've finally lost it, London. Nobody thought you were suitable to be CEO of Breck Global, but we didn't think you were crazy."

Judd rose from his chair, lifted it and then clumped it back on the floor. "Cut it. We know all about the methylene shipments organized by your father to save BGE. We know my father and his partner discovered that BGE was supplying meth labs with the stuff and maybe even went to their superiors. And we know what happened to both of them after that fact—everyone knows what happened to them."

"Meth labs? You're as crazy as London, both of you caught up in some insane conspiracy theory."

"Save it, Niles." She pulled her father's laptop out of her briefcase. "It's on here. This is what you and your father tried to find all those years, isn't it? The proof. This is what you've been looking for—Operation Phoenix—all here. My father made sure of it, made sure he had proof."

Niles slumped in his seat. "My father may have been involved in some illegal activity, but it saved the company. It was your father's company and he didn't have what it took to keep it solvent, and then he pushed Dad out."

"You mean he kept it solvent by getting involved in the drug trade?"

"What do you want from me, London? You have the

company, just like your father always wanted. I always knew he was going to cut me out, just like he cut out Dad."

"Are you going to deny that you know your cohorts kidnapped my daughter to force my hand?"

"I thought he might try something like this." He closed his eyes. "He's desperate and it's been coming for a long while, ever since that psychopath fingerprint tech decided to mimic the Phone Book Killer and get Detective Sean Brody all riled up again."

"The threats to London began after that."

"It was a perfect storm, wasn't it? He knew Spencer Breck had the proof. My father told him that his brother had the proof, and when Spencer died that proof would go to London. Who knew she would hook up with you? Who knew the real Phone Book Killer would step out of the shadows and confess? Who knew the witches' covens in this city would be put on edge by someone trying to get the power of *Los Brujos de Invierno*."

Judd jumped up, knocking his chair to the floor. "What does that coven have to do with this? My brother believes they were responsible for his kidnapping all those years ago."

"He's right. It's all linked." Niles shook his head almost sadly. "Don't you know that by now?"

London took a turn around the room. "You keep mentioning someone, but not by name. Who is it? Who has Maddie?"

"If I tell you, he'll have me killed. He's had others killed for less."

Judd put his face close to Niles's. "He's not going to have that chance. We're going to take him down. We know he's SFPD. He has to be. Again, the proof is in the files on the laptop. We'll put it together eventually, but you could tell us now and do yourself a favor."

"Or what? You have no proof against me of anything."

"We'll set you loose and put the word out on the street that you're talking. How long do you think you'll have before he silences you?"

Nile's Adam's apple bobbed in his throat. "Y-you wouldn't do that. Once you release me from here, I'm probably a dead man anyway."

"Who says we're releasing you from here, Niles?" Judd rolled up his sleeves, the tattoos on his arm snaking up his skin.

"You can't keep me prisoner."

London took Judd's place in the chair facing Niles. "That's exactly what we're going to do—until we get Maddie back to her family and shine a light on this whole sordid affair so that it can't ruin anyone else's life."

"You don't have to worry about Maddie. He's not going to harm her."

Judd growled. "It's only a matter of time before Spencer Breck's files reveal his identity, and he's never going to harm anyone again."

"Give him up, Niles. It'll go easier on you."

London glanced at Judd, who had retreated to the window. He seemed transfixed by the view.

"Judd?"

"I know who it is. He was around twenty years ago, around my father, around yours. He's a member of that club." He jabbed his finger at the glass. "The Bohemian Club. I saw him there."

Niles sputtered and sobbed.

London joined Judd at the window and took his hand. "It's Captain Williams, isn't it?"

Niles groaned from his chair.

Judd nodded at Niles. "There's your answer."

THE FOLLOWING MORNING, the four Brody brothers were scattered across her great room. They'd dropped everything they were doing to help when Judd called. Their intensity permeated the room, the very air thick with their sense of purpose and justice.

Eric, the FBI agent, perched on a stool at the kitchen island. "I told Christina everything last night, and she's convinced Williams is a member of the coven of witches who was responsible for my kidnapping. Members of that coven had definitely infiltrated the Bohemian Club—they're all about power, and he used his connections twenty years ago to have me kidnapped."

London turned to Judd's eldest brother. "Sean, what about you? You worked with Williams."

"He's always been careful to give me what I wanted and needed on the job. Maybe he didn't want to raise my suspicions." He took a sip of coffee. "Ah, about the man in the next unit. You can't hold him, Judd."

Judd snorted. "What are you going to do, arrest me? At this point we're keeping him for his own safety. If Williams finds out we're on to him, Niles is a dead man."

"He won't find out until we want him to." Ryan sat next to London and took her hand in his. "Once we get Maddie back to her home, we'll move in on Williams. He won't know what hit him."

Sean said, "I have a couple of officers with Maddie's parents, the Dillons, right now. They know nothing about the kidnappers' real motives and are waiting for the ransom note."

Judd started. "Williams?"

"Knows nothing about it. These are two guys who owe me a favor."

"I thought you didn't roll like that, bro." Judd winked at Ryan.

"Do the Dillons know these men are cops?" London twisted her fingers in her lap. Her heart ached for Maddie's parents.

"The Dillons don't know they're cops since the kidnappers' note warned them against calling the police. They just know they were sent to help and, knowing their daughter's biological mother, the offer didn't surprise them."

"We've never—I've never interfered before. The Dillons made it clear to my father that they wanted to provide for their daughter themselves, so no secret trust funds or surprise inheritances."

Judd leaned over the back of her chair and massaged her shoulders. "This is different. I'm sure they appreciate the help and concern."

A cell phone rang, and everyone checked their pockets.

Sean held his up and then answered it. "Yeah? Yeah? Is she okay?" He flashed the room a thumbs-up. "That's great. Thanks, guys."

London bounded to her feet. "Is it Maddie? Is she okay?"

"Safe and sound and on her way home."

Judd crushed her in a hug.

Eric said, "Let me guess. Someone dropped her off on a street corner?"

"In a park."

"He kept his promise." London rested her head against Judd's shoulder. "He released her unharmed."

Ryan shook his head. "Now he thinks he's got you where he wants you. He's demonstrated his power and control, and if you step out of line again, he has the means to punish you."

Judd kissed the top of her head and stood tall, squaring his shoulders. "That's before the Brodys got to town—all of them."

They drove in a caravan through the city streets to the SFPD metro division, with London and Judd in the lead on his Harley. Ryan was riding with Sean in his unmarked police car and Eric brought up the rear in his rental.

The five of them trooped through the homicide division

and squeezed into the elevator up to Williams's office. The brothers didn't want to take any chances with any one of them confronting Williams on his own.

When Williams saw them through the window of his office, his face told London everything she needed to know. His face red, his dark eyes darting from Brody to Brody, Williams stammered, "Wh-what's going on? To what do I owe this pleasure? London?"

"Just stop, Captain. We know everything. I know you were behind all the threats against me, and I know you kidnapped my daughter." She patted her briefcase. "I found my father's laptop that has a trail of BGE's involvement in the drug trade and how certain members of the SFPD were complicit in covering it up in exchange for money and positions of power."

He laughed, but it was a hollow sound. "That's insane. Sean, you don't believe any of these ravings, do you?"

"I saw the proof of the involvement by certain officers, and it sickened me."

Williams jumped on their vague accusations. "Certain officers, but not me. My name's not in there, is it?"

Judd widened his stance. "We also have information from Niles Breck."

"That fool?" Williams rolled his shoulders and some of the tension left his face. "You have nothing. I don't know what you're talking about. If your cousin threatened you, London, he's just trying to implicate others now. You have no proof—none of you."

"How about me, Williams? I have proof."

Williams choked and staggered against the doorjamb of his office.

London spun around as the brothers turned slowly.

A tall, lean man with silver streaks through his black hair folded his arms and leaned against a desk.

Sean grabbed the edge of a table. "Dad."

Epilogue

London wrapped her arms around Judd's waist and smiled at the chaos in her condo. It had been Brody, Brody, Brody 24/7 the past few weeks, and of course they'd all congregated at her place, because there were so many of them and Sean's place was small and Judd's even smaller.

And all the activity swirled around a resurrected Joseph Brody, a man who had pretended to jump from a bridge twenty years ago to save his family from the inexorable menace that had closed in on him.

The brothers had forgiven him because to a one, they would've done something similar to protect their loved ones.

Marie Giardano, the records clerk, had come back from her extended vacation, a vacation she'd taken when she realized someone at the police station had been watching and following her.

Now she had her arm linked with Sean's as she shook her finger in Ryan's face, reclaiming her role as the brothers' surrogate mother.

Cynthia Phelps sat on the arm of the couch next to Judd's father, her hand resting lightly on his shoulder. She'd aided and abetted the disappearance of the man who had become her hero. He'd saved her once and she'd returned the favor by saving him. When he'd returned to San Francisco after

a twenty-year absence, when he thought he could safely re-
join his family, Cynthia had again been there for him, acting as a conduit for the two people who could sort out the
lies and deceptions that had affected them both.

London whispered in Judd's ear, "Do you think your
father and Cynthia could be an item?"

"You think because she played matchmaker you can
return the favor?" He touched her nose and followed it
with a kiss.

Joey Brody called to her, "London, it looks like BGE is
going to weather the bad publicity, since your uncle was
the real culprit and your father pushed him out of the company years ago."

"I think the company is in good hands with my half
brother, Wade. He'll right the ship, and Niles is working
out a deal with the D.A. He'll do his time and hopefully
learn a lesson."

Christina, Eric's fiancée, strolled across the room and
gave London a hug. "Your daughter is fine now? No ill effects?"

"I spoke to her parents on the phone, and she's doing
well. Nobody harmed her physically and the kidnappers
didn't try to frighten her."

"I'm so happy to hear that."

London's gaze wandered to Christina's daughter lounging in Eric's lap. "Kendall is adorable."

"She's a handful, but she's happy to have her daddy in
her life."

"And he looks happy to be there."

Ryan came up behind Judd and smacked him on the
back. "I think it's pretty awesome that you of all people
figured it all out in the end."

Judd turned to his brother. "I didn't figure it all out. Really, we didn't have any proof against Williams except for
Niles's confession. Williams's name still hasn't come up

in Spencer Breck's notes and documents on that laptop. It was all Dad, wasn't it? When Williams saw that ghost from his past, he gave it all up."

Kacie Manning, Ryan's girlfriend, joined their group, handing Ryan a beer. "It's an amazing story."

London nodded. "We couldn't have gotten as far as we did without Joey's help. He got Cynthia to get me and Judd together, and then he left the newspaper clipping on Judd's motorcycle and even convinced Otis Branch's cell mate to contact Judd."

Kacie swiveled her head toward the Brody patriarch and bit her lip. "This would be an incredible book, Ryan. Do you think all your brothers would approve?"

Ryan kissed her hand. "I think we need to give this story a rest for now. How about you revisit it in another twenty years?"

Sean held up a glass and tapped it with a fork. "Can I get everyone's attention?"

Eric jumped up and yelled, "Dad's back from the dead. You can sit down now, Sean."

The room erupted in laughter and Sean rolled his eyes at Elise Duran, his fiancée and the woman he'd rescued from a serial killer. "I just want to thank London for her hospitality. I want to thank Cynthia for everything she's done for Dad, and I want to give thanks for having Dad back in our lives after all these years. And finally, I want to thank the three best brothers a man could ever ask for."

Tears were streaming down Elise's face by the end of Sean's speech, and she threw her arms around his neck while everyone clapped and whistled.

Judd pulled London close and whispered in her ear, "Let's blow this joint."

"But this is my joint."

He raised an eyebrow as that lock of black hair fell over his eye. "Are you a CEO or a free spirit?"

Excitement fizzed through her veins as it always would when she looked into the blue eyes of the man she loved.

She tapped her own glass. "My turn. It's been wonderful having you all here, and I've been so honored to be part of this fantastic reunion. Please continue to make yourselves at home, and just lock up behind you whenever you leave."

"And where are you two going?" Joseph Brody stood up, his three eldest sons around him.

Judd met his father's eyes. "It's time for us to hit the road."

Joseph Brody dipped his head once. "You be careful out there, son."

Outside, London snuggled up against Judd's back on the Harley. "Where are we going?"

"Does it matter?"

"Not as long as I'm with you."

He revved the engine. "That's the answer I've been looking for, London Breck."

She rested her chin on his shoulder. "And you're the man I've been looking for, Judd Brody."

As Judd crested the next hill, she tapped him on the shoulder and pointed at the horizon, the Golden Gate Bridge outlined against an orange sky.

Then they really did ride off into the sunset.

* * * * *

Laine was there by the door, waiting for him, and Tucker wasn't sure who made the first move or even how it happened, but she ended up in his arms.

Strange that it kept happening, and it shouldn't. Even a hug of comfort was a Texas-sized reminder that it was Laine in his arms and that nothing good could come of this.

Well, nothing reasonable anyway.

Maybe it was because every inch of him was on edge that he even thought of holding her as a stress reliever. Yeah, for a second or two, it was relief, but what always followed were some crystal clear reminders of why they shouldn't be doing this in the first place.

The heat between them.

The bad blood, too. Hard to hang on to bad blood, though, when the blasted attraction kept getting in the way.

COWBOY BEHIND THE BADGE

BY
DELORES FOSSEN

Published in Great Britain 2014
by Mills & Boon, an imprint of Harlequin (UK) Limited,
Eton House, 18-24 Paradise Road, Richmond, Surrey, TW9 1SR

© 2014 Delores Fossen

ISBN: 978-0-263-91373-6

46-1014

Harlequin (UK) Limited's policy is to use papers that are natural, renewable and recyclable products and made from wood grown in sustainable forests. The logging and manufacturing processes conform to the legal environmental regulations of the country of origin.

Printed and bound in Spain
by Blackprint CPI, Barcelona

USA TODAY bestselling author **Delores Fossen** has sold over fifty novels with millions of copies of her books in print worldwide. She's received the Booksellers' Best Award and the RT Reviewers' Choice Award, and was a finalist for a prestigious RITA® Award. In addition, she's had nearly a hundred short stories and articles published in national magazines. You can contact the author through her webpage at www.dfossen.net.

Chapter One

Tucker McKinnon heard the sound the moment he stepped from the shower. Someone was moving around in his kitchen.

He opened his mouth to call out to his brothers, the only two people who would have let themselves into his house, but then he remembered. His older brother, Cooper, was on his honeymoon, and his kid brother, Colt, was working at the sheriff's office in town.

So, who was his visitor?

He didn't like most of the possibilities that came to mind. Heck, it could even be someone connected to the arrest he'd made just hours earlier. The dirt-for-brains fugitive that Tucker had tangled with could have sent someone out to settle the score with the Texas Ranger who'd hauled his sorry butt off to jail.

If so, the score-settler wasn't being very quiet, and had clearly lost the element of surprise.

Tucker dried off, wincing when he wiped the towel over the cuts and bruises. He wasn't that old, just thirty-four, but he was too old to be getting into a fistfight with the fugitive who'd gotten the jump on him.

Hurrying, Tucker pulled on his jeans and eased open the door so he could peek inside his bedroom. No one was there, so he grabbed his gun from the holster he'd ditched on the nightstand and stepped into the hall.

The sounds continued.

Someone mumbling. Other sounds, too. He heard the click of the lock on the back door. His intruder, whoever it was, had locked them in together.

Probably not a good sign.

Since he was barefoot, his steps didn't make any noise on the hardwood floors, and with his gun ready, Tucker inched down the short hall, past the living room, so he could look into the kitchen.

There was still plenty of light outside, but the trees next to his kitchen window made the room pretty dark and filled it with shadows. None of the shadows, however, looked like an intruder.

He saw the pantry door slightly ajar. A door Tucker was darn certain he'd shut because he was always stubbing his toe on it.

Someone was in there.

He glanced out the window. No vehicle other than his own truck. The sky looked like a crime scene, though. Bruise-colored storm clouds with a bloodred sunset stabbing through them. He hoped that wasn't some kind of bad sign.

"Not very bright," Tucker tossed out there. "Breaking into the house of a Texas Ranger. We tend to frown on stuff like that." He slapped on the lights.

"No," someone said. It was a woman, and even though her voice was only a whisper, there was as much emotion in it as if she'd shouted the word. "Turn off that light. I don't want them to see us."

"Them?" Tucker questioned.

"The killers."

Okay. That got his attention in more ways than one. Despite the whisper, he recognized the voice. "Laine?"

As in Laine Braddock, a child psychologist who sometimes worked with the Rangers and the FBI. Since they weren't on good terms—not on speaking terms, in fact—Tucker had worked with her as little as possible. After all, his mother, Jewell, had been charged with murdering Laine's father. That didn't create a warm, fuzzy bond between them.

Not now, anyway.

Once, when they were kids, Laine and he had played together almost every day. And she'd been on the receiving end of his very first kiss.

That wasn't exactly something he wanted to remember at this moment, though.

Tucker went closer to the door, and despite the fact he knew her, he didn't lower his gun. Everything inside his severely banged up body was yelling for him to stay alert so he wouldn't be on the receiving end of another butt-whipping. Especially since Laine might not be alone.

"What killers?" he asked.

"The ones who could have followed us here."

Tucker didn't miss the *us.*

There was no *us* when it came to Laine and him. Except they had run into each other about a week before, when he was called to assist the FBI with investigating a black-market adoption ring. Laine had been there on standby in case any of the children were recovered, but Tucker and she hadn't exchanged anything other than some frosty glares.

And that told him loads.

Even if so-called killers were involved, he was the

absolute last person on God's green earth that Laine would have come to, and yet here she was.

"How'd you get in?" he demanded.

"Through the back door. It wasn't locked."

Not locking up was a bad habit that Tucker would remedy the moment he got her out of there. "So you let yourself in. Not a smart thing to do, since you knew I'd be armed."

"It was a risk I had to take," she mumbled.

That only added to the whole puzzling situation. Why come here? What risk was worth a visit with the enemy?

Maybe she hadn't come here by choice.

"Come out so I can see you," Tucker ordered, because he wanted to make sure that someone wasn't holding a gun on her. Maybe it was those killers she'd warned him about.

"Turn out the lights first, please. I don't want them to see us."

Her presence, combined with the fear in her voice, was enough to make Tucker do as she said. He turned off the light, let his eyes adjust to the darkness and moved closer in case he had to fight off someone holding her hostage.

The hinges on the pantry door creaked a little when she fully opened it, and she stepped into the doorway. Yeah, it was Laine all right, and even in the dim light, Tucker could see that something was wrong. Everything about her was disheveled, from her brown hair to her clothes. There was mud or something on her jeans, shoes and white top.

She made a slight gasping sound and reached out to touch him, but then she jerked back her hand. "You've been hurt. Did they come here already?"

"No one's been here. I got this while making an arrest."

He must have looked downright awful for her to notice something like that at a time like this. "How'd you get out here? Where's your car? And why would someone have come here *already?*"

Laine pressed her hand to her head as if he'd just doled out too many questions. Heck, he was just getting started.

"I parked in the woods by the road and walked through the pasture to get here," she finally said. "I didn't want them following me, but they could come here looking for me."

Her voice was shaking. So was she. And she latched her hands onto the doorjamb as if that were the only way she could keep on her feet.

That unsteadiness sent a new round of concern through him. "Are you hurt? Do you need a doctor?"

"I wasn't hurt."

She swallowed hard, pushed herself from the doorway and came toward him. Despite the fact he still had a gun pointed at her. She landed in his arms before Tucker could stop her, and she started to cry. Not just any old crying, either. Sobs punctuated with hard breaths that made a hiccupping sound.

Oh, man.

Whatever this was, it was *really* bad.

Tucker would've needed a heart of ice not to react. And he reacted, all right. He slid his left arm around her. He kept his grip loose. Very loose. But it didn't matter. Basically, Laine was plastered against him, and he wasn't wearing a shirt. He could feel pretty much every inch of her trembling body.

"They killed her right in front of me," Laine said through the sobs.

That pushed aside anything he was feeling from the unexpected hugging session. "Who was killed?"

"A woman. I don't know her name."

Tucker eased back, met her gaze. "Start from the beginning. What happened?"

And then he'd want to know why she hadn't taken this to the local cops. After all, his brother was the sheriff, and his brother, Colt, the deputy. Yet, Laine had come all the way there to his family's ranch, which wasn't exactly on the beaten path.

"Remember that undercover assignment I was on last week?" She didn't wait for him to answer. "We were working on it together, but you got me fired."

Yeah, he remembered. "Not fired. I just asked for you to be reassigned somewhere not near me."

"You got me fired," she repeated, sounding not too happy about it. "Anyway, about an hour and a half ago, I got a call from a woman who wouldn't tell me who she was. She said she'd been held captive by guards at the place we were investigating. But she escaped today."

Laine stopped, shuddering, and pressed her fingers to her mouth.

Good grief. He hoped this wasn't going where he thought it was. "Please tell me you didn't go out to meet this woman alone?"

"I didn't have to go anywhere to meet her. She was in the parking lot outside my office in town. Hiding behind my car. She said she was making the call from a prepaid cell phone that she had stolen from her captors."

Tucker groaned and hoped the rest of this conversation would go a whole lot better than what he'd heard so far. "And at that point, you should have called my brother.

Colt's been on duty all day, and he would have responded immediately."

Laine didn't argue with that, even though Tucker was dead certain she didn't trust Colt any more than she trusted him or the rest of his family.

"The woman said not to contact the cops, that I had to see her alone. So I went out to the parking lot," Laine continued.

But she stopped, and the tears returned. Worse, her hands twitched as if she might reach for him again. She didn't, thank goodness. Instead, Laine held on to the counter by the sink.

"What happened?" Tucker pressed. He hated to sound impatient and insensitive, but if a murder had truly taken place, he needed to report it.

"The woman was scared. Terrified," Laine corrected. "And she only had a chance to say a few words to me when a car came screeching into the parking lot. She told me to run and hide. So I did. She said I was to stay in hiding, no matter what happened. I ducked behind the Dumpster."

Tucker knew that parking lot and the position of the Dumpster. Laine's office was on the far edge of Sweetwater Springs, in a small cottage that shared a back parking lot with three other small buildings. Two were empty, and the third was a law office. Tucker hoped someone else was in that office to witness what'd gone on, in case this turned into an investigation.

"If I'd known what was going to happen," Laine continued, "I wouldn't have hidden. I would have tried to get help." She pulled in a long breath, and the trembling got worse. "The car came to a stop, and two men jumped out. They were wearing police uniforms."

That gave him a moment's pause. "What kind?" The cops in Sweetwater Springs didn't often wear uniforms, but when they did, they were khaki-colored.

She shook her head. "I'm not sure. They were blue, and they had badges and guns."

Maybe they had been from another town or jurisdiction and they'd tracked the woman to Laine's office. "Did they try to arrest the woman?"

A sob tore from her throat. "No. She motioned for me to stay put and she ran. She bolted toward the street, and they shot her. Oh, God. Tucker, they shot her."

It didn't matter that he was a lawman. Hearing about a shooting hit him hard. Except something about this wasn't adding up. "Why didn't anyone report the shots? Why didn't *you* report them?"

"They used guns with silencers." She pressed her fingers to her mouth a moment. "They shot her in the back as she was running. She was dead. I could tell by how limp her arms and legs were when they picked up her body and threw her in the trunk of their car."

Hell.

Since it hadn't started raining yet, there'd be blood. Maybe even some other evidence.

Tucker's cell phone was in the bedroom by his holster, and he didn't want to leave the room to go get it. Instead, he reached for the landline on the kitchen wall. He had to call Colt and get him to the scene ASAP.

"Don't." Laine latched onto his wrist. "They had a police radio in their car. I heard it. And if you call the sheriff's office, they'll hear it, too. They'll know I came here."

Tucker blew out a long, frustrated breath. Not good about the police radio, but like uniforms, they could be faked or stolen. It didn't mean cops had actually killed the woman.

"Why *did* you come here?" he asked.

Laine let that question hum between them for several moments. "Because I knew the lawman in you would help me."

Tucker let her answer hum between them a couple of moments, too, even though he couldn't argue with it since it was the truth. "The murder has to be reported, but I'll tell my brother not to put any of this on the police radio. Did you get the license plate on the car?"

"No. Sorry. I wasn't thinking straight." Another sob. "I should have done something to stop them."

"If you'd tried, they likely would have killed you, too." It was the truth, and even though Laine and he were essentially enemies, he didn't wish that on anybody. As it was, this nightmare would be with her for a long time.

He reached for the phone again, but once more Laine stopped him. "I stayed hidden like the woman told me to do. I did everything she insisted that I do." Her voice was frantic now, and she sounded like she was on the verge of a full-blown panic attack. "And the words she said to me keep repeating in my head."

Everything inside Tucker went still. "What words?"

"'Hide them. Protect them.'" She turned, maybe to bolt out the door, so he took her by the shoulders.

"Who's *them?*" He groaned. Were there more women still being held at the baby farm? That wouldn't be good, because if everything Laine had told him was true, their captors were cold-blooded killers.

She pried off his grip and went back to the door of the pantry.

Tucker braced himself to see his pantry crammed with

women who were on the run from the men who'd gunned down one of their fellow captives.

But there were no women.

In fact, because the lights were off, Tucker couldn't see anything other than the food on the shelves.

"I have to protect them," Laine repeated, her voice breaking.

Tucker went closer to the pantry and looked around. On the floor was a rumpled blanket.

Except it wasn't just a blanket.

Wrapped in the center of it was something he'd never expected to find in his pantry.

Two sleeping newborn babies.

Chapter Two

Laine tried to brace herself for Tucker's reaction. By all accounts, he was a good lawman, so she doubted that he would just toss the babies and her out the door. It was one of the reasons she'd come to him. That, and there being literally no one else she could trust.

She wasn't sure she could trust him, either.

But she was certain that he'd do what was right for the babies.

"They need to be protected," Laine said when Tucker just stood there volleying glances between her and the babies. "The killers will be looking for them. And for me."

Tucker shook his head, obviously trying to process this. She wished him luck with that. She'd had more than an hour to process it, and it still didn't make sense.

"Why are you so sure the killers will be looking for you?" he snapped.

"Because if they don't know already, they'll find out I'm the person renting that office space, that it was my car the woman was hiding behind. And that I had a connection to the illegal adoption investigation."

He made a sound of agreement with frustration mixed

in. He tore his gaze from the babies. "How'd this woman know to come to you?"

"I'm not sure. She didn't get a chance to tell me." In fact, the only thing Laine was certain of was the woman's warning that kept repeating through her head.

Hide them. Protect them.

"I don't know anything about these particular babies," Laine said. The panic started to crawl through her again. "But I'm sure they'll be hungry soon. I figured since you have a nephew, you might be able to get some baby supplies."

What Tucker did do was curse and reach for the phone again. Once again, she tried to stop him, but before he could make a call she didn't want him to make, the phone rang. The sound shot through the room and sent her heart slamming against her chest. It also caused the babies to stir.

"Colt," Tucker said when he answered. Someone that she knew well. Colt was his kid brother and the deputy sheriff of Sweetwater Springs. He was also someone else she wasn't sure she could trust. "I was just about to call you."

Tucker still had his gun gripped in his hand, and he turned his steely-gray lawman's eyes to the window when he put the call on speaker.

"I tried your cell phone first and when I didn't get an answer, I called the landline. Good thing you're there. Just had an interesting visit from two San Antonio cops looking for Laine Braddock," Colt continued. "They said they had a warrant for her arrest."

Oh, mercy. It was a lie, of course. There was no warrant out on her, but this had to be the two men who'd killed the woman.

"Are they still there?" Laine blurted out. "If so, arrest them."

"Laine?" Colt mumbled. He said her name like profanity. "Tucker, what the hell's she doing at your place?"

"I'm trying to figure that out now. Why'd the men want to arrest her?"

"Aiding and abetting an escaped felon." Colt paused. "Did she?"

"No!" Laine insisted.

At the same moment, Tucker said, "I'm trying to figure that out, too. Was there anything suspicious about these men?"

"Nothing that I noticed. Why?"

"Just check and make sure they're really cops. I have an old friend in SAPD, Lieutenant Nate Ryland. Call him and make sure these two guys are from his department. Another thing I need you to do is get someone out to Laine's office ASAP and check the back parking lot for any signs of an attack."

"An attack? What the devil's going on?" Colt pressed.

"Just send someone over there and let me know if there's anything to find."

"And don't use your police radio," Laine insisted. "The men are probably monitoring the airwaves, and they might try to go back and clean up before you can investigate the scene."

Colt, no doubt, wanted to ask plenty more questions, but Tucker cut him off. "I'll be in touch after I've made some more calls." With that, Tucker hung up and headed out of the room and into the hall.

"What calls?" Laine asked, following him. She couldn't go far in case the babies started to cry, but thankfully the hall wasn't that long.

Tucker ducked into a room—his bedroom, she soon realized. He grabbed a black T-shirt that'd been draped over a chair. He slipped it on.

No more bare chest.

And she hated that she'd even noticed something like that at a time like this. Of course, it was hard not to notice a man who looked like Tucker McKinnon. That rumpled sandy-brown hair. Those eyes.

That amazing body.

Laine was counting heavily on him using that lawman's body if it came down to protecting the babies.

He looked up at her as he tugged on his boots, and his left eyebrow slid up. Only then did Laine realize that she was gawking at him.

"What calls?" she repeated. Obviously, the murder she'd witnessed had caused her brain to turn cloudy.

"Social services, for one. We have to turn these babies over to the proper authorities."

"What if these killers have connections there, too?" She didn't wait for him to answer. "It's too risky to call anyone now. We need to find someone we can trust before we let anyone know we have the babies."

Tucker gave her a flat look, as if she'd lost her mind. Heck, maybe she had.

"Look, you've been through a bad experience," he said, his tone not exactly placating, but close enough. "And because someone else broke the law, that doesn't mean we have the right to do the same. The babies need to be turned over to social services so they can find out who they are. It's possible the woman who was hiding behind the car isn't even their mother."

That hit her like an avalanche. Because it might be true. God, why hadn't she thought of that? Except she remembered the look of desperation on the woman's face. Her plea for help.

Hide them. Protect them.

And Laine had to shake her head. "She sacrificed her life for them. Only their mother would have done that. A kidnapper would have just handed them over to the killers to save herself."

Tucker stared at her. And stared. Before he mumbled some profanity and snatched up his phone from the nightstand. "A friend of a friend is married to a social worker. I'll arrange a meeting with her."

A meeting like that still wasn't without risks, but it was better than involving the cops. Of course, if Colt found blood or something else in the parking lot, Laine seriously doubted that he would keep the information to himself.

At some point, all of this had to become official.

Laine heard a soft, kittenlike sound and hurried back to the pantry. One of the babies was stirring. The other was still sound asleep. Laine went closer, knelt beside them and tried to gently rock the baby with her hand.

"My friend didn't answer," Tucker said, coming back into the kitchen. "So I left a message." He tipped his head to the babies. "Are they boys or girls?"

"I don't know." She'd been so focused on getting them to safety that she hadn't considered anything else. But Laine considered it now.

Both babies wore full-length body gowns with drawstrings at the bottoms. She loosened the one on the squirming baby and peeked inside the diaper.

"This one's a boy," she relayed to Tucker. She had a look at the other one. "And this one's a girl."

The different sexes could mean they weren't twins after all, though they looked alike and appeared to be the same age. But what if the dead woman had rescued her own child and then someone else's? It could mean there was another woman being held captive.

Or another woman who was already dead.

That sickened Laine even more.

"If my friend doesn't call back in the next few minutes, we'll need to get someone else out here to take them," Tucker explained. "I mean, we don't even have any way to feed them. My nephew's two, and he doesn't drink from a bottle. I doubt we'd even have anything like that around the ranch."

Laine couldn't dispute what he was saying. Nor could she push aside the feeling that these babies felt like her responsibility now.

Tucker mumbled something she didn't catch and went to the kitchen window to look out again. When the baby kept squirming and started to fuss, Laine eased him into her arms.

She had little experience holding a baby, and even though she'd run through the pasture with them, the babies had been wrapped in that bulky blanket. With nothing but the gown and his diaper between them, the baby felt as fragile as paper-thin crystal.

Tucker glanced at her and frowned. "You know what you're doing?"

"No." But the baby did seem to settle down when she rocked him, so Laine kept doing it. "I'm sorry for bringing them to your doorstep, but I drove out of town as fast as I could and didn't know where else to go."

She glanced around the kitchen. "We used to play here when we were kids."

"Yeah. It was my grandfather's house."

The explanation was clipped, as if it were the last thing

he wanted to discuss with her. Maybe because they'd done more than just play in this house. They'd shared a childhood kiss there. She had been ten. Tucker, eleven. Twenty-three years ago.

Just days before her father's murder.

After that, there'd been no kissing.

No more playing together. No more friendship.

Even though she'd just been a kid, it hadn't taken long before Laine had realized what gossip everyone was spreading—that Tucker's mother, Jewell, and her father, Whitt, had done something bad. Later, she would come to understand that *something bad* meant they'd been lovers. And that Jewell had murdered her father when he'd tried to break things off and work on saving his marriage. A murder that Jewell had yet to be punished for. At least now the woman was in jail, awaiting trial.

"Don't," Tucker warned, as if he knew exactly what she was thinking. "I don't want to take any trips down memory lane right now."

Fair enough. His mother was a touchy subject for both of them. From everything Laine had heard, Tucker and his brothers weren't disputing Jewell's guilt. They only wanted the woman who'd cheated on their father and abandoned them to get out of their lives and leave Sweetwater Springs.

Tucker's cell phone rang, causing the baby to fuss again, and Laine leaned in so she could see the caller's name on the screen.

Colt.

The fear returned with a vengeance, and she prayed that Tucker's brother had found something—anything— that would help her keep the babies safe.

Laine leaned in so she'd be able to hear what he said.

Obviously she leaned too close, because her arm brushed against Tucker's chest. He shot her a "back off" scowl and hit the speaker function so she'd be able to hear.

"Just got off the phone with Lieutenant Ryland," Colt immediately said. "He doesn't know a thing about two SAPD cops coming to Sweetwater Springs."

"So they're fake," Laine concluded.

"Looks that way. And there's also no warrant for your arrest."

She hadn't expected to feel as much relief as she did. Laine knew she'd done nothing to have an arrest warrant issued against her, and the last thing she needed right now was real cops trying to arrest her for a fake warrant.

"What about the parking lot?" Tucker asked. "You find anything?"

"I sent Reed to check it out. Still waiting to hear from him."

He was talking about Reed Caldwell, one of the deputies. Laine hoped the two men who'd fired those shots had managed to leave some kind of evidence behind. And then she thought of something else.

"Maybe the dead woman's fingerprints are somewhere on my car? She had her hand on the door when I first spotted her."

"Dead woman?" Colt questioned.

Tucker groaned and rubbed his hand over his face. "Laine thinks she witnessed a murder."

"I don't *think* it. I *know* I did."

"She witnessed a shooting," Tucker said, "by two men dressed as cops. Her car's parked in the woods near my place. When Reed's done with the parking lot, can you send him out to check for prints?"

"Sure. But you know as well as I do, if there was really

a murder, I need Laine down here now to make an official report."

Tucker glanced at her and then at the baby she was holding. "There's a complication. The woman left two babies, and they're newborns by the looks of it. Any reports of missing babies?"

"None," Colt said without hesitation. "If something like that had come in, I would have known."

Yes, he probably would. Amber Alerts got top priority, even in a small-town sheriff's office.

"But I'll make some calls," Colt continued. "Maybe this is a case of parental abduction and the local authorities haven't reported it yet."

Tucker mumbled his thanks. "Hold on a second, Colt." He motioned toward Laine's phone. "Give it to me."

It took some doing, balancing the baby while working her way into her jeans pocket to retrieve the phone. She handed it to Tucker.

Normally, Laine wouldn't have been wearing jeans on a workday, but she hadn't had any appointments. She'd simply gone in to catch up on paperwork and rearrange some things in her office.

As bad as her situation was, she shuddered to think of how much worse it could have been if she hadn't been there to rescue the babies. Either the killers would have found them, or else it would have been heaven knows how long before someone spotted them in the parking lot.

Tucker scrolled through the list of calls she'd received and read Colt the number of the last one on the list. It was the one from the woman.

"It's possible that phone was stolen from those two fake cops," Tucker explained to his brother. "It's also possible that it's a prepaid cell."

It was clear with his *possible* comments that Tucker was withholding judgment about the veracity of her story. But every word of it was true.

Colt didn't respond to that right away, but she heard some movement on the other end of the line. "Yeah, it's a burner all right, and it's no longer in service."

Laine tried not to groan because it might disturb the baby, but it was hard to hold back her disappointment. That phone number could have given them clues about the men's identities.

The dead woman's, too.

"Call me if Reed finds anything in the parking lot," Tucker added. He ended the call and turned to her. "I can't sit on this any longer. If that woman was murdered, then every minute we delay could increase the odds of her killers getting away."

It was the voice of experience. Maybe not just as a Texas Ranger, either. After all, it'd taken twenty-three years for his mother to be brought to justice.

Still...

"Those fake cops were just at the sheriff's office," she reminded him. "What if they come back?"

"Then Colt and I will deal with it." He looked out the window at the sky again just as some lightning zipped across the sky. "We should get the babies in my truck before the rain starts."

Laine glanced out at the clouds, too, trying to gauge how much time they had, but Tucker cursed again and took hold of her arm to push her behind him. The movement was so sudden that she couldn't figure out why he'd done it.

Then Laine looked over his shoulder and out the window.

Her heart dropped to her knees.

There were two men, dressed in blue cop uniforms, walking across the pasture directly toward the house.

Chapter Three

Tucker didn't consider that he might be going out on a limb by assuming the two men stalking toward his house were also the men who'd killed a woman in cold blood.

Well, if she had indeed been murdered.

But believing that wasn't much of a stretch, either. Laine had arrived at his place, scared out of her mind. She must have thought a murder had taken place and that the danger still existed.

These men could be proof of it.

They were both wearing sidearms, both shifting their gazes from one side of the pasture to the other. Keeping watch. Something lawmen would do.

Criminals, too.

The one on the right pointed toward the ground. Probably because he'd spotted Laine's footprints. Too bad the rain hadn't hit to wash them away, because her tracks led right to his back door.

"Oh, God," Laine mumbled, and she just kept repeating it until he was certain she was losing it.

"Get back in the pantry," Tucker ordered her.

He took out his phone to call Colt, but it would take his brother at least twenty-five minutes to get from town to this part of the ranch.

Hell.

That was too long, so he tried to figure out a faster solution.

His other brother, Cooper, wasn't at the main house because he was away on his honeymoon. That would have been his best bet, since Cooper could have gotten to Tucker's house in just a couple of minutes. Without that option, he had to call someone he didn't want to see.

His sister Rayanne.

She was a deputy sheriff on a leave of absence, and by all accounts, she was solid at her job. But since his twin sisters, Rayanne and Rosalie, had been raised by his mother, the girls were on their mom's side when it came to this trial.

Tucker wasn't anywhere near that side.

And that had made for plenty of tense moments in the past couple of weeks since Jewell, his sisters and his stepbrother, Seth, had arrived at the ranch. Because Jewell owned Sweetwater Ranch, he and his brothers hadn't been able to turn them away, but there hadn't been any warm welcomes, either.

However, for now Tucker had to put that bad blood and ill will aside and find a backup. Even if it meant turning to a sibling or a stepsibling who disliked him as much as he disliked them.

Tucker quickly scrolled through the numbers. He tried Rayanne first. He didn't have her cell number, but unlike Rosalie and Seth, she was staying in the main house.

His home.

Because Rayanne had reminded everyone that it was her home, too.

Yeah, calling her wouldn't be much fun.

Mary, the housekeeper, answered, and Tucker asked

her to buzz Rayanne's room. He said a quick prayer that she'd be there and not out visiting Jewell all the way over at the county jail.

"What?" Rayanne answered, sounding about as friendly as Tucker felt.

"I have a situation. Two armed men posing as cops are approaching my house. They're possibly killers...." And here was the hard part. He glanced back at Laine's bleached complexion and the baby she was holding.

No, not that hard. Two babies' lives could be at stake.

"I need your help," he told Rayanne.

Tucker expected her to ask him for more details, tell him a flat-out no, or at least hesitate.

She didn't.

"I'll be right there. Don't shoot me by mistake," Rayanne snarled.

He figured that last part was an insult to his skills as a Texas Ranger, but he didn't care how many barbs Rayanne slung at him. He only needed a warm body who knew how to shoot just in case this came down to a gunfight.

"If you have another gun, I can help," Laine offered.

"No." He didn't want the babies left alone, and he didn't think it was a good idea to give an already shaky woman a gun that she might not even know how to use. "Stay where you are, and if I tell you to get down, do it."

That didn't put any color back in her face, but she nodded and stayed put.

"Where are the men now?" Laine asked. "What are they doing?"

"They're still following your tracks." They were taking slow, easy steps, and only one of them had his attention on the house.

The other was doing the tracking.

Tucker mumbled some profanity when the men drew their guns, and he debated what he could do to try and diffuse the situation. He should probably identify himself as a lawman, but if they were indeed killers, they'd just try to eliminate him so they could get to Laine and the babies.

Then they'd eliminate her.

After all, they'd followed her here, which meant they knew she'd either witnessed the murder or had some knowledge about it or the dead woman.

And that made Laine a loose end.

The seconds ticked with each step the men took, and every inch of him became alert. Tucker had been in situations like this. Facing down suspected killers and waiting for an attack that might or might not happen. But the stakes had never been this high. He had two newborns to protect.

One of the men suddenly stopped, his gaze zooming to the back part of the property. No doubt the route that Rayanne would be taking.

Had they seen her?

If so, he hoped his sister had taken some basic precautions so she wouldn't get herself shot. He suspected she hadn't when the other man pivoted in that direction. Tucker knew he couldn't wait. He had to do something to make sure they didn't gun Rayanne down.

He reached over and opened the door just a fraction so he could see out. "I'm Tucker McKinnon, Texas Ranger," he shouted to them.

Like his earlier call to Rayanne, Tucker wasn't sure what response he'd get from them. But the men stopped and lowered their guns.

That was a good start.

"I'm Sergeant Floyd Hines," the one on the left answered. In his late twenties or early thirties, he was heavily muscled and had nondescript brown hair. "And this is my partner, Detective Norman Hacker." He was on the lean side, with a mean-looking scar running down his cheek.

"We traced a fugitive here," Hines added.

Tucker had to hand it to them—they sure sounded like cops. And maybe they were. Dirty ones. Because he already knew they weren't SAPD.

The rain started. Tucker stayed to the side of the door so they could still hear him, without him needing to put himself in the direct line of fire.

"What fugitive?" he asked the men.

"Laine Braddock. She assisted in helping a federal prisoner escape."

Laine made a sound of outrage, but Tucker motioned for her to stay quiet. Maybe the babies would do the same.

"She's not here," Tucker lied. "You need to be on your way."

The men exchanged glances, obviously not pleased with his lack of cooperation.

"Where is she?" Hines asked, in the way a cop would ask. A demand rather than a question.

"Wouldn't know. I'm not exactly on friendly terms with her."

Hines mumbled something to his partner that Tucker couldn't hear. "We have reason to believe she's inside your house," Hines continued. "We're coming in to check."

Well, they weren't short of gall. But then neither was Tucker. "You got a search warrant?"

That earned him scowls from both of them. "We figured you'd cooperate with your brothers in blue."

"Not this time. Come back when you've got that warrant." Tucker shut the door and kept watch out the window.

The pair definitely didn't turn and leave. They stood there mumbling and looking around for what seemed an eternity. That eternity screeched to a halt when one of the babies started crying.

Not a whimper, either.

A full-fledged cry. Worse, the other one started to cry, too. No way could those men miss that.

Hines raised his gun again and started toward the house. He was no longer moving at a cautious pace. He began to run as if he planned to ram right through the back door.

"Wouldn't do that if I were you," someone shouted.

Rayanne.

Hacker pivoted in her direction. Fired. The shot blasted through the air, and he dropped to the ground behind a tree. Hopefully Rayanne had gotten down, as well.

"Stay on the floor, as low as you can get," Tucker warned Laine again, and he threw open the door so he could return fire.

Hines bolted behind Tucker's truck. That didn't stop the man from shooting, though. This time, the bullet smacked into the door less than an inch from where Tucker was standing.

Hell's bells.

So, he had his confirmation.

These guys were killers, and they were firing shots into a house where they knew Laine and the babies were hiding.

"Don't go out there," Laine whispered as Tucker stooped down and opened the door a little farther.

"I can't let them keep shooting into the house." And anyway, Rayanne was out there. Responding to his call for backup. He didn't intend to let her face down these guys alone.

Laine continued to protest, but the sounds of the babies' cries and the shots drowned her out. Tucker created some sounds of his own by sending a shot at Hines. The bullet smacked into Tucker's truck, very close to his intended target, but the miss got him the results he wanted.

Hines leaned over to fire again.

And this time, Tucker made sure he didn't miss.

He didn't go for a kill shot. He wanted this dirtbag alive so he could explain what the heck was happening here, so Tucker shot Hines in the right shoulder. When the idiot still kept hold of his gun, Tucker put another bullet in his arm.

Even over the noise of the gunfight, Tucker heard Hines groan in pain, and he finally let go of his gun.

Hacker cursed. No doubt because he realized his partner had been shot and was now unable to return fire. Rayanne gave him another reason to spew some profanity. Tucker saw her dart out from behind one of the trees and take aim at Hacker.

"Drop your gun now!" she ordered.

Tucker hurried onto the small porch and took aim at Hacker, as well. A single word of profanity left the man's mouth before he tossed his gun to the side and lifted his hands in surrender.

"Get on the ground," Tucker demanded. "Both of you."

Hines's arm and shoulder were bleeding, and he was clearly in pain, but he eased himself to the ground. About fifteen yards away, Hacker did the same.

Tucker slid his phone across the floor toward Laine. "Call Colt and tell him to get out here now. We'll need an ambulance, too."

Laine gave a shaky nod, and even though she now had both babies in her arms, she managed to grab the phone.

Since Tucker figured the two gunmen could be carrying backup weapons anywhere on their bodies, he kept his own gun aimed and ready when he made his way out the door and down the porch steps. Rayanne kept her gun ready, too, and went to Hacker. Tucker went to Hines.

"Colt should be here soon," Tucker relayed to Rayanne. But maybe he could use the time to figure out who these guys really were.

Tucker took aim at Hines's head. "Start talking. Tell me about the woman you killed."

"Didn't kill nobody," the man snarled. He had his hand clamped to his arm, the pain etched all over his face, but he still managed to look cocky and defiant.

"Wrong answer. Try again." Tucker made sure he sounded cocky, too. "Who sent you here?"

His tobacco-stained teeth came together in a sneer. "Even if I knew that, I wouldn't tell you. Wouldn't be good for my health."

"Neither is bleeding out." Though the man didn't seem to be in danger of doing that, Tucker took his threat a little further. "I can get an ambulance out here real fast. Or real slow. Your choice."

His mouth tightened even more. "You're not gonna let me die."

No. But Tucker figured he could bluff him into thinking otherwise. "You just took shots at me, my sister and a friend of mine."

"She ain't no friend of yours. I know who she is. And

who you are. I know that your mama killed her daddy, and there's bad blood between you two. No reason to protect her."

"I'm a *real* lawman," Tucker snapped.

That only deepened the man's sneer.

The rain started to come down harder. The thunder rumbled, too. Maybe that ambulance would get there before one of them got hit by lightning.

"You don't need this guy alive, do you?" Rayanne called out. She was standing over Hacker, her gun aimed right at him, while he wriggled belly-down on the ground.

"Why'd you ask that?" Tucker wanted to know.

"Because he's got that look, that's why. The one that morons get right before they do something really stupid, like try and go for my gun. If he does, I want to make sure it's okay for me to put some bullets in his head."

The *moron* quit moving.

"We don't need him alive," Tucker assured her.

And that wasn't exactly a bluff. Of course, he would prefer both men breathing so he could try to pit them against each other during the interrogations, but since Hacker's shots could have hurt those newborns, Tucker wasn't feeling very charitable toward the man.

Or toward Hines.

Hines was on his back on the ground. Tucker put his boot against the man's throat. "Talk. Tell me why you came here for Laine."

"Laine," he repeated. "Sounds as if you two have mended some fences."

Not exactly. But being caught in a gunfight together had a way of pushing those old issues to the side.

For a little while anyway.

"Mending fences won't save her," Hines said. His top

lip lifted. It was more sneer than smile, but the warning put a knot in Tucker's gut.

So did the sound.

Behind them, in the house, Tucker heard something he sure didn't want to hear.

Laine's shout.

"Tucker! There's another gunman."

Chapter Four

Laine saw the third man. But it was seconds too late to try to get the babies out of the house. Too late to do anything other than call out to Tucker and hope that would be enough to save them.

The hulking goon must have come in from the front of the house, away from the fight that'd been going on in the side yard with Tucker, his sister and the other two killers.

"Don't do anything stupid," the man warned her. He stepped into the doorway of the pantry, blocking her exit, and pointed a gun right at her.

Just the sight of him caused the skin to crawl on the back of her neck, but Laine forced herself not to panic. She had the babies gripped in her arms, but she put them back on the floor so she could position herself in front of them. Trying to protect them while she prayed that Tucker would get there fast enough to put a stop to this.

If Tucker was able to do it, that is.

She'd heard those shots outside, and one of them could have hit Tucker before he even made it out to stop the gunmen. It sickened her to think of that. She hadn't wanted to involve him or his sister in this, but she'd had no choice.

Laine didn't recognize the guy in front of her, but he was huge. At least six foot four and with a hulking body and wide shoulders. Even if he hadn't had the gun, he would have been formidable.

"The three of you are coming with me," the man snarled, and he used the barrel of his gun to motion for her to get moving. "Now!" he added when she didn't budge.

Laine couldn't risk him firing, because even if he didn't intend to hurt the babies, it could easily happen in such a confined space.

"Please don't hurt them." Not that she thought pleading would help, but it might be able to buy her some time.

Or not.

"I said move!" he shouted.

The man came right at her, caught onto her arm and flung her against the pantry shelves. Her shoulder hit the shelves hard, and the pain jolted through that entire side of her body. In the back of her mind, Laine realized she'd have bruises. Too bad worse things could happen in the next couple of minutes.

Boxes of pasta and canned soup tumbled off the shelves, pelting the floor. Despite the hard grip the man still had on her, Laine dropped back down so she could prevent the babies from being hit.

She didn't stay there long. Once the pantry items had stopped falling, she did the only thing she could do. She came up fighting.

Laine grabbed the first thing she could reach—a large can of mixed nuts—and threw it at him. It hit him on the chin, the can flying open, flinging nuts at him, but the can and nuts bounced off him as if he hadn't even felt it.

She didn't stop. She hurled a can of soup at him next, and received the same reaction as before. Well, almost. She hadn't thought it possible, but the fury in his expression actually went up a notch.

Making a feral growling sound, he came after her again.

But he froze. Then cursed. Without warning, he caught onto her hair and hauled her out of the pantry and into the kitchen.

She heard them then.

The footsteps.

With his gun gripped in his hand, Tucker came in from the living room and took cover by the partial wall that divided the kitchen from the rest of the house. Maybe he'd tried to sneak up on the guy, but if so, it hadn't worked. The man dragged her in front of him and put the gun to her head.

She was now a human shield.

"Put down your gun," Tucker ordered him. Rainwater dripped from his hair and clothes. "Your *friends* are cuffed in the yard, and my sister's guarding them. Or maybe she's killing them," he added. "More backup will be here in a few minutes."

Despite having a gun to her head, relief flooded through Laine. Well, temporarily anyway. The other killers had been caught, and now this guy was the only one left standing. Hopefully not for long, though. Tucker needed to arrest them all so she could find out about the woman these monsters had murdered.

"You won't make it out of here alive," Tucker told the man. He stayed behind cover, using his left hand to bracket his shooting wrist.

"Oh, yeah? With those kids and her, I believe I will," he growled.

Laine could no longer see her captor's expression, but she could certainly see Tucker's. Every muscle in his body was hard and tight. He was a lawman ready for the fight, but this was a fight they could all lose if she somehow didn't manage to protect the babies.

"Escaping with newborns will be tricky at best," Laine reminded the man. "You can take just me and move faster." Not that she especially wanted to play the martyr here, but she didn't have many options.

Obviously, her *option* didn't please Tucker because he shot her a glare. Laine ignored it. If she could do anything to change her captor's mind, she would.

"Taking me and me alone is your best option for staying alive and escaping," she added. "The babies would just slow you down."

She got exactly the reaction she'd expected. Another glare from Tucker when he glanced over at her.

"Laine, if you want to get out of this big hole, you need to stop digging," Tucker warned her. "He doesn't want to take an innocent woman."

"Innocent?" the guy growled. "Yeah, right. You might wanta check your facts there, bud. She's a lot of things, but innocent ain't one of them."

Tucker's glare faded, and for a split second he got a confused look on his face. "What the heck does that mean?"

She couldn't be sure, but Laine thought the guy might be smiling. "It means you need to ask her."

"I'd rather stop you," Tucker fired back. "The questions and answers can come later."

If she made it out of this, and it was a big if, then she obviously had some explaining to do. But for now, Laine had to get the gunman away from the babies.

"Okay," the gunman finally said, "it's just you and me, darlin'. And if you try anything funny, your cowboy here is gonna be the one who pays. Got that?"

That was the only warning Laine got before the man hooked his arm around her neck. He kept the gun pressed to her head.

"Just so you know, cowboy," the man drawled. "I got no problem putting a bullet in her, or you for that matter, so my advice is for you to back off."

Tucker stayed put. But the man maneuvered her forward, each step taking him farther away from the babies. She couldn't see them, but they definitely weren't asleep. Laine could hear them making some whimpering sounds, and she prayed everything was okay.

"This way." Her captor didn't lead her toward the kitchen door, where Tucker's sister was likely holding his comrades. Instead, he dragged her forward, which meant they'd have to go right past Tucker.

Tucker adjusted, moving just out of the guy's reach, but his gun stayed trained on him.

"You're not going to get far on foot," Tucker said. "Especially not with the storm moving in."

The man shook his head. "Won't need to go far."

Maybe because he had a vehicle stashed nearby. But more likely it was because he intended to kill her once he'd used her to escape.

No way would he want to keep her alive, since she'd witnessed the murder.

Even if he hadn't been the one to pull the trigger, he would still be charged as an accessory, which carried the same sentence. He was looking at the death penalty if she stayed alive and could testify against him.

Behind her, the babies began to cry. She desperately wanted to go to them and try to comfort them, but each step she took kept the killer away from them. That's why

Laine didn't resist when the goon practically dragged her past Tucker and toward the front of the house.

Tucker followed, of course. Using the furniture for cover along the way, he kept his attention pinned to the man. They went through the small dining area and into the living room. Without taking the gun from her head, he reached behind him and opened the front door.

Laine immediately felt the dampness of the rain, and even over the sound of it on the tin roof and the babies' cries, she heard something else. Sirens in the distance.

Backup was on the way.

The man's arm stiffened, and he mumbled some profanity. Still, that didn't stop him maneuvering her onto the porch with him.

There were six limestone steps leading down into the yard. A fence and gate, too, and some woods on the other side of the narrow road.

Those woods were no doubt where he intended to take her. And kill her. That meant she had to do something in the next few seconds.

But what?

She looked at Tucker to see if he could give her a suggestion, but he only shook his head. "Sooner or later, this clown will make a mistake, and I'll take the kill shot," Tucker said.

"You wish," the guy growled.

His choke hold on her neck got even tighter, and he began to back down the steps with her. Escaping would take precious time, and with sirens moving closer with each passing moment, Laine could feel the gunman's muscles getting tenser.

He was trapped.

"Maybe you could get a plea bargain," she suggested.

"Maybe you could shut up!"

The moment he cleared the steps, the rain began to swipe at them. Either the rain was cold for September, or it was just her nerves, but Laine immediately started shivering. Unlike Tucker. He was using the doorjamb for cover, but there were no signs that this was anything but routine for him.

Again, the man reached behind them and opened the gate, pulling her through the opening and onto the road. Because of the way he was holding her, she couldn't turn her head, but from the corner of her eye, she saw flashes of blue lights approaching.

It wouldn't be long before backup was in place and ready to help, but Laine didn't know if that would make the situation better or worse. She could feel her captor's anxiety soaring even higher.

The man continued to move, dragging her across the road and directly toward the woods. He didn't stop even when a Sweetwater Springs cruiser braked a few yards away. Colt got out, using the car door for cover, and took aim at her captor. Too bad Colt didn't have any better chance than Tucker did.

Just up the road from the cruiser, there was another set of lights and a siren. An ambulance. However, unlike Colt, the driver stayed back, no doubt waiting until it was safe enough to approach.

"If you get a shot, take it," Tucker told his brother.

"Yeah, do that," the man snarled. "It's a good way to get the shrink here killed. I'm thinking if you shoot me, my trigger finger will automatically tense up. And boom, there she goes."

Laine's shoes sank into the ground when he dragged her off the road and onto the soft shoulder. Just a few steps from the woods. It was now or never. If she didn't try to do something, he'd escape with her.

It was a huge risk, but Laine drew back her elbow and rammed it into his stomach. He cursed at her, calling her a name, and she jabbed him again. All the while, she braced herself in case he chose to retaliate.

He did.

The man pulled the trigger, and the pain immediately crashed through her head.

Laine nearly went to her knees. It took a moment—one terrifying moment—to realize he hadn't shot her. The pain was from the excruciating noise of the bullet being fired so close to her ear. But Laine felt no relief at being spared, because she had no idea where that bullet had landed.

Tucker jumped to the side, still ready to return fire. He didn't appear to be hurt. Neither was Colt. But the shot could have gone into the house. That gave her a much-needed jolt of adrenaline, and she started fighting. At least if he shot her, Tucker would be able to kill the guy.

"This isn't over," he growled.

He shoved her, hard. So hard that Laine stumbled forward and fell at the edge of the road.

"Stay down, Laine!" Tucker warned her, a split second before he pulled the trigger.

Tucker scrambled to the ground near her, but he lifted his hand to fire again. Laine tried to see if he'd managed to shoot the guy, but Tucker pushed her right back down.

Then he cursed.

"He's getting away," Tucker mumbled.

Laine's first reaction to that was, *No!* But at least if he was running, it meant he wouldn't be firing shots into the house. Of course, the downside to that was that if he escaped, he could come after her and the babies again.

"Be careful," Tucker said, and it took her a moment to realize why he'd issued that warning. It was meant for his brother.

With his gun ready, Colt bolted from the side of the cruiser and went after the man.

"The babies," Laine reminded him. "They're in the house alone." And while Tucker had said that his sister had contained the other two men, they could always try to escape and go inside to take the newborns.

Tucker pulled her right back down when she tried to get up, and he kept his attention pinned to the woods where Colt had disappeared. The seconds crawled by. No sounds. No shots. The gunshot had dulled her hearing, but she could feel the steady throb of her heartbeat crashing in her ears.

"Move fast," Tucker finally said, and he stood, pulling her to her feet.

Laine didn't even have time to regain her balance before he started running with her toward the house. Tucker got her up the steps and inside, and then he shut the door.

The babies were still crying, and Laine tried to go to them. Again Tucker moved in front to stop her. He was still the vigilant lawman, his gaze still firing all around.

Mercy, was there another gunman in the house?

They moved slowly, with Tucker checking every corner until they worked their way to the kitchen.

"Stay here," he insisted.

With his gun ready, he first looked out the kitchen window where his sister and the other two men still were. Everything must have been okay there because he started to check out the rest of the house.

Laine hurried to the babies to make sure they were okay. They appeared to be. Since she was soaked to the bone, she put the blanket between the babies and her wet clothes before she scooped them into her arms.

Even though they were too young to understand, they were perhaps sensing the horrible nightmare that'd just happened. She tried rocking them so they would stop crying and she could hear what was going on in the house.

It seemed to take an eternity for Tucker to return, and when she saw him, Laine released the breath she'd been holding. He no longer had his gun raised, and there was some relief in his eyes.

"Are you okay?" he asked. "Did he hurt you?"

"I'm fine," Laine lied. Her scrapes and bruises would all be minor, but it might take a lifetime or two to feel *fine*.

His phone rang, and he yanked it from his pocket. "It's Colt," he relayed to her, and he answered it.

Laine couldn't hear what his brother was saying, but she knew from his expression that it wasn't good news. "The rain washed away the tracks," Tucker explained, a muscle flickering in his jaw.

So they'd lost him.

Laine couldn't stop the sound from making its way through her throat. This wasn't over. The babies still weren't safe.

"We'll get a CSI team out to look for anything to indicate where he's heading," Tucker added, though he didn't sound convinced that it would do any good.

The man probably had a vehicle stashed nearby and was already long gone.

Tucker didn't stay in the pantry. Instead, he went to the back door, opened it and kept watch over the two gunmen they had managed to capture. He also motioned toward the ambulance, obviously giving them the go-ahead to come closer to the house. After he'd done that, he glanced back at her, and this time, there was no relief anywhere on his face.

Just questions.

Well, one question anyway.

"What the heck was that clown talking about back there?" Tucker asked.

Laine knew exactly what Tucker was referring to, and she remembered every word of what the man had said.

You might wanta check your facts there, bud. She's a lot of things, but innocent ain't one of them.

She opened her mouth. Closed it. Shook her head. Obviously that reaction didn't please Tucker, because he mumbled some profanity and snapped back around to face her.

"What did he mean?" Tucker demanded. "And what the heck are you really doing here?"

Chapter Five

Tucker had a dozen other things that he should be doing. For one thing, he should be helping Rayanne guard the two dirtbags she had facedown and cuffed on the ground in the drenching rain. For another, he needed to watch for Colt to make his way back to the house so they could transport the prisoners—one to the jail and the other to the hospital.

Instead, here he was questioning Laine.

And it was obvious from her reaction that she had something to tell him that he didn't want to hear.

"Did you lie to me when you said a woman had been killed?" he demanded.

"No!" She struggled to get to her feet. It wasn't easy with two crying, squirming babies in her arms. "I saw her, and they murdered her."

She sounded convincing enough, but Tucker would wait for some evidence. Still, it wasn't much of a stretch to believe it now that the attack had happened here. Those goons had been trying to cover up something, that was for sure.

"Then, what did the man mean about you not being innocent?" Tucker pressed.

She swallowed hard. "Remember when you had me fired from the undercover investigation?"

He nearly reminded her again that he'd merely asked that she be reassigned because of their old baggage. His supervisor had agreed with him. End of story.

Except it obviously wasn't.

"What'd you do?" Tucker asked, once he got his teeth unclenched.

"The case was important to me," she said, her chin coming up in a defiant pose. Just as quickly, it came down, and she dodged his gaze. "I didn't want to just drop it because you and I couldn't get along. I wanted to help find those women and babies."

Yeah, so had he.

By all accounts, there were dozens of missing women and babies lost in the maze of a massive black-market baby ring. Not just illegal adoptions, but illegal surrogacies, as well. Even pregnant women who were kidnapped until their babies were born, at which point the new mothers were murdered.

Cooper had helped to uncover and shut down a baby farm. That was a start. But there was evidence of many other farms.

And just as many cold-blooded killers operating them.

"Please tell me you didn't do anything dangerous or stupid," Tucker said.

Laine sure didn't jump to tell him that she hadn't. Which meant she had.

Tucker groaned. "What'd you do?" he repeated.

"I used some of the criminal informant contacts from the investigation to try to find another baby farm." She paused, her gaze coming back to his. "And I found one."

"Where?" But unfortunately Tucker had to wave off her answer when he heard a soft whistle.

It was Colt.

And the whistle was a signal they'd used since they were kids playing cops and robbers. It was just to let Tucker know he was approaching so he wouldn't mistake him for a bad guy. Or in this case, shoot him.

Tucker glanced back and spotted Colt making his way across the road. His brother wasn't headed inside the house with them, but rather toward Rayanne and the prisoners.

"What's wrong?" Laine asked, and despite having both arms filled with babies, she hurried to the door beside Tucker and looked out. The medics were lifting the wounded prisoner into the ambulance.

"Rayanne, can you ride in the ambulance and keep an eye on this guy?" Tucker asked. "Colt and I will get someone else there shortly, but first I need to settle some things with Laine."

"Laine?" she repeated in an unfriendly tone. "As in Laine Braddock?"

Tucker nodded, knowing the confirmation wasn't going to help the venom in Rayanne's eyes. Unlike Rayanne, he didn't care much about their mother's upcoming trial, but he didn't want his dad and brothers dragged into it. The Braddocks, especially Laine's mother, had threatened to do just that. She'd tossed around plenty of accusations about obstruction of justice and tampering with evidence.

All unfounded and untrue.

So basically Tucker was caught in the middle. Not a comfortable place to be, especially with Laine right by his side and an estranged sister snarling at both of them.

"You mean you called me out here to save her sorry butt?" Rayanne spat out.

"Not just her," Tucker explained. "She had two newborns with her. Even you wouldn't refuse to help little babies."

Despite the rain and storm winds lashing at her, Rayanne stood there, glaring at him. Glaring at Laine, too, since she was now peering over Tucker's shoulder.

"Let me guess," Rayanne snapped, shifting her glare back to Tucker. "They're your kids?"

Now it was time for Tucker to give her an eye roll. "I'm not exactly the daddy type, now, am I? No, these are babies that Laine rescued."

He hoped.

If he was to believe anything their attacker said, then it was a strong possibility that Laine hadn't told him the truth about the babies. Or about anything else.

Still grumbling something under her breath, Rayanne followed the medics into the ambulance.

"Thank you for helping," Laine called out to her. Not a good thing to say. Anything at this point would have been unwise, especially anything coming from Laine, because it earned her another nasty glare from Rayanne.

"I'll call for more backup," Colt said, getting the second man into his cruiser. "I'm guessing Laine and the babies need a doctor, too?"

"Yeah." At least for a checkup. "I'll drive them to the hospital."

"But what about the missing gunman?" Laine asked the moment Tucker shut the door. "He could follow us into town and attack us again."

"He could, but it's my guess he's in regroup mode. And that means you need to tell me everything you did to cause these goons to come after you. Start with that criminal informant who helped you find the baby farm."

Tucker motioned for her to start talking while he went to the doors and locked them. He didn't intend to be in the house for long, but he also wanted to take a few precautions in case he was wrong about his regroup theory.

Laine didn't jump to answer, something that put a knot the size of Texas in his gut. Tucker motioned for her to get on with it.

"The criminal informant was Gerry Farrow, and he took me to the baby farm," Laine finally said. "He made me wear a blindfold so I couldn't see where we were going, and he drove around for a long time. In circles, I'm sure, so I wouldn't be able to find the place later."

His groan didn't help hush the babies any. "And you thought it was a good idea for a civilian to go walking into something like that with a person you didn't even know if you could trust?"

She glanced away again. "I wanted to find those pregnant captives and save them. I didn't want their babies sold like cattle. And I thought I had a better chance of getting in there than the cops, Rangers or FBI." Laine paused. "I saw two women, including the one who was killed in the parking lot."

Oh, man. "Funny you didn't mention that connection right off the bat. You've told the FBI all of this?"

"I told them about the baby farm, but by the time we were able to work out where it was, it was too late. When they got there, the guards and the pregnant women were all gone."

No surprise there. "You were lucky those guards didn't kill you at the farm."

She made a soft sound of agreement. "I pretended to be a potential buyer for one of the babies."

"And they believed you?" Tucker asked, not bothering to hold back on the skeptical tone in his voice. He motioned for her to follow him to the bedroom so he could do something about their wet clothes.

Laine nodded. Then she lifted her shoulder. "They didn't try to kill me, anyway. They made some calls, did a quick background check and learned that I had indeed been trying to adopt."

Tucker hadn't thought there could be any more surprises today, but he'd been wrong. "You did a fake adoption request for the sake of the investigation?"

"No," she snapped. That put some fire in her ice-blue eyes, but it quickly cooled down. "I can't have children, so I've been trying to adopt for months now."

In a town the size of Sweetwater Springs, it was hard to keep secrets, but Laine had obviously managed to keep that one.

And it caused him to curse again.

"You gave those guards your real name?" The babies didn't like his near shout, and they fussed even louder.

"I figured that was the fastest way to get them to believe I was really there looking for a baby."

There were so many things wrong with that comment that Tucker didn't know where to start. "So, you let them believe you were a customer willing to break the law. Obviously that didn't work out so well, did it?"

"Obviously," she mumbled. "One of the guards told me they'd be in touch, and we left. But they did follow us."

Of course they did.

Tucker rummaged through his closet, locating some dry clothes for himself and a white button-up shirt for

Laine. He dropped it all on the dresser. He also maneuvered her away from the window and helped her put the babies on the bed so she could change.

"They followed you to your office?" he asked.

But he darn near forgot the question when Laine shucked off her wet top. She had on a lacy white bra, but the rain had practically made it see-through.

This wasn't the kid he'd kissed in his granddaddy's kitchen.

Nope. Laine was a fully grown woman now, with real curves he had no business gawking at. She obviously felt the same because she scowled when she noticed where his attention had landed.

"Sorry, I forgot we had this…connection between us," she mumbled.

"There's nothing between us," Tucker jumped to say.

Too bad it was a big fat lie. One that he had zero intention of straightening out. He yanked off his shirt as if he'd waged war on it.

"To answer your question—no, the guards didn't follow me," she snapped.

Because his mind still wasn't where it should be, it took him a moment to remember the question—had the guards followed the CI and her back to her office?

"How would you know if they'd followed you there or not?" he pressed.

Laine huffed, snatched up the shirt. The moment she had it on, she eased down on the bed beside the babies, trying to comfort them. "The CI made sure of that. He drove around with me until they stopped following us, and he said it was safe."

"Well, he was clearly wrong about that, wasn't he?" He

huffed. "Remember, there are two things that make a CI. Being a paid informant and being a criminal."

"What does that mean?"

Her gaze snapped back to his. Probably something she wished she could take back, because Tucker had already stripped down to his boxers. Proving that she was the most stubborn woman in the whole state of Texas, she didn't look away.

"It means the CI could have been looking for a way to earn a few bucks. He could have gone back to the baby farm and told them that he was suspicious of you and that you needed to be taken care of."

Laine opened her mouth, no doubt to deny that, but then she shook her head. Her eyes widened, and she touched her fingers to her mouth. "Oh, God."

"Yeah, *oh, God,*" he mumbled. "You took a serious risk going out there, going anywhere, with that idiot. And even if he was truly trying to help, he put your neck right on the line by taking you into a hornet's nest."

He could have continued his tirade for several more minutes, but his phone rang, and Tucker saw Reed's name on the screen. He hoped the deputy had some good news, because they sure as heck needed it. He hit the speaker button so he could take the call and finish dressing.

"I was just out at the parking lot behind Laine's office," Reed said. "I found some blood."

Tucker cursed, not because he hadn't expected the news. After everything Laine had told him, he had, but that blood was confirmation they were dealing with killers and not just some loons out to kidnap a pair of newborns.

"There's not much blood left because it's raining hard," Reed went on. "Still, I found some spots on the corner of the building beneath the eaves. Found a pacifier, too. Hard to tell, but it might have a fingerprint on it. DNA, too, if the rain hasn't gotten to it."

"Send it and the blood sample to the Ranger lab for immediate processing," Tucker instructed. He glanced at the babies. He needed to know who the dead woman was so he could locate the babies' next of kin.

"Any security cameras nearby?" Tucker asked. "Maybe we can get footage of what happened. In case we don't have a print, we might be able to get some photos of her."

And photos of her killers, as well.

After all, Laine had said they'd gotten out of the car to retrieve the body, and that meant a camera could show the murder in progress.

"Maybe," Reed answered. "That new jewelry store up the street has cameras. Don't know if the angles are right, but I'll call them while I'm driving out to check Laine's car for prints."

"Make the call, but skip the fingerprints on the car for now." With the rain, it was probably a lost cause anyway. Besides, he had something more important for Reed to do. "Come out to my place. I'd like someone close by in case things get ugly again."

That didn't help soothe any of the tension from Laine's face. It wouldn't help soothe his, either, but it was a precaution Tucker needed to take.

Not just for Laine, but for those babies.

The moment he finished the call with Reed, Laine said, "The dead woman could have heard the guards or the CI mention me. She could have heard my name, and that's why she called me."

Yeah, Laine's phone number wouldn't have been hard to find. But why had the woman thought she could trust

Laine? And how the heck had she gotten away from the baby farm and into town?

"She probably heard more than just your name," Tucker explained. "She likely heard the guards say that they didn't trust you, that you could be working for the cops."

Of course that meant assuming the woman was totally innocent in all of this. And that she was indeed trying to protect her babies. But maybe the men killed her for a different reason, and finding that reason would only be possible if they first learned her identity. Hopefully the blood Reed had found would help with that.

"Come on." Tucker grabbed some towels from the adjoining bathroom. "Reed will be here soon, and I need to get the babies and you to the hospital for checkups."

Laine gave a shaky nod, probably because she wasn't thrilled about going outside, where the missing gunman might spot her. "And then what?"

"Protective custody. A safe house."

Another nod. She wrapped the babies each in the towels. Not ideal cover, but it was better than using the damp blanket Laine had used to hold them earlier.

"Can you manage to carry both of them?" he asked. It was a strange question, because she'd carried them across the pasture to get to his house, but she was more shaken up now. After all, she'd just come darn close to dying.

"Yes." And her attention went to the belt holster he'd just put on. Then to the backup weapon he slid into the back of his jeans.

"I'll pull the truck right up to the steps," he assured her. "By the time we make it to the road, Reed should be here."

Tucker had barely made it a step before he heard the sound of a car engine. He hurried to the front window, expecting to see Reed's truck, but it was a black four-door sedan.

"What's wrong?" Laine asked, obviously noticing the change in his body language.

"Maybe nothing." Of course, it felt like something since it could be their attacker returning.

However, the man who stepped out from the car wasn't the escaped gunman. This guy was in his late twenties and had pale blond hair. He was wearing a dark gray suit, with no sign of a weapon. He ducked his head against the storm and ran toward the porch.

The man wasn't alone. There was someone else in the car, but Tucker could only make out a silhouette because of the rain-streaked windows.

"You know him?" Laine asked.

"No. Wait here and stay away from the windows." Tucker didn't move until she had the babies back by the bed before he drew his gun and started for the door. Their visitor knocked just as he got there. He swung open the door and asked the guy to identify himself.

"Martin Hague," the man said, but his voice trailed off to nothing but breath when he spotted Tucker's gun. "I heard on the drive over that you'd had some trouble out here."

"Who'd you hear it from?" Tucker demanded, and he didn't even try to sound friendly.

"A nurse who works at the hospital. Someone from the ambulance called ahead and said they were bringing in a man who'd been wounded here. Good thing I was already on my way to your place."

"Who the heck are you?" Yet another demand.

"Oh, I'm from social services." He reached for his pocket, but he stopped when Tucker lifted his gun. "Just getting my ID." He didn't continue until Tucker gave him the nod, and then he extracted a leather case with his credentials.

It looked official, but Tucker wasn't taking any chances. He didn't lower his gun. "What do you want?"

"I'm a social worker," Hague said, as if the answer were obvious.

He took out a piece of paper and handed it to Tucker just as the other person stepped from the car. A man wearing a uniform and badge that Tucker instantly recognized. He was a Department of Public Safety officer.

"That paper should clarify everything for you," Hague said. "We're here to take the babies."

Chapter Six

Laine stayed away from the windows as Tucker had ordered, but because the babies had finally stopped fussing, she had no trouble understanding what Martin Hague had just said.

He was taking the babies.

She clutched them to her and kept listening. Laine couldn't hear every word they said, but she detected the concern in Tucker's voice. After everything they'd been through, that was probably normal, but this didn't feel normal to her.

Sweet heaven.

Laine hoped that feeling wasn't because she was starting to get attached to the babies. They weren't hers, and she couldn't keep them. Even if it squeezed at her heart to think of handing them over to this social worker.

"You don't have a court order?" Tucker asked.

That got her attention. Laine slipped out of the bedroom and into the living room so she could try to figure out what was going on.

"It's standard procedure to take minors into our protective custody when there's the possibility of danger," Hague argued. "And from what I've learned, there's also a question of the infants' paternity."

"They're already in protective custody," Tucker snapped. *"Mine.* And this is an active crime scene. The babies' clothes need to be processed for evidence. And how the devil did you find out the babies were even here?"

"Your brother, Deputy Colt McKinnon, reported that two babies had been found. We had another anonymous report that a woman had fled an abusive situation with her newborn twins."

Laine inched closer, and as if he sensed she was there, Hague's attention zoomed past Tucker and landed on her.

Or rather it landed on the babies.

"Are they all right? Were they hurt?" Hague moved as if to step around Tucker, but Tucker stepped directly in front of the babies, blocking Hague's path.

"They're fine," Tucker growled. "Their mother, maybe not so much. It's possible she was murdered, and I need to do DNA tests on the babies to determine who they are and if they're connected to the woman in question."

Hague seemed to ignore all of that. He kept his attention fastened to Laine. "You're the one who took them?"

"I *rescued* them." Laine could instantly see why Tucker was stonewalling this man. Maybe it was just because he was inexperienced, but there was something off about him.

"Your Ranger friend seems to think he has jurisdiction here," Hague said to her, aiming a glare at Tucker.

Tucker aimed one right back at him. He was far better at glaring than their guest. "Her Ranger friend is right. Someone just tried to kill us." He pointed to the woods across from the house. "Someone who's no doubt hiding out in there somewhere. Maybe with a long-range rifle."

Hague cast an uneasy glance over his shoulder before

his gaze whipped back to Tucker. "How soon will you release the babies?"

"When I'm finished with them and when you have that court order." Tucker stepped back and slammed the door in the man's face.

"You don't trust him?" Laine asked, inching closer so she could make sure Hague actually left. He did. The man stormed down the porch steps and got back in the car. He sped away much too fast considering the sopping wet roads.

"Right now I don't trust anyone."

Possibly even Laine herself. After all, she'd withheld information about visiting that baby farm. But then Tucker'd had plenty of reasons to distrust her before that.

He took out his phone and sent off a text. Laine only got a glimpse of it, but it appeared that Tucker was asking someone to do a background check on Martin Hague. A few days before, that would have seemed like overkill.

Now, nothing seemed to fall into that category.

"Change of plans," Tucker said. "I'll call Dr. Howland and ask him to come out and examine the babies and you. Not here, though. I'm taking the three of you to the main house where I'll have some help protecting you."

Laine was certain that he'd lost his mind. Now here was an example of overkill, or at least of a really bad idea.

"With your family?" She shook her head, not waiting for him to answer. "Tucker, they hate me. *You* hate me."

For some stupid reason she got a flash of the expression on his face when he'd seen her changing into the dry clothes. It was only a glimpse of this unwanted heat between them, but a glimpse had been enough to know.

"Okay, maybe you don't completely hate me," she amended, "but you certainly don't want me there."

No heated look this time. Just a flat one that let her know she'd stated the obvious. Before Laine could continue the argument, he took out his phone and made a call.

"Mary," he said when someone answered. Mary Larkin had been the McKinnon housekeeper for as long as Laine could remember.

Yet another person who wouldn't want Laine there.

"I've got a situation. Send someone out to pick up bottles, formula, diapers and anything else newborns need. I'll explain when I get there. Oh, and Laine Braddock will be with me…. Yeah, I know," he added a moment later. "Like I said, I'll explain everything."

"Still convinced that taking me there is a good idea?" Laine challenged when he ended the call.

"The house has a security system," he said, obviously ignoring her argument. "The ranch hands can help guard the place."

"But your family—"

"Cooper and his wife aren't there. They're on their honeymoon, and their son, Liam, is staying with his grandmother in Austin. Jewell's in jail, as you well know, and my sister Rosalie and Jewell's stepson, Seth, are in the guesthouse."

"That leaves your father and Rayanne," she immediately reminded him.

"My father won't object to me keeping you safe. I hope," he added. "And Rayanne's opinion doesn't count. She's only living in the house to irritate the rest of us and to rub it in our faces that it's her house, too."

Laine couldn't argue with the reason Rayanne was staying at the ranch. It was pretty much what she'd heard around town, though that wouldn't help with Laine's own situation.

But what would?

She couldn't take the babies and go to her place. The missing gunman could easily find her there. She definitely didn't want to turn the babies over to Hague, either. Not until Tucker and she had figured out what was going on. Her brother was the county sheriff, but he, too, was out of town and wouldn't be back for days.

That left her hiring a bodyguard of some kind.

But that would take time, and she didn't have much of that. It wouldn't be long before the babies would need to be fed, and Tucker had already made plans for that. So for now, Tucker and his family seemed to be her best short-term option.

Heaven help her.

"How long will we have to stay there?" she asked.

"Probably a lot longer than either of us want."

Heck, two minutes would qualify as way too long.

Tucker motioned for them to get moving, but then Laine stopped when her phone buzzed. She tried to balance the babies so she could retrieve her phone from her jeans pocket. She'd managed it earlier with one baby in her arms, but it wasn't possible with two.

Since the call could be important, she handed the infants to Tucker. He didn't scowl, but he did get the look of a man who was way out of his element. He shook his head and tried to hand them back, but Laine ignored him and checked the caller ID on the screen.

It was her mother, Carla.

It wasn't a call that Laine wanted to take. Their relationship was shaky at best, but by now news of the shooting was likely all over town, and her mom had heard about it.

"I'm all right," Laine answered right off the bat.

"Glad to hear that, but why in the world were you out at Tucker McKinnon's place?"

"Who told you I was at Tucker's?" she asked.

"Your sister. One of her reporter friends gave her the details of what happened. She's not happy about you being there, either, so why'd you go running to the McKinnons?"

"It's a long story." And one that she didn't want to discuss with anyone. Well, with anyone but Tucker. Strange that they were finally on the same side about something. "I'll call you later and tell you all about it—"

"A McKinnon killed your father," Carla snapped. "Don't you forget that."

Laine would have a harder time forgetting how to breathe. "I won't be here much longer." And when her mother's tirade continued, Laine worked in a hasty good-bye and pressed the end call button.

She glanced up at Tucker, expecting him to be in a hurry to hand off the babies, but he was no longer looking at the babies as if they were some alien creatures. The corner of his mouth had lifted, and both babies were quietly staring at him. He'd told his sister that he wasn't the fatherly type, but those babies suddenly looked very comfortable in his arms.

"Your mother's not happy about you being here," Tucker commented. He obviously hadn't needed to hear the conversation to know what'd taken place.

Laine made a sound of agreement. "You've no doubt heard the story of Jewell and my father from a different perspective than I have."

"But with the same results. Whitt's dead, and everything points to my mother having killed him. If she did it, then she'll pay."

"If?" Laine repeated. "You're not certain she killed him? Because this is the first I'm hearing about any doubts from you."

"Doesn't matter what I think. I just want her and the kids that she raised to be out of our lives." No longer smiling, he handed the babies back to her. "But I'm glad Rayanne was there to help."

Yes, without her, Tucker and she might be dead and the babies stolen.

"Let's go," Tucker said, and he led her into the kitchen. "Move fast and stay low," he added before he darted out into the rain to get into his truck.

He backed it up and then pulled it close until the passenger's side was almost right against the steps. He threw open the door and motioned for her to hurry.

She did.

Laine didn't want to be out in the open any longer than necessary, for fear the gunman was watching them. The moment she was inside, Tucker took off. Not speeding, as Hague had done. But driving at a slow, cautious pace, probably because they didn't have infant seats for the babies.

Tucker kept watch, his gaze firing all around, and Laine slipped low down in the seat. Despite what was waiting for her inside, she was glad when the massive white house came into view.

The place looked different. Bigger. And there were more barns and other outbuildings than she remembered. About thirty yards from the main house, another structure was going up.

"Cooper's new place," Tucker explained, following her gaze.

It made sense that his brother would want his own

house. After all, Cooper didn't just have a wife now. He was also the father of a toddler boy. Yet another McKinnon male who would no doubt grow up to hate her and her family.

Nope, she didn't feel one bit welcome.

"I'll run background checks on all the construction crew working on Cooper's house," Tucker added.

Good. Because it seemed an easy way for whoever was after them to get onto the grounds. They already had enough security issues without adding that to the mix.

As Tucker had done at his place, he parked right next to the porch. Mary immediately threw open the door and helped them into the foyer. It'd been a while since Laine had seen the woman, but she hadn't changed much, except she now had some threads of gray in her auburn hair.

"The diapers and formula will be here soon," Mary said. The look she gave Laine was frosty, but that frost didn't extend to the babies. Mary smiled and eased the newborn girl into her arms.

Laine hadn't realized just how much her arms were aching until Mary did that, but Laine still wanted to snatch the baby back. To protect both of them. Too bad she was shaking too much to do that. If Tucker hadn't been holding on to her arm, her legs might have buckled.

"This way." He took her into the adjoining living room and forced her to sit on a sofa. In the same motion, he pulled out his phone. "Colt," he said, putting the call on speaker. "Please tell me the fake cops have made a full confession so I can arrest someone."

"No confessions. In fact, they've both lawyered up, and the one in the hospital isn't saying a word. But I did get something from the one we're holding at the jail. His name isn't Hacker. It's Gene Buford. The guy had a record, so I got a match when I fingerprinted him. Anyway, he had three photos in his pocket. One was of Laine, and it looks like it was taken with a long-range camera at some kind of ranch."

"The baby farm," she said. She hadn't seen anyone snap her photo, but there had no doubt been security cameras. "Is one of the other pictures of a blonde woman?"

"Yes. Thin face, short choppy hair."

Laine pulled in her breath. "That sounds like the woman who was killed behind my office."

"That's what I figured. It's the third one that's confusing me. It's a picture of you, Tucker."

"Tucker?" Laine repeated.

She shook her head. Why did the men have a photo of him? There was no way they could have guessed she would have fled to his house. Heck, she hadn't even known that was where she'd been headed until she was actually on the road.

"Send me the photo of the woman," Tucker insisted.

It took several moments for the photo to load on the screen, and Laine got up to have a better look. It was the woman, all right, and just like that, the sickening memories of the shooting returned. The sound of the shots. The blood. The sheer violence of it all.

But she wasn't the only one who had a reaction.

Tucker groaned softly.

"You know her?" Laine asked.

Tucker nodded. "Yeah. Her name's Dawn Cowen." A muscle flickered in his jaw. "And I'm the reason she's dead."

Chapter Seven

Tucker stood in the shower of one of the ranch's guest bathrooms and let the scalding water slam against him. It didn't help. Nothing would. It was his fault that a woman was dead, and no amount of hot water was going to fix that.

The images of Dawn Cowen slammed against him, too. Yeah, she'd been mixed up at times, but all in all she was a good criminal informant, and she'd trusted him.

A big mistake on her part.

Because Tucker had been the one to ask her to assist with the baby farms investigation. And she had. Dawn had managed to get some information that had helped the FBI and Rangers find one of the farms. She had probably saved a life or two.

But not her own.

Someone was going to pay for that, but Tucker figured no one was going to pay as hard as he was. How the heck was he supposed to live with this? A woman was not only dead, but those two babies were now motherless because of him.

Cursing himself and this god-awful situation, he stepped from the shower, dried off and pulled on his jeans.

He was in midzip when he went back into his bedroom…
and quickly realized he wasn't alone.

Laine was sitting on his bed. "Before you say anything, consider just how uncomfortable I must have been
to choose coming up here to your bedroom over being
downstairs with the others."

Tucker smiled, not out of amusement, but because he
was relieved that she wasn't there to dump more bad news
on him. "Where are the babies?"

She hitched her thumb toward the hallway outside his
open door. "Sleeping in their bassinet in the kitchen. Rosalie offered to help watch them again. She's, uh, nice."

"Yeah." It'd been hard to find fault with that particular
sister. Unlike Rayanne, she didn't have a constant surly attitude. "Rosalie's own baby was kidnapped a while back.
From what she's said, she loves kids."

Good thing, too, because it'd required a lot of help to
take care of the babies. Neither Laine nor he had slept
more than an hour's stretch at a time, and it'd taken all of
them—Mary, Rosalie, Laine and him—just to get through
the night.

Tucker wasn't sure how parents managed it. The babies
might be cute and little, but they sure cried a lot. When
they weren't doing that, they drank formula, soiled their
diapers and slept, but not for any length of time.

He'd become an overnight expert in diapering a baby
boy. It required a lot more quickness and dexterity than
he'd ever figured.

Laine stood, her gaze starting at his face and going to
his zipper. Forgetting that he was still partially dressed,
he zipped up and located a shirt he'd had brought over
from his house.

Best not to stand around half-naked with Laine.

His nerves were raw. He was bone-tired. And for just a moment he allowed himself to think of how good and distracting it would feel to put his mouth on hers.

Good, yes. Distracting? That, too. But he'd end up paying a high price for that kind of kiss. Heck, he'd end up paying just for thinking about kissing her.

And for the way she snagged his attention.

No jeans for Laine today. She was wearing a pale green dress that skimmed her body and showed plenty of leg. No doubt an outfit that Reed had picked up from her house and brought out to the ranch. The deputy had obviously brought her some makeup, too, but the dark circles beneath her eyes let him know that she was just as sleep-deprived as he was.

"Want to talk about Dawn Cowen?" she asked, rubbing her hands down the sides of her dress.

He lifted his shoulder and sat on the other side of the bed so he could pull on his boots. "Not much to tell that you don't already know. She worked for me as a criminal informant, and she'd be alive if it weren't for the baby farm investigation."

"Maybe." She paused, fidgeting with her dress some more. "I read the report on her that was sitting on the desk of the office you're using downstairs—"

That brought him to his feet. "You did what?"

"I read it," she admitted, not backing down or even issuing a mild apology for snooping around. "A year ago she was helping you on a case, but then she stopped because she got pregnant."

"Obviously she didn't stop. She was probably kidnapped and held all these months at the baby farm. Months when I didn't bother checking on her."

"You couldn't have known what'd happened to her," Laine said.

"When I didn't hear from her, I should have guessed."

"Yes, because of the ESP that all you Texas Rangers have. I've heard it's standard issue, along with the white Stetson, boots, badge and jeans."

They exchanged flat looks, and Laine was the first to glance away.

"Besides," she continued, "if we're playing the blame game, then Dawn wouldn't have come literally running to my office if it weren't for the unauthorized visit the CI and I made to the baby farm."

"She obviously thought she could trust you. She sure as heck didn't come to me."

And that would haunt him for eternity. Most women held captive at the baby farms were murdered shortly after they delivered. Dawn must have been terrified, not just for her own life but for her newborn children.

Well, maybe they were both hers.

Dawn had indeed been pregnant, but Tucker couldn't rule out that maybe only one of them was hers and the other was one she'd managed to rescue.

"There wasn't anything in your report about Dawn being married or involved with anyone," Laine tossed out.

"The babies aren't mine, if that's what you're thinking."

"I didn't think that. If there'd been any possibility they were yours, you would have said something last night. And you would've given them better nicknames," she added.

It was no doubt her attempt to lighten things up some. It didn't work. Nothing would. But she was right—if they'd been his, he might have called them something better than Jack and Jill.

Okay, now he smiled. "Don't try to make this easier on me," he snarled.

She nodded as if taking that warning as gospel. Hesitated. Then huffed. "I need to figure out some other place to go. Someplace safe, of course."

"With the babies?"

She blinked. "Well, yes. I thought I'd keep them until we figure out where they belong."

"That could be as early as today. It shouldn't be hard to find out about Dawn's romantic interest or the babies' next of kin."

Of course, once the father was indeed found, it didn't mean the babies would be safe. It was possible the people behind the baby farm would want the newborns returned.

They could also want to take their revenge on Laine.

Once they had the babies, they could use them to draw her out. And it would probably work. Any woman who would risk going to a baby farm with a CI likely wouldn't think twice about surrendering herself to save two babies.

"If you take the babies away from the ranch, you could just be putting them in more danger," Tucker reminded her. "If these goons think you can reveal anything about their operation, they won't stop coming after you."

Obviously that was something Laine already knew, but she still flinched. Maybe because hearing the threat aloud really drilled it home. Her mouth trembled a little, and Tucker saw the thin veneer covering her fear.

Ah, heck.

Tears sprang to her eyes, too. She quickly blinked them back, lifted her defiant chin, but Tucker saw something he didn't want to see.

A vulnerable woman.

Usually a woman's tears would send him running in the opposite direction, but in this case, they sent him walking. Directly toward her. To pull her into his arms.

Not the brightest idea he'd ever had.

He blamed that on this stuff going on between them. Not just the stuff with the babies and the danger, but the old baggage, too. If they'd been enemies all their lives, it would have helped, but he kept going back to that time when they'd been friends.

And more.

When he was a kid, stupider than now, he'd spent some time thinking about the two of them being together for life. Not that at age eleven he'd known what life with a girl entailed. Truth was, he'd been more focused on kissing her than on anything else.

Heck, he was still focused on it.

Laine didn't push him away. Big surprise. She looked up at him. "Ironic, huh? When you woke up yesterday morning, I'll bet you never thought we'd be voluntarily touching each other."

Tucker shook his head, hoping that would clear it. It didn't work. Maybe he should try hitting it against the wall. "Who says this is voluntary?"

A short burst of air left her mouth. Almost a laugh. Then that troubled look returned to her eyes. "It's not a good idea for us to be here alone."

"No. It's not."

There. They were in complete agreement. Still, neither of them moved a muscle. Well, he moved some. His grip tightened on her a little, and those kissing dreams returned with a vengeance.

"Besides, I'm no longer your type," she added, as if that would help.

It didn't.

However, it did cause him to temporarily scowl. "How would you know my type?"

Another huff. Soft and silky, though, not rough like his. Her breath brushed against his mouth, almost like a kiss. Almost. "Everyone in town knows. Blonde, busty and not looking for commitment."

He was sure his scowl wasn't so brief that time, but the problem was he couldn't argue with what she'd said. Besides, the reminder accomplished what Laine had likely intended.

Tucker stepped back.

He figured that she'd say something smart-mouthed to keep things light, but she didn't. For a moment Laine actually looked a little disappointed that their hugging session had ended, and that was all the more reason for him not to pick it up again.

Ever.

Even if parts of him were suggesting he do just that.

No, she wasn't blonde or overly busty, and he had no idea if she was looking for commitment or not. His guess was no, especially when it came to the likes of him.

"I should check on the babies," Laine said, and she lit out of there as if he'd set her dress on fire.

Tucker followed her because he wanted to check on them, too, and then head to the ranch office that he'd been using. While he was there, he'd see what Laine had managed to get a look at while she was snooping. He really couldn't blame her for wanting to know what was going on. Nearly getting killed was a huge motivator to finding their escaped attacker.

Laine made it to the kitchen just ahead of him, and Tucker got a glimpse of Rayanne making a hasty exit. Before doing that, however, she scowled at them. Unlike his other sister, Rosalie. She greeted them and then smiled at the babies, who were in a Moses basket on the table.

No white gowns for them that morning. Someone had dressed them in pink and blue. Cute as bugs. They were cuddled against each other, sleeping side by side.

"Sorry about that," Rosalie said, her gaze going briefly to her sister, who was storming toward the guesthouse. Too bad Rayanne wouldn't stay there. "Rayanne wasn't always like she is now."

"Hard to believe," Tucker mumbled. Rosalie and Rayanne had barely been six years old when Jewell left with them. "She had a stubborn streak even as a kid."

That streak was now a mile wide.

"Well, she was always tough," Rosalie amended. "Always trying not to show how much it hurt that she didn't have a dad. Sorry," she immediately added. "Didn't mean to bring up any bad memories."

"She had a dad," Tucker pointed out. "A stepdad."

She nodded. "And he was good to us, but Rayanne could never let go of the anger of having our father toss our mother out of her home." Rosalie winced. "Sorry, again. I keep putting my foot in my mouth this morning."

Laine gave her a pat on the arm. "We all had our lives turned upside down twenty-three years ago."

"Yeah, and they just keep on turning, don't they?" Tucker grumbled. "Like a curse or something."

There'd been nothing but trouble and danger since Jewell had come back into their lives, but since he didn't want to hurt Rosalie's feelings, Tucker kept that little revelation to himself.

Besides, he had something better to occupy his attention. The babies.

It was strange, he'd never considered baby-watching to be very interesting, but it sure was now. Maybe because he thought of himself as their protector.

Temporarily, anyway.

Tucker reached down and touched his finger to Jack's cheek. The corner of his little mouth lifted. A baby smile that Laine and Rosalie had already assured him was just gas. Tucker figured they were wrong.

Hey, a kid who could pee with that kind of accuracy certainly could manage a smile, couldn't he?

"There is something you should know about Rayanne," Rosalie said in a whisper, like she was telling a secret. A secret she obviously wasn't so sure she should share. "I wouldn't bring it up, but Rayanne won't say anything, and it could cause some problems if she's called out to help with another arrest. Or an attack."

Tucker had to shake his head. "What are you talking about?"

Rosalie swallowed hard. "Shortly before we came here, Rayanne got involved with a guy who basically slept with her and then dumped her."

Well, that explained her surly mood. A little bit of the brother inside him kicked in. He had to rein in his protective instincts, though, because Rayanne wouldn't want him to even think about protecting her.

"Anyway," Rosalie went on, "this morning, Rayanne finally got around to taking a pregnancy test. It was positive. She thinks she's about three and a half months along."

Oh, man. That would be a hard blow for any woman, even one with Rayanne's alligator-thick skin.

"Where's the baby's father?" Tucker asked.

"He's dead. He was killed somewhere in Mexico."

Laine made a soft sound of sympathy. "She's had a lot come at her at once. Is there anything I can do to help?"

The shrink in her was coming out. It was like Tucker's brotherly tug, which he was ignoring.

Rosalie shook her head. "Anything any of us could say or do would just make it worse. Rayanne's never had dreams of being a mother, unlike me. I've always wanted children. So this has hit her pretty hard. The only reason I wanted you to know—"

"Was so I wouldn't call her into the middle of a gunfight," Tucker finished. "Let's hope it doesn't come down to that again."

His phone rang, startling the babies and causing them to squirm, and Tucker stepped into the adjoining family room to take the call. Laine followed him, and once Tucker saw it was Colt on the other end of the line, he put it on speaker, since this was something she probably needed to hear.

"Still no sign of our missing shooter," Colt started.

"And the other two?" Laine asked.

"Other than us getting Gene Buford's name, they're not talking, and their lawyers are making sure they stay quiet."

That wasn't good, but maybe there was a way around the mute act from the two they had in custody. Tucker could look at the lawyers themselves and see if they had any connections to those being investigated for the baby farms.

"I made some calls about the social worker, Martin Hague," he told Colt. "Nothing back on him so far, other than he really is a social worker."

"Let me guess—Hague's getting that court order to take the babies?" Tucker asked.

"He's trying," Colt answered. "That's why I've been trying to learn as much about the babies as possible. Both of them have the same blood type as Dawn Cowen, but there's nothing back on the DNA yet to determine if she was really their mother. She doesn't have a next of kin on file so I had Reed chat with some of the other CIs we use in San Antonio. Several of them said she has an aunt somewhere in the state."

"Maybe the Rangers can help track her down?" Tucker suggested.

"I'll ask, but I did find out something else from the CIs. You're not going to believe this, but Dawn was involved with Darren Carty."

Tucker groaned. Not Laine, though. She just stood there looking poleaxed, and her breathing suddenly didn't sound too level.

"My ex-fiancé," she finally mumbled.

She didn't offer more. Not that Tucker needed it. He was plenty familiar with Darren. Same age. Raised just one county apart, they'd competed against each other in high school football and then again on the rodeo circuit.

Tucker pretty much hated the guy, and it had nothing to do with the fact that Laine and Darren had been hot and heavy for a long time before they'd split up about two years before.

"What was Darren doing with someone like Dawn?" Laine asked, her voice a little shaky. "She had a lengthy juvenile record along with some arrests for petty theft and prostitution."

"Darren's apparently been involved with several women like her since you two split," Colt explained.

"But according to a couple of Dawn's friends, it wasn't just a fling. Not on her part, anyway. She was in love with Darren."

Something about that didn't fit. All right, a lot of things didn't fit, but Tucker went with the obvious one. "Then why didn't Darren or her friends report her missing?"

"Because Darren said Dawn had pulled disappearing acts before."

Yeah, Tucker knew that about her, too, but still, someone should have asked her whereabouts.

Including Tucker himself.

"I want to talk to Darren," Tucker insisted.

"Figured you would. I just got to his place, and I'll arrange to have him come in for a chat. Not sure how much he'll cooperate.... Oh, hell—"

"What's wrong?" Tucker couldn't ask fast enough.

"Tucker, you need to get out here right now. I think I found Dawn."

Chapter Eight

Laine looked out at the chaos in front of her, and her stomach tightened even more. Yes, Colt had already told Tucker and her that he'd found Dawn's body.

At her ex-fiancé's house, no less.

However, Laine hadn't realized just how many people would be at Darren's ranch. She spotted the medical examiner's van. A CSI one, too. Then Colt's squad car. Someone from the county sheriff's office was there, as well. Plus four other civilian vehicles, no doubt belonging to Darren and his ranch hands.

Or maybe to his lawyers.

Darren had to know just how much trouble he was in.

Tucker parked behind the ME's van about twenty yards from the house, but he didn't get out. Instead, he turned to her. "They haven't moved the body yet. They're still processing the scene."

She understood what he was saying—if she went outside, she would likely see Dawn. While Laine wasn't anxious to see the dead woman, she did want to hear what Darren had to say.

If he had anything to say.

So far, Darren hadn't said much to Colt, and in turn Colt hadn't volunteered anything about their investigation.

Since Darren's ranch straddled two different jurisdictions, both the county and the Sweetwater Springs cops had agreed to turn it over to Tucker and the Texas Rangers.

Something she was positive Darren wouldn't like.

The two men had never been on friendly terms, and Darren wouldn't have an easy time answering to a man he disliked.

"Stay close to me," Tucker warned her.

It wasn't his first warning of the day. There'd been plenty of them when he had tried to talk her out of coming with him, but Laine had simply reminded him that she would be able to confirm that Dawn was indeed the woman who'd been shot behind her office. That wasn't a lie. But Laine also wanted to see Darren's face when Tucker questioned him about his involvement with Dawn.

She wasn't jealous. Just confused. And more than a little worried that she'd once been engaged to a man who was now somehow involved in a murder.

Just as Tucker reached to open the door, his phone rang, and she saw Reed's name on the screen. He put the phone on speaker when he answered.

"Didn't know if you'd made it out to Carty's place yet, but I just got the background report on that social worker, Martin Hague," Reed greeted. "You want to hear the gist of it now or is this a bad time?"

"You found something?" Tucker immediately asked.

"Maybe. He appears to be living well beyond his means. He recently paid off some huge student loans and bought a house. Can't find any sign of an inheritance or anything. But I did find a connection that makes me uneasy. Remember the name Rhonda Wesson?"

"Yes," Tucker and Laine said in unison. It was Laine

who continued. "She was one of the pregnant women rescued from the first baby farm that was closed down."

"That's right. And she's Hague's cousin."

Laine tried to pick through what she remembered about Rhonda. The woman had a troubled past that included being on the run from an abusive relationship. Or so everyone believed until she'd been found at the baby farm. She delivered the child shortly after being rescued and then had given up the newborn for adoption.

"You think Hague's connected to the baby farm?" Laine asked.

"I just think it's a coincidence that I don't much like," Reed answered.

Laine made a sound of agreement. Of course, just because Hague's cousin had been a victim didn't mean he had been the one who put Rhonda on that baby farm. Still, it was a possible lead that Tucker and she would need to follow.

Well, Tucker anyway.

Laine wasn't sure just how much longer he would continue to let her tag along. Once their missing attacker was caught, Tucker would likely be in a hurry to end their association. Despite the way he'd held her in his bedroom. It'd been, well, nice.

Okay, not nice.

It'd been a *playing with fire* session that she should have never started in the first place.

"You okay?" she heard Tucker ask, and it took her a moment to realize he was talking to her. "You're breathing funny. If you're worried about seeing the body or your ex—"

"I'm not."

He just stared at her, obviously waiting for her to explain what was bothering her. Yes, Dawn's body was part of this mess going on in her head. The spent adrenaline and lack of sleep, too, along with the shocking news that her ex had a possible connection to everything that was going on.

But no way would she mention hugging and playing with fire while Reed was listening.

The town gossip mill already had enough fodder without her adding more, and she definitely didn't want it getting back to her mother that she'd landed not just under Tucker's roof but also in his arms.

"See if you can find the source of Hague's money," Tucker said to Reed. He still didn't take his attention off her, though. "And set up a meeting with Rhonda. I could be tied up here for a while."

"Tied up questioning Darren Carty," Reed supplied. "You arresting him?"

"That depends on how the next few minutes go. Call me if you learn anything else about Hague."

Tucker ended the call. "All right, what's wrong? If you're about to fall apart over seeing your ex, I need to know before you take one step from this truck."

"I look like I'm going to fall apart?" Laine wasn't positive that the falling apart wouldn't happen, but her latest troubled look had sadly been about her situation with Tucker and not about Dawn. "What if I just say this isn't about Darren, and that it's something you don't want to discuss? Would you leave it at that?"

But he didn't leave anything. Not Tucker. He studied her, his attention going from her eyes to her mouth. She saw the *aha/oh, hell* moment flash through his eyes.

"I'm sure it's just nerves," she added. "Better to think about you than what's out there."

"Yeah." He nodded, paused again. "So, should I know why you and Darren split? If I remember right, you two were just a few weeks away from saying 'I do.'"

"There's nothing wrong with your memory." Though it did surprise her that Tucker would remember *that* or any other personal thing about her.

Laine decided to say this fast. Like ripping off a Band-Aid. "I can't have children of my own. I didn't know that when we got engaged, but when I found out and told him, Darren broke things off."

Mercy, it hurt to say that. Hurt more to feel it. The ache was always there, eating away at her. Not because of her failed engagement, but because she would never give birth to the baby that she'd always wanted. The failed relationship was just salt on a wound that would never heal.

Tucker's mouth didn't exactly drop open, but it came close. "I knew Darren was an ass, but that proves it."

Laine shrugged. "He wanted a child of his own and didn't want to adopt. I can't fault a man for that."

"Well, I sure as hell can." He cursed. But then he went still, and Laine knew why. "Hell," Tucker repeated.

"The babies that Dawn had with her could be Darren's," she managed to say. That hurt, too, and it sickened her to think of handing them over to him.

Or to anyone else for that matter.

"Don't borrow trouble by trying to get the truth out of Darren," he warned her. "I'll ask the questions, and if things get too tense, I want you back in the truck." He waited until she nodded before walking with her toward the house.

And toward Darren.

She instantly spotted him. Looking more like a model on a glossy magazine cover than a real cowboy, he was pacing the porch that wrapped around the house. His gaze snapped in their direction as they approached. His ink-black hair was as fashionably disheveled as his jeans and shirt, and she knew he'd had them custom-made.

Darren wasn't alone. There were two men in suits milling around him.

"You know them?" Tucker whispered to her.

"No, but they look like lawyers."

The one on the right did, anyway. He was on the phone having a whispered conversation. The other eased his hand inside his jacket as they approached. He quit easing when Tucker tapped the badge pinned to his shirt and slid his hand over his own weapon.

Laine's attention went to the ME crew on the left side of that massive porch. There, amid some flame-red rosebushes, she spotted the woman's arm. It flung out at an unnatural angle.

Laine went closer. And saw the face. Bloodless.

Now.

The rain had washed her clean and left her bone-white. Her eyes were open and fixed in a permanently blank stare. Laine's thoughts jerked back to those moments in the parking lot. The sound of the bullets being fired. The image of her body being dragged into the car.

"It's the same woman those men shot," Laine managed to say to Tucker. "You're sure it's Dawn?"

"Yeah." Tucker drew in a long breath and maneuvered Laine away from the body. He positioned himself partially in front of her when he faced Darren.

Darren stopped pacing. "Tucker," he greeted. "Laine."

She kept her own greeting at a nod. Best not to trust her voice right now. She no longer loved Darren, hadn't in a long time, but any emotion that came through wouldn't be good.

Mercy, was she looking at a killer?

"I didn't do this," Darren volunteered. "I *wouldn't* do this," he amended.

"Then how'd her body get here?" Tucker asked.

"How the hell should I know?" He groaned, scrubbed his hand over his face. "I just know I didn't put her there."

"Someone did," Tucker snapped. "You didn't hear anyone or see anything?"

"No, and if I had, I would have called the cops." He cursed and started pacing again. "I'm not stupid. If I'd killed someone, do you really think I'd use my own rose bed as a body dump?"

Tucker glanced around, and Laine followed his gaze. No security cameras were visible, but the private road leading to the place was at least a quarter of a mile long. It would have been awfully brassy of the gunmen to bring her body here, but then they'd already shown a brassy streak by attacking Dawn, and then Tucker and Laine, in broad daylight.

Tucker lifted his shoulder. "You might have dumped her body here if you thought it'd take suspicion off yourself."

That brought on a new round of profanity, and one of the suited men on the porch tried to pull Darren aside. Probably to tell him to say nothing else. But Darren only threw off the man's grip and came down the steps. Tucker adjusted, keeping himself in front of her.

"I don't need to take suspicion off myself," Darren said, his teeth coming together. "Because I didn't do this." He glanced at the body, and the color blanched from his face, making the dark stubble seem even darker.

If her ex was guilty, he was certainly putting up a convincing act of being innocent.

"I need you to come in for questioning," Tucker said, using his Ranger's voice now. It wasn't a suggestion. "You can follow my brother to the Sweetwater Springs sheriff's office." He motioned toward Colt, who was next to the body.

Darren just stared at Tucker. "And if I refuse?"

"You won't, because if you're really innocent as you say you are, you'll want to help us catch whoever did this to Dawn."

The staring contest went on for several moments, and Darren finally nodded. "I do want to catch this SOB. And I want to know what happened to the baby Dawn was carrying."

Laine nearly blurted out the question that was on her mind. Were the babies his? But Tucker had already told her to stay quiet. Tucker stayed quiet, too, but he aimed a very intense glare at Darren.

"I have a right to know," Darren insisted. "Because the baby's mine."

"You're sure?" Tucker asked.

"Positive. Dawn told me she was carrying my child, and then she disappeared."

"Maybe Dawn lied," Laine said, and she got a dose of Tucker's glare. Darren's, too. This wasn't exactly a neutral subject for her, so she matched their glares.

"Dawn didn't lie," Darren fired back. "And that means I have a right to the child."

Tucker shook his head. "I'm guessing Dawn wasn't your usual type of woman. I'm also guessing you knew she had a record."

"Yeah, and she was a criminal informant or something."

"She told you that?" Tucker snapped.

"In a roundabout way." Darren paused, and Laine could see the muscles tighten in his body. "What did Dawn have, a boy or a girl?"

Even now, that was important. Maybe more than the dead woman lying just yards away. There was only one person Laine knew who wanted a child more than she did.

Darren.

And he just might have gotten his wish.

It wasn't out of pettiness that she hesitated, even though Darren was perhaps getting the very thing she'd longed for. This was about the babies' safety. She wouldn't have wanted to hand them over to anyone unless she knew they would be safe from danger.

Tucker paused a moment, too. "Just how much did Dawn tell you about the pregnancy?"

That improved Darren's posture. His shoulders snapped back. "That the kid was mine. She was five months pregnant last time I saw her."

"And you didn't think to report to the police that she was missing?"

"I didn't know she was missing!" he practically shouted. Again, one of the suits tried to pull him back, but Darren threw off his grip with far more force than was necessary. The force of a man who was used to getting his way. "Dawn and I had an argument, all right? She left."

"What'd you argue about?" Tucker pressed.

There it was again. That flash of anger in Darren's dust-gray eyes. "A few of my friends had insulted her. Had called her a gold digger. She wanted me to prove my feelings for her by marrying her."

Judging from his renewed scowl, Dawn's demand

hadn't gone over well. Darren wasn't the sort of man who would look kindly on blackmail. Or marrying beneath him. He came from old money, his family practically royalty in the county, and she was betting his parents wouldn't have approved of someone like Dawn.

Heck, they'd barely approved of her, and her family had money, too.

"After Dawn left, I looked for her so I could pay her medical expenses, but I didn't find her." Darren walked closer to them. "And now I want to know if I fathered a boy or a girl."

"I'll let you know when and if we get paternity test results. That's something else you can do when you come to the sheriff's office—give a DNA sample for us to compare. The sooner you get down there, the sooner the test can be done."

One of the suits came forward. "My client has said he fathered this child, and you have no proof to the contrary. He should be allowed to see the baby."

"Normally, he would," Tucker agreed, and then tipped his head to what was left of Dawn. "But in this case, your client could be responsible for that dead body over there."

"I don't have a motive for killing Dawn!" Darren snapped.

"She was your former lover. You admit to arguing with her. And she left you. Now she's dead on your property, and you've got more than enough in your bank account to have hired someone to kill her. That's means, motive and opportunity, and I wouldn't be much of a lawman to dismiss it just because you're telling me to."

Darren's gaze slashed to Laine. "You believe this?"

He didn't wait for her to answer. "Or is this your way of getting back at me? Were you that jealous of Dawn?"

"I didn't even know you were involved with her until today." That made it even more ironic that Dawn had escaped the baby farm and come to her.

Or maybe not so ironic at all.

"Did you tell Dawn about me?" Laine asked.

Darren made a dismissive sound. "She knew you and I were once engaged. She saw pictures of us around the house."

Laine and Tucker exchanged glances, and they didn't have to say it aloud to know where this was going. Maybe Dawn hadn't come to Laine because she'd seen her at the baby farm. Maybe she had come to Laine because of her connection to Darren, her babies' father.

Maybe.

"Why wouldn't Dawn have come to you?" Laine asked Darren. She left out the part about Dawn being held captive at the baby farm and her escape. Laine thought she still might learn something.

And she did.

She saw the pain flash through his eyes. She knew Darren well enough to know that this hadn't been some causal relationship. Too much emotion for that. But was the pain for the death of a woman he'd loved, or for the child he couldn't quite claim?

"I guess Dawn couldn't forgive me for not marrying her," Darren said, shaking his head. "That's why she didn't come here."

"Or maybe she was scared of you," Tucker challenged. Darren howled about his innocence again, but Tucker ignored it. "Be at the sheriff's office in one hour. If not, I'll issue a warrant for your arrest."

"Wait," Darren said as they started to walk away. He waited until they'd turned back around before he continued. "You two aren't together, are you?"

Tucker huffed. "Not like you're thinking. Laine's helping with the case."

Heaven forbid, it sounded like a lie.

Felt like one, too.

Darren kept staring at them, and his mouth tightened. "Just make sure she doesn't help you railroad me straight into jail."

"Has Laine got a reason to railroad you?" Tucker asked. "Or was that just a dig for the sake of slamming an old flame?"

Darren got another look that she knew too well. Cocky, with a mean streak. "She was your old flame, too. At least you had a thing for her when you two were kids. How'd that work out for you?"

"Yeah, it was a slam, just like I thought," Tucker concluded. He tapped his badge again. "One hour. Personally, I'm hoping you'll be late so I can cuff you and haul your butt in."

Maybe because Darren's *slam* had made him ornery, Tucker slipped his arm around her waist. No doubt it was just to get her moving, but Darren wouldn't have missed the little gesture. He probably thought they'd put their differences aside and joined forces against him.

While landing in bed.

Darren had no idea just how much tension there still was between her and Tucker. Tension that would always be there. Except, of course, when there was a different kind of tension from the touching and long looks.

Like now, for instance.

It was all part of the "rile Darren up" act, she assured

herself, but her body kept nudging her to do something more than just look at the man who had her hormonal number.

"You think he had her killed?" Tucker asked.

It took Laine a moment to switch gears and get back to the only thing that should have been on her mind. Finding Dawn's killer. "I don't want to think it could be true. It's easier to believe her death's just connected to the baby farm."

"But Darren could be connected to that, too. A man who wants a baby as badly as he does could have done some desperate things. Maybe when Dawn tried to run away from him, he had her kidnapped and taken to the baby farm until she delivered. If she escaped, he wouldn't have liked that much."

Laine had to process it first, but eventually, she nodded. "It's possible. Darren has a temper, and if he thought Dawn had betrayed him in some way, he could have struck out in anger."

Tucker mumbled some profanity. "And you were going to marry that jerk?"

"Yes." But then she shook her head. "Maybe."

He looked at her as if she'd sprouted wings.

"I wanted a family," she explained. "You know, mom, dad, babies. He wanted the same thing."

Yet another sprouted-wings look. "What about love?"

Here was where things got a little tricky. "I'd just turned thirty, and I thought time was running out for having that family. And Darren was there, pushing for the very life that I desperately wanted. For a while I thought that was enough."

Tucker mumbled some profanity, shook his head. "My advice—never settle for *enough*."

Laine nearly smiled at Tucker giving relationship advice, but she didn't have a chance to respond because his phone rang. They got into the truck before he took it from his pocket and looked at the screen.

"It's Rosalie," he said.

That put Laine on instant alert. "The babies," she managed to say.

All sorts of bad things started running through her head. Obviously through Tucker's, too, because he fumbled with the phone, trying to answer it quickly.

"Tucker, you need to get back here right away," Rosalie said the moment she came on the line. "Martin Hague's here with a court order, and he's taking the babies."

Chapter Nine

Thank God the roads were no longer wet, because Tucker knew he was driving way too fast. Everything inside him was racing, too, and even though he'd sworn to uphold the law, there was no way he was going to let Hague use that court order to take the babies.

The trouble was, he didn't know exactly how to stop him.

It was hardly legal extenuating circumstances for Tucker to say he wouldn't hand over the babies because he didn't trust the social worker.

But he didn't.

And it wasn't just all that unexplained money that Reed had uncovered, or the fact that one of the women rescued from the baby farm was Hague's cousin. It was something else.

Something that Tucker couldn't quite put his finger on.

He'd already called Hague's boss, Rita Longley, as soon as he'd left Darren's ranch, and Tucker had told the woman to back off on the court order. He hadn't outright accused Hague of wrongdoing, but he'd warned Ms. Longley that Hague could have a conflict of interest and that he should be pulled from this particular case.

Tucker hadn't gotten a resounding yes from Hague's

boss, so she might not agree with Tucker's demand. But even if she did, it might not be soon enough to stop what Hague had already set into motion.

"Hurry," Laine repeated.

She was obviously just as distressed about this as he was, maybe more. Tucker hoped like the devil that all their concern was for the babies' safety and not for the babies themselves.

There was a difference.

And it wasn't a good thing for a lawman to lose his objectivity, especially when the babies could belong to a man—Darren—who was just as desperate to get his hands on them as Hague apparently was.

Tucker turned onto the ranch road and immediately spotted Hague's car parked directly in front of the house. Like his other visit, he had a Department of Public Safety officer with him, and the guy was on the steps, along with Hague, Rosalie and Mary. The women each had a baby in their arms, and it was clear from their body language that there was a full-blown argument going on.

The moment Tucker brought his truck to a stop, Laine and he barreled out and headed for the porch.

"You're not taking them," Tucker insisted. "I still don't have the DNA results back yet."

"Then they'll be in foster care while we're waiting for those results," Hague argued. He reached for the baby that Rosalie was holding, and she darted away from him. She no longer had a sweet smile on her face. She looked like a mama hen protecting her chick.

"Does he have the right to do this?" Rosalie asked Tucker.

Yeah, Hague did. But that didn't mean it was going to happen.

Tucker walked past the DPS officer, sending him a back-off glare. Whether he would was anyone's guess, and since the guy was armed, it was a huge concern. If Hague was dirty, then this guy could be, too, and Tucker didn't want any more shots fired.

Laine hurried onto the porch, putting herself between Hague and the others. A maneuver that Hague obviously didn't like, because his cheeks turned to flames.

"I don't understand why you won't let me do my job," Hague argued.

"Because you're a suspect in a murder investigation," Tucker informed him.

Clearly, Hague hadn't been expecting that little bombshell, because he stopped reaching for the baby and snapped toward Tucker. "I have no idea what you're talking about." His eyes widened. "You don't think I had anything to do with their mother's death."

"Did you?" Tucker fired back.

"Absolutely not, and I can't imagine why you'd think there was a connection between Dawn Cowen and me."

"The connection's there. Both your cousin Rhonda and Dawn were held captive at makeshift prisons where their babies would have been sold. Those baby farms were likely run by the same person, or were at least connected to each other."

Hague blinked as if he was hearing this for the first time. And maybe he was, but Tucker wasn't about to take anything he said or did at face value. Not after the attack on Laine and the babies.

"You know where Rhonda is?" Hague asked. "She's been in touch with you?"

Tucker had to shake his head to both, but now he was

the one who was confused. He wasn't faking it, either. "Rhonda's missing again?"

Hague nodded, then sighed. "She's always been a troubled girl. Always disappearing and then showing up when she needs money."

That had made her a prime candidate for the baby farm. No one was out looking for her, and no one would alert the authorities that she was missing. This time there was a reason to send up the red flag.

"Are you telling me you honestly don't know where she is?" Tucker demanded.

"I have no idea. I haven't seen her in weeks."

Hell. Weeks. Tucker wasn't sure who groaned louder, him or Laine.

"Did it occur to you that someone from the baby farm could have kidnapped her again?" Laine asked.

There was no sign that he was the least bit concerned about that. "Why would they take her again? She's not pregnant. She gave birth to a baby less than four months ago and then gave him up for adoption. There's no reason for her to be kidnapped."

Tucker's hands moved to his hips. "Maybe the kidnappers consider her a loose end and want her dead. Maybe *you* consider her a loose end."

That put some venom back in his eyes. "There you go again, accusing me of assorted felonies. Well, I'm not guilty of anything other than trying to do my job."

"Then explain your bank account," Tucker fired back. "Explain where you got the cash to buy a house and pay off your student loans."

He pulled back his shoulders. "You've been sticking your nose where it doesn't belong."

"Yeah, I tend to do that when I'm looking for the truth."

Tucker leaned in, violating the guy's personal space and then some. "Like now. Maybe you're as pure as a saint, but if you're not, it wouldn't be wise of me to hand over those newborns to you. You might just turn around and sell them on the black market."

"I wouldn't do that!" Hague's voice was so loud it caused the babies to jump. Even more reason for Tucker to get this guy off the porch.

"Then explain your bank account," Tucker countered.

"I'll explain nothing to you—" Hague was cut off when his phone rang. Tucker was still close enough to see Rita Longley's name appear on the screen. He hoped Hague's boss was reining him in and not giving him the green light to take the babies.

Hague went to the other side of the porch to take the call. Tucker couldn't hear what he was saying, but he used the time to regroup. "Go ahead and take the babies back into the house," Tucker told Mary and Rosalie.

Both women eagerly nodded, and even though Hague shot them a glare, he didn't stop them. He just continued his whispered conversation with his boss. However, the DPS guy looked ready to intervene.

"There's an escaped gunman on the loose," Tucker reminded the lawman. "It's not safe for the newborns to be out here. Not safe for you, either," he added to Laine.

She only shook her head, not budging, so Tucker moved between her and the road just in case the gunman was stupid enough to make a repeat appearance.

"What do we do now?" Laine whispered.

Only then did Tucker realize just how shaky she was. It'd been a bad morning, what with seeing Dawn's body and then this. Sadly, Tucker couldn't even assure her the worst was over.

"We wait and keep investigating," he answered. "But I'd rather you do your waiting inside."

She followed his gaze to the road. No one was there other than some ranch hands milling around, but someone could easily come driving up.

Someone like the killer.

If that person wasn't already on the porch with them. Either way, Tucker wanted her inside. She nodded, obviously ready to do that, but then she stopped when his phone rang. Colt again.

"I'll bet you're ready for some good news," Colt said, and the moment Tucker heard that, he put it on speaker so Laine could hear, too. Yeah, he was ready for something good. "Gene Buford, the gunman we have in custody at the jail, says he's ready to make a plea deal."

"What kind of plea deal?" Tucker asked.

"Says he'll give us information about Dawn in exchange for immunity and placement in witness protection."

"About Dawn and not the person who set all of this up?"

"Just Dawn," Colt answered. "Anything you don't know about her yet?"

"Probably. But this guy tried to kill us," Tucker mumbled. So, he wasn't sure he wanted the guy to walk, no matter what kind of info he provided. Still, he wanted to hear what the idiot had to say.

"How soon can you have him brought over from the jail?" Tucker asked.

"Soon. I can call there now."

Good. The jail was just up the block from the sheriff's office, but it still would take some time to arrange for a guard to have Buford brought over for questioning. The sheriff's office did have a holding cell in case the timing didn't work out so that Tucker could speak to him right away. If necessary, Tucker could go to the jail, but he preferred to do this at the sheriff's office so he could kill two birds with one stone.

"I'll talk to the gunman when I come in to interview Darren," Tucker told Reed. "See you in about a half hour if I can get things settled here that fast."

Tucker ended the call to see how things were about to play out with Hague, but he, too, had finished his call and was glaring at Tucker again. He slammed his phone shut and jammed it back into his pocket.

"Go inside," Tucker whispered to Laine. "Check on the babies."

That got her moving. Good thing, too, because Tucker thought this situation with Hague might turn even uglier than it already was.

"A plea deal, huh?" Hague made a sound that could have meant anything. "Maybe that means this situation with Dawn will be over soon."

"Maybe." And Tucker left it at that. He wasn't exactly pleased that Hague had overheard that conversation, but something like that wouldn't stay a secret for long, especially since the district attorney would have to be brought into any plea-deal talk.

"My supervisor wants to talk to me," Hague grumbled a moment later. "So help me, you'd better not have done anything to compromise my job."

"And you'd better not have done anything to compromise those newborns' safety."

Hague's mouth tightened, and he started down the steps. "I'll try to find Rhonda, and I'll tell her to get in touch with you so you can hear it from her own lips that I had nothing to do with her kidnapping or the baby farms."

"You said you didn't know where she was," Tucker reminded him.

He threw open the door and looked at Tucker from over the roof of the car. "I don't, but I can call some of her friends on the drive back to my office. When you've heard from her, I want you to back off. I'm not the only one with a conflict of interest here, Sergeant McKinnon."

Since Tucker already knew that, and since he was more than thankful just to put an end to this—even a temporary one—he turned and went inside. Laine was waiting for him by the door, and he wasn't sure who made the first move or even how it happened, but she ended up in his arms.

Strange that this kept happening, although it shouldn't have. Even a hug of comfort was a Texas-sized reminder that Laine was the one in his arms. Nothing good could come of this.

Well, nothing reasonable anyway.

Maybe it was because every inch of him was on edge that he even thought of holding her for stress relief. Yeah, for a second or two, it was relief, but what always followed were some crystal clear reminders of why they shouldn't be doing it in the first place.

The heat between them.

The bad blood, too. Hard to hang on to bad blood, though, when the blasted attraction kept getting in the way.

"What are you thinking?" she asked, her breath and body still trembling.

Definitely something he'd keep to himself. Tucker went with the topic that should be on his mind.

"If I'm wrong about Hague, I'll apologize," Tucker mumbled. He truly hoped he was wrong about the social worker.

He was already battling a major suspect, Darren, without adding Hague to the mix. Especially since Hague could eventually get his hands on the newborns. Not by kidnapping them, either, but with that dang court order. Of course, Darren could take them, too, if it turned out he was the father. Still, it would be hard to claim his babies if he was sitting in a jail cell for killing their mother.

"You need to get ready for your meeting with Darren," she reminded him, easing away.

He nodded. Didn't move. Hated that he felt the loss of her body heat.

Really?

He had to deal with this now. It wasn't as if he didn't have anything to do other than stand there and mentally whine about her body heat. Or her scent. Or the stupidity of wanting her right back in his arms again.

"Where are the babies?" he asked. Yet another subject he should be dwelling on.

She fluttered her fingers toward the stairs. "Rosalie and Mary put them in the crib. They'd just had their bottles before Hague got here, and according to Rosalie, newborns usually sleep after they eat."

"Not much different from the rest of their day, then. They sleep all the time. Well, except at night."

The corner of her mouth lifted. "Fatherhood not suiting you much?"

Tucker found himself frowning before he even realized he was going to do it. "I get that a lot. I'm not sure it's all warranted."

"Really?" Laine said, with far more surprise than was necessary. "You're a player."

Again he frowned and started for the downstairs office he'd been using. Laine followed right behind him. "I'm not a player. I'm just not interested in anything long-term."

She chuckled. "Which more or less qualifies you as a player."

He shrugged, wrestling with another frown. "Haven't heard of you trying to settle down with any one particular guy since you split with Darren."

Of course, he hadn't heard of her sleeping around, either, which was essentially what she'd just accused him of doing.

Tucker couldn't deny it, so he shut up and hoped she'd move on to a different subject.

"I've hit a nerve," she said. "I'm sorry."

So much for her moving on. So much for him shutting up, too. He just kept blathering. "I doubt that. Well, you may be sorry that I'm giving you the stink eye, but I doubt you're sorry you brought it up. I know you don't approve of my lifestyle."

"It's not that." She hesitated, shook her head, mumbled something he didn't catch. "How many real kisses have you had?"

"Excuse me?" Tucker felt another frown coming on. Possibly more blathering, too.

"A real kiss," she repeated. "And I don't mean those *unzip me* kisses with your conquests from the Outlaw Bar. I mean real honest-to-goodness kisses that you feel in more than just one part of your body?"

Okay, so Laine had moved on from semisafe conversation about relationships to this. Whatever *this* was. Well, if she wanted to hold a mirror up to his face, she was about to get one turned right back on her.

"How many?" Tucker repeated. "Two. One was with you right there in the kitchen at my granddaddy's house. Yeah, we were just kids, but trust me, it was real."

She swallowed hard, and her forehead bunched up. "And the second kiss?"

"This one." Before he could talk himself out of it, Tucker slid his hand around the back of Laine's neck, hauled her to him and did the one thing he was pretty sure he shouldn't do.

He kissed her.

For real.

There it was. The slam of her body heat and taste all at once. Yeah, he remembered it from all those years before, but it was even better now. Of course it was, because if it hadn't been, Tucker might have stood a chance of giving this particular mistake a fast ending. As it was, fast didn't even appear to be an option. Not to his fired-up body, anyway.

He dragged her closer and made things even worse by deepening the kiss. That taste set him on fire, and the rest of her didn't help cool him down, either. Probably because Laine did some dragging of her own, pulling him closer and closer until they were plastered against each other. He could feel parts of her that he had no right to feel.

But he did, anyway.

Her breasts against his chest. Her sex close to his. Her taste, her breath. Everything.

It was too much to feel all at once. Too much to stop, too, with parts of him already begging for more. Much more. Like them naked on a bed. That's why he was a little surprised when Laine managed to stop.

She stepped back again, her gaze meeting his, and he saw the same *What the heck did we just do?* expression on her face that was no doubt on his. So much for holding up a bloomin' mirror to her face.

Now he'd be lucky if he could walk.

"How bad are you regretting that?" she asked, sliding her tongue over her bottom lip. That simple gesture caused his body to clench and beg for more.

"As much as you are," Tucker settled for saying.

She shook her head, pushed her hair from her face. "Good."

But she didn't clarify what that *good* meant. Nor did she move too far from him. "Remind me not to play a dangerous game like that with you again."

Right. Maybe he should tell the sun not to rise, too. He might have better success there. "You think a reminder will fix this?"

"This?" she questioned.

The heat. The need. And even the little niggling feeling that it had been more than a blasted kiss. Which it couldn't have been, so he darn sure wasn't about to describe it to her. "I'll explain it if you'll explain your *good.*"

Though he had a pretty solid idea of that *good,* too. Like him, Laine wanted one of them to stay sane during all this close-quarters stuff.

Best of luck with that.

Laine immediately backed up. Smart woman. They were indeed playing a dangerous game, and Tucker couldn't be certain they both wouldn't play another round the next time their guards were down.

His phone rang, yanking him back to his senses. Not exactly where he wanted to be at first, but seeing the name on the screen, he mentally adjusted.

"It's Rhonda Wesson," he told Laine.

He doubted this was a coincidence. Doubted, too, that Hague hadn't known exactly where she was, because obviously he'd managed to get in touch with his cousin shortly after driving away from the ranch.

"Sergeant McKinnon," she greeted. "My cousin said I should call you."

He waited for her to verify that Hague was innocent and had nothing to do with the baby farms.

She didn't do that.

"Are you all right?" Tucker asked.

Rhonda didn't say anything for several seconds. "No. I need to talk to you. I need help."

"What's wrong?" he couldn't ask fast enough.

"I'm in hiding," Rhonda answered. "Because someone's trying to kill me."

Chapter Ten

Laine watched through the observation glass as Tucker
finished up his interview with Darren. Her ex hadn't said
anything remotely incriminating and had instead stuck to
his broken record claim that he was innocent in Dawn's
death.

And maybe he was.

Still, Laine was glad that Tucker was being thorough
with this interview. If he cleared Darren as a suspect,
and the DNA results came back proving the babies were
his, then Darren would walk away with them as fast as
he could. He'd be doing it legally, too.

Hide them. Protect them, Dawn had said to Laine just
seconds before those men had gunned her down, and
Laine intended to do everything she could to carry out
the woman's dying request.

It was odd that Tucker had taken on the same mission.
Not just the investigation. He wouldn't have let go of that.
But he also didn't seem ready to let go of the babies. He
was definitely not the old Tucker.

Well, at least not in that way.

The kiss had certainly been evidence of the charmer
cowboy who'd coaxed plenty of women into his bed.
Laine had to be careful that the same didn't happen to

her. The last thing she needed was to be another notch on his rodeo belt.

Even if that kiss had made her think differently.

For a few heated moments anyway, it'd caused her common sense to take a serious nosedive. Best to avoid future kissing so she could keep a clear head. Too bad just a mental warning wouldn't be enough.

Not even close.

She had to figure out a way to put some physical distance between her and Tucker. Without sacrificing the safety of the babies, of course.

She and Tucker had left them at the ranch with Colt, his father, Rayanne, Rosalie and Mary. In addition, Tucker had put some of the ranch hands on alert. They weren't trained guards by any means, but they were all armed. Hopefully their presence would prevent the missing attacker from trying to get on the grounds.

Maybe Tucker and she would get some other help with that, too.

Just up the hall in one of the other interview rooms, the gunman that'd already been arrested, Gene Buford, was waiting with his lawyer to talk to Tucker about a possible plea deal in exchange for information about Dawn.

"Are we finally finished here?" Darren said, his voice stern enough to snap Laine's attention back to the interview.

"For now." Tucker stood when Darren did, and they faced each other across a gray metal table. "I'll let you know about the GSR test."

Darren mumbled something she didn't catch and scowled, clearly not happy. Tucker had swabbed Darren's hands for gunshot residue—something that could have perhaps linked him to Dawn's shooting.

GSR alone wouldn't be enough to charge him, since Darren could always say he'd fired a gun elsewhere. It wasn't that unusual for a rancher to have to shoot a rattler or some other predatory animal that'd strayed onto the property. But the GSR might cast enough suspicion that Tucker could get a court order to examine Darren's bank account and maybe get a search warrant for his house.

Darren and Tucker were still in a glaring match when Reed appeared in the doorway of the observation room.

"Rhonda Wesson just arrived," Reed told her.

Laine stepped out, not sure she would even recognize the woman. She hadn't been part of the rescue of the women and babies from the farm where Rhonda had been held, but there had been some photos of her in the news. Laine remembered a scraggly looking pregnant woman dressed in green scrubs.

Which was very unlike the woman she saw now.

It took Laine a moment to connect the tall blonde to that rescued woman.

Definitely no scrubs today. Rhonda was wearing dress pants and a white top. Not a strand of her hair was out of place. She seemed more suited to being in a boardroom than to being in hiding, but there was concern in her cool green eyes as they swept around the sheriff's office and landed on Laine.

"You must be Dr. Braddock," Rhonda said, coming toward her with her hand extended. From the looks of it, she'd recently had a manicure.

"Call me Laine." She shook hands with her, and even though Rhonda held eye contact for several seconds, her attention drifted to the closed doors of the interview rooms.

"Excuse me," Rhonda said when she noticed that

Laine's gaze had followed hers. "Police stations make me nervous. Actually, being anywhere in public right now makes me feel that way. I don't want to stay long. I just want to talk to you and Sergeant McKinnon."

Laine was about to assure her that would happen just as one of the interview room doors opened, and Tucker stepped out. Darren and his lawyer were right behind him.

"You need to get off this witch hunt," Darren snapped, looking at Laine, and then at Rhonda. He barely spared her a glance.

Rhonda had a much stronger reaction.

She stepped behind Tucker, her attention fixed on Darren. "I didn't know he'd be here."

"I was interviewing him," Tucker explained.

"Railroading me," Darren corrected. "Is that why you're here, Rhonda? You planning to railroad me, too?"

"You know each other?" Tucker asked.

"Know her? She tried to milk money from me just a few weeks ago."

"I didn't," Rhonda insisted. "I just wanted to talk to you about Dawn, and I wanted to see if you were the person following me." She paused, swallowed hard. "Dawn was terrified of you."

"She wasn't, and you're saying that just because you're riled that I wouldn't pay you off."

Frantically shaking her head, Rhonda turning to Tucker. "We need to talk, but not with him around."

Rhonda threw open the door to the other interview room. Gene Buford was cuffed at his hands and feet, and he was seated with his court-appointed attorney. Both turned in Rhonda's direction, as did the guard who'd brought Buford over from the jail.

The moment seemed to freeze. Gene Buford was in

the process of getting to his feet when he looked into the hall where Laine, Tucker, Rhonda, Darren and his lawyer were standing.

Buford eased back into his chair.

"We've waited long enough," Buford's attorney snapped. She was a petite brunette who looked as if she'd just finished law school. Hardly the voice of authority.

"And you'll wait some more," Tucker snarled back, shutting the door. He tossed Darren one of his hard glares, and both Darren and his lawyer finally left.

"Sorry," Rhonda mumbled. "I'm just shaken up."

"Because of Darren Carty?" Tucker asked.

She nodded. Then shook her head. Her fingers were trembling when she brushed her hair from her cheek. "It's not a good idea for me to be here."

"You're safe," Tucker assured her, and he led Laine and Rhonda into the empty interview room. "Why are you scared of Darren?"

"My cousin Martin told me that Darren was a suspect in Dawn's murder and that he might be the person who's been following me."

Rhonda sat next to Laine, and the woman turned to her when she continued. "I'm pretty sure someone's been following me, and I think it's connected to Dawn."

"How?" Laine asked. "Why?"

"I'm not positive, but I think it has to do with that black-market baby operation where we were held captive."

Laine was almost certain of that. "How well did you know Dawn?" Laine pressed.

Rhonda drew in another shivery breath. "We were held together for a while. Until they moved her to another place. That's around the time Sergeant McKinnon here rescued me." She paused, looking up at him. "I can never thank you enough for that."

Tucker nodded. "We hope you can help us find Dawn's killer."

"You mean it isn't Darren?"

"It could be, but we're looking into several possibilities." Tucker didn't mention that her cousin was one of those suspects. "Tell us what's been happening since you were rescued."

Rhonda put her hand on her stomach. "Well, obviously I had my baby. A boy that I gave up for adoption. I can barely manage to take care of myself, much less a baby."

Laine couldn't argue with that. She'd read through the woman's bio on the drive to the sheriff's office, and even though she was in her early thirties, Rhonda had never held a real job for more than a few months. She was smart, though, and had managed to finish a college degree while serving time for embezzlement and extortion. She'd been out of jail for six years now and in that time had stayed clean and off the radar.

Well, until she'd been taken captive and then rescued at the baby farm.

Of course, Rhonda looked as if she had gotten past her shady roots. At least when it came to her appearance.

"Dawn talked about Darren while you were both being held captive?" Tucker continued.

Rhonda nodded. "She was scared of him and even hinted that he might be the reason she was there. Dawn had tried to get away from him, you see. He didn't really want her, only the baby, and after they had an argument, she told him she didn't want him to raise the child. She'd planned to give it to someone else, someone who'd be a good father."

That meshed with some of the other things they'd learned, but Laine still had a hard time imagining Darren kidnapping his pregnant girlfriend to keep her from giving up his baby. Of course, she also understood this need to be a parent and have a family. Maybe Darren had just taken that need too far.

Rhonda twisted a plain gold ring on her thumb. "What about the baby? Wait, I remember right before Dawn was moved, she found out she was carrying twins." She leaned closer to Tucker. "Are they here? God, please tell me Darren can't get his hands on them."

"No, they've been moved to a safe house," Tucker said.

A lie, of sorts, since the babies were actually at the ranch, but Laine was glad he wasn't giving out their whereabouts. Especially to this woman, who unnerved her. Maybe it was the perfect clothes and manicure, but something about Rhonda didn't feel right.

"Good." Rhonda repeated it as she eased back deeper into her chair. "Dawn would have wanted them kept out of harm's way. Did either of you get a chance to see Dawn before she was killed?"

Tucker shook his head, and Rhonda turned to Laine, obviously waiting for an answer.

"I didn't know her," Laine settled for saying.

"Really? Because I'd heard you were involved with the baby farm investigation."

"I was, uh, removed from the case."

"Oh." Rhonda cast an uneasy glance at Tucker, who thankfully didn't elaborate.

"Tell me about your cousin Martin Hague," Tucker went on. "Any chance he was involved with the baby farm?"

Rhonda's eyes widened, and it seemed to take her a moment to realize Tucker was being serious. "Why?"

"Because he's shown a lot of interest in Dawn's babies, that's why."

Rhonda just shook her head again. She looked to be on the verge of dismissing any possibility of her cousin's guilt. Then she blew out a long, frustrated breath. "Maybe."

That got Tucker and Laine's complete attention. *"Maybe?"* Tucker pressed.

"Martin's always been ambitious. Always looking for an angle to make money."

"Then why'd he become a social worker?" Laine asked.

"I think it was because of the adoption opportunities. There's a lot more money in that than people think, and the job would give him contact with women he could coax into giving up their babies.

"You didn't know he'd helped with some adoptions?" Rhonda added when they just stared at her.

"No, and I'd like some details about that," Tucker insisted.

"Well, there won't be records, that's for sure. Martin's too careful for that. He just connects pregnant women with potential buyers…I mean, parents who'll pay for a private adoption."

"And how do you know this?" Laine asked.

"Because that's what he tried to do to me. He found some family that would have paid me twenty grand for my baby. I didn't like them when I met them so I said no. A couple of weeks later, I was kidnapped and taken to that hellhole of a place that the press dubbed the baby farm."

She and Tucker exchanged relieved glances. Finally, this was some fodder to stop Hague and that blasted court order. Maybe. Rhonda had already said there'd be no records, but it was possible to connect the extra money in Hague's bank account to the adoptions of his clients.

Rhonda shook her head again. "I don't think Martin's responsible for my kidnapping. He's greedy, but I don't think he has the grit to do something like that. Besides, he probably thought he could just set up another private adoption for me. That's what he did after I was rescued and had my son."

"Hague helped with that?" Tucker asked.

"Yes. It was a different family from the first one, and I really liked them."

Tucker frowned. "They paid you?"

Rhonda nodded. "I didn't exactly have any extra cash after you rescued me, so yes, I took some money for the private adoption. That money's almost gone now, and I need a safe place to stay."

Well, that money explained the expensive-looking clothes.

Tucker hesitated a moment. "I'll see what arrangements I can make for a safe house. Wait here." He motioned for Laine to follow him. She did, and when they stepped out into the hall, he shut the door.

"I don't trust her," Laine immediately whispered. "Women in hiding from a would-be killer don't usually have time for a manicure."

Tucker made a sound of surprise to indicate it wasn't something he had even considered. "I want to get Rhonda's accusations about Hague on record." He glanced at his watch. "All this might take a while, and I still need to talk to the idiot who wants a plea deal. I can have someone take you back out to the ranch."

It was tempting, but Laine didn't even get a chance to consider it before Tucker's phone rang.

"It's Darren," he relayed to her. "What do you want?" he demanded, putting the call on speaker.

"I need to tell you something that might pertain to Rhonda."

Whatever it was, it obviously wasn't good, because Laine could hear the doom and gloom in Darren's voice.

Tucker glanced at the door and then the screen, and led her to the break room at the end of the hall. Probably because he didn't want Rhonda or the gunman behind door number two listening in on the conversation.

"What about Rhonda?" Tucker prompted Darren once he was sure the chat would be private.

"I just found a message on my voice mail from Dawn. Things have been so hectic around here, and I just got around to checking it."

Tucker jumped right on that. "When did she call?"

"Yesterday. She sounded terrified and wanted me to come pick her up. She said she was in Sweetwater Springs. Is that where she was killed?"

"You said this was possibly about Rhonda," Tucker reminded him.

"Yeah." Darren sounded more than a little irritated, maybe because Tucker hadn't answered his question. "It's a bit hard to understand what Dawn is saying, but it sounds as if she says 'I'm running from her. I thought I could trust her, but I can't.'"

Tucker huffed. "And why would you think that meant Rhonda?"

"Because why else would she have lied and said Dawn was afraid of me? She wasn't. And the only reason Rhonda would have lied would have been to make you suspicious of someone other than herself. She's a suspect, right?"

"I'm not sure what she is," Tucker admitted. "But I do want a recording of that message. Send it to me here at the sheriff's office so I can get it to the Ranger lab for analysis."

"I will, but so help me, McKinnon, you'd better not try to use this against me in some way."

"You got something to hide?" Tucker was already talking to the air, because Darren had hung up.

Tucker looked at her, and she could practically see the wheels turning in his head. "Her manicure means something, huh?" he mumbled.

"I'd like more proof than that, too," Laine countered, "but maybe it's a start." She paused. "Unless Dawn was talking about me when she said she thought she could trust *her*."

"You?" he challenged. "She came to you for help."

"Maybe. Or maybe she got to my office and thought I'd betrayed her or something. Maybe she even thought that I was the one who sent those killers after her. I could be the *her* in the message she left for Darren."

"She still trusted you enough to ask you to protect her twins." Tucker stayed quiet a moment, then scrubbed his hand over his face. "I need to question Rhonda more about her relationship with Dawn."

Laine agreed, and this time she stayed back, not wanting to compromise what was now an official interrogation of a possible suspect and not just an interview with a possible informant.

Tucker threw open the door of the room where they'd left Rhonda, and he cursed.

The room was empty, and Rhonda was gone.

Chapter Eleven

Well, this day sure as heck wasn't going as Tucker had planned. Rhonda was on the run again, and he was no closer to solving the case than he had been when he'd woken up. Something had to give, and it had to give soon.

"Maybe we can catch up with Rhonda," Laine suggested. "She couldn't have gotten far."

"Not *we*," he instantly corrected. "No way do I want you out there trying to hunt down a suspect."

And since Reed was the only deputy in the sheriff's office, Tucker didn't want him out there, either. He was about to ask Reed to call for someone from the jail to look for Rhonda, but then his phone rang, and he saw the woman's name on the screen.

"Where are you, Rhonda?" Tucker demanded the moment he answered.

"I'm sorry, but I just couldn't stay there. I heard you talking to Darren, and I figured he was setting me up to take the fall for him. Or to be attacked. I don't want to die like Dawn."

Tucker groaned. "No one was going to attack you while you were here."

He hoped. Still, Tucker couldn't rule out the possibility that Rhonda had a legitimate concern. Laine's expression let him know that she felt the same way. Darren had the means necessary to go after anyone who could link him to Dawn's murder, and maybe Laine's ex thought Rhonda fell into that category.

"My offer stands," he added to Rhonda. "I can arrange for you to go to a safe house."

It wasn't a totally selfless offer on his part. Tucker could send her to a place where someone could keep an eye on her if it turned out she'd had some part in the baby farms. A place where he could also keep her alive if she was innocent in all of this.

"I don't want your safe house," she insisted. "I just want to be *safe,* and I'd been doing a good job of that on my own. I hope I didn't make a stupid mistake coming to see you," Rhonda went on, but then she stopped, mumbled some profanity. "I think someone's following me again. I need to go."

Before Tucker could say anything that might stop her, Rhonda hung up. He immediately hit Redial and tried to get her back on the line, but the call went straight to voice mail. She'd no doubt turned off her phone.

Great.

Tucker didn't want to know how long it'd be before he could speak to her and coax her into coming back in for questioning. And besides, maybe it wasn't a good idea bringing her back if someone was truly following her.

Of course, that *if* was just that. An if. Rhonda could be lying through her teeth about everything, especially her lack of involvement in Dawn's murder.

"You still need to talk to Hague," Laine reminded him.

Yeah, because Rhonda's cousin had some things to explain that might shed some light on this case. Or at least some light on Hague himself. Tucker located his number, and the man answered on the first ring.

"I'm on my way there to see Rhonda," Hague said right off the bat. "I'll be at the sheriff's office in about ten minutes, and I'm bringing my lawyer with me."

"Too late. Your cousin's already left. But how the heck did you know she'd be here?"

Hague paused and made a huffing sound, maybe because Tucker hadn't bothered to ask nicely. Tucker wasn't in the mood for stroking egos.

"She called me, all right?" Hague finally answered. "She said she was going to see you, and I thought it'd be my chance to talk to her, to see how she's doing. I also thought she might need a lawyer since she could be involved in something illegal."

Interesting. Especially since Rhonda had her doubts about Hague's innocence. Or maybe she'd just wanted to cast a guilty light on him.

"Illegal, as in the baby farm?" Tucker pressed.

"I don't know. I just know that she's acting even stranger than usual. I figure she's in some kind of trouble. Did she really just leave?" Hague asked, sounding genuinely disappointed. Or else he was doing a good job of faking it.

"She did. She called me right after she left and said someone was following her again. Is it you by any chance?"

"No." Hague stretched that out a few syllables. "And if you're only going to accuse me of more crimes, then this conversation is over."

"It's not over. Not until you explain to me where you got all that extra money in your bank account. Rhonda seems to think it comes from the referral fees that adoptive parents pay you. Is that true?"

It was silent for several long moments. "Rhonda can have a big mouth. She shouldn't have said that."

Maybe not, but Hague wasn't denying it. "Is it true?" Tucker repeated.

"I've done nothing wrong," Hague countered, which was practically code for *Yeah, it's true.*

Now it was Tucker's turn to huff. "I need you back here to give a statement on those funds," he insisted. "Not today, though." One look at Laine's weary eyes, and he figured the last thing she needed was to go another round with Hague. "Be here tomorrow morning, ten o'clock."

"You'll do the interview yourself?" Hague asked.

Normally, a simple question like that wouldn't have put a knot in his gut, but Tucker didn't like the idea of a possible suspect pinning him down to a specific time and place.

It was downright dangerous.

If Hague was guilty, he could use it as an opportunity to attack them again. And even if Tucker left Laine at the ranch for the interview, which he would likely do, it might prompt Hague to go there, knowing that Tucker wouldn't be around to stop him.

"One of the deputies can take your statement," Tucker said. It might or might not have been true.

Tucker hung up, trying to prepare himself to talk with the moron looking for a plea deal, but he needed a moment. Clearly, Laine did, too. Tucker took her back to the break room and poured them each a cup of coffee.

"Uh-oh," Laine mumbled, studying his face. "Are you about to lecture me?"

He was sure he frowned. "A lecture's the last thing on my mind."

Her eyebrows flexed. "Oh."

For a simple little word, it conveyed a lot. So did her gaze, which dropped to his mouth. "Not that, either. I figure it's a good idea if we don't kiss, don't think about kissing and don't even bring up the subject."

The next sound she made was a short *hmm* as she sipped her coffee. "You're right, of course."

It didn't feel or sound right at all.

"Obviously, there's still something between us," he added. "But that kind of something can make a bad situation worse."

An image of her mother flashed through his head. And his family. No one on any side of this mess with Jewell and Whitt Braddock would want to see Laine and him together.

"Maybe that's it," she mumbled. "It's the whole forbidden attraction thing that's drawing us together."

Tucker thought about that a moment. Dismissed it. And because he clearly didn't have much of a brain left, he leaned in and brushed his mouth over hers.

It was nothing—just a touch of their lips. At least it should have been nothing. But as usual with Tucker, things were never simple.

"Nope, nothing to do with anything forbidden," he assured her. "It was there a long time before we ended up on opposite sides."

A knock at the door caused him and Laine to fly apart as if they'd been caught doing something wrong—which they were. It wasn't Rhonda or either of their other suspects. It was the dirtbag's lawyer. The woman was pale, and had beads of sweat above her upper lip.

"I'll be there when I'm ready," Tucker snapped.

"No need. My client's changed his mind. Mr. Buford doesn't want a plea deal after all."

The lawyer would have just darted right out of there if Tucker hadn't snagged her by the arm. "What gives?"

She looked over his shoulder and then shook off Tucker's grip. "I'm not at liberty to say. My client wishes to be returned to his cell now. He's advised me that he intends to remain silent."

Tucker cursed when the lawyer walked away, and he went back through the past half hour to try and figure out what'd gone wrong.

It didn't take him long to come up with something.

"Buford saw Rhonda when she opened the door to the interview room," Tucker said with a groan. "Darren, too. If one of them is his boss, Buford could have seen their presence as some kind of veiled warning for him to keep quiet."

"Well, it worked," Laine said. "What about the one in the hospital? Any chance he'll be willing to make a plea deal?"

"Maybe. But I need to make sure both Darren and Rhonda stay away from him. Hague, too, because Hague could have called Buford's lawyer and told him he was on the way here."

Maybe Buford had thought he could make the deal and be placed in witness protection before his boss learned what was going on. Now something—or more likely, *someone*—had spooked him.

Tucker took out his phone to call the private security company that was guarding the guy, but before he could make the call, his phone rang.

"It's the Ranger crime lab," he relayed to Laine, and he answered it.

"We just got back the results of the babies' DNA tests," the tech said.

Tucker had hoped they'd be back this soon, but he hadn't realized just what an emotional punch it would be when the crime lab called. His stomach tightened again, and when his lungs started to ache he realized he was holding his breath.

"And?" Tucker managed to ask.

"They're fraternal twins, and their mother was indeed the dead woman, Dawn Cowen."

Laine sucked in a lot of air. Not that this was a surprise to her. After all, Dawn had brought the babies to her office, but still it was hard hearing it all spelled out for them.

"And the babies' father?" Tucker asked, though he figured the tech wouldn't have that info. There was no reason for Darren to be in the system, and there wouldn't have been time for his DNA sample to be processed yet.

"It's a man named Kurt Laverty."

Tucker looked at Laine to see if she knew who the man was, but she only shook her head. "You're positive?" he asked the tech.

"Yeah. This is standard paternity test, and it was an easy match since we have Laverty's DNA on file."

There were only a few reasons why the DNA would have been in the system, and knowing Dawn's history, Tucker was betting Laverty wasn't a state or federal employee. It was because he was a criminal.

"Tell me Laverty's in jail," Tucker added, because he didn't want to hand over the babies to some sleazebag who just happened to get Dawn pregnant.

"Oh, he's in jail, all right, and he's been there for the

past four months. He pled out on a double murder charge so he could get the death penalty off the table. He got two consecutive life sentences."

Good. Well, not *good* for the twins. It would have been better if they'd had a decent father who could give them a good life. But at least this way, Laverty wouldn't get his hands on them.

Nor would Darren.

"Now we know," Laine mumbled when Tucker ended the call. She opened her mouth, closed it, then started to pace. "I want to adopt them."

It wasn't exactly a surprise. Tucker had seen her getting attached to the babies, but attachment and motherhood were two different things.

"Dawn could have next of kin who would want them," Tucker reminded her. And if any of Dawn's or Laverty's family members were around, they would have a legal claim.

For that matter, so would family services.

With the results from the DNA test back and the confirmed death of the birth mother, the state could and would take the twins while they sorted it all out.

"Sleep on that," Tucker advised her. Though part of him—an obviously stupid part—hoped she didn't change her mind. Laine would be a good mother.

He didn't have any doubts about that.

Tucker had seen the way she'd handled the babies. He'd also seen how much she'd wanted a child, especially since he now knew she couldn't have one of her own.

"I'd planned on adopting anyway," Laine continued, as Tucker led her out of the break room and toward the front of the building.

"Twins," he reminded her. "They're double the work."

She looked up at him. "Do you really want them to go to strangers?"

"No." Tucker didn't even have to think about that. "I just want what's best for them. And for you."

He groaned, hating that Laine now factored into this. It darn sure didn't help things that he was thinking of what was best for her, rather than what was best overall.

That dang kiss had changed everything.

He stopped by Reed's desk and waited until the deputy had finished a call. "Laine and I are heading out," Tucker told him. "Any word on Dawn's next of kin?"

Reed shook his head. "Her parents are both dead, and she has no siblings. Her mother has a sister, but the Rangers haven't had any luck tracking her down so far."

"Does she have a criminal record?" Laine asked right off the bat.

Another head shake from Reed. "She's a secretary at a bank in San Antonio, but she's on vacation and isn't answering her phone." His eyes widened. "You don't think she's been hurt, do you?"

"No." At least Tucker hoped she hadn't been. "But just in case, have someone from SAPD drop by her place for a welfare check."

Reed nodded, assured him that he would.

So, the babies had an aunt. Maybe one who would want them and crush Laine's dream of adopting them. Tucker hated how this could all turn out, but he especially hated that they had no control over the fate of the newborns they'd been protecting.

"Come on," Tucker said, opening the door.

He glanced around to make sure no one suspicious was lurking in the halls, including Hague, who was still possibly on his way over. Tucker didn't see anyone, so he got Laine moving toward the side parking lot. They were halfway between the sheriff's office and his truck when he spotted movement on the roof just across the street.

But it was too late.

The shot came right at Laine and him.

Chapter Twelve

Laine didn't even have time to react. But Tucker did. He pulled her to the ground.

They landed hard, the concrete scraping against her hands and knees and nearly knocking the breath right out of her. Before Laine could even regain that breath—or think—Tucker had gotten her moving again. He hooked his arm around her, and they rolled to the side of a cruiser.

Barely in time.

Another bullet slammed through the air, landing in the spot where they'd just been.

Cursing, Tucker drew his gun and took aim at the diner across the street. The front of the small building was a wall of windows, and Laine got just a glimpse of the stunned expressions of the diners before Tucker pushed her even farther to the ground.

Sweet heaven. Was the shooter in there with all those people?

If so, not only did Tucker not have a clean shot, but it was also possible he could hit an innocent bystander. At this time of day, there could be families inside.

"You see the shooter?" Reed shouted, and it took her a moment to realize he'd shouted it from an open window in the sheriff's office.

"He's on the roof of the diner," Tucker answered, but then he cursed again when another bullet slammed into the concrete just inches from them.

So the gunman wasn't actually inside, but he could do a lot of damage from the roof. Worse, some of the diners were obviously starting to panic. Laine could hear their screams and shouts for help, and she prayed none of them would run out into the line of fire.

"Call the jail and have them send some guards for backup," Tucker yelled. "Did the guard already leave with Buford?"

"No. Buford's still in the interview room talking with his lawyer."

That obviously didn't please Tucker because he groaned. "Tell them to stay put."

That's when Laine remembered that Reed was the only deputy inside the sheriff's office. Colt was back at the ranch guarding the babies, and Cooper was away on his honeymoon. The night deputies wouldn't be coming in for several hours, and there was no way Tucker would want Buford left alone. It would be too tempting for him to try to escape.

In fact, that might be why this attack was happening.

If someone connected with Buford had been watching the sheriff's office, then they would have known this was the perfect time for an attack. A gunman could take out her and Tucker while freeing Buford, and it likely wouldn't matter to this shooter how many innocent people could get caught up in the cross fire.

"Unlock the cruiser," Tucker called out to Reed.

More shots came, and in between the loud blasts, Laine heard the slight clicking sound. A moment later, Tucker threw open the passenger's-side door of the cruiser. Obviously, Reed had managed to unlock it from inside, no doubt using a remote key. The police car wasn't ideal cover because it was parked out in the open, but Laine was thankful for anything that would get her and Tucker out of the path of those bullets.

"Get in and stay down," Tucker told her.

He stayed perched behind the door and in front of her, his gun ready. And with his left hand, he pushed her into the cruiser.

Laine scrambled across the seat, reaching for Tucker to pull him in with her, but he stayed put and adjusted the aim of his gun.

Tucker fired.

The sound was deafening. It was so close that she could have sworn it rattled the windows.

Laine couldn't tell if his shot hit its target, but she guessed it hadn't when the next shot flew into the cruiser's front windshield. The glass was obviously bullet-resistant, but it still cracked and webbed, making it even harder for her to see what was going on.

Tucker levered himself up to fire another shot, but then immediately flattened himself on the ground when a bullet slammed into the cruiser door. The sound of metal ripping through metal caused her heart to pound against her ribs. The door might be bullet-resistant, too, but if the shooter kept it up, the shots could eventually get through, and Tucker could die.

"Get inside the car," she insisted.

Of course, he ignored her and leaned out of the door again.

This time, he didn't even get off a shot before a bullet smacked into his gun. For one heart-stopping moment, Laine thought he'd been hit, and she heard herself call out his name again. The sparks flew, and Tucker dropped his weapon only to snatch it back up again.

"I'm pretty sure this is the moron who tried to kill us at my house," Tucker relayed to her.

It didn't surprise her that he'd come back for them. Laine could still feel his arm around her throat and his gun jammed to her head. He wasn't close enough to do that now, but he could continue to blast his way into the car.

But why?

Why had he or his boss targeted Tucker and her to die?

Laine had gone back to that question over and over, and the only thing she could come up with was Dawn. Maybe the gunman thought Dawn had told her something incriminating. Something that would link back to the person behind not just these attacks but the baby farms themselves. But Dawn had barely managed to say anything before the killers had come for her.

"What the hell's he doing here?" Tucker mumbled.

Laine lifted her head just a fraction and caught a glimpse of Darren across the street. He was in front of the antique store just to the left of the diner. He had his back flat against the store's door, and he, too, had drawn his gun.

Tucker had asked a great question—what was he doing there?

Darren had left the sheriff's office a good half hour before, and while Laine wanted to think that maybe he was still in town just doing errands or something, she didn't like the timing of this.

Was Darren there because he'd hired that shooter on the roof, or was he in the same wrong place/wrong time situation as the diners?

"Get inside the store, Darren!" Tucker shouted to him.

Even over the din of the gunfire, Laine was fairly certain that Darren had heard him, but he ignored Tucker's order and stayed put. Sweet heaven, Tucker didn't need to have that kind of distraction now.

"Two guards are on the way!" Reed shouted out to them.

Good. But they wouldn't be able to get close enough to the shooter without running the risk of being gunned down.

Tucker fired another shot, took out his phone and tossed it to her. "Tell Reed to get those guards at the back of the diner. I want this idiot stopped now."

Laine managed a shaky nod, and with equally shaky hands, she scrolled through the numbers until she located Reed's. The deputy answered on the first ring, and she relayed Tucker's message. Tucker no doubt hadn't wanted to shout it out because he didn't want the guy to have any warning as to what was about to happen.

Maybe he hadn't wanted to alert Darren, either.

"The guards will be at the rear of the diner in just a couple of minutes," Reed confirmed after she heard him make a call. "But we got another problem. That social worker, Hague, and his lawyer just came running into the back of the sheriff's office. He claims he heard the shots and figured this was the safest place to be."

Oh, God. Definitely not good. "He could be there to help Buford escape."

"That's what I figured. I'll keep an eye on him."

That wouldn't be easy because she could still see Reed at the window. He had his gun ready, and his attention was focused on the shooter.

The bullets continued to come at them, but the direction changed a little. Instead of the door, they all seemed to be coming through the windshield. Each one chipped away at the glass and sent her adrenaline soaring.

"Get on the floor," Tucker told her.

He fired some shots at the gunman, reached in the glove compartment, reloaded with a fresh magazine and fired again. Still the bullets kept tearing through the glass, and one finally broke through just as she dropped to the floor. It tore through the car and slammed into the rear windshield.

The shooter might have seen her move, because again the shots shifted and he began to fire into the engine. Where the bullets could eventually reach her. Maybe reach her before the guards got to the diner.

"Do you know how to hot-wire a car?" Tucker asked. Because of the gunshots, he had to yell it.

Laine shook her head.

"Then you're about to learn, because there's no remote starter for the cruiser. Stay on the floor, get that Swiss Army knife in the glove compartment and use it to open the ignition cover." He motioned toward the plastic panels above and below the steering column.

Laine cursed her hands, which were shaking even harder now, and despite her out-of-control heartbeat and breathing, she tried to tamp down her responses. Hard to do with that with those bullets eating their way through the car. Even if she managed to hotwire it, those bullets might have already disabled the engine.

It took some doing, but she finally managed to get the panel off, and some wires spilled out.

"Take the red one—" Tucker's explanation was cut off by more shots.

Different from those that had been coming at them.

Laine hadn't thought the noise from the gunfight could get any worse, but she'd obviously been wrong.

She glanced out at Darren again to see if he was responsible for this new round of gunfire, but he was still in place against the antiques store. He was holding his gun in both hands against his chest with the barrel pointed up. The stance of a man who was waiting, not firing.

"Disconnect the red wire from the cylinder," Tucker continued. "And strip off the plastic ends." His voice was calm enough, but she saw the concern in his eyes. If she didn't get the cruiser started soon so they could escape, they'd be killed.

That gave her another shot of adrenaline that she desperately needed. Laine used the knife again to start scraping off the plastic. She'd barely gotten started when Tucker's phone rang.

"It's Reed," she told Tucker. She put the call on speaker and kept working on stripping the wires. Obviously she wouldn't make a good car thief because she was working at a snail's pace.

"There's a second shooter," Reed said the moment he came on the line. "And he's covering the rear roof. The guards can't get close enough to take out either of the men."

Tucker cursed. Laine groaned. She kept working.

"Tell the guards to stay in place and wait for a shot," Tucker told the deputy. In the same breath, he tipped his head to the wires again. "Twist the ends together, but don't let it touch anything else. Then strip the brown wire."

Even though the instructions were simple, the shots were more than enough of a distraction to make the task next to impossible. Laine grabbed the brown wire just as a shot slammed through the engine and made it all the way into the interior. It nicked the sleeve of her shirt.

Maybe her arm, too, since she felt the stinging pain.

That didn't stop her. In fact, it caused her to speed up, and the moment she had the brown wire stripped and the ends tied together, she glanced over at Tucker.

"What now?" she asked.

"I'll finish it." That was the only warning she got before he finally climbed into the cruiser and threw himself across the seat.

Laine hadn't ended the call, so she could still hear Reed yelling something. And she could also hear another voice.

Hague's.

That put her heart in her throat, and she hoped the man wasn't launching some kind of attack inside the sheriff's office. But she also heard something else.

A scream.

Not from Hague. This was from a woman, and Laine couldn't be sure, but it sounded like Rhonda. Mercy, had all their suspects managed to converge on this spot?

And if so, why?

It was a sickening thought that they could all be in this together. But if that were true, why would they have shown up right in the middle of this attack?

Ignoring the scream, Tucker touched the ends of the wires together. There was a spark, and the engine roared to life. Laine said a quick prayer of thanks that the bullets hadn't damaged it. He didn't waste even a moment maneuvering himself behind the wheel.

"Hold on," Tucker warned her.

There was no clear spot left on the windshield for him to see, but he hit the accelerator, and the cruiser practically flew out of the parking lot. There were no oncoming vehicles, thank goodness—probably because the sound of those gunshots had kept everyone at bay.

The bullets kept coming at them, even as the cruiser screeched away from the diner. The shooters adjusted their positions and continued to fire, but the bullets didn't go into the interior of the car.

They went into the tires.

Laine couldn't be sure, but it felt as if at least two tires had been shot out. Tucker had no choice but to bring the cruiser to a stop, and he got out.

"Stay on the floor," he warned her, and he started back toward the diner.

"It's too dangerous for you to do this," Laine called out to him.

"I won't go far. Can't risk those shooters coming out here to kidnap you."

That caused the skin on the back of her neck to crawl. The killer had come too close to taking her last time, and if they were bold enough to attempt another attack in broad daylight, then they'd have no problem gunning down Tucker and anyone else who got in their way.

Tucker kept a firm grip on his gun and shooting wrist as he inched away from the car. There were no more sounds of shots. Just eerie silence punctuated by an occasional shout.

Laine tried to keep watch. Tried to keep the panic in check, too. Still no shots. She figured it was too much to hope that the guards had managed to capture them. It was more likely that the shooters were on the move.

"You'd better be down," Tucker said to her over his shoulder, and he pivoted in the direction of one of the buildings just up the street from the diner.

He fired.

Tucker immediately jumped to the side behind a concrete park bench. Laine couldn't see who or what he was aiming at, but she certainly heard what followed.

Shots.

Not just a couple of them, but enough to make an all-out gunfight. And they were close. Maybe just yards away.

She put her hands over her ears to muffle the noise, but she kept watch of Tucker. "Stay put!" she yelled, though she doubted he even heard her.

He certainly didn't listen if he did, because he took aim again and fired off another shot.

This time she saw something. A man staggering out from the alley between two buildings. He was dressed all in black and was carrying some kind of rifle. Definitely not someone from the diner. No, this was almost certainly one of their attackers.

"He's headed right for you!" someone shouted, and it took her a second to realize it was Reed's voice coming from the phone.

"The gunman's coming your way," she warned Tucker.

Again, he took aim, but before Tucker could even pull the trigger, someone else fired.

The shot blasted through the air.

Chapter Thirteen

Tucker heard the shot, and for a split second, he thought he was a dead man.

No pain, no feeling of having a bullet blasting through him. It took him another split second to figure out what the heck was going on.

Ahead of him, he spotted Darren, his gun still drawn, and he had his attention nailed to the man on the ground to the right of him.

The second shooter.

And someone that Tucker might not have spotted in time before he got off a shot. But Darren had obviously seen and shot him.

"Don't get out of the car yet," Tucker said to Laine. "And call the ranch to make sure everything's okay there."

Tucker spared her a glance from over his shoulder to make sure she'd heard him. She had. But she was ghostly pale and shaking. Laine had come way too close to dying—again—and while Tucker needed to make sure she was all right, he first had to be certain that the threat had been neutralized.

And that the threat wasn't still standing directly in front of him.

Darren moved toward the man on the ground. Tucker

made his way to the gunman he'd shot, keeping his eye on Darren.

When Tucker reached the gunman, he knew he was dead.

Tucker didn't even have to check for a pulse to know that, or to notice that it was the same man who'd tried to kidnap Laine back at his place. After what the moron had done to her, it was hard to wish this had turned out differently, but a dead man couldn't tell them why he'd done it.

Or who'd hired him.

Even though on the surface, it appeared that Darren had helped him, had maybe even saved his life, Tucker wasn't about to dismiss him as a suspect just yet. Once the two jail guards had made it to the diner, it was highly likely that the gunmen would either be killed or taken captive.

Their boss definitely wouldn't have wanted the latter. Better dead than talking and naming names.

"How bad is Laine hurt?" Darren asked.

The question threw Tucker for a moment. Her ex's concern could have been real or faked—that wasn't what threw Tucker. It was the tone that Darren used, like that of a man who was certain she'd been injured. Or worse.

Tucker reeled around and looked past the lack of color in her face to the blood on the sleeve of her pale blue blouse.

"Call an ambulance," he shouted to Reed.

Hopefully, the deputy could hear Tucker's order. And hopefully, an ambulance was already on the way. Surely someone in that diner had called 911.

Despite the fact he had an armed suspect nearby, Tucker ran back to Laine and crawled into the shot-out cruiser with her.

"I'm fine," she insisted, probably because he looked ready to lose it. "So is everyone at the ranch. I just talked to Colt, and he said there's been no sign of attackers."

That was good, but it was the only good thing about this mess.

"You're not fine. You're bleeding." It turned his stomach to see that blood, and he ripped open her sleeve so he could see just how bad it was.

"It's a scratch. The bullet just grazed me."

"And you didn't say anything." Yeah, he definitely sounded like a man on the verge of losing it.

Tucker forced himself to take a deep breath. Forced himself to look at this like a lawman and not like some guy who'd, well, kissed her. The wound didn't appear to be serious. It was a graze, as she'd said. But she still needed to see a doctor.

"I'm sorry," Tucker managed to say.

"Sorry for saving my life?" Laine huffed, and in an instant her color got a whole lot better. "*Right*. Don't you dare apologize for what just happened. There's no way you could have stopped this."

Not true. If he could just get to the bottom of this investigation and arrest the idiot who'd put her life in danger yet again. It would happen. He would find this piece of dirt and make him, or her, pay hard.

Tucker heard the wail of the ambulance. Not just one from the sound of it, but several. Good. He had no idea if anyone else was hurt, but there was plenty of potential for civilian injuries with all those shots that'd been fired.

"Just wait until the ambulance gets here," Tucker told Laine when she started to get out. "I need to make sure this is finished."

And *finishing* it started with Darren.

"What the heck were you doing out here?" Tucker demanded, his narrowed gaze zooming right in on the man.

"I got a text saying there was trouble going down, and that you were going to use that trouble to set me up."

Tucker wasn't sure whether to curse or laugh. "Who sent that?"

Darren shook his head. "The name and number were blocked."

Now Tucker did curse. "And you believed anything an anonymous source had to say after your girlfriend was murdered and her body was dumped on your ranch?"

Tucker let his question hang in the air and thought about just how stupid—or calculating—Darren had been. For now, he motioned for Darren to hand over his gun.

"Really, we're gonna do this?" Darren challenged.

"Yeah," Tucker said with attitude, tapping the badge on his shirt.

One way or another, Darren was handing over that gun. No way did Tucker want an armed suspect wandering around to pick off him and Laine.

"I'll want it back when you're finished playing lawman." Scowling and cursing, Darren handed him the gun, and Tucker put it in the back waist of his jeans.

The two ambulances pulled to a stop, and the medics darted out. So did Laine, and despite Tucker warning her to stay put, she walked toward them.

"I'm okay," she insisted again. She held up his phone. "But Reed's not. There's a problem in the sheriff's office."

Of course there was. Nothing about this day was going to be easy.

"Don't go far," Tucker ordered Darren, and he gently looped his arm around Laine's waist so he could get her moving toward the ambulance.

"This can wait," Laine said, leading him toward the sheriff's office instead. "Reed needs you now."

"Is someone hurt or dead?" he snarled. The moment he asked the question, Tucker knew exactly what'd happened. "Buford escaped."

She nodded. "And Hague ran out, too, supposedly to chase after him."

Great. Just what he didn't need. A suspect trying to help round up a fugitive.

Tucker hoped Laine was right about being able to wait to get to the hospital, because he didn't take her directly to the ambulance. However, he did motion for one of the medics to follow them into the sheriff's office.

Yeah, it was chaos inside, all right. Reed was on the phone, yelling for someone to send out a search crew. Rhonda was sitting in the chair next to his desk, sobbing. Twin steaks of mascara tears streaked down her cheeks. The gun cabinet was open, and papers were scattered on the floor.

Another dark-haired man dressed in a suit paced the floor. Hague's lawyer, no doubt. His cold, gray eyes landed on them as if he blamed them for the shooting and his client's hasty departure. Tucker glared back. He wasn't in the mood to take anyone else's mess off their hands. Especially someone who had Hague for a client.

"What happened?" Tucker asked Reed the moment he finished his call. He holstered his gun, eased Laine into one of the other chairs and again motioned to the medic to tend to her. The guy hurried right over.

"I was at the window, trying to get a clean shot at the gunman on the roof when she came running in." Reed tipped his head to Rhonda. "Then she started screaming."

"That prisoner came out of the room," Rhonda said

through a sob, "and he worked his hands around his lawyer's neck so that his chains and cuffs were choking her. He dragged her out the back door like she was a rag doll."

Hell. He should have seen this coming. In fact, this entire attack could have been designed just to free Buford. Now Buford had a hostage.

Maybe.

And maybe the lawyer had been in on this, too, and had just been pretending to be his captive so she could get him out of there.

"Did Buford manage to get a gun?" Tucker asked.

Reed shook his head. "But Hague grabbed one. He said he wasn't going to let that innocent woman get hurt."

That was admirable, if it was the truth. With all the other insanity going on, it was possible that Hague took the gun so he could give it to Buford.

"I tried to talk my client out of this," the pacing suit said.

"And you are?" Tucker snapped.

"Steve Wilkey," he spat out, as if it wasn't any of Tucker's business.

"Well, Mr. Wilkey, your client has earned you a little stay here until we can get all of this sorted out."

As expected, that didn't put a pleasant expression on the man's sour face. His expression got significantly worse when Tucker led him down the hall and locked him in one of the interview rooms. He couldn't hold him for long, and the guy was already making a call before Tucker stepped away. Still, it would get Hague's eyes and ears away from Rhonda in case the woman had anything else to tell them.

"Right after the attack started, I called the sheriff from Appaloosa Pass," Reed continued. "He's sending over all his available deputies. The Rangers are sending someone, too. They should be here soon."

Good. That was a start, and Tucker hoped that *soon* would be soon enough. "Buford shouldn't be hard to find. He's wearing an orange jumpsuit and is cuffed at the hands and feet. He can't get far like that."

Well, unless someone had a vehicle waiting nearby to whisk him away. Which was entirely possible.

Tucker took out his phone and called the Ranger crime lab to make sure they were on their way. They were. And with that taken care of, he turned his attention back to Laine.

She was making a face, and it took him a moment to realize it was because the medic was dabbing her arm with antiseptic. She softened her expression when she caught him looking at her.

"I'm fine," she repeated.

"She is," the medic agreed. He took out a bandage strip and pressed it to the wound on her arm. "It's just a deep scratch, but as a precaution, she should drop by her doctor's office and get a tetanus shot."

"I will," Laine mumbled. She pointed to the diner. "Now, go take care of the people who really might be hurt."

The medic waited for Tucker to give him the nod before he rushed out. Hopefully, there wouldn't be any injuries, but at the very least, some folks would be in shock.

Maybe Laine was, too.

She suddenly looked very calm for a woman who'd come close to dying. It wouldn't last. Tucker figured she was holding herself together for his sake, so he wouldn't feel like kicking himself for allowing something like this to happen again.

"You want me to go out there and check on things?" Reed asked, volleying glances between Rhonda and Laine.

Tucker nodded. "Just make sure the back door and windows are locked." Buford likely wouldn't come back, but Tucker didn't want to risk him, or anyone else for that matter, having another go at trying to kill Laine. "And get Darren's phone. I need to check something on it."

Once Reed was outside, Laine stood and pushed her hair from her face. "I'll get you out of here as soon as possible," he promised.

"And I'll leave, too," Rhonda insisted. "As soon as it's safe."

Heaven knew when that would be.

"Why'd you come back to the sheriff's office?" Tucker asked her.

"My car wouldn't start." Rhonda's breath broke and she wiped away more tears. "I'd parked up the street in the grocery store lot, and I got worried that maybe someone had tampered with the engine. I came back so I could ask you to check it for me."

Either it was another bad coincidence, or Rhonda had come back to watch her hired guns in action. Of course, that would pretty much make her a psycho.

Something he couldn't completely rule out.

"I didn't know my cousin would be here," Rhonda went on, "or I wouldn't have come. I don't like the things Martin's been saying about me."

Tucker figured Hague felt the same way about her. But which one of them had reason for concern?

Maybe neither.

Tucker glanced out the window at their third suspect, Darren, who was handing over his phone to Reed. Darren clearly wasn't happy about that, and as soon as he slapped it in Reed's hand, he started to pace on the sidewalk.

"By any chance, did you call Darren earlier?" he asked Rhonda.

"No." Her forehead bunched up. "Why, did he say I did?"

"No. Just wondering."

She stared at him, the tears welling up in her eyes again. "Darren did say that I had. I don't know why people always accuse me of things I didn't do."

Her hands were shaking like crazy, but she clutched her purse against her chest like a shield. Tucker nearly drew his gun again when she reached inside. But instead of a weapon, she pulled out a bottle of firecracker-red polish and proceeded to give her nails another coat.

Rhonda followed Laine's gaze to her hands. "I saw you looking at my nails when I was in here earlier. Couldn't figure out why at first, but it was because of the manicure, wasn't it?" She didn't wait for an answer. "It's just something I do when I'm stressed. It's like you looking at Sergeant McKinnon."

Tucker blinked. "Excuse me?"

"Laine always looks at you when she's stressed. Like the conversation we had with Darren—whenever something hit a nerve with her, she'd look at you. You're like her security blanket or something."

He glanced at Laine to see if this made a lick of sense. Tucker didn't get much of an answer. Just a deer-caught-in-headlights look from Laine, and even that vanished when two people approached the door.

Reed and Darren.

Since Tucker didn't trust Darren any farther than he could throw him, he stepped in front of Laine and put his hand on the butt of his gun. He'd already taken Darren's gun, but that didn't mean the man didn't have a backup.

Coming through the door, Darren scowled at Tucker's stance. Tucker just scowled back. No way was he going to apologize for protecting Laine.

Reed handed Tucker the man's phone and then stepped away to make a call. Tucker scrolled through the recent calls on Darren's phone until he got to one with an unknown name and number. It'd been made about an hour earlier—just about when those gunmen would have been setting up their attack.

"I told you the person blocked the name and number. Satisfied?" Darren took back his phone. "I think after everything that just happened, I should take the babies to my ranch where I can keep them safe. When you get the DNA results back—"

"I got the results," Tucker interrupted. He tried to figure out a good way to share them, and just decided to blurt it out. "Dawn's the mother, but you're not the father."

Darren looked as if someone had slugged him. "You're lying."

Tucker shook his head. "DNA proves otherwise. Their father's a convicted murderer named Kurt Laverty. Did Dawn ever mention him?"

"No." Darren scrubbed his hand over his face and dropped down in one of the chairs. "I guess Dawn lied to me."

"Yeah. I'm sorry about that." And he was. Tucker knew how he would feel if he'd thought those kids were his, only to learn they were someone else's, and they were about to be legally snatched away.

"Some good news," Reed announced. "The medic said no one else was hurt in the shooting."

Tucker blew out a breath of relief, a breath that would have been a whole lot bigger if Buford had been caught. The man was a killer and would no doubt try to kill again if he wasn't stopped.

"Go ahead and start taking statements," Tucker said to Reed, and he helped Laine to her feet. "I need to check on some...things."

Laine herself was one of those things, but he also needed to call Egan Caldwell, a Ranger friend. The minute he had her in the break room, Tucker checked her arm. Because of the pristine white bandage now covering it, he could no longer see that angry-looking cut, but the images of it in his head were way too clear.

"Don't say you're sorry again," she blurted out, and Laine came up on her tiptoes and brushed a kiss over his lips.

Tucker hadn't known just how much he needed that kiss until she gave it to him. He eased his arm around her and kissed her right back.

Yeah. It was what he had needed all right, and judging from the little sound Laine made, she had needed it, too. And that wasn't good. They had enough going on without adding kisses. That's why he stopped this time, but Tucker wasn't the sort of man who lied to himself.

He would kiss her again.

And more. They'd soon land in bed to take up where they'd left off all those years before. Later, that is. For now, he had to tell her something, and he was really going to have to sell it.

"I need to arrange a safe house for the babies," he started. "One away from us. It doesn't have to be far, but they can't be under the same roof as us."

Tucker got the reaction he figured he'd get. Her shoulders slumped, and her mouth began to tremble. "We've kept them safe so far."

"Yeah. But we've gotten lucky. We can't continue to rely on luck when it comes to them. With Buford out there again, he or his boss could already be planning another attack on us. He wants us dead, and I don't want the twins getting caught in the middle of another gunfight."

Hell, he didn't want Laine caught in one, either. That cut on her arm was proof of just how close these morons had come to killing her. Next time, it could be a thousand times worse.

"I'm the one the killers want most," she said. "You need to distance yourself from me."

Oh, man.

The tears came again, and Tucker pulled her back into his arms.

"I'm not doing that, okay? They want us both. Those shots today proved that." He shook his head. "For now, we stay together and try to figure out who's behind this. Once we've done that, there'll be no need for the babies to be in a safe house."

She seemed relieved, for a moment anyway, but then she had to blink back tears. "How soon would the twins be moved?"

Best not to sugarcoat it. "Pretty much now."

He stepped a few feet away from her and called Egan. It wasn't exactly a surprise call. Tucker had contacted him the night before and asked him to make preliminary arrangements. It was time to make those arrangements final.

"I just heard about the shooting," Egan said the moment he answered the call.

"Yeah. We need to move the babies ASAP. Don't tell me where you're taking them."

Tucker didn't think there were any leaks in the sheriff's office, but he didn't want to take any chances. Buford had had access to that particular room since he'd used the back door to escape, and Tucker didn't want to risk Buford or his lawyer planting some kind of eavesdropping device.

"Just promise me the babies will be safe," Tucker added to Egan.

"They will be. I'll get a team out to your family's ranch now to pick them up, and we'll drive them to the safe house."

So everything was set into motion. Well, partly, anyway. "I want to see them before the Ranger moves them," Laine insisted.

Tucker didn't argue with her. He wanted her out of there anyway, but he had to make sure everything was as secure as he could make it.

When he went back into the squad room, he saw that Reed was on the phone. Rhonda and Darren were seated and writing their statements. Better yet, a guard from the jail and the night deputy had come in to help.

Good.

That freed him up to get Laine back to the ranch.

"Call if you need me," Tucker said to Reed. "And once we're out of here, then you can let Hague's lawyer go." He started for the door.

Reed held up his hand in a "wait a second" gesture. Tucker couldn't tell who the deputy was talking to, but judging from his expression, this wasn't good news.

"How bad?" he asked, the moment Reed finished his call.

"Bad." Reed drew in a long, weary breath. "We've got two dead bodies on our hands."

Chapter Fourteen

Laine's heart dropped when Tucker pulled in front of the Sweetwater Ranch. There was no sign of the Ranger team who'd come and collected the twins, and that meant she hadn't been able to see them.

Maybe for the last time.

It shouldn't have felt like a big deal since they weren't hers. Might never be. And it wasn't as if she didn't have other things to occupy her mind, especially after the news of the two dead bodies. A horrible ending to what had been a horrible attack.

One had been Penny Wilmer, Buford's attorney.

Her body had been found on the side of the road just outside of town. Since they'd known that Buford had taken her hostage, it wasn't a total shock. Still, it'd been a reminder that they were dealing with killers.

And one of those killers had been killed.

Tucker and she didn't have all the details yet, but it appeared that someone had gotten past the guard at the hospital who was watching the injured gunman, Hines, and had given the man a lethal injection. He could no longer tell them the identity of the person who'd hired him or any details about the black-market baby operation.

Neither could the man who'd launched the attack from

the roof of the diner because he was dead, too. Reed had shown Laine a photo of the dead man, just to verify it was their missing gunman who'd tried to kidnap her at Tucker's place. It was.

Now, Buford was the only one who could give them those details, and they'd have to find him first. So far, there'd been no sign of him.

"I'm sorry," Tucker said as he brought the truck to a stop in front of the house.

He didn't have to clarify that apology. Laine knew. He, too, seemed sorry that they'd missed saying goodbye to the babies.

"You're sure they'll be safe with the Rangers?" Laine asked him.

"Yeah. And the babies will be well cared for. The team has a nanny from the Safe Cradle Agency."

An agency that Laine knew well. It provided bodyguard nannies to at-risk infants and children. Sadly, the twins definitely fell into that category.

Because she and Tucker were also in danger, he didn't waste any time getting her into the house. Colt was in the foyer, waiting for them.

"The Rangers left about ten minutes ago," Colt said, checking his watch. "Now that you're back, I need to head to the office and help Reed. There's a mountain of paperwork from the two murders."

Tucker nodded. "Thanks for everything." He glanced around the empty rooms that flanked the foyer. "Where are the others?"

"Rosalie went up to her room. Mary, too. They were a little upset to see the babies leave. Dad's out with one of the hands checking on some new calves."

Colt headed for the door, and the moment he was outside, Tucker locked up and set the security system. "Come on," Tucker added. "You've got to get some rest."

Laine was too exhausted to argue, and besides, the look on his face was troubled enough without her adding more to it by protesting.

"I know you don't want to worry about me," she mumbled as they worked their way up the stairs. "And you don't have to. I'm not going to fall apart or anything."

She hoped.

Tucker made a noncommittal sound that rumbled deep in his throat, and he just kept her moving until they reached the guest room. Laine expected him to deposit her inside and head to the ranch office to work, but he stepped inside with her.

"Rest," he ordered, tipping his head to the bed.

She blindly started in that direction, but then stopped and placed her hand on the side of his face. "Rest would do you some good, too."

His eyebrow moved up, and she knew what his answer would be. No way. Tucker would work himself into the ground to try to make things right.

But maybe she could do something about that.

Without thinking it through, Laine came up on her toes and brushed her mouth over his. She should have thought it through. Or rested, as Tucker had ordered. Because she'd only meant for it to be a kiss of comfort.

However, their kisses weren't the comforting sort.

Nope. Just the simple touch sent a lightning bolt of heat through her entire body. It probably didn't have that same kind of impact on Tucker, but it did put some fire in his eyes.

"Really?" he challenged.

She lifted her shoulder. "I figure I've made so many

mistakes already. Going to the baby farm with the CI. Getting involved with Darren. Running to you for help. What's one more?"

He didn't lift his eyebrow this time, but he did tighten his mouth. "You think coming to me was a mistake?"

"Of course." Not that she'd had other solid options, but she should have come up with something. *Anything*. "Buford wouldn't have tried to kill you if I'd managed to go to someone else."

"No, he would just have tried to kill that *someone else*." Tucker mumbled some profanity, slipped his arm around her waist and eased her to him. "So, no mistake there. But the other three things, yeah, definite mistakes."

She flinched a little. "You lumped that kiss in with those other huge mistakes?"

He stared down at her. "Yeah, because it wasn't just a kiss. You're tired. I'm tired. Our defenses are way down, and anything including a simple kiss will feel as if it's full-blown foreplay."

Laine couldn't argue with that, either. Her nerves were right there at the surface, and it would feel so good to lose herself in Tucker's arms.

In his bed.

The timing was all wrong, though.

She shook her head, rethinking that. The timing would always be wrong with Tucker. His mother's trial would start soon, bringing all those old memories to the surface. While neither she nor Tucker seemed to have much emotional stake in the outcome of all that, it would mean having to deal with their families' reactions.

Especially her mother's.

And his father's. And those of half of his siblings.

"Talking yourself out of it, huh?" Tucker drawled.

She started to nod, but rethought that, too. The timing would never be good for them. Her family was never going to accept him, and the same was true for his accepting her. Besides, there was no telling when this investigation might be over.

No telling when they'd have a chance to be alone again like this.

Or when she'd have an opportunity to add another mistake to the ones she'd already made.

Laine reached up, slid her hand around the back of Tucker's neck and pulled him down to her. No hesitation. No resistance. From either of them.

Just the sizzling kiss that she knew meant there was no more turning back.

TUCKER HAD SOME serious doubts about this. Man, did he. But he just shoved those doubts aside and kept on kissing Laine as if he had a right to do just that.

He didn't.

The only thing he had a right to do was protect her, and while kissing her wouldn't do that, Tucker couldn't see any way around it.

Laine and he had been eyeing each other for a while now, and the heat had been building with each passing second. He'd have an easier time stopping his lungs from needing air than he would putting a stop to this.

So, knowing he was making a huge mistake, Tucker decided to make it worth whatever the hell price they were going to pay for this. And there would be a price. Laine was all worked up now, but soon she'd realize it was impossible for the two of them to be together.

That put a knot in his gut, and gave him a few much-needed seconds of hesitation. He pulled back just a little, his gaze meeting hers.

"What?" she said, her voice warm and breathy. "Please tell me you're not stopping."

"No."

But Tucker likely would have given a little more thought to that *no chance of making this work* notion if she hadn't latched onto his neck and pulled him back to her for a kiss. She didn't stop there. Laine pushed up his shirt, her hand landing on his chest.

Heck, that did it.

No more time for thoughts or doubts. He deepened the kiss and did some shirt-tugging of his own.

Tucker pulled off her top and sent it sailing over his shoulder. He got a good look at those curves that'd been driving him crazy. A good taste, too, when he lowered his head to kiss the tops of her breasts.

Oh, man. He'd figured this would be good, but he'd way underestimated it. She was perfect—not just her breasts, but the rest of her, too.

Laine made a helpless little sound of surrender, and she sagged against him. Tucker pinned her against the closed door and kept kissing her until soon, very soon, it wasn't enough.

The lacy white bra went next, and he got a punch of sizzling heat when he kissed her bare breasts. And lower, to her stomach.

Laine made more of those sounds when his mouth reached the front of her jeans. He unzipped them, pulling them off her. Her panties, too. The next kiss caused her moans to get significantly louder.

"Get up here," she mumbled, grabbing onto his shoulders and hauling him back up the length of her body. "I want us to do this together, with you inside me."

Tucker had no objections to that, but he was more than a little concerned that *together* was going to happen pretty darn fast. Laine didn't just tug at his clothes. She started fighting to get him undressed, and Tucker intended to help her do just that.

But she stopped him with a kiss.

Her clever mouth landed on his neck, just below his right ear, and Tucker darn near lost what little breath he had left. He was rock-hard and ready, but that did it.

For just a moment, he allowed himself to get lost in the heat. In those neck kisses she was so good at giving. He hadn't needed anything else to fire him up, but Laine delivered anyway.

While she continued to grapple with his jeans and make him crazier with those neck kisses, Tucker maneuvered her away from the door, somehow remembering to lock it. They moved together without stopping the kisses and without breaking the hold they had on each other. By the time they made it to the bed, Tucker was sure he was hot enough to burn to ash.

"Now," she insisted.

He couldn't have delayed this if he'd tried, but he did hope there would be a second round somewhere in their future. One not driven by this insanity to finish all of this at lightning speed.

Laine finally got him unzipped just as they dropped down on the mattress. A new wrestling match began, and they managed to get off his boots so the jeans could go next. However, Tucker put another pause to the frantic pace when he caught sight of a naked Laine beneath him.

Yeah, she was a beauty, all right.

Over the years when he hadn't been able to stop it, he'd imagined her like this. Naked, beneath him, flushed with arousal and waiting for him to take her. Good thing they didn't have a lot of time, because he had to have her *now*.

Clearly, Laine felt the same way. She slid her legs around the back of his, and Tucker had no choice but to sink deep and hard into her.

His vision blurred.

His heart started galloping a mile a minute.

Everything inside him urged him to finish this and bring them both to a climax, but even through the crazy haze of fire in his head, he knew this wasn't just sex.

Hell.

Tucker wanted to remind her that he wasn't the more-than-sex type. But he didn't get the chance to say anything. He started to move inside her, and every logical thought flew right out of his head.

The only thing that mattered now was taking Laine.

"You're much too good at this," she mumbled, matching him thrust for thrust.

Tucker wanted to say something, anything, but he was past the point of coherent speech. Past the point of anything except racing toward the finishing line. First for Laine. And then for himself.

The feel of her release roared through him. Driving him harder. Pushing him closer. Until he couldn't hang on to the pleasure even a second longer. The last thing Tucker heard before he went over was Laine.

Whispering his name.

Chapter Fifteen

The slow-burning hunger was finally quiet. For a little while, anyway. Laine's body was slack from the pleasure, but she had no doubts—*none*—that the sizzling need would return with a vengeance. Maybe in a day or two, when she and Tucker had this investigation under control.

Or sooner.

The heat trickled through her again when he lifted his head and looked down at her. She'd never been immune to that handsome face. Never would be. Those alarmingly good looks made her want him all over again.

Too bad it wasn't only his looks that drew her in.

Sadly, it was the man himself, the total package, and she wondered if she'd ever get over this thing she had for Tucker.

Probably not.

Making love with him had only strengthened her desire. And that meant she was setting herself up for a broken heart.

"Man," Tucker mumbled. "When I mess things up, I go for broke."

Laine dredged up a smile, located his mouth and kissed him. "I should probably be insulted by that."

He made a sound of disagreement. "You should probably slug me and toss me out of your bed."

Slugging and tossing Tucker were the last things she wanted. Well, unless he continued to talk like that. Yes, it was a mistake, but it certainly hadn't felt like one, and she wanted him to feel the same conflicted emotions she was—but not for another few minutes.

Tucker groaned, moved off her and flopped onto his back beside her. Laine braced herself for more chatter about how wrong all of that had been, but he merely leaned over and returned the kiss she'd given him earlier.

"I can't stay," he mumbled, easing off the bed.

And she wondered just how many times he had said that to a woman. Tucker certainly wasn't the sort to linger after landing in bed, but she'd hoped for a little more time.

Well, at least she had a view to admire.

Mercy. How could any man look that good with so little sleep, especially after all the stress they'd been through?

"I want to call Egan and make sure the twins arrived at the safe house," he added.

That got her moving off the bed, too. Laine certainly hadn't forgotten about the babies, but she hadn't thought they'd be able to contact them so soon. Or at all.

"Will they be there already?" she asked.

"Maybe. I doubt he'll take them too far away since there are several safe houses in the area. But if they haven't gotten to one of them yet, I'll find out when they're due to arrive and how much backup Egan has with him."

Good. She wanted every precaution to be taken. "A call will be secure?" The last thing she wanted was for the kidnappers to find the twins and go after them again.

"Our phones are secure." And he pressed the Ranger's number. Sergeant Egan Caldwell answered on the first ring.

"We're still driving around," he volunteered. "The kiddos are fine."

Laine prayed that it would stay that way.

"Someone did try to follow us," the Ranger went on. "The guy was darn persistent, too, but I managed to lose him about fifteen minutes ago."

Had her heart stopped for a few seconds? It'd certainly felt like it. She'd known the kidnappers were likely watching them. Would perhaps try to follow them, too. But it was gut-wrenching to hear it spelled out.

"You're certain you lost the guys following you?" Tucker asked Egan.

"Positive. And I won't go anywhere near the safe house until I'm sure they haven't picked up our trail. It's not that far from town so I'll call you once I have everyone settled."

Tucker thanked him and ended the call, but then he just stared at the phone. The muscles in his jaw started to work hard against each other.

"If you decide to adopt them, I'll help." He didn't exactly look comfortable with that offer, but when his eyes met hers, Laine could see that it was genuine. "Not that I know much about babies, but—"

"But you care for them," she finished for him. "I understand."

Her mind immediately started to weave a fantasy. Of the two of them taking care of the babies together. Of them landing in bed for another mind-blowing round of lovemaking. But Laine forced aside those images. Tucker's offer certainly hadn't included playing house with her.

Had it?

The fantasy took off again like a bee-stung horse, but this time it was the sound of Tucker's phone that nipped it in the bud. Laine's attention snapped to the screen, where she thought she might see Sergeant Caldwell's name, but instead she saw Colt's.

"We found Buford," Colt announced the moment Tucker answered.

Both fear and relief jolted through her. She wanted the monster found, but Laine prayed he was nowhere near the babies.

"Where is he?" Tucker asked his brother.

"At your house."

Laine did a mental double take. Tucker's house was only a quarter mile away. Way too close.

The muscles in Tucker's face tightened again. "Please tell me you have him under arrest."

"Not yet. One of the deputies from Appaloosa Pass spotted Buford and went in pursuit. Buford ditched his truck not far from the ranch and ran on foot through the pasture to get to your house. He's inside, but we have him surrounded. Some of the ranch hands are coming to help so Buford won't be able to sneak out."

"Good. I'll be there in a few minutes." Tucker ended the call and immediately finished dressing. "You'll stay here," he insisted before she could say a word.

Not that Laine wanted to go with him. But she also didn't want him rushing out into possible gunfire.

Even if it was his job.

She got a solid reminder of that when he put on his shirt, badge attached, and then slid on his shoulder holster. As if it were the most natural thing in the world, he dropped another kiss on her mouth, and Laine had to hurry to keep up with him when he rushed out of the room and down the stairs.

"Reset the security system and stay away from the windows when you go back up to your room," Tucker instructed at the front door. "I'll call my dad and let him know what's going on so he can come upstairs and stay with you. Rosalie's in the house, too."

He rattled off the security code, and just like that, Tucker was gone.

Laine watched him from one of the sidelight windows. It was already dusk, but she had no trouble seeing him get into one of the trucks parked alongside the house. And he wasn't alone. Two armed ranch hands got in with him, and they sped away. Another ranch hand stayed, standing guard in front of the house.

She hadn't realized she was shaking until she locked the door and pressed in the security code. Once she had that done, Laine didn't waste any time getting upstairs. She turned off the lights, and despite the fact she wanted to see if she could spot Tucker's place from any of the windows, she stayed back.

And she waited.

The seconds crawled by. So did the thoughts in her suddenly wild imagination.

This time it was not a fantasy of playing house with Tucker, but rather a stream of images of another gunfight. She seriously doubted that Buford would just surrender, and that meant Tucker, his brother and anyone else out there were in danger because Buford would have come armed and ready to kill.

Since she couldn't see what was going on, Laine tried to level her breathing so she could hear. Tucker's place was just up the road. Thankfully, she didn't hear any gunshots.

Laine was so focused on listening for those shots that she nearly jumped out of her skin when there was a knock at the door. She eased it open to see Tucker's father. He had a gun tucked in the waist of his jeans.

Roy slipped a phone into her hand. "Tucker said he'd call you on this number when he had Buford."

"Thanks." She must have looked even more terrified than she felt because Roy gave her arm a gentle pat. A generous gesture, considering what had gone on between their families.

"I'll be in my room right across the hall." He started to turn, but then he stopped and caught her gaze. "I'm old but I'm not blind. I can see what's happening between Tucker and you."

Uh-oh. She braced herself for another lecture like the one her mother had given her, but that wasn't a lecturing look in Roy's eyes.

"For what it's worth, I've always thought you were a good woman. Good for Tucker, too."

Laine had to stop her mouth from dropping open.

"Neither of you can probably see that because of the way circumstances put you in the middle of a mountain-sized mess," Roy went on. "Still, if I were you, I wouldn't give up on him just yet."

She shook her head. "But what about the rest of your family?"

He lifted his shoulder, gave a weary sigh. "Sometimes folks don't know what's best for them until it knocks them upside the head."

They shared a smile so brief that when Roy walked away, Laine wasn't even sure it'd happened. Once Roy was inside his room, Laine went back into hers. However, she'd barely managed to get the door shut when she heard a sound.

Not gunfire.

This was a loud humming noise, and it took her a moment to realize what it was. The security alarm. Someone had opened a window or a door.

She forced herself not to panic. After all, Rayanne, Rosalie and Mary were in the house, and any one of them could have gone outside. She stepped into the hall, waiting for someone to punch in the access code so the humming wouldn't go to a full wail.

But that didn't happen.

The alarm blasted through the house, and Roy hurried out into the hall. Soon other doors opened, too, and Rosalie came out from the guest room that she'd been using when the babies had been at the ranch.

"Where's your sister?" Roy immediately asked.

Rosalie shook her head. "She went back over to the guesthouse right after the Rangers took the twins. She said something about going through some of Seth's notes for the trial. Mary's in town. As far as I know, we're the only ones here."

Roy hurried to the keypad on the wall near the front of the stairs. "Someone triggered the alarm in one of the downstairs windows."

That sent Laine's stomach to her knees. Rayanne and Mary wouldn't have come in that way. She grabbed her phone and saw that she had no service.

Had someone managed to jam it?

Laine knew there were devices that people could use to disrupt phone signals. There'd been news reports about them. Had that happened now? And if so, who'd done it?

"Mary? Rayanne?" Roy shouted. "Who's down there?"

No one answered.

But even over the screech of the alarm, Laine heard the footsteps on the stairs. Someone was coming directly toward them.

TUCKER STEPPED FROM his truck, and with the two ranch hands following, he made his way to Colt, who'd taken cover behind his sheriff's cruiser.

Parked next to Colt and also behind cover was the deputy from Appaloosa Pass. With two hands guarding the back of the house, hopefully there was no way Buford could escape.

"Any sign of where he is in the house?" Tucker asked his brother.

Colt shook his head. "But Deputy Grange said he saw him go in through the back door."

A door that Tucker had likely left unlocked in his hurry to get Laine and the babies out of there the last time Buford had paid them a visit. Not that a simple lock would have stopped a man like Buford, but it might have slowed him down enough for the deputy to make an arrest.

Or kill him.

"Deputy Grange said Buford seemed to be staggering when he ran inside," Colt added.

Tucker shook his head. "You mean staggering like a wounded man?"

"Maybe. He couldn't tell. But it's possible Buford hurt his ankle or something."

Too bad the injury hadn't been enough to make him collapse in the yard. Being inside put the man in the catbird seat since there were plenty of windows through which to take shots at them.

Colt glanced at Tucker and did a double take. "You okay?"

Tucker automatically scowled, since he really didn't want to be questioned about his state of mind. Or maybe it was the well-pleasured vibe he might be giving off. "Yeah. Well, okay for someone about to face down a killer. Why?"

"You just look funny, that's all." And Colt took another long glance.

Probably at Tucker's messed-up hair, wrinkled clothes and few missed buttons on his shirt. Tucker probably had Laine's scent all over him. A brother would pick up on that.

A smart brother would keep his mouth shut about it, though.

Especially since Laine was a topic on which Colt and he would probably never see eye to eye.

Heck, two days before Tucker and she hadn't seen eye to eye, either. Sex changed things. It broke down barriers. Put the past in a different perspective. It was also distracting the heck out of him at the worst possible time.

Obviously, Colt was a smart brother, because he didn't push the subject.

"Right before all of this happened, I got a call about the twins," Colt continued a moment later. He reached into the cruiser and took out a tear-gas-canister gun. "SAPD talked with Dawn's aunt. She's sixty-four and about to retire. She doesn't want to raise the twins."

Despite everything else going on, that was a relief. It would be for Laine, too, and he couldn't wait to tell her the news.

Except it might only be temporary good news.

"What about Laverty's family?" Tucker asked. After all, Laverty was the birth father, and his kin would have a say in custody. "Is it possible they'll want to claim the babies?"

"No next of kin. He has some distant cousins, all in jail. None of them would pass a background check, much less qualify to get custody of his offspring."

Again, that was good, and once he had Buford out of the house and back in custody, it might be something Laine and he could celebrate.

Maybe with more of that distracting sex.

"I can put the tear-gas canister through the front window or the side," his brother said. "Can't guarantee it won't cause something to catch on fire, though."

Yeah, Tucker already knew that, but he also didn't want this to turn into a long standoff. The sooner they got Buford out of there, the better, and the tear gas should send the killer running outside. With Buford's record, though, it was likely the man would come out shooting.

"Don't worry about the house. But if possible, I need him alive," Tucker reminded Colt. With the other gunmen and Buford's lawyer dead, this man was his best shot at learning the truth about who was behind these attacks.

Colt nodded, took aim and fired. The tear-gas canister crashed through the window to the right of the front door, and Tucker heard it clank to the floor. Seconds later, wispy white gas started to ooze through the gaping hole in the glass.

Tucker took aim, waited.

Only a few seconds passed, but he suddenly got a bad feeling about all of it.

Why wasn't Buford running out?

He glanced at the main house. Tucker could see the lights stabbing through the twilight, but the place was too far away to tell if anything was wrong. He reminded himself that his father and sisters were in there. If Buford had somehow managed to escape and get to that house, they'd protect Laine. And besides, if something went wrong, one of them would call him.

Still, the skin crawled on the back of his neck.

"I'm speeding this up," Tucker warned his brother. He fired a shot into the eaves of the house. Then another.

No response.

Certainly no sign of Buford.

Tucker waited another couple of seconds, hoping that the front door would burst open, and Buford would come staggering out.

He didn't.

"Something's not right," Tucker mumbled. He took out his phone and pressed Laine's number. No answer. He tried again with the house phone.

Nothing.

Hell. This was some kind of trap.

"Call me when you have Buford out of there," Tucker said to his brother, and he didn't wait for the ranch hands who'd come with him. He jumped back in his truck, started the engine and hit the gas.

In his rearview mirror, he saw Colt and the others moving toward the house, guns raised. Ready in case Buford came out shooting. Tucker hated to put this on other people's shoulders. Buford was his problem, and he wanted to be the one to take him down. But he couldn't ignore the fact that Laine and the rest of his family might be under attack.

The short drive seemed to take an eternity, and when

he pulled to a stop in front of the house, Tucker still didn't see signs that anything was wrong. However, the moment he threw open his truck door, his phone rang.

Colt's name popped up on the screen.

"You have Buford?" Tucker immediately asked.

"We have him, all right." Colt paused. "But he's dead."

Oh, man. That was not what he wanted to hear. "You had to shoot him?"

"No. I think he was poisoned or something. I haven't examined the body yet, but I can see him through the window. He's on the floor in the kitchen, and there's foam around his mouth. He looks like he had a seizure."

Both concern and relief roared through Tucker. On the one hand, this meant Buford couldn't come after Laine and the babies again. But it also meant someone had likely murdered the one man who could give Tucker answers.

Who'd done that?

"There's more," Colt went on. "You can thank Deputy Grange for spotting it. There are trip wires on both the front and back doors. Someone's rigged them with explosives. They're small enough to fit in a man's pocket, but they probably would have gone off if we'd barged in there. That's why I haven't had a good look at the body yet."

Hell. If this dirtbag had set explosives at his place, maybe he'd done the same at the main house.

Tucker looked up at his family's home again, and he heard something he damn sure didn't want to hear. First, the sound of the security alarm blaring, and over that, he heard something else.

Laine shouting.

"Get down!"

Her shout was followed by a gunshot.

Chapter Sixteen

Laine saw the shadowy figure at the top of the stairs. And the gun pointed directly at Roy.

She shouted for Roy to get down, and she tried to pull him into the room with her.

But it was already too late.

The person fired a shot at him.

Thankfully, the guy missed, but he took aim again at Roy.

Rosalie screamed, and both Laine and she shoved Roy into the guest room and shut the door. They locked it and moved to the side in case the gunman tried to shoot his way through.

Laine braced herself for more shots, but they didn't come. In fact, other than the security alarm, there were no sounds of any kind, including footsteps.

Was the killer trying to sneak up on them?

If so, he'd certainly lost the element of surprise. But maybe he was trying to figure out a way to get to them other than breaking down the door. After all, he had to figure that at least one of them would be armed.

Her pulse was racing now, and the air felt still, as if everything was holding its breath. Roy started to open the door, no doubt to have a look at what was going on in the hall, but Laine pulled him back.

She didn't hear footsteps, but something caught her attention. A smell.

"Smoke," she mumbled.

Oh, mercy. Had he set the place on fire? If so, that would explain why he hadn't come after them. It also meant they could be trapped.

"Laine?" someone called out. *Tucker.* The alarm quit clanging, probably because he'd put in the code to stop it. "Dad?"

There were still no shots, but Laine knew she had to do something in case Tucker was walking right into a setup. The person who'd set the fire could ambush him.

"There's someone in the house!" she shouted. She prayed that would help him get out of the path of any bullets this monster intended to send his way.

Was it Buford out there? Had he managed to escape from Tucker's house and come for them? If so, he wouldn't stop until Tucker or one of them forced him to.

"It's getting thicker," Rosalie said, tipping her head to the milky-gray smoke oozing beneath the door.

It was also getting harder for her to breathe, but Laine didn't know what to do about that. If they hurried out into the hall, they could all be shot. But they couldn't stay put, either, because they were starting to cough. Besides, the fire could consume the house and burn them alive.

"Don't shoot. I'm coming up," Tucker yelled. He, too, was coughing.

Laine pulled in her breath, waiting and praying. Without the blare from the alarm, she had no trouble hearing the racing footsteps on the stairs and in the hall.

"It's me," Tucker said through his coughs.

Laine threw open the door and was so relieved to see him that she had to fight from launching herself into his arms. Tucker didn't give her a chance to do that anyway, because he moved them away from the door again.

"Is anyone hurt?" he asked, giving all three of them a quick glance.

Laine shook her head. "The man fired a shot at your father."

Tucker cursed, gave his dad another look. "I didn't see anyone downstairs. Just the smoke."

"Where's the fire?" Roy immediately asked.

"Don't think there is one. Looks like this bozo set off some smoke bombs downstairs."

Part of her was relieved, but the smoke could turn out to be just as deadly as the fire if it meant they couldn't breathe.

"I think the phones are jammed," Laine told him as Tucker motioned for them to come out of the room. He kept his gun aimed in the direction of the stairs.

"Yeah, someone used a signal zapper, and it's not Buford's doing. He's dead back at my house."

The sickening dread raced through her. Laine certainly hadn't wanted to come face-to-face with Buford again, but if he wasn't the one doing this, then who was?

She had a horrible thought that they would soon find out.

Leading the way, Tucker hurried them up the hall and toward the stairs, where the smoke was the thickest. Roy started coughing so hard that Laine and Rosalie each took him by the arm and tried to keep up with Tucker. By the time they made it to the bottom, her lungs felt ready to burst, and her eyes were watering so badly that she couldn't see more than a few feet in front of her.

"Not that way," Tucker said when she reached for the front door.

Probably because he thought the killer was out there waiting for them. And he or she could be. The smoke could have been a ruse to draw them all out of the house and into the line of fire. But the ruse would also work if they all passed out from smoke inhalation.

Then they'd be sitting ducks for a killer.

Instead, Tucker hurried them toward the back of the house. Not to the kitchen, either, where she knew there was a door to the backyard.

With his attention firing all around them, they went into the family room, and he hurried to the window on the far exterior wall. The smoke was still thick—there was more than enough to keep them all coughing—but Tucker still didn't throw open the window to let in the fresh air.

"Keep watch behind us," he said to his father. Roy turned, pointed his gun in that direction.

Tucker looked out the window, eased it open and then shoved out the screen. The night breeze immediately started to pour in, and Laine gulped in several long breaths before Tucker climbed out. As he'd done in the hall, he looked around, his gun ready, and then motioned for them to come out.

Laine helped Rosalie through first. When it was her turn, she tried to hurry in case their attacker came after Roy. The moment they all had their feet on the ground, Tucker got them moving again.

They only made it a few steps before Tucker stopped, pivoted and took aim.

A shot cracked through the air.

TUCKER FIRED AT their attacker, who'd just leaned out from the corner of the house.

He missed.

But thankfully so did the shooter.

His bullet slammed into the ground, but Tucker figured the idiot would soon pull the trigger again.

And he did.

Another shot immediately came their way, and instead of shooting back this time, Tucker knew he had to get Laine and the others out of the line of fire.

"This way," Tucker shouted, and he caught onto Laine's arm to run toward a pair of oaks about ten yards away. They had only made it a few steps when the shots returned.

Man, did they.

They came at them nonstop.

The shooter was obviously using some kind of assault weapon to be able to get off that many rounds that fast. It also meant he wouldn't have to pause to reload anytime soon. That wasn't good news.

Tucker kept moving, and the moment he reached the trees, he dragged Laine to the ground so he could cover her and help his dad and Rosalie.

But his heart dropped.

Rosalie and his dad weren't there.

It took Tucker a moment to pick through the darkness to spot them. Alive, thank God. They'd gone in the other direction. Probably because of the path of those bullets around them. And they were now behind some shrubs and a large stone birdbath. It wasn't much cover, but at least they weren't out in the open.

Tucker wanted to call out to them, to ask if they

were okay, but if the shooter didn't have them pin-pointed, that would give away their position. Besides, his father was a smart man, and he knew how to defend himself. Still, Tucker didn't want him or Rosalie to have to do that.

Because Laine was pressed right against him, he could feel the tightened muscles in her body and could hear her ragged breaths.

"Shhh," he said, trying to soothe her. It didn't work.

She was obviously terrified, and so was he. He wished he could assure her that he'd get all of them out of this alive. But a reassurance now would be a lie.

Tucker took out his phone to call Colt, but then cursed when he saw that he had no service. Laine had been right about someone jamming the phones. It wasn't hard to do, but it meant their attacker had not only brought jamming equipment and an assault weapon, but had also likely been the one to set the explosives at Tucker's house.

This had not been a spur-of-the-moment attack. It'd been well planned, and that meant Tucker had no idea what other things this idiot could throw their way. Or how many goons he'd brought with him to finish the job.

The shots kept coming, all of them aimed at Laine and him. Each bullet tore through the trees. It wouldn't be long before the gunman chipped away at enough of their cover to do some serious damage.

But the angle of the shots was a little off.

Not by much. Just enough for Tucker to think this guy didn't want them dead. Well, not both of them, anyway. Still, even if he wasn't trying to kill them, it didn't mean a stray bullet wouldn't finish them off.

"I'm sorry," he mumbled to Laine.

She lifted her head just a fraction and glared up at him. "This wasn't your fault."

He disagreed. "I sure as heck didn't stop it from happening."

But he could do something about stopping it now. If he could just maneuver himself into a better position, he might be able to get off a decent shot and put an end to the triggerman.

Tucker knew the side yard like the back of his hand. There were more trees and shrubs, but nothing that would get him into a position to fire. His brother's house was about forty yards away and was still under construction. It would give Tucker the right angle, but the odds were sky-high that the shooter would see him and stop him before he made it there.

That left one of the vehicles.

Several trucks were parked on the grounds. None would be ideal, but he somehow had to make it work. The biggest problem with the plan was that it involved leaving Laine alone.

He hated that.

Because this moron could have someone else out there, waiting for him to make a move just like that. Still, Tucker would likely be able to shoot anyone who attempted to kidnap Laine again.

"Wait here and stay down," Tucker told Laine.

She immediately started shaking her head. "You're not going out there."

"I don't have much of a choice." He motioned toward his dad's truck, which was about halfway between where they were and the front of the house.

The head-shaking continued, and when it finally stopped, he saw the tears shimmering in her eyes.

Oh, man. Not tears. It tore at his heart to see her cry, but it would tear at him even more if he didn't do everything possible to get her out of this alive.

Tucker leaned in, pressed a kiss on her mouth. He figured it wouldn't help. He was wrong about that, too. It sure helped him, and it was a good reminder of just how much was at stake. Not just his father's and sister's lives.

But Laine's.

He gave her one last look. There was no way he would say goodbye, but Tucker knew in the back of his mind that this could have a very bad ending. He got ready to move, but the moment he leaned out from the tree, he spotted the headlights from a vehicle barreling up the road toward the house.

Colt.

Thank God. His brother must have heard the shots and come to help. Maybe he'd brought the deputy and the ranch hands with him, too, in case the shooter had reinforcements.

The shooter reacted to those headlights, all right. He stopped firing, and Tucker saw him pivot in Colt's direction. Tucker couldn't let him shoot at Colt, so even though he was way out of position, he double tapped the trigger to get the shooter's attention.

It worked.

The person dropped to the ground.

It was exactly the distraction Tucker needed, and it meant he didn't have to leave Laine alone and unguarded behind the trees. He hauled Laine to her feet and got her moving toward his dad's truck.

Tucker tried to keep watch all around them to make sure the shooter didn't have backup planted around the ranch. With the distraction that Buford had created at

Tucker's place, it was possible several gunmen had come undetected onto the ranch. They could be waiting anywhere, ready to ambush them.

Laine and he ran, but they were still yards from the truck when the shots started again. They weren't going toward Colt. They were going toward him and Laine.

Tucker cursed and kept running. It wouldn't do any good to pull Laine back to the ground, since that's where most of the shots were landing. The bullets were kicking up dirt all around them. The truck was off-limits now, too, because the shooter had moved in that direction.

Mercy, he and Laine were trapped.

Tucker just tightened his grip on her and kept running toward his brother's house.

The place looked like a giant skeleton with the moonlight bouncing off the pale wooden frame. The walls were only partially up, but there were plenty of places for him and Laine to take cover. So Tucker ran as if their lives depended on it.

Because they did.

The shots kept coming closer and closer, but missing their mark.

Maybe.

Either this guy was a bad shot, or the bullets were meant to drive them to a specific place.

Not a comforting thought.

That's why Tucker tried to see if there was anyone lurking in the shadows of all that construction. But he saw nothing. So, as soon as he reached the front of the house, he pulled Laine inside.

Just like that, the shots stopped.

Tucker was partly thankful for that. It meant he could

hear anyone trying to sneak up on them. But it also meant the shooter could be coming in pursuit.

Laine and he needed to find better positions.

It'd been more than a week since he'd been to the construction site, and Tucker wasn't familiar with the layout. He glanced around, spotted the stairs that he figured would lead to the yet-to-be-completed second floor. The height would give him a good vantage point from which to spot the shooter and anyone else he'd brought with him.

"This way," he said. Keeping Laine close, he made his way up the stairs. Tucker paused at the top and looked around, but again didn't see anyone.

The walls had been framed on the top floor, and there were gaping holes where the windows would eventually go. It wasn't enough cover for one person, much less two, but he'd been right about the vantage point. He had a bird's-eye view of the surrounding pastures and the house.

Tucker spotted his dad and Rosalie, still cowering where he'd last seen them. Colt was in the front driveway of the main ranch house positioned behind the door of his truck.

No sign of the shooter, though.

But the guy was still nearby because he sent a shot in Colt's direction, pinning his brother down.

Tucker maneuvered Laine behind a stack of lumber and away from the stairs, in case someone tried to get to them from that direction. He inched his way toward the front, still looking for the idiot who'd tried to kill them. It sickened Tucker to think of the guy getting away or hurting Colt, but it sickened him even more that he or one of his cronies could already be in place to strike again.

Tucker hadn't even gotten in place when he heard a strange sound. Not footsteps or gunshots, but almost a groaning noise. His gaze flew to Laine, praying he'd been wrong about the sound coming from her direction.

But he wasn't wrong.

The groaning sound turned to a loud snap. The floor gave way, and Laine called out for Tucker as she fell through the broken wood.

Chapter Seventeen

Everything happened so fast. Much too fast for Laine to do anything to break her fall.

One second she was standing on the second story of Cooper's future house, and the next she was slamming into the floor below her. She landed on her back, and with nothing to break her fall, she had her breath knocked right out of her.

The pain shot through her, and with her lungs clenched, she had to fight just to sit up.

"Laine?" Tucker shouted, and she could hear him running on the floor above.

But Laine also heard something else.

Movement to her right.

Despite the pain, she shifted her attention in that direction and saw something she definitely didn't want to see. The same shadowy figure from the stairs at the McKinnon house.

He took aim at her.

Laine forced herself to move. Not easy to do with every muscle in her body aching, and maybe even a broken bone. Still, she moved. She scrambled behind a partial wall.

Barely in the nick of time.

A bullet came right at her.

The shot smacked into one of the wooden studs, rattling the wall and also rattling her even though the shot itself hardly made a sound. The gunman was now using a silencer. Maybe so that none of the McKinnons would know that she and Tucker were being attacked again.

This couldn't be happening.

Tucker, his family and she were right back in the middle of danger. The only bright spot in it all was that the babies were at the safe house, far away from the bullets. She was thankful that Tucker had had the foresight to get them out of harm's way.

Of course, he wouldn't see it that way.

He'd see it as a failure on his part, since he hadn't been able to protect everyone else. Her included. But she knew the only reason she was alive at all was because of Tucker.

"Laine?" Tucker shouted again.

She could tell he was at the top of the unfinished stairs. No railing. Just bare steps that jutted up to the opening that would become the landing. The shooter obviously could tell where Tucker was, too, because the next shot swished in his direction.

Laine nearly shouted for him to stay down, but she didn't want to risk him answering, since it was clear the shooter was gunning for him.

She tested her legs, and even though she had cuts and bruises, there didn't seem to be any broken bones, so she started moving. She inched her way along the partial wall, trying not to make a sound.

Above her, she heard Tucker moving again. At least she prayed it was Tucker. This monster could have brought more killers with him, and it was possible he had them close enough to go after Tucker again.

Still listening for any movement from their attacker, Laine reached the end of the wall, and she peered up at the gaping hole above her. It was the edge of the stairwell, and she could just make out Tucker. He had his gun aimed and his foot positioned as if he were about to make his way downstairs.

Laine shook her head, hoping he'd see her. She didn't want him walking directly toward a killer, and she was certain he was nearby, ready to strike.

But Tucker didn't stay put.

He paused when he landed on the first step. Paused again as he made his way down.

He was on the third step when the shot zinged through the air.

Even though the gunman was still using a silencer, there was no mistaking that the shooter had been aiming at Tucker, because the bullet bashed into the drywall right next to him, sending powdery dust raining down on her. Since she was dragging in air through her mouth, she dragged that in, too, and had to choke back a cough.

Two more shots came at Tucker. Then in the blink of an eye, the shooter's direction changed.

The bullets started coming at her.

They went right through the drywall. Right at her. Laine was forced to scramble deeper into the house so she wouldn't be hit.

There was no light in this part of the structure because of the exterior wall and floor above, so she crashed into some tools. The clanging noise was practically deafening.

But not loud enough for Laine to miss the sound of footsteps.

These weren't coming from the stairs where she'd last seen Tucker. They were coming from behind her.

Laine didn't bolt, though she had to hold herself back from doing just that. It was too dark for her to see much of anything, and if she ran, she could land right in the arms of a killer.

She felt around on the floor and located a screwdriver from the toppled tool case. It wasn't much of a weapon, but it was better than nothing. So was the long nail she snatched up. Holding the screwdriver like a knife, Laine eased up a little, trying to sort through the murky shadows and spot the killer.

Nothing.

No footsteps, either, though it was hard to hear with her own heartbeat crashing in her ears.

"Laine?" Tucker said again.

It wasn't a shout, but rather a whisper. She couldn't pinpoint his exact position, but it sounded as if he was still near the stairs. It definitely hadn't been Tucker's footsteps that she'd heard earlier.

And that meant their attacker had moved closer.

Laine tried not to make a sound. Hard to do, though, since she was breathing through her mouth. She clamped her teeth over her bottom lip, prayed and glanced around, looking for the monster who'd put them in the middle of this nightmare.

Another sound.

More footsteps.

Definitely coming from the stairs. Either their attacker was going after Tucker or Tucker was trying to make his way downstairs to her.

Again, she nearly called out to warn him not to do anything that could get him killed, but the debate came to a crashing halt when she heard the next sound.

It was close.

Too close.

She reeled around, prepared to use the screwdriver to defend herself, but she didn't get the chance. Someone from behind her knocked the screwdriver from her hand, hooked an arm around her neck and dragged her to her feet.

Laine wasn't able to fight off the attack before she felt the barrel of a gun against her head.

TUCKER HEARD LAINE'S GASP, and he figured that wasn't a good sign.

With his gun ready, he inched down the stairs. His instincts were yelling for him to get to her—fast—but it wouldn't help either of them for him to go charging into a situation that could get them both killed.

He reached the bottom step, his gaze slashing from one side of the building to the other. No sign of the shooter or Laine. But he could hear her.

Quick jolts of breath.

She was obviously terrified, and that got him hurrying. Tucker had to get to her.

With his shooting wrist bracketed with his hand, he moved to the left side of the stairs, keeping cover behind a stack of building materials. Tucker's heart went to the floor. He'd found Laine all right, and she was alive.

For now.

But she might not be for long if Tucker didn't do something. The dirtwad holding a gun to her head could pull the trigger and kill her with one shot.

"Let her go," Tucker ordered. He couldn't see the person because of the spotty darkness, but he was pretty sure it was a man.

Maybe Hague or Darren.

However, it could also be just another hired gun like Buford. If so, then Rhonda could be calling the shots—literally.

Tucker inched closer but stopped when the person jammed the gun harder against Laine's head. He had no trouble seeing her face. The ghost-white moon seemed to land on her like a spotlight, and he could see the absolute terror in her eyes.

He could also see something else.

She wasn't surrendering. No, there was plenty of fight left in her body, and that could be a bad thing. He didn't want her fighting back.

Not now, anyway.

After all, if this creep had wanted her dead, he would have already shot her. Tucker, too. And he hadn't fired a shot. That meant he wanted something from both of them, and Tucker got a good idea of what that was when the man started to drag her back, deeper into the shadows.

He was kidnapping Laine.

"Stop," Tucker warned him. He tested his theory that this guy wanted him alive by taking one step out from cover. He could always dive back if the creep fired.

But he didn't.

"What do you want with us?" Tucker demanded.

Silence.

The guy just kept moving, although Laine wasn't exactly cooperating. She was struggling. Well, she was until the guy whispered something in her ear. That stopped her. She practically froze. And there was probably only one reason for her to do that.

Her attacker had threatened to shoot Tucker.

And he might try. But Tucker didn't have any plans

for Laine and him to die tonight. Or for Laine to be kid-napped by this trigger-happy nut job.

He hadn't seen any unusual vehicles parked around the house or the ranch, but that didn't mean this man didn't have a car stashed somewhere. If he managed to get Laine away from there, God knew what he would do to her.

"You know I'm not just going to let you take her," Tucker said, moving right along with them. "Just tell me what you want, and we can settle this right here, right now."

Still nothing.

Hard to bargain with the devil when he didn't know what the devil wanted. Of course, as long as he stayed quiet, Tucker didn't know who he was dealing with. It could be either Darren or Hague, trying to conceal their identity.

So far, it was working.

The man dragged her toward one of the spaces where the windows would soon be. Right now, they were just giant holes, with plenty of space for someone to slip through. And that was obviously the plan, because while keeping a firm grip on Laine, he ducked down a little.

Just enough for the moonlight to glint across his face.

Martin Hague.

Tucker cursed. Hague wouldn't exactly have been a formidable foe, *if* he hadn't been armed. But that gun was the ultimate equalizer. Desperation, too. Tucker was betting Hague must have been desperate to come to the McKinnon ranch and pull a stunt like this.

"He told me he wouldn't hurt you if I go with him," Laine said.

"Yeah, right," Tucker mumbled. "I'm thinking Hague's not a credible source when it comes to a comment like that."

Judging from Laine's expression, she wasn't buying it, either, but she didn't exactly have a lot of options. She wasn't armed, and even though Hague wasn't a hulking brute like Buford, he was still bigger and stronger than her.

"Buford's dead," Tucker told Hague, just in case he didn't know.

But obviously he did. There was still enough moonlight for Tucker to see that Hague didn't even react to that. Too bad. Tucker had hoped it would shake him up enough to make a mistake. Any mistake.

All Tucker needed was one clean shot.

"You killed Buford," Tucker concluded. "He was your own hired gun, and you made sure he was dead."

Hague didn't confirm or deny that. He just kept moving. A few more steps and he'd be at the window. If Tucker couldn't talk him out of this before then, he'd have to take drastic measures.

Anything to stop Hague from leaving with Laine.

"I'm figuring you told Buford to set the explosives," Tucker went on, hoping anything he said would slow the guy down or distract him. "They were small enough for him to have carried them in his pocket when he was running from the deputy and into my house. But he didn't know you'd already given him poison that would kill him."

Again, Hague didn't confirm it. Not verbally, anyway. But he clearly wasn't surprised by anything Tucker had said.

"What was Buford going to do—blackmail you or something?" Tucker asked. "Or maybe you were worried about that plea deal he tried to make before all hell broke loose."

"Maybe," Hague mumbled.

Since it was the first thing Hague had said to him since the whole ordeal had started, Tucker figured he'd hit a nerve. He took another swing at it.

"When you deal with criminals, it shouldn't surprise you when one tries to backstab you. You hired Buford, Hines and the other gunmen. So what happened? Did Buford want more money from you to keep his mouth shut and to take the plea deal off the table?"

"Don't know why you'd care," Hague snarled.

"I care because I'm wearing a badge. And because you're holding an innocent woman at gunpoint."

"She's not innocent!" Another nerve.

But Tucker didn't like the result of this one that he'd managed to hit.

"She started all of this by sticking her nose where it didn't belong," Hague grumbled. "She should have never shown up at the baby farm."

True, but if she hadn't, the twins might not have been rescued. Of course, Laine was paying a high price for saving them, and Tucker didn't doubt that she'd pay the ultimate price if it came down to it. There were a lot of lawmen who weren't as brave as she was.

Hague's grip tightened on Laine's neck, and he dug the gun deeper into her temple. She made a sound of pain that she clearly tried to bite back. No doubt so it wouldn't send Tucker into a rage. He wanted to think he wouldn't do that, but it was Laine at the end of that gun barrel.

Laine made another small sound when Hague jerked

her back, putting her in a choke hold. Tucker heard the sound of pain loud and clear, and it ate away at him. Hell. He couldn't let Hague keep hurting her like this.

"Laine isn't the reason your baby farm was closed down," Tucker went on, though he figured it wouldn't do any good. Still, he had to try. "You were breaking the law, and she was only doing her job."

"She got in the way," Hague fired back. "And now I'll use her to fix what she messed up."

That put some ice in his blood. "Use her how?"

"You'll soon find out." Hague lifted his left leg and put it through the window slot. "I'll be in touch with the ransom demand."

"What ransom?" Tucker snapped.

"The one you'll pay if you want to get her back alive."

Part of him wanted to believe this was for real, that Hague had no plans to kill them, that he could be appeased with just money. But Tucker couldn't see how that would happen. Both Laine and he were loose ends, and even though he didn't know Hague's plan, he wouldn't want to leave witnesses like them behind.

"Tell your brother and any of the others to back off," Hague warned him. "If they don't, I'll hurt Laine."

Tucker hadn't actually seen Colt, but he figured now that his brother wasn't being pinned down by gunfire that Colt would quickly make his way to Cooper's house. Maybe Hague had figured that, too. Most of the ranch hands, however, would probably stay at the main house to guard Roy and Rosalie.

"Tell them!" Hague repeated, shouting this time. Mercy, the man was quickly losing control of his icy composure.

Not good.

Because in a fit of temper, Hague could start a gun-fight that would get Laine killed.

"Colt, hold your fire," Tucker called out.

Maybe his brother was close enough to hear him, and if he was, perhaps Colt would indeed hold his fire, unless he had the perfect kill shot aimed at Hague. That wouldn't be easy with the darkness and with Hague gripping Laine so close to him. Still, it could happen, and Tucker had to hold on to that thought like a lifeline.

"I'm sorry," Laine said, and Tucker knew she was talking to him.

He gave her his best flat bad-boy look to let her know an apology would just piss him off. But the look fell short when he saw her moving her left hand.

And Tucker saw what she was holding.

A nail.

Laine gave him a slight nod, and he knew then that she was about to do something that was a thousand steps past being dangerous.

"No," Tucker mumbled.

But it was too late.

Tucker saw Laine draw back her hand and jam the nail into the side of Hague's thigh. Before the man could even react—or pull the trigger—Tucker did the only thing he could do.

He launched himself at Hague and prayed he would be able to stop him in time.

Chapter Eighteen

It was all a blur of sounds and movements for Laine.

Hague howled in pain, cursing her in the same breath, and she felt his hand tense on the gun. Laine braced herself for him to pull the trigger.

But he didn't get the chance to do that.

Hague was already off balance with his one leg out the window opening, but his precarious position got significantly worse when Tucker rammed full force into them.

The pain was instant, like an explosion going off inside her head, and it took Laine a moment to realize the pain wasn't from a bullet but rather from being bashed into the wall. Hague jerked her back, using her to break his fall, and the side of her head slammed into the wooden frame.

Before she could react or even catch her breath, she felt herself falling right along with Hague, and all three of them landed on the ground just outside the window.

She was trapped between them.

Worse, Hague still had his gun. It was jamming into her neck, and if he pulled the trigger, she'd be dead.

Laine tried to do something about that.

No way did she want to just lie there while Hague killed both her and Tucker.

She had somehow managed to keep a grip on the nail

so she thrust it at Hague again. His shout of pain was almost deafening since his mouth was right against her ear. Obviously, she'd done some damage, but it only seemed to enrage him even more. It certainly didn't slow the man down, and he was fighting like a wildcat, using her body as a shield to keep Tucker from attacking him.

Tucker wasn't exactly his usual calm self, either. He was cursing Hague and fighting, too, trying to push Laine out of the way so he could get to the man. The only thing she could do was try to stay out of their way in case Tucker got the chance to pound Hague to dust.

Hague shifted his gun away from her neck. Aiming it right at Tucker. Her heart jumped to her throat, and Laine hit him with the nail again.

And again.

She would have hit him a dozen times if he hadn't hit her. Cursing, Hague latched onto her hair with his left hand and yanked it back so hard that she was the one yelping in pain.

It only made Tucker fight harder.

She saw Tucker's fist come right at her. Except it wasn't coming at her, but rather at Hague's jaw. Tucker connected, and Hague's head flopped back for an instant. It was just enough for him to let go of her hair so she could stab him with the nail again. This time she went after his neck, hoping to hit an artery.

But she didn't.

Hague moved at the last second, and the nail glanced off his shoulder.

He didn't even seem to react to the new wound, though Laine was certain she'd drawn more blood. Probably because the adrenaline was fueling him. It was fueling her, too, but Hague was still stronger than she was, and he dragged her back in front of him. He then bashed his gun against her hand so hard that the nail went flying.

Laine was ready to drop down so she could hopefully give Tucker enough room to fire. But Hague put her back in a choke hold, even tighter than the one before. If this kept up, she'd soon lose consciousness. Or worse. He'd crush her windpipe and kill her. She had to do something.

But what?

She was fighting as hard as she could, and Hague was holding Tucker at bay by keeping the gun to her head.

Without warning, a shot cracked through the air.

Laine screamed and tried to get to Tucker. She was positive that Hague had shot him, but the bullet hadn't come from Hague's gun.

It'd come from the front of the house.

Maybe from Colt, or from one of the ranch hands. Laine prayed it hadn't been fired by one of Hague's henchmen. At least it hadn't been Buford, because according to Tucker, that particular killer was already dead. Still, Hague might have others out there helping him.

"If you want her dead, go ahead and fire another shot," Hague shouted. He had complete control of her again. She was positioned in front of him, the gun digging into the back of her head.

"Hold your fire," Tucker said to whoever was out there. Whoever it was, maybe he could get into a position to shoot Hague since the angle was all wrong for Tucker.

Hague waited a moment, his heartbeat thudding against her back and his breath gusting in her ear. He had the smell of fear, blood and sweat all over him. She'd lost count of how many times she'd struck him with that nail or how many times Tucker had punched him, but from the corner of her eye, she could see the blood trickling down his face.

"Now drop your gun and get on the ground," Hague ordered Tucker.

Tucker shook his head. "I can't let you take her, and that's exactly what you'll do if I'm not armed and ready to stop you."

"You don't have a choice. You already know I'll do anything to put an end to this. Anything, including pulling the trigger that'll kill her."

Again, Tucker shook his head. "It doesn't have to be this way. We can work something out."

Laine didn't know how Tucker managed it, but he kept his voice calm. She'd heard that tone before, when she had been on the scene and he'd had to negotiate with a parent who'd taken his own child hostage. Tucker had managed to save the child, and she prayed he could do the same thing now.

Unless her staying alive would somehow endanger the twins. Was that it?

That put her heart right in her throat.

"This is about the babies," she said. "You're going to exchange them for me. Except we both know you aren't going to let me live."

That earned her another hard jab from his gun. "I told you to put down your weapon," Hague repeated to Tucker.

And he moved the gun to her already injured arm.

"I'll put a bullet in her," Hague threatened. "It won't kill her, but I wonder just how long you'll be able to stand there with her screaming in pain."

Laine tried to brace herself for the shot. She doubted she could stay quiet if Hague carried through with that threat, but she hated that he would use her pain to manipulate Tucker.

The muscles in Tucker's jaw stirred. "If you hurt her again, you die."

"If you don't put down your gun, I'll hurt her," Hague countered.

They stood there glaring at each other, and she saw the moment that Tucker surrendered to the demand. Without taking his eyes off Hague, he stooped down and eased the gun onto the ground just inches from his own boots.

"I can't watch while he hurts you," Tucker said, his voice barely a whisper.

He sounded plenty sorry about that. And he probably was. This was personal for him now, and she could blame their lovemaking for that. He'd lost his objectivity, and it was now playing into how he was handling this.

It was playing into how she was handling it, too.

If Hague killed her, at least it'd be fast, but she would die a thousand times over if he turned that gun on Tucker. Thankfully, Hague seemed to want her.

"If it's really just the money you want," Laine offered the monster with the gun to her head, "I can get it for you."

"Oh, you will," Hague assured her. "Tucker will, too. I need all that you two have and a lot more. Now, stand up," Hague ordered Tucker. "And keep your hands where I can see them."

Tucker stayed stooped down, his hand near his gun where he could hopefully snatch it up if necessary. "If you owned the baby farm, why are you being pressured for money?"

"Stand up!" Hague shouted.

Cursing, Tucker had no choice but to do just that.

Hague started inching her backward. Away from Tucker and the house. Also away from Colt or whoever had fired that shot. Laine hoped there was some way someone could sneak up behind Hague, but unfortunately, there was only open space around them since Cooper's house was being built on the edge of the pasture.

"Let me guess," Tucker went on, glaring at Hague. "You borrowed money from the wrong people to fund this sick operation of yours."

"Why do you care?" Hague snapped, still moving.

"I'd just like to know the reason you're planning to demand a ransom." Tucker lifted his shoulder. "That, and I'm puzzled about something that Buford said right before he died."

Hague froze. It was the first time she'd felt him that still since the attack had started. "What the hell did he say?" Hague snapped.

Tucker lifted his shoulder again, as if this were the most mundane subject. It obviously wasn't, and Laine had no idea if Tucker was bluffing or if Buford had indeed managed to say something incriminating.

"Buford said he had some info stashed away in a safe-deposit box. Said it would prove it was you working the baby farm." Tucker paused. "I'm pretty sure Buford figured out you poisoned him. I'm also sure he didn't trust you any more than you trusted him."

Because Hague was so close to her, she felt the change in his breathing, and even though she hadn't thought it possible, his muscles tensed even more.

Obviously, this was a glitch he hadn't expected.

"You're lying," Hague said.

"Don't have to. Buford was almost dead when I got to him, but trust me, almost dead men can do plenty of talking. Especially since he wanted his killer to pay for poisoning him."

Hague stayed quiet a moment, his breath gusting even harder. "What safe-deposit box? Where is it?"

Tucker shook his head. "Didn't say. But I'm thinking it won't be hard to find once my brother gets the search warrants. Oh, wait. Were you planning on involving my brothers and the Marshals' service in this?"

Clearly, that was the last thing Hague wanted, and his profanity proved that. He'd likely wanted to make a clean getaway, and then he could use her to get money from her own family and from Tucker.

And then he would murder them.

Hard to kill dozens of people who could come in contact with what might be in a safe-deposit box.

"If Buford left any kind of evidence, and that's a huge *if,*" Hague said, "then my advice is for you to leave it hidden away. There's someone other than me who'd kill to keep all of this under wraps."

Laine tried to figure out if that was a lie, but there was no indication that it was anything but the truth. Worse, it made sense for someone else to have been involved in the baby farm operation.

With his bombshell dropped, Hague got her moving again.

"Who'll try to kill us?" Tucker pressed.

Hague laughed, but there was absolutely no humor in it. "Just giving you his name would be bad for all of us. He plays dirty, and if I don't turn over Dawn's babies to him, a lot of people will die. Myself included. He's the one who put the hit on her—not me—when he didn't get the twins he'd been guaranteed. But even if he hadn't wanted her dead, I couldn't allow her to stay alive. She could have spilled details about the baby farm."

That put some more fire in Tucker's eyes. His mouth tightened. "This piece of dirt you're talking about paid for the babies?"

"Hey, I run a business, not a charity."

"You *ran* a business," Tucker said, his teeth coming together. "That's about to end. And there's no way in hell I'm letting you give those babies to the person who ordered a hit on their mother."

"You don't have a say in the matter, McKinnon. Ditto for giving me whatever amount of cash I demand. No say whatsoever. Without the money, you don't get Laine back, and even a fool can see you'd do anything to stop her from being hurt."

"You're wrong," Laine insisted. "There's too much bad blood between Tucker and me. He's just doing his job here, but he'd sacrifice me in a second if it meant taking you down."

Tucker didn't argue. In fact, he didn't say a word. He just kept that fierce glare nailed to Hague.

In the distance, she heard a slight whistle and remembered that Colt had made that same sound when he'd gone into the woods looking for Buford after he'd tried to kidnap her. Tucker must have heard it, too, but he didn't react.

Hague did, though.

He looked in the direction of the sound. Just a simple movement of his head. The moment seemed to freeze, but Laine could almost feel the attack before it happened.

With Hague distracted, Tucker scooped up his gun and charged toward them. Laine did her part and prayed it was the right thing to do.

She fell backward, throwing all of her weight into Hague and hoping to topple him.

Maybe because he was already distracted, Hague clearly hadn't expected it, and she felt herself falling again. Hague latched onto her, and in the same motion, he slammed the butt of the gun against her face. Laine could have sworn that she saw stars, and it knocked her to the ground.

Hague went after her again, clawing at her and trying to put her back in front of him.

Tucker came at them, not saying a word, but she could feel the rage in him. He dropped down onto his knees and punched Hague full force with his fist.

And he just kept on punching.

His fists flew along with the profanity that left his mouth, and Hague could do nothing but drop the gun and let go of her.

"Don't kill him," Laine managed to say. Not because she wanted this piece of slime to live but because she didn't want Tucker to have to deal with the aftermath of killing an unarmed man. He was too good of a lawman for that.

Tucker landed one last punch and moved back just as Colt and two ranch hands rushed up. The three took aim at Hague, but it was clear the man wasn't going anywhere. He could barely move.

"You okay?" Colt asked, volleying glances at Tucker and her.

Tucker nodded but cursed again when his attention landed on her face. Laine felt it then, the trickle of blood on her cheek from where Hague had hit her with the gun. Tucker uttered a single word of really bad profanity, and she caught onto him to stop him from launching himself at Hague again.

"I'm fine," she lied.

She would have said anything at that point to put an end to this, but the truth was her legs were shaking so hard she thought she might collapse.

Tucker solved that problem for her. He slipped his arm around her, supporting her weight, and they started back toward the main house.

"Take this snake to jail," Tucker told his brother.

"Gladly. Maybe he'll even resist arrest so I can add some bruises to his face. It takes some kind of jerk to hit a woman."

Laine was glad Colt hadn't qualified that with *"any woman."* Even one his family considered an enemy. That was indeed progress when it came to the McKinnons.

"I'll call the doctor," Tucker whispered to her. "How bad are you hurt?"

"Not as bad I could have been. Thanks." She tried to brush a kiss on his cheek, but the emotions were still too raw, as if it hurt him to see her, to touch her.

"You need to find Steve Wilkey," Hague shouted back to them.

Laine stopped and shook her head. The name was only vaguely familiar, and it took her a few seconds to realize where she'd heard it before.

"You mean the lawyer you brought to the sheriff's office?" she asked.

"He's a lawyer, all right, but he's not mine." Hague winced and cursed when Colt dragged him to his feet. "He insisted on coming with me because he was sure I'd screwed things up. You're lucky he didn't have all of you killed that day, because those were his hired guns who shot at you."

Despite the steamy heat, that sent an icy chill through her. She wanted to believe that Hague was lying, that there was no other person involved in this. But it didn't sound like a lie.

Tucker turned and faced Hague, but he kept a gentle grip on her. "You owe this man money?"

"Yeah. Plenty of it. Find him and arrest him, because he'll send someone after me even if I'm behind bars. At best, he'll kill me. Or else he'll make me wish he had."

"And why should I be concerned about that?" Tucker fired back. Laine wanted to ask him the same thing. After everything he'd done, she didn't care an ounce what happened to Hague.

"You should be concerned, because Wilkey's after the twins."

Laine was sure her heart skipped a beat or two. Tucker and she exchanged glances, and she prayed he would have some reassurance that it wasn't true. But he only looked as thunderstruck as she felt.

"What'd you mean?" Tucker demanded.

"He has a buyer for the twins," Hague fired back. "A big buyer. Wilkey has men out looking for them now, and there'll be a huge payout for whoever finds them. With Wilkey's resources, if I were you, I'd hurry. Maybe you can get to them before he does.

"Maybe," Hague repeated, his voice and the threat echoing in the darkness.

Chapter Nineteen

Once again, Tucker was watching a medic tend to Laine. This time, they weren't at the sheriff's office but rather in his family's home.

That cut and god-awful bruise that Hague had put on her face turned his stomach. So did the still-haunted look in her eyes. But he knew that look wasn't just from the pain of the attack or the thorough job the medic was doing of cleaning the wound.

No. It was from a different kind of pain and fear.

For the babies.

Tucker was right there on the same page with her. No way could he stand the thought of someone taking those children. Somehow they had to stop this Steve Wilkey from getting close to them.

Or close to Laine, for that matter.

Tucker had already beefed up security at the ranch. The hands were all armed and were patrolling the grounds in case Wilkey came their way. He'd also spoken to Sergeant Egan Caldwell and had learned that Wilkey and his henchmen hadn't come to the safe house.

Thank God.

Tucker hadn't wanted to move the twins. Instead, he

had sent out several Texas Rangers to look for the lawyer and haul him in for questioning.

Hague could have been lying about Wilkey's involvement, but Tucker wanted no stone left unturned when it came to Laine's and the babies' safety.

They'd gotten somewhat lucky tonight. Everyone was alive, and his dad and Rosalie were all in one piece. Thankfully, none of them had tried to play hero and come storming into Cooper's house, where Hague had been holding Laine at gunpoint. Roy and his twin sister had stayed put on Colt's order, and instead of injuries—like Laine's—all they would have to deal with were the horrible memories of the attack.

That was more than enough, and was likely the reason Rosalie had gone back to the guesthouse as soon as Hague had been taken away. She'd already been through so much with the kidnapping of her own baby that this could have brought it all back to the surface. He made a mental note to check on her.

Once he'd seen to Laine, that is.

"I think she'll be fine," his dad said to him. Again. Roy could no doubt tell that this had shaken him to the core, but it was a surprise that his dad and Colt were being so, well, friendly.

They certainly weren't giving Laine any signals that they wanted her immediately out of there. And that was good. It was a start, anyway. Because after everything that'd gone on tonight, Tucker couldn't see himself giving Laine the heave-ho.

Maybe they could even date or something.

Images of her naked flashed through his head. Okay, so they were well past the dating stage, but he had no intention of letting this go back to where it'd been a few days before. The trouble was he didn't know how to go about making sure that she stayed in his life.

"You're staring at me again," Laine mumbled, turning away from him. "I must look pretty bad for you to keep doing that."

"You look amazing," Tucker blurted out, catching both his father's and Colt's attention despite the fact that Colt was on the phone talking to Reed, who had Hague in custody at the jail.

The corner of Laine's mouth lifted for just a brief moment, but it didn't take more than a couple of seconds for her to get that haunted look again. Tears came, too, and then nothing in the world could keep Tucker from her side. He didn't elbow the medic aside. Not exactly, anyway. But he put himself between the guy and her so he could pull Laine into his arms.

"We can't let that man get to the babies," she whispered, and the tears came streaking down her bruised cheek. Tucker tried to gently kiss them away. They just kept coming. All he could do was stand there and let her get it all out.

"We won't," he assured her.

He led her to the other side of the room. It wasn't exactly private, but it was better than the center of the foyer. The medic looked at them as if he might come over and resume whatever he'd been doing, but Tucker waved him off.

"Egan's a good man," Tucker added, trying to soothe Laine. "No way would he let anyone get to the twins. Jack and Jill," Tucker added because he thought they could use some levity.

It worked a little. Laine tried to smile anyway.

Roy groaned softly, shook his head. "You gotta come

up with better names than that, especially since Laine said she was planning to adopt them."

"I am." That helped, too, and she brought her chin a little higher. "Any ideas?"

Now it was Tucker who groaned. If Rosalie had been in the room, at least there would have been some possibly good input, but he wasn't expecting much from his dad and brother.

And he didn't get much, either.

"Frick and Frack," Colt suggested. "Or maybe Trouble One and Trouble Two?"

Laine winced, but there was actually a little lightness beneath it.

"Laine, I always thought your grandmother had a pretty name," Roy spoke up. "Mattie. She was a fine woman. Good heart."

It was the first time in twenty-three years Tucker had heard anyone say a kind word about the Braddocks. But his dad was right. Tucker remembered Laine's paternal grandmother, and even though she'd long since passed away, she deserved a namesake.

Laine nodded. "Mattie it is." And she swallowed hard, as if she had a sudden lump in her throat.

Tucker didn't dare suggest using her father's name for the boy. Too much pain there yet, especially with the renewed memories from the upcoming trial.

"Matt goes pretty good with Mattie," he offered.

Another nod, and this time she gave a little smile. "I like it. Thanks." She mumbled the same to Roy and gave Colt a mock scolding glance, which he probably didn't even see because he got another call from Reed. Colt stepped away to take it.

The moment didn't last long, and Tucker saw the fear

creep back into Laine's eyes. Before he could start another round of reassurance, or distraction, his phone rang. Not Egan, thank God, with news that they'd had a *visitor* at the safe house. It was another Ranger, Griffin Morris.

"We found Steve Wilkey," Griffin said the moment Tucker answered. "I'm pretty sure your prisoner, Hague, was telling the truth about this jerk funding the baby farm. I pulled up his rap sheet on the way to his house, and he's corrupt all the way to the bone. He's been disbarred for years now and always seems to be one step ahead of the law."

Tucker had been doing a lot of cursing lately, but he added some more. "Why didn't Wilkey show up on the radar before now?"

"Maybe because his only association with the baby farm was through Hague."

That was possible. Heck, Hague hadn't even been on their radar until he'd shown up and tried to take the twins.

"What's Wilkey saying about all of this?" Tucker went on.

"He's not saying much of anything. We showed up at his house, and it didn't have a pretty ending. Before we could even tell him why we were there, he turned two goons on us. They shot at us, and we had to return fire."

Hell. Wilkey was obviously a violent man and had been there with Laine at the sheriff's office. Just a few feet away from her. And Tucker had been so focused on their other suspects, he hadn't realized they had a second snake in their midst.

"Wilkey joined the gunfight," Griffin went on, "and he and both of his men are dead."

The relief was overwhelming. Wilkey and his henchmen couldn't go after the babies now. But it would have been nice to get some answers from one of them so they could tie this up into a neat little package. Maybe he could get those answers from Colt after he finished his call with Reed.

"While he was shooting at us, Wilkey yelled out that he was going to kill Hague for setting us on him," the Ranger continued. "That's why I figured any part he had in the baby farm was only between Hague and him. Wilkey didn't name anyone else, and he was sure doing a lot of yelling."

"Yeah. Hague said that Wilkey had a buyer for the twins so maybe he'd already paid Hague and wanted him to deliver on the goods."

A sickening thought. Hague and Wilkey had treated the babies like livestock, ready to be sold to the highest bidder, and Tucker didn't even want to go with the rest of that thought. God knew what the highest bidder actually wanted with the twins. He figured if they'd been loving parents without police records, they would have taken a more normal route to adoption.

"I've already had someone call Egan to tell him the danger's passed," Griffin added. "The safe house is just five miles or so from you. Figured you'd want the babies brought back to you ASAP. Unless you want them to go to social services. If so, I can call Egan back."

"No." Tucker didn't even have to think about it. "I want them brought here to the ranch. The woman who's adopting them will take custody."

That would be possible now that there were no other obstacles in her way. No one in Dawn's or Laverty's family to stop her petition to get custody of Mattie and Matt. With Laine's position in the community, it appeared to be smooth sailing, despite her being a single mom.

"Oh, and tell Egan to hurry," Tucker added to Griffin. "We're anxious to see them." It would help Laine to be with them and hold them.

Heck, it'd help him, too.

When he finished the call, he could tell that Laine had heard every word of the conversation because she smiled and nearly launched herself into his arms. The medic must have decided he didn't want to be part of the little celebration because he packed up his things.

"Her injuries aren't that serious," the medic said to no one in particular. "She should make an appointment with her doctor, though."

Tucker assured him that would happen. And it would. Laine would get a thorough checkup. After they'd celebrated a little, that is.

The medic mumbled something about needing to get back to the hospital, and he let himself out.

"They're safe. We're safe," Laine said. She kissed him, and Tucker realized it helped his raw nerves and spent adrenaline hugely.

However, they still had an audience.

Something that Tucker didn't remember until he heard his dad clear his throat. He broke the kiss, fully expecting Roy to give him a look or some kind of reminder that this wasn't a good thing.

That didn't happen.

Roy reached out and gave Tucker's arm a pat. The sort of pat a man gave his son when he was proud of him.

But he couldn't be proud.

Could he?

"You won't hear any complaints from me," his dad offered. "Or from the rest of the family, if I have a say in it."

And then he did something else that surprised the heck

out of Tucker. Roy leaned in and brushed a kiss on Laine's cheek. The unbruised one. If there was any trace of that bad blood, it didn't show now.

Tucker was still in a bit of shock. He didn't notice that Colt had finished his call and was staring at them as if he couldn't figure out what to make of it.

Then his brother shrugged. "I guess I won't complain, either. Well, not much, anyway."

Laine smiled, nodded. "I'll try not to make a nuisance of myself."

Tucker frowned. He sure didn't like the sound of that, but before he could voice it, Colt pointed to his phone, reminding him that there were some darn important ends to tie up.

"Hague's cooperating big-time with Reed. Yakking his head off in the hopes of getting a plea deal."

"He's not getting one," Tucker argued.

At the same moment Laine said, "Not a chance. I want him in prison for life."

"That's the plan. Reed told him the same thing, but he's talking anyway. Hague said he convinced Dawn and Rhonda that Darren was the bad guy. That's why they were afraid of him."

Well, that explained some things. Not all, though.

"But what about the recording Darren had?" Tucker asked. "Dawn used the word *she*. Does that mean she was afraid of Rhonda, too?"

"Probably. Hague wouldn't have wanted the women to be too chummy, because they might put one and one together and figure he was in charge of the baby farm. If he'd lie about Darren being bad, I don't see why he wouldn't lie about Rhonda, too."

True. And while it was good that Darren hadn't done

anything wrong, Tucker wouldn't have minded a few minor charges thrown at him.

Okay, that was the jealousy talking.

He wasn't just riled that Laine was avoiding making a *nuisance* of herself, but he was also irritated that she'd once been in love with that selfish rat who'd treated her like dirt. Laine wasn't Darren's. She was his.

Whoa.

That brought him skidding to a mental halt.

Laine wasn't his and hadn't been since they were kids. Though he was pretty sure he wanted her to be. He was also sure he wanted a lot more than a kiss from her in his granddaddy's kitchen.

"Could you excuse us a moment?" he said to his dad and brother, leading Laine out onto the porch.

Even though there were plenty of ranch hands still milling around, it was a better place from which to watch for the babies. It was also a better place for him to make a fool out of himself with what he wanted to say.

Tucker wasn't exactly sure of the words. They might not even have made sense, but he knew he couldn't let Laine leave with Mattie and Matt.

"Look, I know I'm not exactly daddy material, but I was serious about my offer to help you raise them."

It was a start, but judging from the way the corners of her mouth turned down, it wasn't the exact offer she wanted to hear.

"Or not," he said, testing it. That didn't test well at all, and Tucker found himself frowning. It was obvious he needed to say something, but he wasn't quite sure what that was.

She huffed, and her hand went on her hip. "For Pete's

sake, we've been through this, and you already need a reminder."

"Yeah, I guess I do." He didn't want to make an ass out of himself and assume that Laine was asking for a whole lot more than just a commitment to help with the babies.

"When was your last real kiss?" she asked.

Oh. Tucker knew exactly what to do with that question.

He eased her to him and kissed her. It was long, hard and pretty darn satisfying. Well, until oxygen became an issue. "That one."

She made a dreamy little sound of pleasure before she pulled back her shoulders and stared at him. "Well, at least you're better with your mouth than you are with your words. Have you ever told a woman you love her?"

Tucker had to shake his head. He'd had women in his life, but he'd never wanted to lie to them. And saying "I love you" would definitely have been a lie.

Until now, he realized.

The corner of her mouth kicked up as if she knew she'd just hit pay dirt. Probably because he had a goofy look on his face. Hard to keep his cocky bad-boy look when he'd just figured out what exactly was going on in his head.

And in his heart.

She wadded up a handful of his shirt and pulled him back to her. "Here's the deal," Laine said, her mouth against his. "I'm in love with you. Always have been, always will be. Yes, I want your help raising the twins, but I want more than just that."

Laine paused, kissed him. "Tucker McKinnon, I want it all. I want *you*."

Well, heck. More pay dirt. Tucker figured he should just keep quiet since she was saying all the things that he wanted her to say. All the things he wanted to hear.

"You're in love with me?" he asked, just to make sure he hadn't misheard her. And because he wanted to hear her say it again.

"Yes. Of course I love you." Her smile got even wider. He had to have a sample of it to see if it tasted as good as it looked on her.

It did.

Like his birthday and Christmas all rolled into one.

She pulled back, obviously waiting, and Tucker wanted to say to her what he already knew in his heart. But before he could do that, he saw the approaching headlights of a vehicle making its way up the road.

Because of the nightmare they'd just gone through, Tucker automatically stepped in front of Laine and reached for his gun. But it was a false alarm.

The best kind.

It was Egan in an SUV, and he was no doubt bringing the babies home. Tucker and Laine made it all the way down the steps before Tucker decided that this was indeed their home.

Well, hopefully.

He might have to convince Laine of that first.

Tucker let her make it to the SUV ahead of him, and the nanny bodyguard stepped out. She handed one of the babies to a waiting and eager Laine. Since the baby was dressed in a blue gown, he figured it was Matt.

He was glad they'd taken the time to come up with better names.

Laine pressed a flurry of kisses on the baby's sleeping face and then handed him to Tucker so she could do the same to Mattie. Heck, he hadn't thought it possible, but they were cuter than they had been a few hours before when they'd left for the safe house.

Since Tucker figured this kissing, oohing and aahing could go on for a while, he thanked Egan and the nanny, and while they drove away, he got Laine moving back toward the house.

"I want to do more than just help with them," Tucker blurted out. "I want to be with them all the time. I want to feed them. Play with them." He paused. "Yeah, I'll even change 'em, often, but I'll let you know up front that's not something I especially want to do."

Though it no longer seemed like the chore it had been just a few days before. In fact, spending any kind of time with the pair would be something special.

"What exactly are you saying?" Laine asked.

Tucker fumbled around with this thought a moment and finally plucked out words that he hoped made sense. "I think we should make this legal and all. You should marry me and move into my house. Or your house. The location's irrelevant. Your answer, well, it isn't."

She stared at him as if he'd lost his mind, and for a few heart-stopping seconds, he thought he'd gotten this all wrong. That Laine's "I love you" hadn't meant the whole big dream that was now playing out in his head.

"Say yes," he prompted.

"Well, of course I'll say yes."

The relief caused him to make a funny breathing sound. Thank goodness it still managed to sound manly.

"Yes," she repeated.

Laine leaned in, kissed him. And that simple motion reminded him that once they had the babies put to bed, he wanted to strip off her clothes and make love to her again.

Plenty of times.

But first, he had to get something else off his chest.

"I'm in love with you, too, Laine."

The words felt darn good for something that'd never slipped past his tongue before. Tucker thought he'd be saying them for a long, long time.

Like the rest of their lives.

Laine pulled him to her and let him know that it was exactly what she had in mind, too.

* * * * *

USA TODAY *bestselling author Delores Fossen's new miniseries,* SWEETWATER RANCH,
continues next month.
Look for RUSTLING UP TROUBLE

MILLS & BOON®

Why not subscribe?

Never miss a title and save money too!

Here's what's available to you if you join the exclusive **Mills & Boon Book Club** today:

✦ *Titles up to a month ahead of the shops*
✦ *Amazing discounts*
✦ *Free P&P*
✦ *Earn Bonus Book points that can be redeemed against other titles and gifts*
✦ *Choose from monthly or pre-paid plans*

Still want more?

Well, if you join today we'll even give you
50% OFF your first parcel!

So visit **www.millsandboon.co.uk/subs**
or call Customer Relations on **020 8288 2888**
to be a part of this exclusive Book Club!

SUBS_2014

Snow, sleigh bells and a hint of seduction

Find your perfect Christmas reads at
millsandboon.co.uk/Christmas

MILLS & BOON®

Why shop at millsandboon.co.uk?

Each year, thousands of romance readers find their perfect read at millsandboon.co.uk. That's because we're passionate about bringing you the very best romantic fiction. Here are some of the advantages of shopping at www.millsandboon.co.uk:

* **Get new books first**—you'll be able to buy your favourite books one month before they hit the shops

* **Get exclusive discounts**—you'll also be able to buy our specially created monthly collections, with up to 50% off the RRP

* **Find your favourite authors**—latest news, interviews and new releases for all your favourite authors and series on our website, plus ideas for what to try next

* **Join in**—once you've bought your favourite books, don't forget to register with us to rate, review and join in the discussions

Visit **www.millsandboon.co.uk**
for all this and more today!